Critical acclaim for Graham Hurley

Deadlight

'This is how a crime novel should be written, and it pushes Hurley right to the forefront of British crime writers, where he richly deserves to be'
Mark Timlin, *Independent on Sunday*

'Uncompromisingly realistic . . . this series grows in stature with each book'
Susanna Yager, *Sunday Telegraph*

'As serious as ever in its social concerns . . . it's got a great plot, rich in detail' Mat Coward, *Morning Star*

Angels Passing

'Splendidly gritty . . . most enjoyable' *FHM*

'It is difficult to believe that Graham Hurley could write a better novel than *The Take*. But he has done it. This is tough, gritty, and unsparing'
Margaret Cannon, *Toronto Globe & Mail*

Graham Hurley lives in Portsmouth with his wife, Lin. After twenty years as a TV documentary producer, he now writes full-time. Visit his website at www.grahamhurley.co.uk.

By Graham Hurley

RULES OF ENGAGEMENT
REAPER
THE DEVIL'S BREATH
THUNDER IN THE BLOOD
SABBATHMAN
THE PERFECT SOLDIER
HEAVEN'S LIGHT
NOCTURNE
AIRSHOW
PERMISSIBLE LIMITS
TURNSTONE
THE TAKE
ANGELS PASSING
DEADLIGHT
CUT TO BLACK

TURNSTONE

Graham Hurley

An Orion paperback

First published in Great Britain in 2000
by Orion
This paperback edition published in 2001
by Orion Books Ltd,
Orion House, 5 Upper St Martin's Lane,
London WC2H 9EA

5 7 9 10 8 6 4

A CIP catalogue record for this book is available
from the British Library.

ISBN-13 978-0-7528-8113-2
ISBN-10 0-7528-8113-3

Typeset by Deltatype Ltd, Birkenhead, Merseyside

Printed and bound in Great Britain by
Clays Ltd, St Ives plc

The Orion Publishing Group's policy is to use papers that
are natural, renewable and recyclable products and
made from wood grown in sustainable forests. The logging
and manufacturing processes are expected to conform to
the environmental regulations of the country of origin.

www.orionbooks.co.uk

To
Tony and Willy
with love

Acknowledgements

Among the many individuals who have been more than generous with their time and expertise are William Bowman, Scott Chiltern, Ian Corney, Roly Dumont, Fran Foster, Bill Flynn, Bob Lamburne, Barry Little, George Marsh, Colin Michie, Nick Pugh, John Roberts, Ian Rose, Christina Waugh and Charles Wylie. I thank them all. My thanks, as well, to my agent, Antony Harwood, and my editor, Simon Spanton. Credit for the softer passages belongs, as ever, to my wife, Lin.

'Every contact leaves a trace'
– *Edmund Locard,* 1910

Prelude

The only time she'd ever been inside a police station was the day someone had stolen her bike. Luckily, it had turned up several weeks later, recovered from a second-hand shop near her home, and afterwards she'd realised how worthwhile that trip to Kingston Crescent had been. The police were there to chase the bad people. They knew how to get things back. So who was to say it wouldn't happen again?

She stood for a minute or two on the kerbside, clutching her white envelope, waiting for the traffic to part. On the police station steps, kids from the estate were trying to cadge fags from a couple of bigger boys. By the time she'd darted across the road, they'd drifted away.

Inside the police station, the waiting room was full. She wedged herself beside a huge man with a dog on a length of rope and blood down the front of his shirt. There was a lot of noise from phones ringing and the banging of doors. The big man tried to talk to her a couple of times but she pretended she hadn't heard.

At last, the policeman behind the counter called her forward.

'How can I help you?' he said, looking down at her.

In her head she'd been trying to work out what to say, but now the time had come words failed her.

'Has something happened you want to tell me about?'

'Yes.'

'Would you prefer to see a policewoman?'

'No.' She could feel the outlines of the photo in the envelope. 'No, thank you.'

There was another long silence. She shuffled from foot to foot. She felt hot and awkward.

At length, the policeman pulled a big pad towards him and reached for a pen.

'I think you've lost something,' he said, 'and I expect you want to tell me about it.'

'I have.'

'What is it, then?'

She glanced round. Everyone was looking at her. Everyone was listening. She closed her eyes a moment, took a deep breath, and then reached up, putting the photo from the envelope on the counter.

'It's my dad,' she whispered. 'We can't find him anywhere.'

One

Asleep at last, Faraday dreamed of the frigate bird. From wingtip to wingtip, it measured a full seven feet. Its tail was long and forked. In silhouette, in the pages of his bird books, it looked like the avenging angel, and for months on end it carved breathtaking hundred-mile arabesques across the world's great oceans, a flying machine perfectly adapted in the lie of every feather and the tiny corrective tug of every sinew.

People called the frigate bird a born thief, and Faraday loved that too because this glorious creature spent its entire life stealing height and distance from the elements around it. The frigate bird cared nothing for gravity, nor for the crushing routines of daily life. Instead, it soared aloft on those long, delicate, scimitar wings, as free and beyond reach as any creature on God's earth. It offered limitless possibilities. It spoke of hope.

A slow smile warmed Faraday's sleeping face. *Fregata magnificens*, he thought. Total release.

The trill of the phone brought Faraday back to earth. It was Cathy Lamb, the weekend's duty CID sergeant.

'We've got a G-28,' she said briskly. 'I'll be round to pick you up.'

A G-28 was office-speak for a dead body. Faraday hauled himself out of the armchair, the mobile clamped to his ear. His first-floor studio looked east, over the gleaming expanse of Langstone Harbour. This morning the tide was on the ebb, sluicing out between the tall wooden posts that marked the

3

navigable channels, and on either side, busy amongst the stranded boats of local fishermen, were the birds that feasted on the rich harvest from these glistening mud flats. Normally, through the scope on the tripod beside his chair, Faraday could rely on half a dozen species at a single sweep: egrets, lapwings, curlews, oyster-catchers, cormorants, turnstones, all of them carefully assembled bricks in his wall.

Cathy was detailing the background to the discovery of the body. The dead man's name was Sammy Spellar. He lived in Paulsgrove, a council estate to the north of the city, sprawled across the lower slopes of Portsdown Hill. A neighbour had raised the alarm after hearing sounds of a struggle next door. Uniform had attended and found Spellar on the carpet in the front room. Scenes of Crime had already secured the premises and the police surgeon had confirmed that Spellar was dead. He was an old man, seventy at least. Most of the injuries had been to his head.

Cathy paused for breath. Her ability to marshal so many facts in so few seconds had never failed to impress Faraday.

Now, he glanced at his watch. Nearly one o'clock.

'Give me the address,' he muttered. 'I'll meet you there.'

'You can't, sir.'

'Why not?'

'Your car's buggered. You told me last night.'

She was right. Down in the kitchen, trying to wrestle a slice of bread into the toaster, Faraday used his mobile to phone the garage. He'd known the older of the two mechanics for years. When he explained the problem, the man groaned.

'It's the brakes again,' he said. 'I thought I told you to go easy.'

Easy? Faraday snorted, pocketed the phone and left the kitchen. The big lounge was flooded with sunshine

4

and he stood by the full-length glass doors for a moment, gazing out at the harbour. Year after year, he could set his watch by the arrival of the spotted redshanks from their breeding grounds in the far north and he looked for them now, still waiting for the toaster to pop.

Cathy appeared minutes later. She was a big woman, one year short of thirty, with cropped brown hair and the easy grace of a natural athlete. Most weekends would have found her afloat – either canoeing in Wales, or water-skiing with her husband over on Hayling Island – but lately CID had been stretched to the limit, and the concept of time off had become an increasingly sour joke. Not that Cathy was the sort to complain.

She drove north through the choked city streets, declining a bite of Faraday's bacon sandwich. Lunch could wait.

'When did all this happen?'

'This morning. The neighbour says about half nine.'

Faraday was gazing out at the pasty-faced mill of shoppers. The hottest summer for years seemed to have passed the inner city by.

'So how come you took so long?'

'I've been out on another job. It's been hectic.'

'They couldn't raise you?'

'No, sir, they couldn't.'

Something in Cathy's tone warned Faraday against inquiring further. She'd come from the Paulsgrove estate herself and at moments of stress it showed. When he asked whether the Scenes of Crime Officer, the SOCO, had managed to keep things nice and clean she said she'd no idea, and when he inquired about the detail of the dead man's injuries she just shrugged. She'd got the brief by phone from the uniformed sergeant on the spot. Some of his blokes had already

5

started on house-to-house. Beyond that she was in the dark.

Faraday grunted, wondering whether he shouldn't push Cathy for a proper explanation for the delay in contacting him. Some days she seemed as preoccupied as he was. Some days, indeed, she was so tetchy, so defensive, that he'd begun to consider the possibilities of a serious conversation.

The lights changed to green and Cathy swore as she made a mess of slipping the clutch. While she restarted the engine, Faraday stared up at the line of flat roofs above a parade of shops. Two sparrows were having a noisy squabble in the guttering, raising tiny clouds of dust. Territory, he thought, and the incessant need to confirm the pecking order.

Sammy Spellar's council house lay at the top of Anson Avenue, one of a grid of streets that featured regularly in the quarterly divisional crime stats. Paulsgrove was a council estate where post-war good intentions – decent housing, clean air, brand-new start – had slowly given way to the tide of social anarchy that had engulfed so much of the city. In his glummer moments, Faraday likened CID work to fire-fighting. You attended the blaze. You did your best to limit the damage. But about the underlying causes – poverty, ignorance, family breakdown – you could do absolutely nothing.

Now, Faraday made his way through the crowd of watchers gathered in the road. The uniformed constable held up the blue 'Police No Entry' tape and then unclipped a pen to note his arrival on the Scenes of Crime log. Faraday paused outside the house. The gate to number seventy-three was hanging off its hinges and a dismantled bed frame lay rusting in the long grass beyond it. Beside the front door was a row of uncollected milk bottles. None of them had been washed and whoever had kicked over the nearest one hadn't bothered to clear up the shards of glass. On the doorstep, Faraday studied them a moment. His instinct was to tidy them up, to gather them in a twist of newspaper and chuck them in the rubbish bin, but he knew the Scenes of Crime protocol backwards. The SOCO was king here until the forensic checks were complete and anything that spoke of violence was potential evidence. Even the remains of a week-old milk bottle.

The front door was open and the sour, rank breath of the house brought Faraday to a halt. The narrow, uncarpeted little hall smelled of damp and neglect, of re-used chip fat and unwashed bodies. Kitchen rubbish spilled from a bulging black sack and Faraday caught a blur of movement as a cat bolted upstairs. The SOCO's row of metal stepping plates flagged a path into the front room.

'Jerry?'

The door was ajar and it opened further when Faraday gave it a push. Peering round, he looked in vain for Jerry Proctor, the duty SOCO. Sammy Spellar was still lying on the carpet, a frail, thin little body in stained brown trousers and a grubby nylon shirt with his knees drawn up to his chest where he'd tried to protect himself. There were taped plastic bags over his head and hands. The side of his head was matted with blood, his mouth was torn, and through the thin film of plastic it was possible to see that one of his eyes was hanging out of its socket. For Faraday, still rooted by the door, a single glance was enough. Fifteen years of Portsmouth murders told him that Sammy Spellar had been kicked to death.

A movement behind him brought Faraday out of the room. Detective Sergeant Jerry Proctor was a big, heavy-set, bear-like man with a bone-crushing hand-shake and a developed sense of territory. Like most

SOCOs, he insisted on keeping live bodies at the scenes of crime to an absolute minimum and was fearless about imposing his ground rules on more senior officers. As a detective inspector, Faraday had shared dozens of murders with Proctor and knew there was no better way of getting himself up to speed. The man would have been here for hours, carefully logging every last particle of evidence.

'What have we got then?'

Proctor slipped off a plastic glove and wiped the sweat from his face. He was wearing a white, one-piece paper suit and Faraday knew from experience how hot they could get.

'The neighbour called at half nine,' he said. 'Her husband had looked in through the window and saw the old boy on the floor.'

'Cathy mentioned some kind of row.'

'That's right. There'd been fighting. Par for the course, apparently. The old boy's son lives here too. Nothing but trouble according to next door.'

Sammy's son was called Mick. He'd left the house shortly after the fight. Asked for a description, the next-door neighbours had come up with rat-face, dog-breath and piss-head. They'd tried to be nice to him for more than three years but seldom got anything but abuse for their troubles.

'Guy's a scrote,' Jerry concluded.

Faraday was looking back along the hall. Outside he could see Cathy making notes as she talked to a uniformed sergeant. Already Mick Spellar's details would have been flashed to every patrol car and beatman in the city. As a kicking-off point for CID inquiries, he sounded deeply promising.

'Anyone else live here?'

'Mick's got a son, Scott. Nice lad, according to next door.'

'Was he around?'

8

'No idea. He certainly wasn't here when we turned up.'

'Has he got a room of his own?'

'Upstairs. I had a brief look this morning, but it'll be this afternoon before we get round to it properly.'

'What was it like?'

'Neat. Tidy. And the lad's mad about football. Kit and banners and stuff everywhere.'

Proctor's grunt of approval brought a smile to Faraday's face. Until very recently, the SOCO had turned out for the divisional rugby team, laying waste to a long list of opposing forwards. People foolish enough to take on Jerry Proctor seldom made the same mistake twice.

Faraday glanced at his watch. According to Proctor, the house would be off-limits for the rest of the day. There was a hands-and-knees search of the front room to organise once the body had been removed and he wanted more photographs of bloodstains on the wall around the fireplace. Fibre collection and then finger-printing the room to eliminate intruders would take God knows how long, and on top of that there was the post-mortem to arrange. The local hospital was offering ten o'clock in the evening but he'd yet to pin down the Home Office pathologist. The guy lived down in Dorset and had taken his daughter to some gymkhana or other.

'And the old boy?' Faraday nodded at the front room.

'Fractured skull probably. Whoever did it will need a change of footwear.'

Proctor wiped his nose on the back of his hand and shook his head. Eleven years on the Scenes of Crime unit had armoured him against the more obvious forms of shock, but the sight of Sammy Spellar had added yet another cooling body to the sad tally of broken lives that no amount of hi-tech forensic investigation could put together. People were screwing up more and more. And he had a thousand photographs to prove it.

On the point of leaving, Faraday paused. He'd heard something from the back of the house. It sounded like the splintering of wood. He glanced at Proctor. He'd heard it, too. Both men were setting off down the hall when the kitchen door burst open in front of them. The intruder was in his forties. He had a bony, yellowing face and a snake tattoo down the side of his neck. He carried a Thresher's bag in one hand and a carving knife in the other.

Without warning, he dropped the bag and lunged at Faraday with the knife, narrowly missing his shoulder. In the tiny hall, the smell of booze was overpowering. Faraday took a step backwards, waited until the knife hand came up again, then kicked the intruder's knee as hard as he could. The knife skittered down the bare boards of the hall while the intruder grabbed at his knee, bellowing with pain and rage. Hobbling, he came at Faraday again but it was child's play this time to turn him. Moments later Faraday had an armlock on his neck, tightening it to throttle-point every time he tried to struggle.

Proctor was squatting in the hall, studying the man's trainers and the bottom of his jeans with interest. The bollocking he was about to give the uniforms outside, the ones who were supposed to have sealed off the house, could wait. He glanced up at Faraday, shaking his head in amazement, then stood upright again, towering over the intruder.

'A name would help,' he said. 'Just for the record.'

Faraday relaxed the armlock enough to permit speech. When the intruder lashed out at Proctor with his feet, he tightened it again.

'Get the neighbour in here,' Faraday said. 'It'll be quicker.'

Proctor went to the front door and called to one of the uniformed PCs. A couple of minutes later, the neighbour confirmed that the intruder was Mick Spellar. By now, he was sitting on the stairs, taking great gulps of air. He'd been down to the offie for a couple of bottles of vodka. He'd treated himself to a mouthful or two on the way home. Coming in through the back, he'd heard voices. Round here you were barmy to investigate without taking precautions. Hence the knife.

Faraday told him to turn his pockets out. From his denim jacket, with some reluctance, he produced a debit card. Faraday took it outside to the daylight to be sure of the name on the bottom. It read 'S. Spellar'. Spotting Cathy, he threaded his way through the crowd and told her to call off the search for Mick.

'Why?'

'He's turned up. Pissed as a rat.'

'You're serious?'

'Yes.'

'Then he's a dickhead.' She stared at Faraday. 'Isn't he?'

Back inside, he showed the dead man's debit card to Proctor. By now, Mick Spellar had surrendered his jeans and runners to the SOCO, who was sealing them carefully inside heavy-duty plastic evidence bags. Even in the gloom of the hall, Faraday could see where dark gouts of blood had splashed over the frayed denim.

At length, Jerry Proctor glanced up. He saw the debit card in Faraday's hand and nodded. Motivation. Opportunity. And now arrest.

'Subtle, this isn't,' he muttered.

Two

Paul Winter loved informants. He loved their vulnerability and their bent little ways. He loved the smell of greed and needfulness they brought with them for their periodic meets. He loved the way they stitched each other up, all the time, for nothing more than a drink, a couple of quid and the chance to settle a score or two. And most of all, he loved being the conductor of this extraordinary orchestra of fuck-wits, and whingers, and no-brain low-life. He called them his Chorus of Dwarfs. And he taught them to sing better than any other detective in the city.

On this particular Saturday, he was due to meet a new prospect. On the phone she'd called herself Juanita and for a change she even sounded foreign. Lately, local girls had taken to using exotic names in a bid to rid themselves of being Tracy or Sharon. Informants were like that. Losers since birth.

Now, sitting in an Old Portsmouth pub around the corner from the cathedral, Winter watched the tourists flocking in for lunch. The venue for the meet had been her idea. Normally informants liked to choose somewhere closer to their own territory, not *too* close in case they got clocked by someone they knew, but close enough to avoid the traumas of crossing the class divide. The American Bar was as close as Pompey got to posh, the haunt of lawyers and architects and sharp-suited young entrepreneurs from the glitzy Gunwharf Quays development across the road. Most of the informants Winter ran would die of social exposure the moment they stepped in through the door.

On the phone this woman Juanita had offered a handful of names for collateral. They were good names, names that Winter recognised from the eighties, young thugs who'd run with the 6.57 crew, packing the first-class carriages of Saturday's early train out of the city, terrorising rival fans in football grounds all over the country. A decade later, in a development that would have won plaudits from the Harvard Business School, these psychopaths had transferred their considerable talents to the supply of Class A narcotics, calling on that same nationwide network of hardcore football hooligans to underwrite the deal. In the process the best of them had become very rich indeed, but what made this success story so very Portsmouth was the fact that they refused to change their ways. They still wore knock-off Armani suits. They still preferred the Stanley knife to the corporate lawyer. And however gaudily they flaunted their new wealth, they still lived in the backstreets of Buckland and Paulsgrove, a constant taunt for a police force increasingly bound hand and foot by paperwork, legislation and the nervous hand of the headquarters performance management team.

Take informants. Winter was forty-seven. In the early days, he and his colleagues had enjoyed a virtually free hand with the men and women who wanted to trade information for cash, or revenge, or any of the thousand other reasons they'd pick up the phone or pass the word. Now, though, the handling of informants had become as complicated and bureau-cratic as everything else in the force. You had to fill out dozens of forms, get witnessed receipts, pull your poor bloody grass through a receiving line of account-ants, and line-managers, and God knows who else before he got a chance to squirt a confidence or two your way. That, in Winter's opinion, was a criminal waste of a prime CID asset. In Portsmouth, with its on-going tribal feuds, informants were often the shortest cut to a result. Without informants, detectives like him were dead in the water. Hence his quiet determination to carry on running them the way he knew best. Meetings in pubs. Lots of pressure. And the promise of a quid or two if things worked out.

By twenty past two, Juanita hadn't showed. Half-way through the *Daily Telegraph* for the second time, Winter was on the point of leaving when a small, squat figure in jeans and a leather jacket emerged from the restaurant. He must have had the longest lunch in history. Winter hadn't seen him go in and there was no other exit from the conservatory area where the food was served. The pub was beginning to empty now and Winter was about to fold his paper and head for the door when he realised who the diner was. The man was standing over his table, staring down at him. Money might have bought him a decent leather jacket but it couldn't do anything for his tiny, lopsided face, or the two long razor scars that bisected his shorn scalp.

He pulled out a chair and sat down.

'Long time,' he said, 'no see.'

Winter summoned a smile. Marty Harrison was the closest Portsmouth could offer to a big-time drug baron. According to the latest intelligence, he was wholesaling serious quantities of cocaine. He had supply lines of the stuff established from Liverpool, Manchester and London. He had a house in Puerto Banus, another somewhere in Northern Cyprus and a £340,000 motor yacht moored up at Port Solent. Even the Drugs Squad found it hard to get close to him, but narcotics had very definitely become the hottest ticket in town and nicking Marty Harrison was any detective's wet dream – just one of the reasons Winter was determined to win himself a posting to the squad before age and retirement caught up with him.

'Marty.' Winter gestured at his empty glass. 'What can I get you?'

Harrison ignored the offer. Years ago, he and Winter had had protracted dealings over a seizure of cannabis. Not a lot of money had been involved, and for months Harrison had resisted the idea of even talking to CID, but in the end, in return for certain information about a newcomer moving into heroin and cocaine, Winter had destroyed the file. Like most good deals, both parties had walked away happy – though Harrison had made a point of not talking to him since. Winter had occasionally wondered whether Harrison's subsequent rise to fame and fortune hadn't somehow dated from that moment. Other people's success was like that. It made you feel cast off. And it made you feel envious.

Now, with a chilling theatricality, Harrison put his hands on the table, bunching them into fists. He had huge hands, navvy's hands, and the skin of each finger between the first and second knuckle was tattooed with a single blue letter. The left hand read NOEL. The right, including the thumb, spelled BLAKE. Noel Blake was a legendary Pompey defender in the '88 promotion-winning side, a towering centre-back who cut off visiting attackers at the knees. Marty, according to word on the street, did the same.

Harrison studied Winter a moment longer, then smiled.

'Message from Juanita,' he said simply. 'Sorry to stand you up.'

Winter did his best to look concerned.

'Nothing serious, I hope.'

'No, mate.' Harrison shook his head. 'Nothing a good dentist can't sort out.'

Minutes later, through the pub window, Winter was watching Harrison climb into a dented BMW when his mobile rang. It was Cathy Lamb, the duty CID sergeant.

'We've pulled a bloke in for murder,' she said briskly. 'Boss wants you to talk to him.'

The first interview with Mick Spellar began at seventeen fifty-three. He'd spent the last four hours at the city's Bridewell police station, sobering up in one of the cells. A police surgeon had given him a full examination, and taken scrapings from under his fingernails. Sealed in plastic containers, these would be readied for despatch with the blood samples from Mick Spellar's runners and jeans to a forensic laboratory in Chepstow. A match with Sammy's DNA would help seal the case against Mick Spellar. Son kicks father to death. Another home defeat.

The interview rooms at the Bridewell had recently been repainted and the tang of white emulsion still hung in the air. An audio feed was relayed through speakers to the room next door, and Faraday settled himself on the edge of the bare table, a pen and scrap of paper beside him. Putting together an interview team had been less than easy. At full strength he had five detectives at his disposal, but a couple had been extracted to join a major inquiry up in Aldershot while another was on leave. That left just two bodies. And one of them, to Faraday's infinite regret, was Paul Winter.

Not that Winter lacked interviewing skills. On the contrary, he was bloody good at it. He knew how to build relationships, how to lard a conversation with a smile and a wink, how to worm his way into someone's confidence, and win their trust, and lead them ever so gently towards the series of yawning traps he'd dug in their path. On the edge of that first abyss he'd let them pause, and glance down, and when they reached out to steady themselves – as they inevitably did – it would always be Winter's hand they found first.

In the eyes of some of his fellow detectives, Winter had turned duplicity and verbal sleight of hand into an art form, scoring a series of amazing results, but as far as Faraday was concerned, the man was an affront, the living proof of how corrupting CID work could be. It wasn't only that he was dishonest or untrustworthy. It was the way he regarded trust as just another currency – to be accumulated, invested, and then spent. To Faraday, Winter was a man without any shred of morality. Give Winter too much rope and you'd be dangling from the nearest tree by nightfall.

His voice came through the speakers at Faraday's elbow, warm, intimate, the kind of guy you'd open up to in a pub. He was inviting everyone to grab a seat. There followed the scraping sound of chairs and then another voice Faraday recognised as the duty solicitor. Fenwick was new to the city, an ambitious young northerner who'd already badged himself with a V–reg BMW, and it was obvious to Faraday that he regarded the case as a windfall challenge. Keep Mick Spellar out of prison, and Fenwick would be the toast of the legal community within hours.

'My client would like to make a statement,' he began.

They took the first break at seven o'clock, standing around the table in the room next door while Winter sorted a tray of coffees from the machine down the corridor. The other interviewer was a young female detective, Dawn Ellis, a slight, pretty twenty-six-year-old with a cap of auburn hair and the clearest eyes Faraday had ever seen. She'd only been on the division since Christmas, but already she'd earned herself a reputation for shrewdness and a certain tenacity. In her previous life, Dawn had been a hairdresser.

Anyone who could survive eight months of jokes about blow jobs in the CID room would have few problems with the likes of Mick Spellar.

'He's making it up as he goes along,' she said to Faraday, 'and Fenwick knows it.'

According to Mick Spellar, his son Scott was responsible for the old man's death. He'd found the pair of them scrapping in the front room. He'd pulled the lad off and given him a good talking to, but he'd no idea how bad the damage had been. Of course the blood on his shoes had been Sammy's. The stuff had sprayed everywhere.

Winter returned with the coffees. He'd tuned in to the conversation on his way back down the corridor.

'Early days, boss.' He handed Faraday a brimming polystyrene cup. 'Might help to find the lad, though.'

Faraday grunted agreement. The neighbours next door were positive that they hadn't seen Scott leave but, as Fenwick had whispered to Mick Spellar, the rear access would have been an obvious escape route. The suggestion had drawn a sharp rebuke from Dawn Ellis but already it was obvious that getting a confession out of Spellar was going to be tougher than anyone had anticipated.

Winter was still looking at Faraday. Both men were aware of the gulf between them, but to Faraday's intense irritation Winter handled it far more effectively than he did. Indeed, the older man often seemed to take an active delight in the thinness of the DI's skin.

'Where are we looking, then? For little Scottie?'

'Cathy's circulated a photo. Jerry Proctor found it in the boy's bedroom.'

'Good one, is it? Recent?'

'Last week. Since you ask.'

It was true. Jerry had come across a strip of passport photographs, each dated on the back. A couple of them showed a cheerful, crop-haired youth in his late teens. He had a crooked grin and the suggestion of a bruise under one eye. In the other two photos, he'd been joined by a girl of the same age. She had long black hair, three nose-rings and a smile even wider than Scott's. In one of the shots, her tongue was in his ear.

'We'll find him,' Faraday muttered. 'But it would be nice to put Spellar away first.'

Once the interview began again, Ellis and Winter started to make progress. For one thing, Spellar was exhausted. He had the attention span of a gnat and keeping track of all the lies he was obliged to tell was obviously beyond him. Time and again, Winter encouraged him to go over the events of the morning, gently-gently, the way you might ask someone about their holidays, slowly widening the focus until Spellar began to trip himself up. As the sequence of events became more and more chaotic, Spellar's voice got lower and lower until Faraday had trouble making out exactly what he was saying. No, he couldn't explain why he hadn't called an ambulance for his father. And no, he should never have left him lying there while he went down the offie for a bottle or two. Even Fenwick's murmured protests started to lack conviction.

The interview had degenerated into near-silence when Faraday's mobile began to trill. He fetched it out of his pocket, listening hard as Dawn Ellis tried to concentrate what was left of Spellar's mind.

'Joe? Harry Wayte.'

Faraday reached for a pen. Harry Wayte always wanted a favour. He was the DI in charge of the area Drugs Squad, a big, bluff career detective who hid his determination to smash the local drug supply networks behind a robust sense of humour and a bottomless thirst.

'What can I do for you?'

Harry had just seen the details on Scott Spellar. He wanted to know more. Faraday bent to the phone, explaining that the lad was a potential suspect in a murder case. He was alleged to have kicked his grandad to death. Picking him up had become a priority.

'When did all this happen?'

'This morning. Around half nine.'

'Where?'

'Up in Paulsgrove.'

'No chance.'

'How do you know?'

'The lad was in Whitechapel by then, scoring half a kilo of coke. We tailed him up the A3. He left Paulsgrove around six this morning.'

Scott Spellar, according to Wayte, was working as a courier for Marty Harrison. He'd started a couple of years ago, nicking mobile phones to order, but now he'd graduated to drugs mule. The going rate for an excursion to London was around a hundred and fifty pounds. Some weeks Scott was making the round trip twice.

Faraday permitted himself a smile. As well as the passport photographs, Proctor had found nearly eight hundred pounds in cash and a couple of airline tickets for Ibiza in the boy's bedroom. This afternoon, Faraday had wondered where Scott had got the money from. Now he knew.

'You tailed him back as well?'

'No. We lost him in Walton-on-Thames.'

'But he still came back?'

'He was carrying, Joe. He had to. Harrison gets funny about late deliveries.'

'So where was he taking the stuff?'

'That's exactly it. That's what we don't know. That's why we were on him in the first place.'

There was a long silence. Next door, Paul Winter was telling Spellar that his story was a load of old bollocks. At length, Faraday cleared his throat.

'You want me to sweat the lad? Assuming we pick him up?'

'I'm just saying he'll need an alibi.'

'You're suggesting he'd give me chapter and verse on the likes of Harrison?'

'I'm suggesting the prospect of a murder charge might concentrate his tiny mind. Grassing Harrison wouldn't be the cleverest thing he ever did, but the alternative might be worse.'

'But he didn't do it, Harry.'

'Of course he didn't. We know that. He knows that. But he can't be certain we're not playing games. Who else is in the frame?'

'His father.'

'And what's the strength?'

'One hundred per cent. We're talking to him now – and the way things are going we may not bother waiting for the forensic.'

'How much time have you got? Can you get an extension?'

Faraday glanced at his watch. Getting an extension meant keeping Spellar longer than the permitted twenty-four hours. And that, in turn, meant going to the superintendent with some bullshit story about needing to test the man's alibi.

'I can't do that, Harry. If he coughs, I'll have to charge him.'

'And you think he will?'

'Yes.'

There was a long silence. Then Harry Wayte suggested delaying a formal charge until tomorrow morning. Just in case.

'Just in case what?'

'Young Scottie turns up.'

Twenty minutes later, with Mick Spellar ever closer to confessing, word came from Paulsgrove that Scott Spellar had appeared at the house in Anson Avenue. Recognising his face from the circulated photo, the young PC guarding the place had arrested him. As soon as transport was available, he'd be taken down to the city. Where would Faraday like him delivered?

'The Bridewell,' Faraday grunted, listening to the exchanges next door as Winter dismantled the last of Spellar's fairy tale about defending his poor old dad. The truth, suggested Winter, was much simpler. He'd gone to bed pissed. He'd woken up pissed. And when the old boy wouldn't part with his debit card to buy more booze, Spellar had lost his rag. No?

The silence that followed was broken by yet another call. This time it was Faraday's CID boss, Detective Superintendent Arnold Pollock, a thin, intense high-flyer with a Cambridge degree and little time for moral nuances. He was obviously at some party or other because Faraday could hear laughter and the clink of glasses in the background.

'How far have you got with Spellar?'

'Nearly through, sir. I'd give it another half hour at the most.'

'What about this lad, Scott?'

'He's on his way down.'

'Get what you can from him, will you? Red Rum's costing us an arm and a leg.'

Red Rum? Faraday stared at the phone. It sounded like the codename for some kind of major operation but he couldn't be sure.

'It's the drugs job Harry's running,' Pollock explained. 'And if Harry says he wants the squeeze on the boy Scott, then that's good enough for me. Just do it, Joe. OK?'

Abruptly, the phone went dead. Next door, through

the speakers, Mick Spellar was at last agreeing that he'd kicked his father to death.

Three

The photos arrived shortly afterwards from the Scenes of Crime office at Cosham police station. With Mick Spellar back in a holding cell, formally charged with murder, the interview team had reconvened in Faraday's makeshift office. He tore the manila envelope open and shook the photos on to the table. They were big, ten by ten inches, full colour, perfect focus, and each of them offered incontestable evidence of the consequences of Mick Spellar's rage. In one photograph, the old man scarcely had a face at all.

Winter was studying the photos with interest. At length he looked up at Faraday. By now Scott Spellar was occupying a locked office down the corridor.

'What has he said so far?'

'He's denied it. As he would.'

'Has he asked for representation?'

'He's been offered the duty brief.'

'And?'

'He was outraged. He says he's got nothing to hide and he thinks that getting himself a solicitor is halfway to pleading guilty.'

Winter beamed, saying nothing. Then he slid the photos back into the envelope, making sure that the most graphic shot was on top. Against his better judgement, Faraday had decided that it made sense to keep the interviewing team intact but the decision filled him with disgust. Winter, as he knew only too well, loved challenges like this, bluff piled on bluff, until the moment came when he could turn an interviewee upside down and empty him of everything he knew. The Police and Criminal Evidence Act should have put a fence around individuals in situations like these but PACE made no allowances for artists like Winter.

Now, the detective emptied his coffee cup, wiped his mouth with the back of his hand, and then stood up.

'No point delaying it,' he said silkily. 'Is there?'

By the time Scott Spellar was inside the interview room, his anger was coming close to physical violence. He was wearing stone-washed Levis and a blue Pompey football top and he bent forward over the table, practically nose-to-nose with Winter. No way would he ever lay a finger on his grandad. What kind of fucker would suggest a thing like that?

'Your dad. That kind of fucker.'

'He says I killed him? How?'

'He says you kicked him to death. On the front-room carpet.'

'That's what he's saying?'

'Yes.'

'And you believe him?'

'I don't know what to believe. That's why you can help us, son. Here . . .'

Next door, Faraday heard a rustling noise as Winter stripped the cellophane from a packet of cigarettes. After the scrape of the match came a long silence. Then the boy's voice again, lower this time.

'When's all this supposed to have happened?'

'This morning. Around nine o'clock.'

'And he's really dead? This ain't some wind-up?'

'No.'

'Then I can't have killed him.'

'Why not?'

'Because I wasn't even fucking there.'

'Fine, then you're off the hook son. Just as long as

we know where you were.' Winter paused. 'So where were you?'

For the next half hour or so, Winter played the boy like a fish, allowing him plenty of line, allowing him the illusion of freedom, letting him mumble on about spending the night at his girlfriend's, or his mate's place, or getting up early and going out for a walk, or any of a dozen other fictions all of which fell apart when Winter, the voice of sweet reason, asked for corroboration.

Finally, past nine o'clock, the interview came full circle with Scott simply protesting his innocence, a plea untarnished by anything as helpful as an alibi.

'No fucking way,' he kept saying. 'Why would I ever do a thing like that? I wasn't even there.'

'So where were you?'

'Told you. I was out.'

'But where? Help me, son. Tell me where you were.'

'Can't. Doesn't matter where. Just out.'

Winter was edging towards closure. Faraday could feel it. At length, he sighed, letting fear and silence do his work for him. He'd done his best for the boy. He'd tried to see it his way, tried to offer him the benefit of the doubt, but in the end he had a job to do, no matter how distasteful that job might be.

'I don't believe you, son,' he said at last. 'I think you were there in that house and I think this is down to you. Maybe your dad helped. Maybe the pair of you did it. But that's no defence, not in a court of law, not with something as horrible as this.'

Faraday stiffened, recognising Winter's cue to show Scott Spellar the contents of the manila envelope. There was a soft shuffling noise as the photographs spilled across the table, then a moment of absolute silence as the boy tried to make sense of the pulped remains of his grandfather's face. The work of the

Scenes of Crime photographers was seldom pretty. They weren't paid to disguise the truth.

Scott's voice was low, barely audible, pain salted with disbelief.

'Jesus . . .' he said.

Another silence. Then Winter. He was playing it stern this time, the father figure with young Scottie's best interests at heart.

'I hate to say this, son, but you should maybe take a good look at yourself. It doesn't matter whether or not you meant it. It doesn't matter whether or not you lost your temper. All that matters is these, because all that's left of him is this. Take a look at the next one. Go on, look at it.'

'Told you already. I was with my girlfriend.'

'Name? Address? Phone number?'

'She . . . oh shit . . .'

'You don't want us to talk to her?'

'No fucking point, is there?'

'Why not?'

'Because . . . oh, Jesus, forget it.'

'We can't Scott, we can't forget it. That's not the way things work here. You're down for murder, son. And even worse, you're down for kicking the shit out of your own grandad. You know who gets a copy of this lot? Of every single photograph? The jury. And you know what they'll do when they see what you're seeing?'

He let the question hang in the air. Faraday got up and went to the little wired glass window in the door. He felt cheapened. He felt trapped. He felt as banged-up as Scott Spellar. This was grotesque.

The boy was talking again, but in a different tone of voice, confidential, private, treating his interviewer the way Winter had always designed it, as a friend. He'd been to London. He was involved with some guys. They were dealing dope. Nothing heavy. Just an ounce or two of weed. He'd brought the stuff back and dropped it off and naturally he wasn't keen to go a whole lot further. Not because it hadn't happened but because you never grassed on your mates.

'Not even when you might be facing a murder charge? Your own grandad?'

It was a reasonable question, but Scott ducked it.

'No way,' he said. 'No fucking way.'

'Then I don't believe you.'

'You have to.'

'No, I don't.'

'Yes, you do.'

'Why?'

'Because it's true.'

The exchange went on and on, Winter pushing harder and harder, tearing layer after layer of fancy wrapping off Scott's pathetic little parcel. First it was dope. Then it was something harder. Finally, by the time Cathy Lamb knocked on Faraday's door and stepped inside, it was cocaine, a lot of cocaine, and guys so heavy that only a lunatic would cross them.

Faraday looked inquiringly at Cathy. A break from this would be more than welcome.

'The post-mortem starts in twenty minutes, boss,' she said. 'I'll run you up there.'

The sight of Sammy Spellar's thin little body under the pathologist's knife compounded Faraday's growing sense of despair. What had happened up on Anson Avenue was bad enough, graphic evidence of a society gone mad, but what was even worse – and what he'd become part of – was the tawdry piece of theatre down in Interview Room One. The fate they were about to inflict on Scott Spellar didn't bear contemplation. Not if he bent the knee to Paul Winter.

Stepping out of the hospital morgue, Faraday

thanked the pathologist for the sacrifice of his Saturday night. The post-mortem had yielded no surprises – Sammy Spellar had died from a massive brain haemorrhage – but the procedure was mandatory and Faraday would be getting the typed report within days. Before he said goodbye he inquired how the pathologist's daughter had done at her gymkhana. Her name was Susie and this was her first pony.

The pathologist took his time peeling off his surgical gloves.

'She won,' he said proudly.

Back at his listening post at the Bridewell, Faraday knew at once that Winter had also posted a victory. He was helping Scott Spellar piece together his trips to London, still using the threat of the murder charge to squeeze every last particle of information from the boy. The addresses he visited in London, the amounts he carried back to Portsmouth, the drops he used in the city, even the times of the trains he caught when he couldn't be bothered to take the car he'd bought on the proceeds of his first six months. Every last detail Winter wrote down, making sure he had it right and making sure that Scott Spellar knew it. These notes of Winter's were handcuffs, binding the youth hand and foot. Henceforth, if he was sensible, Scott Spellar would do exactly what Winter decreed.

The formal interview over, he offered Scott another cigarette. The boy told him he didn't want it. This time last night, life had been really kushti. He'd had money, a job, respect, a girlfriend, the lot. Now, he'd lost everything.

'It's over, isn't it?' he muttered. 'You'll bang me up. I'm fucked.'

'Bang you up for what?'

'For drugs. Possession. Supply. The whole fucking lot.'

29

Faraday heard Winter's soft chuckle. This was the moment he savoured most of all. This was the moment that would change Scott's life for ever.

'We could do a deal,' he murmured. 'Sweet for you, sweet for me.'

'How's that, then?'

'You keep me in touch, street-wise. You give me names, addresses, who's carrying what for who, just like you did just then. In return I give you money. Maybe quite a lot of money.'

'That's grassing.'

'You're right. But that way you'll get paid twice. Once by us and once by Marty Harrison.'

The name drew an audible intake of breath from Scott. It was the first time that Winter had mentioned Harrison and Faraday could picture the fear in the boy's eyes. After a moment or two, he tried to laugh it off, pretending he'd never heard of Marty Harrison, but his denial fooled nobody, least of all Paul Winter.

'We know,' he said softly. 'We know about you and Marty.'

'How?'

'Surveillance. Obs. We've got you clocked, son. You want the date and times?'

'You're winding me up.'

'You think so? You want to give Marty a ring? Check it out?' There was another silence, longer this time, then Scott's voice came through the speakers again. He sounded like a child. He sounded close to tears.

'You think I'd grass up Marty?' he whispered. 'You must be off your fucking head. The guy'd kill me. He'd chop me up in little pieces and feed me to his dogs. You know what he's like. Jesus . . .'

Faraday shot a look at Cathy then bent to the speaker again as the shuffle of paper came from the room next door. Winter was sounding positively cheerful.

'These notes stay with me,' he purred. 'I'm not after a statement, nothing formal, nothing you'll have to sign, but remember what you've told me, and remember that I'm the mate you need if things get out of hand. At the end of the day, son, my gang's bigger than Marty's.' Faraday heard the scrape of a chair, then Winter's voice again, brisker and more business-like. 'You're right about Class A drugs, by the way. Carrying that stuff in those sorts of quantities is serious shit. Here.'

'What's that?'

'My mobile number. Ring me when you've had a think.'

Cathy drove Faraday home. On the face of it, he'd done a good day's work. A murder solved, some priceless intelligence on its way to the Drugs Squad, and every prospect of an informant at the very heart of one of the city's major drug rings. In anyone's book, that was a result. But it felt very different.

'Come in for a drink.'

Cathy followed Faraday into the house. She could count the number of times this had happened on the fingers of one hand. Of all the detectives on the division, she liked to think that she was by far the closest to Faraday, but the kinship they shared had rarely extended to anything remotely social.

The big lounge occupied most of the ground floor. Framed photographs, most of them black and white, hung on the walls. Faraday waved vaguely in the direction of the kitchen and told Cathy to help herself.

'There's Scotch and all sorts,' he said. 'Open a bottle of wine if you'd prefer.'

It was a single man's kitchen, organised, indexed, neat. Faraday stored spaghetti in tall glass jars and had a blown-up copy of the tide table Blu-Tacked to the fridge. Cathy found the Scotch and poured half a tumbler for Faraday before making a coffee for herself. By the time she got back to the sitting room, Faraday was slumped in his favourite armchair, his body half-turned towards the darkness beyond the tall glass sliding doors.

The ice clinked in the glass when she gave it to him. His gloom was almost visible, a heavy aura that a child would colour black in a picture book.

'It's J-J, isn't it?'

Faraday didn't answer. He loved this house, perched on the edge of the harbour. He loved its silence, and its space, and the way it had looked after them both for the entire span of the boy's life. The house, like Joe-Junior, had been a fixed point in an ever more chaotic world. The one had gone with the other. Until last week.

'Yes,' he said.

'Because you miss him.'

'Yes.'

'Because he's never been away before.'

Faraday nodded, taking a pull at the Scotch, closing his eyes for a moment as it burned its way towards his belly. Once again, he felt like Scott Spellar. Nowhere to turn. No place left to go.

'Gone is a good word,' he said slowly, 'and you know what? I don't think he'll ever come back.'

'You told me he had a return ticket.'

'He does. He's due back next week. I'm meeting him off the ferry. But it won't be the same. I know it won't.'

'How can you say that?'

Faraday shot her a glance. She was standing beneath a line of Janna's framed photographs, nursing a cup of black coffee, ever solid, ever sensible. If it hadn't been the police force, Faraday thought, she'd have made a brilliant community nurse.

Cathy asked the question again, not bothering to hide her impatience. Faraday was behaving like a child and she wanted him to know it.

He studied her a moment, weighing some inner decision, then got to his feet and went upstairs. When he came back he was carrying a sheet of paper.

'This came last night,' he said woodenly. 'He took his laptop with him.'

Cathy's head bent briefly to the paper.

'He's twenty-two for God's sake,' she said, looking up again. 'He's allowed to fall in love.'

'He's deaf, Cath. Deaf kids never grow up.'

'Who says?'

'I do. And twenty-two years alone with him tells me I know the lad, believe me.'

Cathy nodded, watching Faraday empty the tumbler. She was tempted to sympathise, to offer him the comfort he undoubtedly needed, but she knew the truth was long overdue.

'Maybe that's the problem,' she said lightly.

'What?'

'The twenty-two years. That tells me you don't want him to grow up.'

Cathy was home by midnight. She and her husband lived in a modern house at Portchester, fifteen minutes' drive from the top of the island. She parked her Escort in the carport, wondering what had happened to Pete. This morning he'd mentioned an evening session with his sailing buddies, but said he'd be back by ten. Despite the usual staffing crises at Fareham nick, he'd managed to wangle the entire weekend off.

She let herself into the house, turned off the alarm and dumped her keys by the fish tank in the lounge, wondering whether she could manage another coffee.

Pete should be back soon. It might be nice to sit up and wait for him.

She looked round, not able to make up her mind, suddenly wearied by all the decisions she seemed to get wrong. Only last year she'd repainted this room. She'd gone for a shade of mid-grey described as 'dove' in the colour charts, and on sunny days she liked to think it gave the lounge a certain sophistication. Lately, though, it had just looked cold.

She drifted across to the phone. There was a single message waiting on the tape but her finger hovered over the replay button. On the table beside the phone was the little collection of mementos she'd harboured to remind herself of the special times. A pebble from the beach at Weymouth, picked up the afternoon Pete had so nearly won the Laser Nationals. A dried cornflower, pressed between two wafers of perspex, plucked from a meadow in the Austrian Tyrol where they'd spent their honeymoon. She'd met Pete as a probationer. From the moment she'd first set eyes on him, there'd been no one else she'd ever wanted.

Was he really having an affair? She simply didn't know. She had evidence in spades – the occasional scent of perfume on his shirts, unexplained absences, mysterious phone calls – but the parts of her that would never be a detective were determined to ignore the clues. Maybe he was under stress. Maybe he was going through some early mid-life crisis. Maybe there was some other reason for his drinking and his endless silences. God knows, regular two-week stand-bys for the force Tactical Firearms Unit – on top of everything else – would surely stretch any man to breaking point.

At last, she listened to the message tape. It was Alan, the skipper of the little twenty-nine-foot yacht the lads had entered for the Fastnet. The race began in exactly a week's time, a round trip of more than seven hundred miles to Southern Ireland and back, and

Cathy knew how much Pete was looking forward to it. It would be a chance to get away, to leave his demons behind and concentrate on what he did best. Winning.

The message was timed at ten-fifteen. Alan asked Pete to give him a ring. Something about a new set of bottle screws for the standing rigging. Something they needed to sort out before Monday. Cathy scribbled a note on the pad beside the phone and went through to the kitchen to fill the kettle. She was still washing up the breakfast cups when she heard tyres on the drive.

Pete came in through the back door, shutting it with his heel. She could tell he'd been drinking because he had a big grin on his face. He gave her the briefest peck on the cheek and then headed at once for the fridge. The fridge was where they kept the vodka.

Cathy turned the kettle off. It was pointless offering him coffee.

'Good evening?' she inquired.

'Brilliant.'

'Where have you been?'

Pete was pouring himself a hefty slug of Smirnoff, not bothering about ice. She noticed a tiny tremor in his hand. Raising the glass, he faced her from the other end of the kitchen.

'Alan's,' he said. 'Cheers.'

Four

Next morning, Sunday, Faraday got up late. He showered, dressed, swallowed two paracetamol, binned the empty Scotch bottle and went out to the garage. On the point of starting the engine, he remembered the brakes.

The cab took him up through the city, over the creek at Hilsea, and on to the mainland. By the time he got to Anson Avenue, it was nearly eleven o'clock.

Downstairs, Jerry Proctor was preparing to call it a day. He'd been back at the Spellars' house since seven. All that remained now was to arrange for specialist cleaners to call early next week, and to find a time for a uniformed inspector to give the place a once-over in case of any damage claims. With luck, he could be back home in time to watch last night's recorded football highlights before his wife dished up lunch.

Mention of the football prompted Faraday to ask about Scott Spellar.

'I need to see his room.' He nodded towards the stairs. 'OK by you?'

Jerry had been right about the state of the lad's bedroom. Compared to the rest of the house, it looked pristine: neatly fitted wardrobe, fold-down desk, and a huge Pompey poster Sellotaped to the wall over the single bed.

Faraday edged around a pile of football shirts by the door and examined the mosaic of cuttings and photos that decorated the wall above the desk. One shot in particular caught his eye. It showed a pub side from one of the Sunday leagues. According to the carefully scissored *News* cutting beside it, they'd just won a Fair Play award. Scott Spellar was sitting in the middle of the front row, the ball clamped between his knees, grinning fit to bust. The cutting was only months old, but he looked about fourteen. Fair play? Faraday turned away, shaking his head.

The bedroom window faced south. The sun was strong through the glass and from here, on the slopes of Portsdown Hill, he could see the hazy sprawl of the city stretching away towards the gleam of the Solent, and the low swell of the Isle of Wight. There were a hundred and fifty thousand people down there, jig-sawed together in street after street of terraced housing. The parking was non-existent. The traffic was impossible. The schools were falling apart. The kids were out of control. And if you found yourself a job, the pay rates were often pitiful. Yet still folk hung on, glued to the island city by something deeper than habit.

More and more Faraday found himself asking what it was about the place that made it so particular, so infuriatingly special, but none of the sensible answers did it proper justice. He'd lived here for over twenty years and he'd grown to love the seafront, with its busy views, and the quiet, shadowed cobblestones of Old Portsmouth, still haunted by the tramp of the press gang, but this was the tourist's Pompey, Flagship Portsmouth, the image that the council loved to peddle on posters nationwide. What it didn't capture, or explain, were the subtler glimpses of a very different city. Even at the distance of two generations, poverty and war still seemed to shape the people he dealt with. They expected, and got, very little. A certain stoic resignation seemed to go with the turf. Yet still they managed a smile and a joke with people they trusted. Islanders were like that. Given any kind of choice, they always looked inward.

Was Scott Spellar as hemmed in as the rest of them? Or would he have the sense to pack his bags and get on a train and put several hundred miles between himself and Marty Harrison? Faraday didn't know, but that was hardly the point. What the lad needed now was the means to make a decision. Under the circumstances, he might not come back to the empty house for days – and in an area like this, break-ins were practically guaranteed.

A quick search through the chest of drawers drew a blank. The wardrobe was full of clothes but the pockets were largely empty. Faraday had begun to strip the bed when Jerry Proctor appeared at the door. He was finally through. He wanted to lock up and go home.

Faraday was still gazing at the bed.

'That eight hundred quid,' he began. 'Where is it?'

'Second drawer down.' Proctor nodded at the chest beneath the window. 'Brown doeskin wallet.'

'And you put it back?'

'Of course.'

Faraday went through the drawer again. Football socks, underpants, a couple of towels, a packet of Rizla cigarette papers, petrol coupons, a DJ Shadow cassette, an old Lottery ticket. But no wallet.

Proctor was frowning.

'It was definitely there', he said. 'Yesterday afternoon it was in there with the rest of the stuff. I took it out, counted it, and then put it back again.'

'Anyone else been up here?'

'Not to my knowledge.'

'What about the PC outside? Was he on all night?'

'Yes. It was still a scene of crime.'

'Where's his log?'

'At the station.'

Proctor clattered downstairs for his mobile. He was still deep in conversation, minutes later, when he returned. Finally he grunted a thank you and slipped the mobile into his pocket.

'DC Winter.' He was staring down at the open drawer. 'Logged in at 23.14. Stayed ten minutes and left.'

Faraday was back home by the time he made the call to Winter. He'd sat in his study for the best part of an hour, wondering whether this wasn't the opportunity he'd been waiting for, wondering whether it wouldn't be better to let Winter dig himself in even deeper before springing the trap.

Removing private property without going through the formal procedures was a primary breach of regulations. Winter knew that, and every next day that passed would compound the transgression. Money – cash – was especially sensitive. The Met were forever being accused of helping themselves to suspects' property and Hampshire's new Chief Constable had recently organised a task force to ensure that allegations like these didn't spread south. In the current climate, Winter might even lose his job.

The prospect of life without Paul Winter was deeply tempting, but the longer Faraday thought about the implications the more he knew he had to make the call at once. The priority, as far as he was concerned, was Scott Spellar. The lad was no angel but losing his grandfather in circumstances like yesterday's was quite enough grief for one day. The money, tainted though it might be, still belonged to him. Strictly speaking, Faraday should have notified Harry Wayte, who would doubtless regard it as evidence, but the stroke the Drugs Squad DI had pulled through Pollock still rankled, and eight hundred pounds – sensibly spent – might just put Scott Spellar beyond the reach of Marty Harrison. The last thing the boy needed was more trips to London.

Winter answered his mobile on the second ring.

'I'm at the garden centre,' he said cheerfully, 'with Joan.'

Joan was Winter's wife, a plump ex-teacher who dressed almost entirely in beige. The marriage had survived Winter's many affairs and appeared to be in ruder health than ever.

'Where did you get to last night,' Faraday began, 'after you left the Bridewell?'

Winter didn't answer for a moment. Faraday could hear his wife in the background asking about bedding plants.

'I went up to Paulsgrove,' Winter said at last. 'Spellar's place.'

'Why?'

'Why do you think? The kid's running serious dope. I needed a look through his stuff. It's what detectives do, boss.'

'And did you find anything?'

'Yeah, matter of fact I did. Eight hundred quid in notes.'

'And?'

'I seized it.'

'Did you register that with the PC outside?'

'Of course not. What's the doorman got to do with it?'

Faraday was watching a pair of mallards at the water's edge. Conversations with Paul Winter never went the way he intended and this one was no exception.

'So what happens to the money?' he said at last. 'Given that it belongs to Scott?'

'He gets it back.'

'When?'

'When he gets his shit together and gives me a ring and agrees to see me.'

'Ah . . .' Faraday began to pick at a loose thread on

the arm of the chair. 'So his own money buys him a meet? Is that the way it goes?'

'No, boss, me. It buys *me* a meet. That's why I took it. You think he'd see me otherwise?'

'That's hardly the point. There are rules here. Regulations – '

'I know that.'

'So why didn't you follow them?'

'Follow what?'

'The rules.'

'Are you serious?'

The tone of Winter's voice, weary, incredulous, brought a sudden blush of colour to Faraday's face. The man was treating him like a child. Real life was out there on the streets. Real life had fuck all to do with rules and regulations. Faraday had heard the phrases over and over and this time he'd had enough.

'Maybe we should continue this conversation in my office,' he said thickly. 'Just as soon as you can get there.'

There was another silence, briefer this time, before Winter began to chuckle.

'A pleasure, sir,' he said, 'then you can check the dosh yourself.'

'You'll be bringing it with you?'

'No need. I booked it in last night. Brown doeskin wallet. The night-shift skipper put it in the safe. Should be in the crime property store by now, if you'd like to check.'

Faraday ignored the sarcasm.

'I want the money back to the lad,' he said carefully. 'And I want proof that you've done it.'

Pete Lamb was out in the garden when Cathy went through to the lounge to take the call. Two mugs of coffee and a thick bacon sandwich had mopped up the worst of his hangover, and any minute now he'd be suggesting a stroll to the pub. What on earth had happened to day-long hikes across the Isle of Wight? To windsurfing at Hayling Island and a barbecue afterwards on the beach?

Cathy picked up the phone. It was the duty sergeant at the firearms range over at Netley. The leader on the duty Tactical Firearms Unit had gone down with a virus. Could Pete stand in while they sorted out a replacement?

'He's booked leave from the end of next week,' she said quickly. 'He's doing the Fastnet.'

'I know, love. It's just for a day or two.'

Cathy glanced out of the back window. Pete's long frame was sprawled in a deckchair, his face invisible behind the *Mail on Sunday*. She was about to go out there and ask him for a yes or no, but then she had second thoughts. Members of the duty TFU weren't allowed to touch alcohol. That would put the mockers on another gloomy lunchtime in the pub.

'He says it's fine,' she said brightly, 'as long as he can still do the race.'

Faraday spent the afternoon on Farlington Marshes, an RSPB nature reserve at the top of Langstone Harbour. He went there for the walk as much as anything else, a three-mile trek along the harbour edge that emptied his mind of the conversation with Winter. Years ago, he'd tried to ring-fence at least one day a week from the pressures of the job. Sundays had always been the obvious firebreak and if he'd wasted half of this one, then that was his own fault. The fact that Winter had promised to hand over Scott's money without insisting on a long meet with the boy was some small satisfaction.

The afternoon was hot and windless, and there was little activity amongst the birds. Wedged in his favourite spot against the seawall, Faraday watched a pair of newly arrived redshanks for a while, dancing in the shallows, but then he adjusted the focus on his Leica Red-Spots and swept the binoculars back along the harbourside path until his house swam into view, shimmering in the heat.

It was a two-storey construction, dating way back to the early nineteenth century, red brick at the bottom, white clapboard and glass at the top. It had been built for one of the barge-masters who'd used the ill-fated Portsmouth Canal and Faraday had often wondered whether this man, too, had been fascinated by the pageant of wildlife – birds especially – constantly unfolding on the wide, bright spaces of the harbour. The upper floor of the house was where Faraday had installed his study, tearing down a couple of inner divides to make a big, oblong space, with rugs on the polished floorboards and views out through the windows on three sides. From his first glimpse of the water, he'd known that there was nowhere else he ever wanted to live. The house was, at once, a delight, a shield, and a solace.

The freehold on the house had been a gift from Janna's American parents after she'd died. They'd both come over for the funeral, staying with Faraday and the baby in the damp little bungalow on the Isle of Wight that he and Janna had turned into their first real home. It had been obvious to both Julie and Frank that Faraday was going to have trouble coping with a four-month-old baby, and after their return to Seattle they'd sent him a long letter and a cheque for two hundred thousand dollars. Within a year, Faraday had become a police probationer, posted to Portsmouth, and the prospect of a career had encouraged him to put down roots. The bulk of the money had paid for the barge-master's house and with the rest he'd hired a nanny to look after Joe-Junior when he was on shift.

Several months after they'd moved in, Faraday had

taken photographs of the house, trying to frame it the way that Janna would have done. Janna had made a name for herself as a professional photographer with a very distinctive take on her subjects, and one of her many bequests to her husband was the equipment she'd collected over the years. Faraday had used the simplest of the cameras, rising early to capture the spill of the yellow sunrise over the front of the house, and he'd sent half a dozen of the resulting photos across to his in-laws in Seattle. *This is your investment in our future*, he'd written. Too damn right.

He gazed at it now through the binoculars, his elbows braced against his knees, half-imagining the shelves of books against the back wall, and the big roll-top desk where he and J-J had first tiptoed into the world of birds.

Confirmation that the child was deaf had come days before his first birthday, and for years after that Faraday had knocked on endless doors, hunting for advice. He'd wanted a way of talking to the child, a way of getting through. Signing was fine, and – once J-J was established at the special school – the daily diary they'd shared had been a godsend, but Faraday had never been as close to any other human being, not even Janna, and he sensed instinctively that there had to be a better way.

In the end it had been a friend's suggestion that had taken him to the city's Central Library. She'd faced a similar challenge and she recommended a particular bay on the second floor, three along from the photo-copier. Faraday had found it in minutes. The middle shelf was full of picture books. About birds.

He'd brought them home by the armful – and early evenings and weekends had found Faraday and Joe-Junior sprawled in various corners of the study or the downstairs lounge, poring over shots of waders and warblers, of harriers and kites. The beauty of the house was its harbourside location. The view from the window was the pictures brought to life. Shelduck, mergansers, godwits, curlews, all real, all moving, and – as far as J-J was concerned – all totally mute.

For the boy, though, that hadn't mattered in the slightest. What he woke up to, what he pressed his nose against on cold winter mornings, was a world that belonged exclusively to himself and his dad. Faraday understood this, not because some expert had told him, but because he'd seen it in the child's eyes, heard it in the strange, tuneless cackle that served for him as laughter. J-J loved his dad very much, and the birds – with their thousand different shapes, plumages, habitats, breeding patterns – were the messages they passed back and forth.

By the time J-J was ready to leave the special school and ride his luck with ordinary kids, those messages had become a language, expressive, flexible, capable of infinite nuance. When J-J made gannet wings, his arms arrowed back from his thin little shoulders, it meant that he was hungry. When Faraday posed as a heron, one leg tucked up as he fought for balance in the middle of the kitchen, it signalled another trip to Titchfield Haven, a bird reserve along the coast where J-J had made special friends with the man who sold the ice creams.

By the boy's eleventh birthday, Faraday knew he'd turned the numbing double-trauma of those early years – his wife's death, his son's deafness – into something infinitely precious, and to mark the occasion he'd bought J-J the first volume of the birder's bible. The books were called *Birds of the Western Palearctic*. At £85 each they weren't cheap, but nine birthdays later J-J had the full set on a shelf of his own beside the ancient roll-top desk. Even now, the sight of those books still gladdened Faraday's heart.

*

It was later, when he was back in the house, that Harry Wayte phoned. For once, the Drugs Squad DI had no favours to ask. Instead, he just wanted to say thank you. The stuff they'd got from young Scottie was priceless. Red Rum was back on the rails for the gallop to the line and if things went well, then some of the credit belonged to Faraday's team.

Faraday resisted the temptation to inquire further about Harry's impending drugs bust. The thought of Paul Winter buying everyone celebratory drinks in the police bar turned his stomach.

On the phone, Harry changed tack.

'Understand you're up to HQ for interview tomorrow. Going for one of the MI Teams? Is that right?'

Faraday was watching a cormorant preening its feathers on a piling at the water's edge. A posting to one of the force's three Major Incident Teams was regarded as a plum assignment, though Faraday had his doubts.

'That's right,' he confirmed. 'But it's their idea more than mine.'

'Don't you fancy it? Pick of the good quality crime?'

'Yeah, of course I do.'

'What's the problem, then?'

Faraday grunted something about management structures but refused to go any further. Harry began to laugh.

'It's true, then,' he said. 'The man who hates delegating can't take orders either.'

Faraday didn't reply, letting the conversation trail away. It was probably fair to say that he put too much faith in his own judgement, and it was truer still that he had little respect for most of his superiors, but this was neither the time nor the place to share confidences. Finally Harry wished him good luck and rang off. Faraday was still staring out of the window. The cormorant had gone.

Five

The fact that Scott Spellar phoned first thing in the morning was a good sign. He wasn't pissed and there was nothing that Winter had yet come across to suggest that he was sampling the merchandise he delivered to Marty Harrison. No, the boy just wanted a meet.

Winter was up in his bathroom, having a shave. He named a big department store in the city centre and then glanced at his watch.

'The coffee place is up on the top floor. Be there for ten.'

He wiped the foam from his mobile, returned it to the glass shelf under the mirror, and carried on shaving.

Scott Spellar was already in the store cafeteria by the time Winter arrived. The moment he sat down, he made it plain why he'd rung.

'Someone's nicked some money of mine,' he said, 'and I want it back.'

'I've got it.'

'How come?'

'Safe keeping.'

'You took it? Just like that?'

'Yeah. Call it a favour, area like yours.'

Scott stared at him for a moment or two. He hadn't shaved for several days and the shadow added years to his face. He looked pale and drawn, and the way his eyes kept flicking towards the top of the escalator spoke volumes about the state of his nerves. He could be a tout already, Winter thought.

'How much was there?' Scott asked.

'Six hundred pounds.'

'There was eight hundred on Friday.'

'Are you telling me I can't count?'

'No. I'm just saying someone's nicked two hundred quid of my money.' He paused. 'So where's the rest?'

Winter reached inside the breast pocket of his jacket and laid the wallet on the table between them. Scott tore it open. Apart from his driving licence and a carefully folded photo of Steve Claridge, it was empty.

He stared at Winter.

'Where's the money?'

'I'd like to talk about Marty Harrison,' Winter said softly. 'I've got a proposal that might interest you.'

The boards for the MIT job took place at police force headquarters in Winchester, and Faraday was very nearly late. A crash on the motorway at Eastleigh delayed him half an hour, and he sprinted the two flights of stairs to the ACCO's office on the first floor.

There were three men waiting for him behind the big conference table. Henderson, the Assistant Chief Constable (Operations), waved him into the empty chair, accepted his apologies, and gave him a moment to get his breath back. With him were Detective Superintendent Pollock, Faraday's CID boss, and a uniformed superintendent from Southampton.

Faraday produced a handkerchief and blew his nose, doing his best to get his thoughts in order. He'd got up to find another e-mail from J-J. His son was thinking of selling the return half of his ferry ticket. Did he mean it? Or was this just another step into fantasy land?

Across the table, Henderson was offering his congratulations on the speedy resolution to the Paulsgrove murder. One of the words he used was 'exemplary'.

Faraday at last forced himself to concentrate.

'We were lucky,' he said. 'The guy virtually gave himself up.'

'Not the way we heard it.' Henderson glanced sideways at Pollock. 'Eh, Det. Supt.?'

'It was certainly neat, sir.' Pollock's smile was bright with self-congratulation. 'It just shows what you can do when you keep the channels open.'

Faraday stared at him, remembering the curt instruction on the phone and the tinkle of party voices in the background.

'Channels?' he queried.

'Talking to each other. Sharing intelligence. Looking for synergies. Getting our act together, if you'll excuse the *argot*.'

Faraday studied his knuckles in disgust. Pollock had a habit of spicing his conversation with little morsels of French. He owned a place down in the Charente somewhere and it was rumoured that Henderson was one of many summer visitors.

Henderson was looking hard at Faraday. Two years on the fourth floor hadn't quite robbed him of his street instincts.

Taking his cue, Pollock leaned forward over the desk.

'What's the matter, Joe?'

'Nothing, sir. Except the kid was innocent.'

'Of murder, of course he was. We knew that. He just happened to be running Class A drugs. Doesn't that come into the equation somewhere?'

'Cocaine's a career opportunity to kids like Spellar. As far as he's concerned, it's a way of getting out of Paulsgrove.'

'You're defending the boy?'

'Not at all. I'm doing the job his brief would have done. Had he had one.'

'He refused, so the custody sergeant tells me.'

'That's right.'

'You'd have preferred the duty brief there?'

'In his own interests, yes.'

There was a long silence. Henderson was bent over his pad. At last, he looked up.

'I don't think this is getting us very far, Joe,' he said carefully, 'unless there's something you haven't shared with us.'

After the second cup of coffee, Winter took Scott Spellar for a walk. Victoria Park was in the city centre, bounded by the railway line on one side and a couple of major roads on the other. In the middle, where it was quieter, Winter pulled the boy to a halt. There was a big aviary only metres away and Scott couldn't take his eyes off a gaudy, mad-eyed toucan.

'What do you say, then?'

'I dunno.'

'There's no pressure, absolutely none.'

'You're joking. You think this isn't pressure?' He gestured hopelessly at the space between them, then his gaze returned to the aviary. 'Tell me again about Marty.'

'Blokes that carry for him are under surveillance. You know that. You've worked that out for yourself. Them being under surveillance can only mean one thing. You've worked that out, too.'

'Yeah?' Scott shot him an ironic look, his chin tilted up. 'Remind me.'

'It means he's under the cosh. If he's got any sense, he'll be taking' – Winter shrugged – 'precautions.'

'Like what?'

'Like cleaning up his premises. Like making sure he doesn't get nicked with anything silly. If it comes to it.'

'He does all that anyway. He's really careful.'

'Then he's got nothing to worry about. But look at

it this way – if you break the news gently you may spare him a nasty surprise.'

'What are you talking about?'

'These busts, son. They can be heavy. I've been on them myself. Half past four in the morning? That can ruin your whole day.'

'You're telling me they're going to bust Marty?'

'I'm telling you it's a possibility. I'm telling you lots of people are spending lots of money keeping tabs on blokes like him. And money like that doesn't get spent without a result at the end of it.'

Scott blinked. He seemed to be having trouble keeping up.

'Are you sure about this?'

'No, son, *you* are. It's what you sussed in the Bridewell, the night we put you through the mangle over your grandad. It was Saturday night, remember? Half of Paulsgrove was in there with you.'

'I know.' Scott nodded. 'That's what's doing my head in. Loads of guys saw me down there. And half of them know Marty.'

Winter nodded, saying nothing, letting the situation speak for itself. Harry Wayte's little bust would happen regardless. Wouldn't Scott do himself a favour by passing on the news before Harry's boys went in?

Scott dug his hands in his pockets. A tall, well-built blonde girl sauntered past, but he didn't give her a second glance.

'I dunno,' he said again. 'This is mad.'

'Listen, son.' Winter took his arm and began walking. 'Look at it like this. You *have* to do it. If you don't, and if he gets done, Marty will think you've grassed him up anyway. And just imagine where that could lead.'

'Yeah, but . . .' Scott stared at him. 'What the fuck happens after that?'

Winter smiled.

'Nothing,' he said.

'*Nothing*? I just walk away? And you won't come hassling me any more?'

'Absolutely not.' He reached into his jacket and produced a plain white envelope. 'Count it, will you?'

Scott looked at the envelope and then ripped it open. The money was in ten-pound notes. He counted it twice and then scribbled his signature on a pad that Winter held open for him.

'About this little meet you're going to have with Marty . . .' he began.

Scott shook his head and tried to take a step away, but Winter stopped him. Scott stared at Winter's hand on his arm.

'What's this about?'

'Money,' Winter said easily. 'You'll be paid for your trouble.'

'Yeah? How much gets me a new face?'

'Two hundred.' Winter flashed a sudden smile. 'Cash.'

Faraday was back at his desk in the inspectors' office by early afternoon. There were mountains of paperwork to sort out from last week, and an urgent message from Jerry Proctor asking about the deadline on the Paulsgrove DNA report. He had the samples from Mick Spellar and his dead father ready for despatch, but the charge the labs made for the 48-hour turnaround had just gone up to £2400. Was Faraday happy to authorise the sum?

Faraday was still trying to get through to Jerry to tell him to hold off when a secretary called Bibi stuck her head round the door. Bibi worked for Superintendent Neville Bevan, the uniformed boss of the division and Faraday's immediate superior. He wanted a word as soon as possible.

Faraday asked Cathy to talk to Proctor and plucked

his jacket from the back of his chair. Bevan's office was up on the next floor, and when Faraday appeared at the open door, he glanced up from his computer screen and beckoned him in.

Bevan was a squat, robustly built Welshman with a reputation for plain-speaking. He and Faraday would never be social buddies but a measure of mutual respect made for a solid working relationship. Bevan always drew the straightest line between two points, and for that, Faraday was eternally grateful.

Bevan finally turned from his computer screen. Over his shoulder, Faraday scanned a line or two of rotund managerial prose before Bevan switched it off.

'I've had ACCO on about your interview,' Bevan said briskly. 'I think "mystified" covers it nicely.'

'Mystified about what?'

'You. Why you even bothered turning up this morning. Waste of time was one of the phrases he used.'

'Theirs or mine?'

Bevan threw back his head and barked with laughter. A couple of his teeth were missing, combat damage from some long-forgotten rugby match, and the fact that he'd never bothered with cosmetic dentistry spoke volumes about the man. Bevan measured himself and everyone else in terms of results. The rest, in his phrase, was conversation.

'They're pissed off,' he went on in his Swansea lilt. 'They don't understand you and they feel a bit insulted and they've asked me to have a word. They think there might be a stress problem.'

'Who with?'

'You.' He frowned, peering hard at Faraday with his muddy little eyes. '*Is* there a stress problem?'

Faraday wondered where to start. Should he tell him about J-J? About the lad's fantasy affair with some French social worker? Should he tell him about the nights he lay in bed, listening to the lap-lap of the tide, trying to work out where the last two decades had gone? Should he describe the moments when he sometimes paused on the stairs, frozen by the memories behind one of Janna's photographs? Should he share the bewilderment and disgust he increasingly felt, tidying up the wreckage of other people's lives? Should he confess, just occasionally, to an anger so intense and so deeply rooted that he felt capable of murder himself?

'No,' he said softly, 'there isn't a stress problem.'

'Good,' Bevan nodded. 'That's what I told them. I said you were a difficult bastard and tricky to handle and much better off where you were. That kind of stuff really throws them. Dishonesty they can cope with, and incompetence, too, but blokes like you leave them in the dark. They think it's lack of ambition and that's something they most definitely don't understand. You know the eleventh commandment? *Better* thyself. Aggressively, boyo. And at all times.'

He barked with laughter again, shaking his head. Like Faraday, he viewed headquarters with a certain derision. They were too remote from the real business of policing. Like bosses everywhere, the uniformed hierarchy had begun to believe all the New Labour clap-trap about community partnerships and transparency and best value. The latter, according to Bevan, was a smokescreen for wholesale cuts in budget. This year alone, he was supposed to find a two per cent budget reduction through a mysterious mechanism headquarters termed 'efficiency savings'. Two per cent of Bevan's budget would keep five beat men on the streets for a whole year.

Now he produced a red file from a drawer and slid it across the desk towards Faraday. The heart-to-heart was obviously over.

'I've got the Port Solent lot on my back again,' he

said. 'Someone's having a go at all those fancy motors and they don't think we're doing enough to stop them. And you know what? I think they're probably right.'

Faraday returned to his office with the file. The marina development was tucked into the northern corner of Portsmouth Harbour. Apartment blocks and water-side executive houses ringed a yacht basin with berths for over a hundred boats, while pubs, restaurants and a multiplex cinema drew in crowds every night from the city. Port Solent was where you went for tapas and a chilled bottle of Becks, for deck shoes and the latest chinos, and, according to some, it offered exactly the kind of leisure experience that would shape the city's future. The irony that it lay a stone's throw from the wastelands of Paulsgrove, hollowed out by poverty and crime, was largely ignored.

Faraday flicked through the file. By page three of the report, he'd lost count of the number of BMWs that had been burgled or vandalised in the big public car park, and it was no surprise to find the letter at the end. It had come from the desk of Nelly Tseng, Port Solent's chief executive, and it was blunt to the point of terseness. She was sick and tired of waiting for the police to do something about the current influx of hooligans. They were making life a misery for her and her staff. More important, they were starting to drive customers away. Developments like hers depended on their reputation, and Portsmouth – in turn – depended on developments like Port Solent. Was it really asking too much of the police to expect a little action?

Faraday tossed the report on to the desk, only too aware of the opportunity he'd squandered at head-quarters. A posting to one of the Major Inquiry Teams would have freed him from the daily grind of shoplift-ing and car crime. Guys on the MITs never got out of bed for less than serious rape, kidnapping or murder, and if he was honest with himself, he yearned for something more challenging than sorting out Nelly Tseng's gripes. So why hadn't he put up a better performance in front of the Assistant Chief Constable and his buddies? Why hadn't he taken their questions seriously? Why hadn't he even *tried* to please them? He thought about it for a moment or two and then shrugged. Maybe Harry Wayte was right. Maybe he was just too bloody-minded.

When Cathy Lamb passed the open door of the inspectors' office, he called her in and showed her the file. He wanted her to put together a small task force. Bevan had promised enough budget for a couple of nights' surveillance and some modest overtime. What he wanted was a rapid result and Faraday had promised him exactly that.

Cathy tried not to laugh. One of her missions in life was to bring men down to earth.

'Have you seen the backlog?' she said. 'Domestic burglaries are going through the roof. There are families in Buckland going barmy thinking their kids are smoking heroin. We're still clearing up the paedophile ring from April and every DC in the office is handling a CPU overspill. Most days it's like a war zone in there. And you want a task force for a couple of scratched Beamers? On the strength we've got? Are you serious?'

'Always, love. Just do it.'

Faraday turned away, refusing to take the file back, wondering which of his three in-trays to tackle first. Exchanges like these with Cathy always exhausted him, partly because she was so tenacious, but mainly because she was right. It was a fact of life that those with the fattest wallets and the loudest voices always got more than they deserved. Sadly, even Neville Bevan wasn't immune to pressure from the likes of Nelly Tseng.

*

When Paul Winter hadn't heard from Scott Spellar by four o'clock, he decided to drive to Anson Avenue and try and find him. The deal had been explicit. As soon as he'd seen Marty, he was to give Winter a ring. He wanted to know what Harrison had said, how he'd reacted, what plans he might have shared. Only then would Winter start serious negotiations about the promised two hundred pounds.

Crawling north through rush-hour traffic, Winter knew that he was up against the clock. The Drugs Squad was based at Havant nick and rumours were sweeping through their CID room that a bust was on for first light tomorrow morning. Winter had been on the phone to a mate only an hour ago. The canteen manager had been asked to prepare fifty-five doggy bags. Doggy bags contained the sausage rolls, apples, crisps and Kit-Kats that would fuel the guys on the sharp end, and an order that big could only mean that Harry Wayte's boys were going to execute a number of warrants, four or five different addresses at least. For an operation as major as Red Rum, it made perfect sense.

Anson Avenue was in its normal state of torpid chaos: abandoned cars, sullen kids, and a lurching drunk who was doing his best to piss into a pillar box. Winter gave him a toot and waved a finger as he drove past. The guy could barely get the thin yellow stream up above waist level.

At the top of the road, Winter turned the car round and then parked outside number seventy-three. He killed the engine and then gazed up at the house. Word must have spread about Scott's appearance at the Bridewell on Saturday night because someone had already been at the front door with a spray can. 'Scum' went the simple message.

Winter checked his watch, wondering whether the boy was in. One way or another, he badly needed to get him alongside Harrison. If Scott came back with serious intelligence – a sudden change of address, say – then Winter would make his name with the Drugs Squad. If, on the other hand, he simply passed on the warning then Winter would have planted his very own grass bang in the middle of the city's number one network. A tip like that, as long as the boy kept his nerve, would guarantee Scott Spellar a place in the sun. Harrison would owe his young gopher. Big time. And where, Winter wondered, might that lead?

Getting out of the car, Winter smiled. These were the kinds of strokes he enjoyed pulling most, stepping outside the system, turning his back on the paperwork, running private informants, inching his way into the heart of the action without anyone – *anyone* – being any the wiser. Then, at a time of his choosing, he would cash in all that information, all those carefully harboured secrets, step into the spotlight and take the applause he so richly deserved. Criminals, serious criminals, needed detectives like Paul Winter. The fact that there were few of his breed left was one of the reasons crime was getting so out of hand.

He pushed in through the gate and rapped on the door. The paint from the spray can was even fresher than he'd thought. At length, a girl appeared, opening an upstairs window. She had nose rings and long black hair.

'Yeah? What is it?'

Winter asked for Scott. She said he wasn't in.

'Where is he?'

'Downtown somewhere.'

'Doing what?'

'No idea.' She peered down at him. 'Are you the filth, then? Only he said you were a fat bastard.'

For once, Winter didn't know what to say. Then he gave her the finger, turned on his heel and went back to the car. Gone downtown, he thought. Good sign.

Faraday was home by seven. Upstairs, in the study, he checked the PC but there were no more e-mails from J-J. Was he really going to flog his return ticket? Was this really the time to pack up twenty-two years of fatherhood and start again?

There was an unopened bottle of malt in the drinks cabinet in the lounge. Faraday poured himself three fingers, added ice, and drank it in the garden, watching a distant jet-ski trailing curtains of water on the Hayling side of the harbour. With pressure high, the breeze was from the east, and the insect-buzz of the jet-ski finally drove him back indoors. His glass recharged, he put on some music – the Goldberg Variations – and tried to bury himself in the tinkling arpeggios. Anything to stop him thinking about J-J. Anything.

Twenty minutes later, the glass empty again, he abandoned Glenn Gould, hauled himself upright on the sofa and headed for the stairs. The diaries were in a cardboard box at the back of J-J's wardrobe. He hesitated for a moment, then opened one at random, settling himself on J-J's bed. The diaries had been written up in school exercise books with drawings and text from J-J's class teacher, and from Faraday himself. This daily tally of events had passed back and forth between home and school for years, bridging the gap between the child's two worlds, and as J-J had learned to write, his own scrawled contributions had appeared as well.

This one was an early diary, June 1981, and looking at the crayoned sandcastle, Faraday was suddenly back on the beach at Eastney. J-J was four, a boisterous little blond kid with his mother's grin and his father's patience and a bunch of friends from the neighbourhood kindergarten who spoke the rumble-tumble language of infants world-wide. J-J's nanny had the weekends off. Dad was in sole charge.

The kids were building an elaborate fortification against the rising tide. At Faraday's prompting, it had drainage channels, paper Union Jacks and a big fat sand palisade behind a semi-circular apron of pebbles to cushion the breaking waves.

The kids had danced around, shrieking with excitement, determined that their castle should survive, and then suddenly there came the heavy drone of Merlin engines and a Lancaster bomber appeared, flying parallel with the shore, and the other children ran down to the tideline, pointing up at the huge plane as it soared into a graceful wingover, leaving J-J squatting on the wet sand, slowly patting a turret into shape, quite oblivious of the commotion behind him. That was the moment when Faraday realised that J-J would always be different, that there would always be parts of the world beyond his reach. And that was the moment, too, when J-J glanced round, and saw that his buddies had left him. By the time he joined them in the shallows, the Lancaster was a speck in the distance, heading for an anniversary fly-past over the naval dockyard. He tried to share his friends' excitement, to pretend that he too had seen the huge black beast, but Faraday recognised the bright little smile for what it was. The boy was being brave.

Walking home that afternoon, he clung to Faraday's hand. At tea, he barely touched his boiled egg. With the plates and cups cleared away, Faraday drew big fat aeroplanes on the A4 pads he kept everywhere to hand, and when the sketches drew no response, he began to circle the room, his arms outstretched, banking and weaving around the furniture, until the sight of J-J's face brought him to a halt. The child was weeping – and the moment etched itself deep into Faraday's unconscious because his tears were silent. He made no show of his grief. He didn't howl, like normal kids. He just sat there, with the tears rolling slowly down his face, utterly inconsolable.

That night, with J-J in bed, Faraday had sought advice and, days later, as soon as his shifts permitted, he made the visit to the library. Within a week, birds had begun to appear in the diary, little stick creatures flying over the smudgy blues and greens of the harbour and the foreshore, and by the end of the year Faraday had recognised the wisdom of his friend's suggestion. When he met her at the school carol service, an oddly joyous event scored for kids who hadn't got the faintest idea about music, she'd been delighted by J-J's progress. He was happy again, and secure, and watching him trying to figure out what to do with a tambourine, she put Faraday's own thoughts into words. Birds can be kinder than people, she'd said.

Six

Faraday, for once, had left his mobile downstairs. Roused from deep sleep, he fumbled his way towards the bedroom door and then negotiated the stairs one by one in the half-darkness. Beside the sofa, he struggled to get the world into focus.

'Who is it?'

'Cathy. There's been a shooting.'

Faraday rubbed his eyes. The paleness of the light beyond the curtains told him that it was still early.

'A shooting? Where?'

'I'm still trying to find out. It's complicated.'

'Who's dealing with it?'

'Nobody.'

'Nobody?'

'Not from our end, no.'

Faraday could sense the panic in her voice. Cathy never panicked. He glanced at his watch. 06:39.

'I'm on my way,' he said. 'I'll meet you at the office.'

Cathy was sitting on her desk, swallowing her second coffee by the time Faraday arrived. Her face was the colour of putty.

'It's Pete,' she said at once. 'He's shot a guy.'

'And?'

'Nearly killed him. It's still touch and go.'

Harry Wayte had called the bust for four-thirty. The priority address had been in North End and Pete had led the five-man TFU up the stairs after Harry's boys had done the front door. In the master bedroom he'd found the target tucked up with his girlfriend. The guy had dived for something under his pillow and Pete had

62

yelled at him to freeze but he'd taken no notice. Suspecting a gun, Pete had opened fire.

'And?'

Cathy looked away.

'It was a sim card,' she muttered. 'I guess the guy was going to swallow it.'

Faraday eased her into a chair. A sim card sat in the back of a mobile phone. It stored the numbers from previous calls and – recovered intact – it could save hours of painstaking investigation.

Cathy pushed hopelessly at the desk, making the chair revolve.

'So far they've found nothing in the house,' she said quietly. 'No gear, no money, no paperwork, absolutely nothing.'

'What about the sim card?'

'Just a list of numbers. Nothing to warrant a charge. And it gets worse. There was a baby in the bedroom, too. Little kid of fourteen months in a carrycot on the floor. The *News* are on to it already.'

'How come?'

'The girlfriend phoned them. She's the mother. She's gone potty, as you can imagine.'

Faraday looked at the ceiling a moment, wondering how much worse the damage could get. The *News* was the city's local paper. A circulation of seventy thousand gave it considerable weight and it used every tabloid trick in the book to fatten daily sales still further. Given Cathy's brief description of the morning's events, Faraday shuddered to think about the midday placards on the city's streets. Bevan, as senior uniformed officer on the division, would be well and truly in the firing line.

'There's more.' Cathy nodded towards the open door. 'Do you mind?'

Faraday shut the door with his foot. It was way too

early for the eight a.m. shift and even the cleaners had yet to arrive. He turned back to Cathy.

'Well?'

'I think Pete had been drinking.'

'What?'

'He came in very late last night. I could smell it on him.'

'Anyone else know this?'

'I dunno. Apparently they've asked him for a blood sample, but so far the doctor hasn't turned up. He phoned me from Havant nick. He's well choked.'

Faraday nodded. Requests for blood samples were automatic after a shooting, part of the inquiry procedure, though Pete Lamb had a legal right to refuse.

'I know,' Cathy said, 'but it doesn't look great, does it? Not if you've got something to hide.'

Faraday had to agree. Driving under the influence was bad enough. Going in mob-handed with a sliding-stock Heckler and Koch and a headful of last night's booze was unthinkable.

'They'll throw the book at him. Any trace of alcohol, and he's fucked.'

Cathy stared up at him, shocked. Faraday rarely cursed.

'You think so?'

'I know so. And for the record I have to say it makes sense.'

Cathy's eyes widened still further. She made a loose, slightly pathetic gesture with her right hand, bridging the gap between them. Was it OK to talk like this? Could Faraday respect a confidence?

'No problem,' he said at once, reaching out for her hand and giving it a little squeeze. 'I'm just telling it the way it is.'

He paused a moment, wondering what on earth had driven Pete Lamb to the bottle. The TFU guys went through extensive psychological profiling before they got anywhere near the firing range. Any hint of a drink problem, or poor resistance to general stress, and they were chopped from the course. Pete Lamb had always struck him as ideal TFU material: level-headed, self-confident, cool under pressure. So how come he'd ended up in a state like this?

Cathy was staring blankly at the wall.

'There's one question you haven't asked me.' She looked up at Faraday. 'Don't you want to know who Pete shot?'

'Go on.'

'Harrison.' Cathy swallowed hard. 'Marty fucking Harrison.'

Faraday phoned Paul Winter at home.

'What's this about then?' he asked sleepily. 'World War Three?'

Faraday told him about Harrison. He wanted to know whether Winter had caught up with Scott Spellar since the night they'd threatened him with a murder charge.

'Yeah. I saw him yesterday morning.'

'And?'

'Gave him his money back. Like you said.'

'Anything else?'

'Nothing. We had a little chat, you know, but nothing you'd want to get excited about.'

'He's not working for you?'

'He's not working for anyone. If he's got any sense, he'll fuck off out of it. He's convinced that half of Paulsgrove have him down as a grass and he's terrified Marty Harrison will get to hear of it.'

'I doubt it. Not for a while, anyway.'

'How come?'

'Harrison's in intensive care. Harry's boys busted him this morning. He took a bullet from the TFU.'

Faraday told Winter what little he knew. Then he

went back to Scott Spellar. Harrison's premises had been clean. Just the way you'd expect if someone had tipped him off. He let the thought sink in, then wondered aloud whether Winter hadn't had a longer conversation with the lad than he'd let on.

'I'm not with you. You think I'd tell him Harrison was under the cosh?'

'I think you'd want to run him. It may be the same thing.'

'But you really think I'd jeopardise an operation? For a scrote like Spellar?'

'It's a question. That's all.'

There was a long silence, and Faraday began to suspect he'd pushed it too far. An allegation as serious as this, if it was to lead anywhere, needed hard evidence – evidence that Faraday simply didn't have. Finally, he heard Winter stifling a yawn.

'I'm back to bed, boss,' he said. 'If that's OK by you.'

The *News* broke the Harrison shooting in their midday first edition. Placards outside the city's news-agents read 'Police Shoot Father In Dawn Raid'. The bust had happened on Neville Bevan's patch and all morning the phones had been ringing in the superin-tendent's outer office with inquiries from other branches of the media. Local radio and television wanted briefings on the background to Red Rum. For how long had the raids been planned? How good was the intelligence that underpinned them? How come armed police had burst into a house that sheltered a sleeping baby?

With immense patience, Bevan referred each of the callers to the headquarters press office at Winchester, but a couple of the more persistent journalists man-aged to pin him down for a quote or two. The drugs war, he pointed out, was both dirty and dangerous.

The men and women on the Drugs Squad, though not directly his responsibility, regularly put their lives on the line. If mistakes occasionally happened then it was deeply regrettable, but the police invested enormous amounts of time and effort in operations like Red Rum and there'd been absolutely no reason to doubt the intelligence. Other addresses raided across the city – many of them occupied by people who were close to Harrison – had yielded a rich harvest of Class A drugs. That, strictly off the record, might help to put the thing into some kind of perspective.

Just after lunch, Faraday bumped into Bevan in the corridor. The superintendent looked him in the eye and then beckoned him into a nearby office which happened to be empty. The hospital was putting Harrison's chances at sixty-forty. Given the passage of the bullet – three millimetres beneath his heart – that made him a very lucky man. In the meantime, a senior officer from another force had been called in to investigate the circumstances of the shooting and Pete Lamb had been suspended from duties while the initial inquiries got under way. How was Cathy coping?

'I've sent her home, sir. She's pretty upset.'

Faraday was trying to work out whether Bevan knew about Pete drinking. He'd reluctantly agreed to take the blood test and it would only be a matter of days before the results came back.

'I understand Lamb's doing the Fastnet.' Bevan was looking at a calendar on the wall. 'Is that the case?'

'Absolutely. He's had leave booked for months.'

'And when does it start?'

'This Saturday. Though I think he's over in Cowes from Thursday evening.'

'Good.' Bevan nodded. 'Best bloody thing.'

Late afternoon, Faraday made time to drive up to Cathy's Portchester house. The curtains were drawn in the front room and he thought at first that she must be asleep, but eventually she came to the front door. She was wearing patched jeans and an old T-shirt with a print of Freddie Mercury across the front. She looked drawn and weary, and the mascara under her eyes had smudged where she'd been crying.

'Pete?' Faraday gestured beyond her, into the gloom of the tiny hall.

Cathy shrugged.

'Out somewhere,' she said.

'Like where?'

'I haven't a clue. I'm only his wife.'

She looked at him for a long moment, wanting him to go away, but Faraday didn't budge. Finally, she invited him in. A small table lamp in the lounge threw a soft light on to the sofa. The cushions were still indented with the shape of Cathy's long body.

Faraday settled himself in the armchair beside the fireplace.

'What's the problem, Cath?'

Cathy shot him a look, refusing him the satisfaction of an answer.

'Are you here as a friend?' she said at last. 'Or should I phone for a lawyer?'

'Depends what you want to talk about.'

'I don't want to talk about anything.'

Faraday shrugged, then lay back against the plump headrest of the armchair, peering up at the clip-framed photos around the wall. Cathy's grin spoke volumes about her personality. Big-hearted and spontaneous, it lit up her entire face. Most of the photos featured Pete as well, though his smile was more guarded.

'Things been OK between you?'

Cathy closed her eyes and shook her head. Her voice was very low, as if she was talking to herself.

'I don't need this,' she whispered. 'Truly, I don't.'

'You may have no choice, love.'

'I do, and I'd like you to leave.'

Faraday studied her a moment, nonplussed.

'You phoned me this morning,' he pointed out.

'I was upset.'

'And now?'

'I'm knackered. I'm serious. I'd like you to go. I'm grateful and everything, and I know you mean well, but I'll sort this on my own.' She stood up, reaching out to the mantelpiece for support. 'No offence,' she said, 'but I'll be better by myself. It's nothing new, I promise. I've been rehearsing for weeks.'

She offered him a weak smile and nodded towards the door. Faraday got to his feet and turned to go, then paused.

'I know how you feel,' he said, 'if that helps.'

Cathy nodded.

'I know you do,' she said wearily. 'That's what frightens me.'

Back at the station in Kingston Crescent, Faraday found a note from Bevan Blu-Tacked to his computer screen. He'd had yet another call from Nelly Tseng, the woman who ran the Port Solent management company. She'd made time in her schedule for a meeting tomorrow morning at eleven and she was expecting the pleasure of his company. At the bottom of the note Bevan had added a scribbled order. *Be there*, it read.

Next door, the CID room was empty. When he finally located Dawn Ellis, she confirmed that Cathy Lamb hadn't done anything about organising a surveillance task force for the Port Solent car park. With Cathy away, the current CID strength was now down to just two bodies, herself and Paul Winter. What did Faraday want her to do?

Faraday was looking at the big white board beside the door on which individual detectives tallied current jobs. The board was covered in black squiggles, crime after crime that was still awaiting attention, and gazing at it Faraday felt a sudden weariness. Would they be chasing shadows for ever, their pitiful resources divided between an ever-growing army of shoplifters, burglars, con men and car thieves? Or might there, one day, be a chance to take the initiative? To turn this depressing game of catch-up into something altogether more bold?

Dawn Ellis was still waiting for a reply.

'Eleven o'clock tomorrow,' Faraday grunted. 'You, me and a woman called Nelly Tseng.'

An hour and a half later, on the point of going home, Dawn Ellis took a call from Paul Winter. She liked Winter. He was old-style, and shameless, and didn't much care who knew it. Plump and balding, he ambled around in his car coat, winding everyone else up with his boasts about all the quality criminals he'd nicked. Anyone who wore aftershave that awful deserved her admiration.

Just now, typically, he seemed to be in a pub. She could hear conversation and the clink of glasses.

'Dawn, love? I'm after a favour.'

'What is it?'

'Come here and I'll tell you. Don't be long, though. There's snooker on the telly tonight.'

She found him deep in conversation with the barmaid at a pub beside the level crossing. He ordered Dawn a Bacardi breezer and another pint of Kronenberg for himself.

In the corner beneath the telly he explained what he was after.

'The lad we talked to on Saturday, Scottie.' He beckoned her closer. 'I took a look round that shitheap of his up in Paulsgrove. All those trips to London, he must have made a bob or two.'

'And?'

'I found eight hundred quid stashed in his bedroom and I seized it. It's been in the nick safe all weekend, but I gave him six hundred back yesterday morning. Guvnor's orders.'

'Where did the money come from?'

'Harrison. Must have.'

'In person?'

'Probably. He doesn't trust anyone else.'

'Then it's evidence, isn't it, the money?' Dawn frowned. 'Didn't anyone mention this to forensic? Shouldn't we be looking for prints here?'

'I told you, love. I had to give it back.'

'*Had* to?'

'Yeah, guvnor's orders.' He spread his hands wide. 'You tell me.'

'What about the rest?'

'He gets that now. I just need a witness.'

'Why?'

'Because Mr Faraday thinks I need watching.' He leaned across the table and patted her arm. 'This job used to be fun once. Remember?'

He drove her to Anson Avenue in his car. Someone had been at work with the spray can again, turning 'Scum' into 'Scummer'. Scummer was a local term of abuse for anyone born in Southampton. Round here, genuine Scummers had a life expectancy measured in minutes.

Winter knocked a couple of times and then stepped back, looking up at the top windows.

'Someone's in,' he said. 'I can hear them.'

He tried again, harder this time, and a moment later the door was pulled open by a thin, pale-faced man in his mid-twenties. He was wearing jeans and a leather waistcoat, and his throat was necklaced with a daisy-chain tattoo.

'Scott around?'

The man shook his head and flicked the remains of a roach past Winter's left shoulder. Then he looked at Dawn.

'You that desperate for company, missis?'

'No, unless you're offering.'

He laughed, exposing a mouthful of blackened teeth. Winter ignored him. He wanted to know about Scott. Where was he? When was he expected back?

'Why's that then? You got something for him?'

Dawn Ellis glanced at Winter. This was a conversation they shouldn't be having. Not in front of a total stranger. Winter had his hand in his coat pocket. He began to pull out an envelope and then had second thoughts. The man on the doorstep was watching his every move.

'Wanna leave it, do you?' He nodded at Winter's pocket and then leered at Dawn again. 'Only I'm bound to see him later. Me and a few mates.'

Seven

All the way to Port Solent, next morning, Faraday was trying to forget that J-J was due back on the evening ferry but even Dawn Ellis, who regarded her boss as seriously remote, noticed how fretful and preoccupied he seemed.

'Is anything the matter, sir?' she inquired, as they turned into the big car park at the marina complex.

'Nothing, love.' He gestured at the line of bars and restaurants that fronted on to The Boardwalk, keen to change the subject. 'Amazing, isn't it?'

Walking across the car park, Faraday mused about the brutality of the social contrasts. Millions of pounds' worth of yachts tied up beside one of the UK's most deprived council estates. Knick-knack shops selling pot-pourri at six pounds a throw when kids half a mile away couldn't afford new shoes.

Dawn let him get it off his chest, then nodded across at the big UCI cinema complex.

'Ever tried it, sir?'

Faraday gazed at her, wrong-footed.

'No,' he said, 'I haven't.'

'Then maybe you should.' Dawn risked a smile. 'They sell great popcorn and the sound system's brilliant.'

Nelly Tseng was a slight, intense, exquisitely dressed Hong Kong Chinese in her mid-forties with a big desk, lots of gold jewellery, and perfect English dusted with just the trace of an American accent. Her eyes were as cold as her handshake and she had absolutely no time for small talk. Faraday had scarcely sat down before she was telling him how successful Port Solent had become. The place was an absolute smash. The bars and restaurants were packed every night and she had a queue of heavyweight merchandisers itching to get into the retail outlets. The last thing she needed now was pondlife.

'Pondlife?' Faraday inquired mildly.

'Kids from across the tracks. As far as food and beverage is concerned, we're covered. They can't afford the prices, not in the bars, and certainly not in the restaurants. But they still come. God knows why, but they do. Have you checked with that superintendent of yours?'

'Of course.'

'Then you'll know about the cars. My security guys keep a log. Here.'

Faraday took the proffered sheet of paper. Talking to Nelly Tseng was like trying to survive in a gale-force wind. Unless you gave a little, you were doomed.

'Terrible.' Faraday knew the list of vandalised cars by heart. 'Must be a real pain.'

'Too right. And you see that last one? The top-of-the-range Mercedes? Guy over from Monaco, big investor, looking to fund the next major expansion. And you know what happens to his car? He leaves it outside the multiplex for an hour and when he comes back it's scored from end to end.'

'I expect it was hired, wasn't it?'

'That's hardly the point, Mr Faraday. He's thinking clientele. He's thinking Joe Public. A family spending eighty pounds in a restaurant or the evening in the cinema doesn't expect to find their car trashed.' She tapped a perfect nail on the desk. 'So my Mr Mercedes wants to know why. And so do I.'

'You've got CCTV?'

'Of course we have. You'll have seen the cameras.'

'Then maybe you should upgrade the system.'

'We're looking at it, Mr Faraday, but you're talking serious money. My commercial tenants already pay a fortune in rates. So do the residents. So do we. To put it crudely, Inspector, that buys them you.'

Faraday stole a glance at Dawn Ellis. She looked spellbound.

'I'll need more than this.' Faraday gestured at the list of cars. 'I'll need times, locations. We look for patterns in cases like this. DC Ellis will be your point of contact.'

Dawn Ellis mustered a smile. Nelly Tseng didn't take her eyes off Faraday. She wanted the organ grinder, not the monkey.

'Let's understand each other, Inspector. We talk the language of results here. That's why we're so success-ful. That's why we're setting the tone. Your city needs a future, Mr Faraday, and we're happy to oblige. No one wants to go back to the swamp, do they?'

'Swamp?'

'Portsmouth. You've been thinking small-time too long, Inspector. Things have to change around here.'

She gestured vaguely towards the window, dismiss-ing the cranes and the tower blocks beyond the low sweep of the motorway, and Faraday gazed at her, masking a hot surge of anger behind a puzzled smile. At length, he got to his feet.

'Swamps can be interesting,' he murmured, 'if you're into birdlife.'

Before returning to Kingston Crescent, Faraday drove to Paulsgrove. He'd phoned Bevan from Port Solent, asking for an update on Marty Harrison, and when the superintendent had told him that the surgeons had done a second operation and that Harrison would definitely pull through, he felt obliged to pass on the news. The least he owed Scott Spellar was a nudge on the elbow. Get out now. While you still can.

Outside Spellar's house, Faraday gestured at the scrawled message on the front door.

'Nice area,' he grunted. 'No wonder the kids go off the rails.'

Dawn Ellis nodded, but said nothing. This was her second trip to Anson Avenue in less than twelve hours, but one of the many lessons that CID work had taught her was the need for discretion. Never say more than you have to. No matter what kind of company you keep.

There was no response to Faraday's knock at the front door. Round the back, he peered in through the kitchen window but there was no sign of life. Someone had left a copy of the *News* on the window sill and Faraday wondered whether it might have been Scott. Over a grainy photograph of five handcuffed men being bundled into the back of a police van, the headline read 'Drugs Bust – More Arrests', and Faraday was still wondering what young Scottie must have made of the story when he returned to the car.

'You interviewed the lad,' he said to Ellis. 'What's the verdict?'

Dawn Ellis took time to frame her answer.

'Straight,' she said at last. 'I just thought he was dead honest.'

'But bent as well?'

'As far as the coke and stuff was concerned, of course. But it was a job for him. It paid well. It was pretty exciting. And round here that's a definite result. He hated us getting at him, hated it. Poor little sod didn't know what to do.'

'He grassed Marty Harrison,' Faraday pointed out. 'Did that surprise you?'

'Not really.'

'Why not?'

They were waiting at traffic lights at the entrance to the estate. The conversation was going further than Dawn Ellis had intended.

'Paul can be very persuasive,' she said carefully. 'He's clever in situations like that.'

'That's what he's there for. That's why we get results.'

'Of course, sir. I know that. It's just' – she shrugged – 'the kid was really upset about his grandad, you could tell. When he saw those photos . . .' She shook her head, and looked quickly out of the window.

The lights changed to green and Faraday turned on to the dual carriageway. Minutes later, speeding into the city on the spur motorway, he glanced across at Dawn again.

'Harrison's place was clean,' he told her.

'I know.'

'So why was that, d'you think? Did young Scottie tip him off?'

Dawn frowned. She'd been asking herself exactly the same question, ever since she'd accompanied Winter to the house last night. Had Scott put two and two together about the imminence of a drugs bust, then he might well have passed the message on to Marty Harrison. But if that was the case, how come Paul Winter was handing him an envelope stuffed with cash, albeit his own? None of it made any sense, and in the end she thought it best to be honest.

'I don't know,' she said. 'He may well have done, but I simply don't know.'

'Do you think we frightened him?'

'Definitely.'

'And do you think he'd relish a meet with the likes of Harrison? Given the fact we'd pulled him in?'

'Obviously not.'

Faraday nodded in mute agreement. The conversation died while he swooped past a big continental lorry and tucked into the slow lane again.

'Winter knew Harrison personally, didn't he? Way back? Before my time?'

'I think he'd had dealings with him, yes.' Dawn was frowning. 'But they were never mates, not so far as I know.'

'I don't mean mates. I mean acquaintances. He got a favour or two out of Harrison, the way I heard it.'

'Is that right, sir?'

'Yes.' Faraday seemed oblivious to the sudden caution in her voice. 'And I understand it helped our clear-up rate no end.'

Dawn stared at him for a moment, then looked away. They were nearly back in the city before she broke the silence.

'You want me to tell Paul that? Pass a message?'

Faraday permitted himself the beginnings of a smile.

'You'll do it anyway,' he said softly, 'whatever I say.'

Back at the station, the inspectors' office was empty. Faraday draped his jacket on the back of the chair and gazed at his desk, struck yet again by the way that command seemed to guarantee such total isolation. He'd been a DI for four years now, winning the promotion after a long stint as a DS in neighbouring Waterlooville. The move back on to Portsea Island had brought him much closer to home, and he'd treasured the freedom of being his own boss in a division as busy and varied as Portsmouth North, but he'd never anticipated the distance he'd have to keep between himself and the rest of the squad.

In part, he'd learned to recognise this gulf as inevitable. It was true what his old guvnors had told him – that the investigative buck well and truly stopped with the DI – but there was something else, too, and the older he got, the more difficult it was to define. It had to do with laughter and a degree of irresponsibility. It had to do with the knowledge that each working day was finite and that a limit existed to what one man could reasonably achieve. Get yourself promoted to detective inspector, and those comforts disappeared. Faraday's responsibility was no longer one part of the jigsaw, or even two, but the whole bloody puzzle. It was his job to piece it together, his job to conjure administrative order out of chaos, and the longer he did it the harder it was to resist the conclusion that the job was impossible. Being a successful DI meant learning how to survive under a state of constant siege – not just from the criminal fraternity but from his own bosses as well. And in war, as Faraday was beginning to understand, no plan survives contact with the enemy.

Enemy? Faraday sat back at his desk, visualising his squad next door, the fellow campaigners on whom he had to depend. The fact that most of them had either been poached by other divisions, or were sunning themselves on foreign beaches, was yet another irritation, but Faraday had long since stopped believing that the CID room would ever be up to full strength, and simply counted himself lucky to have acquired such an extraordinary bunch of individuals.

Big Cathy Lamb with her bursting heart and limitless, headstrong loyalties. Little Dawn Ellis with her trophy rugby shirts and chaotic love life. Then the older guys like Rick McGivern and Bev Yates. Bev had swapped dreams of football stardom for a brace of jet-skis and marriage to a woman half his age. Invited to the reception, Faraday had marvelled at Bev's sheer nerve. Melanie, his new wife, was beautiful, and educated, and came from a solid naval family in the

Meon Valley – at least three reasons for giving Bev a very wide berth indeed.

Faraday smiled at the memories. They'd all clubbed together to buy the happy couple a jumbo-sized fridge. They'd filled it with champagne, *foie gras*, truffles, Belgian chocolate – plus a year's subscription to *Loaded* – and after Rick McGivern's best-man speech in the big reception tent behind the family spread, they'd all got drunk together. Even Faraday had succumbed and for one glorious afternoon he was able to shed the job title and most of the rest of his life, and simply marvel at the daftness of it all. Bev Yates. In the bosom of a family like this.

Even Paul Winter had made an effort. Bumping into him in the hired de luxe Portaloos behind the stables, Faraday had mumbled something about Bev not being able to believe his luck. Winter had grinned his evil grin, unzipped his fly, and then laughed.

'Neither can we, boss. Neither can fucking we. Good, though, innit?'

And it was.

That night, Faraday drove down to the ferryport to meet the incoming boat from Caen. A final check on the PC at home had revealed no further e-mails and Faraday could only assume that J-J hadn't – after all – decided to flog his return ticket. Now he stood in the window of the arrivals' hall, watching the towering, slab-sided hull nudge alongside.

Already, it seemed like months since he'd seen the boy. Twenty-two years together had imposed a certain pattern on the way they'd lived, measuring out the beginnings and ends of each day with the small courtesies of a shared life. An early-morning cup of tea for J-J before he struggled upright from the wreckage of his bed. An exchange of signs on the state of the shopping list. A couple of early-evening beers and a chat before tackling the supper. With J-J so suddenly gone, these routines had lapsed, and with the boy due back again Faraday had become aware of a fluttering in his stomach that he'd at first put down to indigestion. Only towards the end of the afternoon, with his in-tray down to manageable proportions, had he realised the truth. That he was nervous.

A couple of pints in the pub round the corner from the ferryport had helped. He'd settled in a corner of the bar, trying to read the evening paper, telling himself that this was absurd. J-J was his son, not his lover. But even the second Guinness, normally so reliable, had failed to achieve the right degree of numbness. Six days ago, J-J's departure had thrown him into confusion. Now, with the ferry moored alongside, Faraday was even further from any kind of peace.

Cars from the crossing began to whine past. Faraday left the window and walked towards the mouth of the arrivals' tunnel. Back-packers appeared in twos and threes, then came a big group of French schoolkids, chattering away to each other. A couple of families followed in their wake, and a moment or two later a small, plump priest arrived, gazing across the concourse through thick pebble glasses. Faraday watched him for a moment, wondering if his son had, after all, sold his ticket, when he felt a tiny pressure on his arm. He spun round to find himself looking at J-J's lopsided grin.

Awkwardly, the boy held out a bony hand. He was tall, taller than his father, and the blond curls had darkened since his days making sandcastles on the beach at Eastney, but he had Janna's eyes – big and candid – and that same knack of defusing a potentially awkward moment.

'Got ya,' he signed.

They had a private vocabulary of sign, father and

son, letting the years add little flourishes to the repertoire that they'd both picked up at J-J's special school. 'Got ya' was two fingers tapping the soft skin beneath J-J's right eye, followed by the index pointing at Faraday, and now, as always, Faraday ducked the way you might try and duck a bullet, miming a chest wound over the heart to signal that the boy had, indeed, taken him by surprise.

Recovering, he picked up the heavier of J-J's two rucksacks, absurdly pleased that the newly arrived priest had witnessed the exchange, and looped one strap over his shoulder. J-J was wearing a brand new denim jacket and jeans, but he hadn't shaved for days and the dark growth of beard gave his long face an entirely new cast. The boy loped beside him towards the sliding exit doors and they were out in the car park before Faraday realised exactly what difference the beard had made.

'You look French,' he signed, touching the newly sewn tricolour on the back of J-J's rucksack.

J-J beamed back, delighted, and when he shifted the weight of the rucksack on his back Faraday saw the thin silver chain around his son's neck. J-J had never expressed the slightest interest in rings or chains or any other kind of bodily ornament. Never. Now, aware of his father's curiosity, he reached behind his neck and undid the clasp, offering the chain for Faraday's inspection.

'A present,' he signed, 'from Valerie.'

On the way home, Faraday stopped to pick up fish and chips. They ate it together in the kitchen, straight from the paper, not bothering with plates, but when Faraday delved in a cupboard and emerged triumphant with a brand new bottle of his son's favourite brown sauce, J-J shook his head. For the first time in his life, he'd stripped the fish of batter, picking daintily at the plump flakes of cod, and Faraday watched him with a deepening sense of bewilderment. Already they seemed to have run out of things to say to each other. It was like eating with a stranger.

After supper, he made a renewed attempt to find out what had happened in Caen. Had he got on with Valerie's family? With the French in general? Had he made friends out there? Had he seen anything in the way of birdlife?

The latter question produced a derisory shake of the head. He and Valerie had been far too busy for birds. They'd been out every night, out to bars, and clubs, and the flats of Valerie's friends. J-J had met lots and lots of people and he'd loved them all, especially the ones who knew how to sign. Signing was international. Signing meant that you didn't have to speak French to understand the people. He'd made friends, lots of friends, real friends, and some of them had belonged to a troupe of street actors, so he'd joined too. He'd gone to rehearsals, and worn a costume, and had his face painted white. The play was about life after a nuclear holocaust and he'd been cast as an elder, the morning after the end of the world. The four tribes of the earth had come together in the ashes, determined to build a new society. Valerie was going to teach him the guitar. They'd drunk lots of wine.

The stories spilled out, a torrent of free association, and it had taken Faraday a while to realise just what it was that bound all this passionate reminiscence together. J-J was digging a moat. Not the inch-deep little rivulets he used to scrape in the sand at Eastney but something infinitely deeper and wider, the depth and width – indeed – of the English Channel. J-J loved France, loved the French, loved Valerie. And he plainly couldn't wait to get back.

At ten, after a series of theatrical yawns, J-J headed for the stairs. Half a bottle of Scotch later, prone on the long sofa, Faraday fumbled for the phone. Cathy answered on the second ring. As soon as she heard Faraday's voice she told him she was OK. Things were getting better. She'd heard the good news about Marty Harrison pulling through. She'd even managed to have a sensible conversation with Pete. He'd left for Cowes already and was staying with his Fastnet mates, looking forward to the race. It was good that he'd managed to get away.

Faraday let her finish. The tumbler of Scotch beside him was beginning to blur.

'This isn't about you, Cath,' he muttered. 'It's about me.'

Eight

On Saturday the Fastnet Race got under way from Cowes. Nearly three hundred yachts crossed the start line, then tacked down the western Solent into a steady ten-knot breeze. By the following morning the lead boats were already closing on Land's End and the Scilly Isles when Faraday left his sleeping son and drove the forty miles to Pennington, a bird reserve on the coastal fringes of the New Forest.

On the edge of the tidal saltmarsh, he settled down with a groundsheet, a flask of tea and his binoculars. Across the Solent, the last of the yachts from Cowes Week were streaming out of the Medina River in bright sunshine, and he watched them as they raised sail and ran before the breeze under bulging spinnakers. All morning, weather forecasts had been warning of a sudden drop in barometric pressure over the eastern Atlantic, a portent of a major storm. Back in 1979, fifteen men had died on the Fastnet Race when hurricane-force winds tore into the fleet. No one wanted it to happen again. Least of all, Cathy Lamb.

On the phone the other night she'd been more than generous with her time. They'd talked for more than an hour, Faraday trying to sort out the muddle of emotions the boy's return had stirred, Cathy offering the kind of unvarnished home truths Faraday knew he needed to hear. There was no point wallowing in a past that had gone. J-J was a man now. Of course he had problems, of course it would be hard for him, but that was the way life took most people. He'd fled the nest. And the sooner Faraday grasped that simple truth, the sweeter life would be for all of them.

Deep down, Faraday knew she was right. Calmer now, he spent the morning watching groups of waders. Their feeding was frenzied. They moved quickly from area to area, pausing to peck and worry at the rich soup of nutrients beneath the glistening mud flats, and as Faraday eased the binoculars from bird to bird he wondered whether they were aware of the weather that might be soon sweeping east.

From Pennington, in mid-afternoon, Faraday drove north to a car park deep in the New Forest, and walked across the heath into the woodland. The woods were cool and dark after the blaze of sunshine. He sat beneath a beech tree, watching a redstart chasing flies, then smiled as the little bird darted into a holly bush, disturbed by the brief shadow of a sparrowhawk circling overhead. The forest was in full leaf and overhead the trees were beginning to stir, a constant muted rustling that spoke of deep unease.

Faraday felt it on his nerve ends. All morning he'd done his best not to think about J-J, but here in the woods it was impossible not to let the last few days crowd in on him. A week in Caen had changed the boy beyond recognition. Time after time, Faraday had tried to revive the old rapport, the old easy ways, but to no avail. J-J had become evasive, hard-edged, calculating, wary. His vulnerability was as evident as ever but he wore this new persona like a baggy, off-the-peg coat bought for him by a stranger. It didn't fit. It didn't suit him. And sooner or later, Faraday knew that he'd have to take it back.

In the meantime, though, Faraday had come to realise that there was no point worrying about what might happen next. Maybe the old relationship, the old rapport, would come back. Maybe it wouldn't. Either way, it was probably beyond his control. Cathy

Lamb had been right all along. The boy was twenty-two years old. Real life had consequences for us all. It was time to let his precious J-J work it out for himself.

Faraday had supper alone in a pub in Lyndhurst. Driving back to Portsmouth, he turned on the radio to check on the weather. The isobars were tightening into a dizzy whorl off the west coast of Ireland and the Fastnet Race committee had issued an advisory notice requesting yachts to report in hourly. Should the weather worsen over the next twenty-four hours, some commentators were calling for the race to be abandoned completely.

At home, J-J was back in bed. Faraday sat out in the darkness, listening to the eerie plaint of a distant curlew. It was low tide in the harbour and on the hot breath of the exposed mud flats came the tarry smells of driftwood and the tang of drying seaweed. Overhead, the moon was gauzy behind a thin layer of high cloud but the wind seemed to have died completely. Perhaps the storm has gone away, thought Faraday. Perhaps, like so much else, it was nothing more than make-believe.

The next morning, Monday, he knew at a glance that the forecasters had got it right. From his bedroom, the last of the sunshine had acquired a curiously livid cast and the waters of the harbour were gun-metal grey. Little flurries of wind were raising the dust along the waterside path and the birds were flying low, skittering from bush to bush. On the morning news, there were reports of huge seas in the Western Approaches and it seemed that dozens of boats on the Fastnet were already in trouble, overwhelmed by the storm's leading edge.

Before he got round to a shave, Faraday phoned Cathy. She'd been up since five, listening to the radio, wondering whether she ought to phone the Rescue

Co-ordination Centre in Plymouth, but something had stayed her hand.

'They know what they're doing,' she kept saying. 'I don't want to tempt fate.'

Forty minutes later, on the point of leaving for work, Faraday bumped into J-J on the stairs. He'd taken to wearing a black T-shirt in bed. Another innovation.

The boy wanted money, quite a lot of money, and Faraday knew why.

'I haven't got it,' he signed.

J-J didn't believe him. He turned his back on his father but Faraday followed him into the kitchen. It was a revelation how sulky he could get.

J-J's eyes found his in the mirror over the spice rack. He held up five fingers.

'Fifty?'

'No.' The boy shook his head before spelling it out with his hands. He wanted five hundred.

Faraday studied him for a moment. J-J had a job at a factory on the Hilsea estate, packing hair dryers into boxes for transit. It wasn't the most exciting challenge in the world, but for an assembly line it paid well.

'Why don't you ask them for a loan at work? Or save up for a couple of months?'

'I hate that place.' J-J pulled a face.

'Then try the bank.'

'They'll say no.'

'How do you know?'

'They always say no.'

Faraday wondered who had planted this idea in J-J's head. His son hadn't been inside a bank for years. Finally, Faraday bunched his fist, touched it lightly with his middle finger, and shrugged. J-J stared at him a moment, openly hostile, then turned away again. The bunched fist had always been the gesture one or other of them made when they'd run out of options. In plain language, it meant 'Tough'.

At Kingston Crescent, Faraday attended morning prayers. The regular nine a.m. update on developments overnight in the city took place in the police station social club, with as many CID and uniform as possible attending. Today, with cover stretched to the limit, there were just three bodies. Dawn Ellis, a worried-looking Cathy and the crime desk clerk looked lost amongst the dozens of circular tables.

'Paul Winter was duty over the weekend,' Cathy told Faraday the moment he appeared. 'He'll be back tomorrow.'

Faraday made no comment, shredding a beer mat while the clerk went through the usual tally of arrests for shoplifting, attempted thefts from cars, neighbourhood mayhem from drunk and disorderlies, and half a dozen reported burglaries. Only at the end, almost as an afterthought, did she mention the reported misper that had come in from the duty reception officer.

Faraday abandoned the remains of the beer mat. 'Misper' was CID-speak for missing person. A city the size of Portsmouth received misper reports at the rate of two or three a week, but most of them came from the regular band of teenage runaways who simply got bored with living with mum and dad, or who fled from one or other of the city's children's homes. Their details would be circulated through the normal channels and they'd normally be back as soon as their money ran out. This report, though, hit a different nerve. For a start it had come from a child.

'*How* old was she?'

'Eight.' Dawn was peering at the form 'Emma Maloney'.

'And she'd lost her dad?'

'So she said. The reception officer phoned her

89

mother to check. She lives in North End. Her name's Sandra. She and her husband are divorced.'

'And he's disappeared?'

Dawn nodded. There wasn't much detail, but it seemed that father and daughter spent lots of time together. The arrangement had worked perfectly for months, until Saturday.

'And?'

'It was the little girl's birthday. She and her dad were going out somewhere. He never turned up.'

Faraday reached out for the form, making a note of Sandra Maloney's address and phone number. Cathy Lamb was watching him over the rim of her coffee cup. Priority mispers were normally those deemed to be especially vulnerable: the elderly, the very young and the mentally afflicted. A middle-aged divorcee who'd missed out on his daughter's birthday didn't appear to fit into any of these categories.

The meeting over, Cathy caught up with Faraday on the stairs.

'You want me to put someone on that?' Cathy indicated at the form in Faraday's hand. 'Only we're a bit stretched today.'

'I know. That's why I thought I'd do it.'

'*You*? With everything else on our plate?' For one brief second Cathy seemed to have forgotten about the Fastnet Race.

Faraday smiled, and paused beside the open door to the inspectors' office. A phrase from their recent heart-to-heart had come back to him.

'I need to get out more,' he said. 'You're absolutely right.'

Outside, the wind was swirling around the police station car park and there was a hint of rain in the air. Sandra Maloney and her daughter lived in a tall, bay-fronted Victorian terraced house with Greenpeace stickers in an upstairs bedroom window. Faraday sheltered in the lee of a dripping privet hedge, waiting for an answer to his knock at the front door. It was raining hard by now.

Eventually, the door opened. Sandra Maloney was a tired-looking blonde woman in jeans and a grubby sweatshirt. Her hair was tied up with a twist of blue ribbon and there were scabs of white emulsion on her hands. Faraday explained about the missing-person report. She nodded, checked his ID more carefully than most, then let him in.

The hall smelled of fresh paint. There were dust sheets on the carpet and an open tin of primrose gloss beside a wooden step ladder.

'Long holidays.' She gestured at the mess. 'One of the perils of being a teacher.'

She took Faraday through to the lounge. There were books everywhere, ranged on shelves along the wall. Sandra Maloney waved Faraday into an armchair by the window. The glass was blurry with rain.

'I hope to God he comes back soon,' she said. 'It's breaking Em's heart.'

Faraday was looking at a row of school portraits arranged on the mantelpiece. The latest showed a freckle-faced eight-year-old with wispy auburn hair and a slightly crooked grin. In five years, she'd barely changed at all.

'He sees her a lot?'

'At least twice every week. Often on a Tuesday night, because that suits him, and then again at the weekend, normally Saturdays. Sometimes she stays over with him. In fact she's got a key of her own.'

'To his place?'

'Yes, he's got a flat on the seafront near the pier. It's a conversion. It used to be a hotel. She loves it there, takes a friend sometimes.'

There was another photograph, bigger, on the piano

behind the door. It showed Sandra standing on a footpath, her eyes narrowed against the sun. The glum figure in the red anorak beside her looked older, his face shadowed by a baseball cap, his upper body bent under the weight of an enormous rucksack. Cliffs rolled away behind them, plunging into a deep-green sea.

'That's a friend of mine, Patrick,' she said at once. 'If you're after a photo of Stewart, I'll see what I can find.'

She got up and rummaged in a drawer before producing a battered album. Stewart Maloney had the kind of face that belonged in an advert for French cigarettes. He had a three-day growth of beard and a pair of wraparound sunshades hid his eyes. He wore a white T-shirt under a black leather jacket and he was sitting astride a heavily laden motorbike. His smile, to Faraday, spoke of pride of ownership and a deep sense of mischief, not necessarily in that order.

'That was eleven years ago,' Sandra said. 'We were touring in Germany.'

'Has he changed much?'

'Hardly at all. Sadly.'

'How do you mean?'

'Some men never grow up. Stewart is one of them.'

Faraday considered the statement for a second or two, then pocketed the photo and pushed the conversation along. The last thing he wanted was a lengthy analysis of Sandra Maloney's divorce.

'Has he been under any stress lately that you know of? Anything at work?'

Sandra shook her head. Stewart Maloney was a lecturer at the city's university. He specialised in fine art, with an emphasis on representational drawing skills.

'They seem to think the world of him. He's a great communicator. Always has been.'

Faraday asked for a contact at the college, scribbling the name in his pocketbook. Jan Tilley.

'Money troubles at all?'

'Not that I'm aware of.'

'Who does he bank with?'

'NatWest.'

'Branch?'

'Southsea.'

Faraday scribbled another note, then looked up again.

'Anything in his private life?'

'Stewart doesn't have a private life. That's always been his problem. Was then. Is now.'

That same edge was back in her voice. Her gaze strayed to the pocket where Faraday had lodged the photograph.

'I'm not with you,' Faraday said softly. 'No private life?'

'Stewart never knew the meaning of private. He's a terrible show-off. Whatever he does, he does it in public. He's a child that way. He says he can't help himself but that's just an excuse.' Sandra pursed her lips, suddenly the schoolmistress. 'This isn't very helpful, is it?'

Faraday did his best to look non-committal. Sandra Maloney was doing her best to play the cool, well-adjusted divorcee but her emotions kept letting her down. Faraday sensed that the over-burdened pack-horse beside her on the clifftop was very much second-best, a poor substitute for the wild man astride the motorbike, and what made it worse was the fact that she very probably knew it.

'You say he can't help himself,' Faraday murmured. 'Can't help himself how, exactly?'

'Friends. Relationships. His career. Even the bike, lately. He's got a Honda now, a huge thing, and he fell off it on Wednesday, according to Em.'

Faraday leaned forward, wanting the details. Maloney had been over on the Isle of Wight, racing in Cowes Week. He regularly crewed aboard a yacht called a Sigma 33. At the end of Cowes Week he'd been due to do the Fastnet, but he'd crashed the bike on Wednesday night and broken his arm.

'Bad break?'

'Bad enough to need a replacement on the boat. The hospital must have sorted him out over on the island. I gather he came back afterwards.'

'When would that have been?'

'He phoned Em Thursday lunchtime, from the flat. She insisted I drove her down to see him.'

'What was he like?'

'I don't know. I waited outside.'

'But your daughter . . .?'

'Said he was fine. Same old daddy. You know what kids are like.'

Faraday nodded. Didn't he just.

'And after that? After Thursday?'

'Nothing. We haven't heard from him since. Saturday was Em's birthday. Now he wasn't doing the race, he was going to take her to London on the train. When he didn't turn up, she was terribly upset. You can imagine.'

'Did you phone him?'

'Of course. The answerphone thing was on.'

'Did you go round?'

'Yes.' She bit her lip. 'I did.'

'And?'

'The place was empty. He hadn't . . . you know . . . collapsed or anything.'

She got up again and left the room. When she came back she had a pair of keys on a loop of scarlet ribbon. Faraday stared at them. He'd done exactly the same thing the first time he'd given J-J the key to their little house by the harbour, tying it to a length of ribbon.

Red for the great spotted woodpecker, J-J's favourite bird. Red for love.

Sandra was still dangling the keys to Maloney's flat.

'You should go and look for yourself. It's number seven, Solent View Mansions. The bigger key fits the main door to the street.'

Faraday took the keys and pocketed his notebook. What sounded the loudest alarm bells was the routine Maloney had kept, that pattern of obligation he'd laid upon his life, and Faraday knew only too well how important his daughter would have become. Who wouldn't give up a couple of evenings a week for the dimpled grin on the mantelpiece?

'They were pretty close, then,' Faraday said, 'Emma and her dad?'

Sandra took a tiny step backwards, then ducked her head. It had been Em's idea to try and find her dad, Em's idea to raid her jam jar full of coins, get on a bus and ride down to the police station. The first she'd known about the child going to Kingston Crescent was a call from the officer she'd been talking to. They were sending her back by squad car. And they wanted to check the name of her father.

Sandra finally raised her face to Faraday and nodded.

'Em loves him,' she sniffed, 'to death.'

Nine

The taxi dropped Paul Winter outside Le Dome several minutes late for his appointment. The rain was sheeting down by now, and Winter made the mistake of trying to open his borrowed umbrella for the dash across the pavement. Within seconds, the wind had turned it inside out and he pursued it into the shelter of the shadowed café-bar.

The venue had been Templeman's idea. The partnership offices were three doors down the street and he'd made it plain on the phone that he could spare Winter the time for a double espresso and not a second more. Why he didn't come to the offices like everyone else was beyond him.

Winter shook himself like a dog by the door. Morris Templeman was waiting for him at a table near the back. He lifted a thin hand in greeting and then gestured limply at the waiting cappuccino. Winter always drank cappuccino.

'Crap weather.' Winter indicated the wreckage of the umbrella. 'Any idea how much these things cost?'

Templeman ignored the question. The onset of emphysema had practically bent him double.

'What's the problem?' he wheezed.

'There isn't one. Or not yours, anyway, and not mine, either.'

'So why are you here, Paul?'

Winter smiled at the question, and took a cautious sip at the cappuccino, wiping his mouth on the back of his hand. Lawyers were always the same, even ones as physically wrecked as Morry Templeman. They were

96

forever dividing their time up, pricing each segment, mesmerised by the need to account for each passing hour.

Winter leaned forward. The cuffs of his suit left damp marks on the tabletop.

'You'll be representing Marty Harrison,' he said.

'Yes.'

'And I expect you'll be framing some kind of claim.'

'Without a doubt.'

Templeman nodded. He was interested now, Winter could see it in his pouched little eyes, in the way they'd stopped straying to the door, in the way his yellowing fingers had suddenly stilled over the coffee spoon. Greed always gave men away. Always.

'Seen him yet? Marty?'

'Of course not. He's still in the ICU.'

'But getting better?'

'Definitely. He's off the danger list. As of yesterday.'

'Talked to the girlfriend at all?'

'Of course.' Templeman frowned as he sucked in another breath. 'These are clients of mine, Paul. There's a protocol here, as well you know.'

'Absolutely.' Winter sat back, his hands in the air, a mute gesture of apology.

A waitress approached with an armful of menus. Templeman waved her away.

'Well?' he said.

Winter had his eyes on the retreating waitress. He'd got up too late for breakfast and he was starving. At length, he looked at Templeman's pinched face.

'The pillock on the TFU who shot Marty was a guy called Pete Lamb,' he said carefully. 'If I was to tell you he was pissed at the time, might we stretch to a spot of early lunch?'

Faraday stood in the window of Maloney's third-floor flat, listening to the wind. Already it was blowing hard enough to hunch the tiny figures below him on Southsea Common, their dogs in tow, while out beyond the seafront the Isle of Wight was no more than a smudge behind the dirty, ragged skirts of low cloud. Tuned in to the police traffic net in the car driving down, he'd heard the controller warning about high-sided vehicles coming to grief on exposed sections of the motorway. Now, looking at the horizontal sheets of rain, he could understand why.

He turned back into the room, drawing a mental curtain over the view. He was here to do a job: to note, and assess, and – if possible – draw conclusions. In Faraday's experience, every room told a story, and this one would be no exception. The image that haunted him more than any other was that of Maloney's daughter, Emma. To do what she'd done – to jump on a bus, find the police station and report the loss of her dad – required either courage of a high order or simple desperation. The least he owed the child was the possibility of a happy outcome.

He looked round. The decor was aggressively minimalist – white emulsion on the walls, black carpet, single leather sofa and a round glass table – but the intended effect was spoiled by the clutter of a life very obviously interrupted.

On the table was a litter of bills, letters, circulars and various other items including an exposed roll of film and an appointments card for the fracture clinic at the city's Queen Alexandra Hospital. Faraday gazed at the debris, fixing the image in his mind: an open bottle of ibuprofen, a half-drunk cup of coffee, a Ricard ashtray brimming with cigarette ends, a half-eaten and very stale Danish pastry, a copy of Friday's *Guardian* with pages five to fourteen missing and a barely touched packet of cheese and onion crisps.

Settling on the sofa, Faraday stared at the wall opposite. In a neat line across the wall hung a series of aluminium-framed black and white photos. He examined them one by one, recognising the locations immediately.

Each of the photos captured one of the city's landmarks. There were shots of the harbour mouth, of the Guildhall steps, of HMS *Victory* glimpsed from the bottom of the dry dock in which she sat. There were studies of a breaker's yard – a resting place for generations of naval junk out beside the motorway – and of the Tricorn Shopping Centre, a brutal essay in unadorned concrete that had won prizes for the ugliest building in western Europe. This was a very different city from the Portsmouth of Nelly Tseng's dreams, infinitely more real, and there was something about the photographs – their framing, their texture, their refusal to compromise – that reminded him of Janna, his dead wife. As a photographer, she'd had a similar eye, a similar fascination with the awfulness of things. Odd, really, remembering how vivid she'd been, and how alive.

More photos lined the wall behind the sofa, but these were gentler in subject and treatment: minutely detailed studies of flowerheads, beach shells, and the deeply etched grain on lengths of ash-grey driftwood. Towards the window, beneath a hook on the picture rail, was an empty space, an oblong of white emulsion bigger than the photo frames and perceptibly brighter than the rest of the wall. Faraday gazed at it a moment, wondering where the missing item had gone.

Maloney's bedroom lay at the back of the flat. A big unmade double bed occupied most of the space but there was still room for a wardrobe, a chest of drawers and a smallish desk on to which he'd managed to cram a PC and a keyboard. Propped against the monitor screen was a nicely framed pen-and-ink drawing of sailing boats in a boisterous wind. The setting, instantly recognisable, was the entrance to Portsmouth

Harbour and the artist had caught the chop and curl of the ebbing tide with absolute precision. Though unsigned, it was a beautiful piece of work, strangely out of place in this claustrophobic little bedroom, and Faraday took it to the window for a closer look. It was far too small to have hung in the vacated space in the front room. What was it doing here?

A cable snaked down from the PC to a printer on the floor. Behind the printer was a big leather briefcase. Faraday hauled the briefcase on to the bed. Inside he found an address book and a manila envelope full of bank and credit card statements, but a cursory check found no obvious debts or financial embarrassments. On the first of every month, Maloney made a series of standing-order payments, and one of them – for £280 – was to his ex-wife, Sandra. Faraday made a note of the sort code and account number, then returned the envelope to the case.

In a side pocket of the briefcase, he spotted Maloney's passport. The photograph at the back showed the same close-cropped face he'd seen astride the motorbike at Sandra Maloney's house. This time, the pose was deliberately pugnacious – chin tilted, head thrown back – but Maloney wasn't wearing sunglasses and Faraday recognised something in the eyes, something almost playful, that many women would find attractive. Slipping the passport back, Faraday's fingers snagged on a curl of something faintly plastic. He pulled it out and found himself looking at a strip of photographs. There were four. They came from a photo booth. And they all showed the freckled face which had decorated Sandra Maloney's mantelpiece.

Faraday stared down at them. Why had Maloney's daughter got herself photographed this way? And what were the prints doing in her father's briefcase?

Back in the living room, Faraday went through

Maloney's pile of correspondence on the table. Towards the bottom, he found a half-completed passport application form made out in his daughter's name. The new passport was to replace the current arrangement whereby Emma travelled as a named child on her mother's passport, but the section requiring a parent or guardian's consent had been scored through with a thick black Pentel. Attached to the form was a yellow Post-it with a handwritten message. 'You know there's no way I'm going along with this,' it read, 'and *please* don't discuss it with Em.'

For the first time, Faraday felt a tingle of excitement. On the face of it, Maloney was locked into a dispute with his ex-wife about their daughter's passport. His disappearance had been reported not by his wife, who might well have worries about continuing maintenance payments, but by his eight-year-old daughter. So what did that suggest?

Faraday returned to the front room and checked the messages on Maloney's answerphone. They included calls from Sandra, his ex-wife, and a plaintive inquiry from a man named Marcus, wondering why Maloney hadn't shown up for his barbecue on Sunday.

None of these messages offered Faraday any clues to Maloney's disappearence, but when he pressed the 'redial' button on the phone, the voice on the other end turned out to be a despatcher at Aqua Cabs, one of the city's biggest taxi firms. Faraday made a note of the details, then returned to the window and gazed out.

Any serious investigation flagged various paths forward. There'd be checks to make on neighbouring flats, interviews to arrange with friends and employers, leads to pursue with banks and phone companies. Every single one of these actions carried a price in time and manpower – manpower that Faraday simply didn't have. Was he serious about Stewart Maloney? Was there really enough evidence to warrant launching a full-scale inquiry? He simply didn't know, but the longer he stared at the watery blur of the common and the seafront, the clearer became the image that swam towards him. Maloney's daughter, at the very least, deserved some kind of result.

Winter and Templeman were outside Le Dome. In the end, to Winter's immense satisfaction, the meal had extended to three courses and a bottle of Chardonnay. Now, inevitably, only one question remained.

They were both sheltering beneath Le Dome's ample canopy.

'So what do you want out of this?' Templeman was still studying the bill. 'Marty's bound to ask.'

Winter gave the question some thought.

'A conversation,' he said, 'once he's up to it.'

He watched Templeman pocket the bill, turn the collar of his jacket up and limp out on to the pavement, his tiny hunched figure braced against the wind and the rain. Then he called the lawyer back.

'By the way' – he beckoned him closer – 'who's Juanita?'

'What did they tell you?'

Faraday had found Cathy Lamb in the empty CID room, standing by the window, staring out at the rain. She'd finally phoned the Rescue Co-ordination Centre in Plymouth and the news had been far from reassuring.

'They're trying to get calls through to all the yachts. Some answer. Some don't.'

'And Pete's?'

'Didn't.'

'You mean hasn't. So far.'

Cathy glanced back at him, seizing on the change of tense.

'That's right.' She nodded, briefly warmed by the thought. 'No word. Yet.'

Pete's boat was called *Tootsie*. At twenty-nine feet Cathy knew it was far too small to be out in weather like this and a snatched five minutes with the midday television news had done nothing for her peace of mind. Yachts on the Fastnet dismasted, capsized, abandoned. Huge seas swamping life rafts. Rescue helicopters battling eighty-knot winds. If anything, said one survivor, it was already looking worse than '79.

Desperate to change the subject, Cathy nodded at the roll of film in Faraday's hand.

'You want that developed? Only I've got something else to go up to photographic.'

Faraday gave her the film and told her about Maloney, and the accident that had kept him out of the Fastnet. On the way back from the seafront, he'd been trying to piece together the kind of man he was, and competitive was one of the obvious conclusions. You could see it in the face in the photographs, sense it in his ex-wife's bitter reminiscence. Here was a guy with a mind of his own, a guy who didn't give in easily. Might a sudden decision to rejoin the crew explain the hastiness of his exit from the seafront flat? And his subsequent failure to turn up for Em's birthday?

Cathy wasn't convinced. If it was a serious boat they'd never carry a casualty like that. Never.

She was looking hard at Faraday, trying to gauge the strength of his interest. Was he really going to pursue this thing? With a queue of jobs stretching halfway down the corridor?

Faraday slipped behind the nearest desk and reached for the phone.

'Who organises this race?' he queried. 'Who do I talk to about Maloney?'

The official race office for the Fastnet was over in Cowes. The girl with access to the data base needed only the gentlest persuasion to enter Maloney's name. The check took barely seconds.

'Stewart Maloney?'

'That's him.'

'He was on a Sigma called *Marenka*. He only crewed on Tuesday and Wednesday. Then another guy took over. A Sam O'Connor.'

Faraday was scribbling down the names.

'Tell me about this *Marenka*.'

'It's a Sigma 33.'

'Thirty-three?'

'Feet long.'

'Is that big?'

'Not really, not for the Fastnet. Nice boat, though.'

Faraday explained about Maloney's injury. With a broken arm, would there be any chance that he'd still made it on to the Fastnet?

'On a boat like that?' Faraday could hear the girl laughing. 'They don't come more competitive than *Marenka*. Her skipper was looking for class honours on the Fastnet. We had him in here a couple of times last week, sorting out the crew change. No way he'd take a guy with a bust arm, absolutely no way.' She paused. 'Lucky him, really, given what's happening.'

Faraday thanked her and put the phone down, aware of Cathy watching him.

'Believe me now?' she muttered.

Back in his office, Faraday glanced through the list of waiting messages. Bevan, his superintendent, had rung three times. When he phoned his secretary, Bibi, she told him the meeting was due to start at two.

'What meeting?'

'I'd pop along if I were you,' she said dryly, 'and he might tell you.'

Bevan was in his office, looking glumly at a cheese salad sandwich. His wife had put him on a meat-free diet and he'd grown to loathe the sight of lettuce. When Faraday appeared at the door, he pushed the plate to one side and tossed a file of press cuttings across the desk.

'Trying to find you is ceasing to be a joke,' he said. 'Read those.'

Coastlines was a local freesheet, the brainchild of a young journalist-turned-entrepreneur called Spencer Weatherby. Like every other householder in the city, Faraday got the paper delivered twice weekly, and on a couple of occasions he'd even found time to read it. Weatherby's bright idea had been to marry an aggressive civil-rights agenda to a peppy, hard-hitting tabloid journalism – and *Coastlines*' resulting profile had pulled in bucketloads of advertising.

Faraday began to leaf through the cuttings. It was no secret that the police force had been one of Spencer Weatherby's prime targets, and over the last year he and Bevan had inevitably crossed swords. The headquarters press office, alarmed by the size of *Coastlines*' readership, was trying to broker a peace between the two men and at their insistence Weatherby had been invited along for an off-the-record background briefing in a bid to get the paper onside. The meeting was scheduled for two o'clock. Faraday's role was to talk about CID.

'So what do you think?'

Faraday was still looking through the cuttings. Most of them were pretty innocuous – undergraduate drivel about aggressive policing – but Bevan had ringed some of the more colourful phrases in red Pentel. Not a good sign.

'It'll be fine, sir,' he murmured. 'These people need us more than we need them.'

'You really think so, boyo?' Bevan shook his head. 'That makes you as naive as I was.'

The meeting got off to a disastrous start. Spencer Weatherby had been called to attend an important client meeting and he'd sent his news editor to stand in. Kate Symonds was an outspoken twenty-four-year-old with an absolute determination to antagonise Bevan just as soon as she could. She handed him her long, belted raincoat, sat down uninvited, and complained that down her street no one had seen a beat officer for months.

'I thought you guys were into community policing,' she said, producing a small lined pad and putting it carefully on the table. 'Round our way, coppers are an endangered species.'

Bevan ignored the remark. Waving Faraday into the chair beside him, he tabled his peace terms. Decent access in return for responsible coverage. Prior briefings on important policy issues. Maybe even a tip or two about major initiatives at street level. And all this as a down-payment on a new partnership.

'Is any of that beyond us?' he asked briskly.

'Us?' The girl bridled at once at Bevan's choice of pronoun. 'We have a duty towards our readers, Mr Bevan. If you're talking partnership, our partnership's with them.'

This was classic media-studies tosh, flaunting the precious independence of the fourth estate, and Bevan wasn't having it. Twice in the last month, front-page splashes in *Coastlines* had headlined alleged police harassment. At best, went the editorial line, our coppers are lazy and inefficient. At worst, they're no better than the louts and bullies who rule our streets. Unlike Faraday, Bevan had a thin skin as far as the media was concerned. *Coastlines'* accusations had wounded him deeply and only a last-minute intervention from the press office at HQ had stopped him from taking up the cudgels in earnest. Now, at last, he had a chance to set the record straight.

The girl was talking about journalistic ethics. Bevan leaned forward across the table. He was never more dangerous than when he was smiling.

'That's a joke,' he said softly. 'And an oxymoron, too.'

'A what?'

'An oxymoron. A contradiction in terms. The day you convince me that gutter journalism and ethics go together is the day you start wising up about grammar.' He reached for the file and began to lay the cuttings out across the table. Then he looked up again. The smile had gone. 'My people bleed because of your incompetence. I'd just like you to know that.'

The girl was staring at the cuttings. Many of them carried her own byline.

'I can defend every one of those stories,' she said hotly.

'No you can't, love. And you know why? Because they're not true. People like you want headlines, not real life, not the stuff we deal with. You want grief and sensationalism. You want widows and orphans. And when they're not available, you think it's smart and street-wise to have a pop at us. You're reckless and lazy and you have absolutely no idea of the damage you do. Here. Let's start with this one.'

Bevan reached for yesterday's front-page coverage of the Harrison raid. The headline read 'In Cold Blood?' Then he found another about an alleged strip show at the police social club. He'd hit his stride now, citing example after example of facts unchecked, circumstances misunderstood, phone calls never made.

At last, Symonds managed to hit back.

'You're saying yesterday's raid wasn't a tragedy?'

'I'm saying it was a mistake.'

'Shooting someone? With a baby in the room? A *mistake*?'

'We never like shooting anyone. Even scum like Harrison. Far too much paperwork for a start—'

Bevan broke off, shaking his head, knowing he'd gone too far. Symonds was still staring at him when her mobile phone began to ring. She hesitated, before retrieving it from her bag. Bevan was watching her closely across the table. Faraday had never seen him look so wary before.

Symonds began to nod. Someone was talking very fast at the other end. Finally she glanced up at Bevan.

'Of course,' she said on the phone. 'I'll be right back.'

She slipped the mobile into her bag and got to her feet. Bevan hadn't moved.

'Who was it?' he asked stonily.

'The office. The Search and Rescue blokes are pulling bodies out of the water from the Fastnet. A lot of these guys are local. I have to get back.'

'More widows? More orphans?' Bevan glanced sideways at Faraday as she made for the door. The smile was back on his face. 'You think we made a friend there, Joe?'

Ten

By late afternoon, Faraday was back outside the seafront apartment block where Maloney had gone missing. His first visit had ended with checks on neighbours who might have been able to shed light on Maloney's disappearance, but most of them were either out or unhelpful. Only one lead had seemed remotely worth pursuing. Maloney had been on good terms with the lady in the flat across the hall. Her name was Dorothy Beedon. Every Monday she was in the habit of going to a local bridge club but she was normally back around four.

By now, the full force of the storm had engulfed the south coast. Sheltering beneath the big porch while he fumbled for Emma's keys, Faraday watched huge waves battering the seafront, livid explosions of foaming brown water that dwarfed the lamp posts on the promenade. From a distance it felt as if the city was under bombardment and he shuddered to think what it must be like out at sea.

At last he found Em's keys and let himself in. The woman at number eight answered his knock within seconds. Dorothy Beedon was a tall, thin, elderly woman with a slight cast in one eye. She peered at Faraday's ID, then let him in.

'I thought you were the builder,' she said, gesturing helplessly at the window.

They were standing in the big front room. A semi-circle of buckets and saucepans in the bay window were carefully positioned beneath a line of steady drips through the ceiling. More rain bubbled through the seals on the windows themselves.

'It's been like this for an hour. You'd think he'd be here by now, wouldn't you?'

Faraday couldn't take his eyes off the view. The boiling sea had turned a sinister shade of yellow-brown and at last he understood a phrase he'd treasured from his childhood reading.

'Evil weather,' he murmured, turning back into the room.

He accepted the offer of an armchair and explained that he was making some inquiries about Mrs Beedon's neighbour, Stewart Maloney. He understood that the two of them were friends.

'Am I right?'

'You are.' She offered him a vigorous nod then glanced towards the window. 'My goodness!'

A length of bladderwrack, seaweed the colour of iodine, had briefly flattened itself against the glass, blown hundreds of metres across the common. They both gazed at it.

At length, Mrs Beedon struggled to her feet.

'He's broken his arm, you know. Would you like some biscuits?'

She left the room without waiting for an answer and returned with an open packet of custard creams. Young Stewart had popped in first thing Friday to borrow some milk. That's when she'd seen the way they'd strapped him up.

'He broke it here. Not nice.' She touched her cardigan lightly with one gnarled finger, high up on her right arm.

'Was he OK?'

'Not at all. Would you be?'

'I meant in himself. Apart from the arm.'

Mrs Beedon went across to the window bay, examining the buckets one by one. Thinking she hadn't understood the question, Faraday tried to rephrase it, but he could have saved himself the breath.

'How was little Em's birthday?' Mrs Beedon was back in her chair. 'They went to London, didn't they?'

'No, they didn't,' Faraday said. 'That's why I'm here.'

He explained briefly about Maloney's disappearance. Something had happened to call him away from the flat across the hall. Had Mrs Beedon seen him after he'd borrowed the milk?

'Not to talk to, no.'

'But?'

'I did see him go out. Friday afternoon it must have been. After the other chap had popped in.'

'What other chap?'

'Well now . . .' She bent her head, frowning with the effort of recollection. 'An older chap I think he was, thinnish. He came on Friday afternoon, arrived in a taxi.' She nodded towards the bay window. 'It's the view, Inspector. I sit here most days. Not much gets by me.'

'And this man? Had you seen him before?'

'Never.'

'What time would this have been?'

She frowned, looking at her watch.

'The big P&O ferry had just gone out. Say half past three.'

Faraday asked her how long the stranger had stayed. She thought ten minutes, no more.

'And Mr Maloney was in?'

'Oh yes, definitely.'

'How do you know?'

'Well, this other chap couldn't have got in otherwise, whoever he was. Not without Stewart. But there was the shouting, too.' She nodded, disturbed by the memory. 'They were having an argument, a real set-to.' She bent towards him, her knuckles white on the armrests of the chair. 'I was quite worried, to tell you the truth.'

'What were they saying?'

'I don't know. But they were both . . . you know . . . pretty angry.'

'Was there any other noise? Bumps? Crashes?'

'Fighting, you mean?' She shook her head. 'No, thank goodness.'

'And you saw this person leave?'

'Yes, and this time he was carrying something big, wrapped in newspaper.' Her hands sketched an oblong in the air. 'He didn't take a taxi this time. He just walked off.'

Faraday leaned forward in the big armchair. The shape she'd just made would have fitted the empty space on Maloney's wall. Almost exactly.

'This man,' Faraday said, 'would you recognise him again?'

'Maybe . . .' She hesitated. 'But the eyes aren't as good as they were.'

'What was he wearing?'

'Outdoor clothes, you know, one of those anorak things. Red it was, and a nice red, too . . .'

Faraday stopped writing for a moment. Sandra Maloney's boyfriend wore a red anorak. He'd seen it in the photograph on the piano. He was tall, too, and on the thin side. He glanced across at Mrs Beedon. She was saying that Maloney had left shortly afterwards. In another taxi.

'Can you remember the firm?'

'No, I'm afraid I can't.'

The two of them looked at each other for a moment then a brief flash of white drew Faraday's gaze to the window. A gull, he thought, desperately trying to spill air and regain some kind of control before the storm tossed it over the rooftops. The touch of the old woman's hand on his arm made him jump. She was peering at him in the gloom.

'Tell me something.' She was looking anxious again. 'Do you think the builders really will come?'

Faraday let himself into Maloney's flat with Emma's key. Ignoring the clutter in the sitting room, he went straight to the bedroom at the back. Stored computer files on a PC had rapidly become one of the CID's first ports of call in situations like these and normally the search teams downloaded everything on to floppy discs for later analysis. Faraday could organise this if he felt it necessary, but a quick trawl might save him precious man-hours later. Settling himself on the end of the bed, he fired up the computer. Within minutes, he scented success.

Maloney had stored a correspondence file tagged 'Emmy' on his hard disc. There were three letters, all of them addressed to one of the city's biggest legal firms. The first letter was by far the longest and told Faraday everything he wanted to know.

According to Maloney, his ex-wife had started a new relationship. Her partner's name was Patrick McIlvenny. He was Canadian by birth and taught at a local comprehensive. His own marriage had foundered a couple of years ago and now he wanted to go home. Home was Vancouver. He was determined to take Sandra with him. And Sandra was equally determined to bring Emma, Maloney's only daughter.

The letter bristled with righteous anger. 'There's absolutely no possibility,' Maloney had written in the final paragraph, 'that I will ever let this happen – and they both know it. Legally, I need to know that I can stop them. If this proves impossible, there have to be other ways.'

Other ways?

Faraday bent to the box of copier paper on the floor

and fed a sheet into the printer beside it. If the threat was this explicit in a letter to a solicitor, then God knows what Maloney must have told his ex-wife. No way do you get between me and my daughter. No way do you crate your belongings, flog the house and steal off to Heathrow to start your new life. Not with Em. Not with my precious daughter. No way. Not now. Not ever.

And Sandra? Or – more importantly – Patrick McIlvenny? What might they have done? Say their plans were cast in concrete? Say they'd even got a deadline, a leaving date, a buyer for the house? What would you do about a man as intransigent as Stewart Maloney? Might you try sweet reason? Might you try and buy him off? And if that failed, and you were that desperate, might you just phone for a cab? And come round to sort the issue out?

Faraday retrieved the letter from the printer and walked through to the front room. The presence of the passport application form was much clearer now, Maloney's bid to regain some control in this situation. With a new passport, Em could exercise an element of choice. Maloney could even keep the passport himself, making it impossible for her to leave the country.

Faraday sifted carefully through the correspondence on the table, sorting out the uncompleted form and putting it on one side. There comes a moment in every investigation when instinct begins to harden into conviction and he knew that this was it. Beyond any reasonable doubt he'd established a motive. Where that motive might lead was still largely guesswork, but at least it was a start.

By the window, he paused, listening to the howling wind, thinking of Maloney again. There were holes in this theory of his and one of them had to do with Sandra, Maloney's ex-wife. If her new lover was really responsible for Maloney's disappearance, then how come she'd volunteered the keys to this flat so willingly?

Faraday shook his head, not knowing the answer, and then picked up the passport form. Next stop would be another visit to Sandra Maloney and the chance to put his suppositions to the test of a second interview. Faraday glanced at his watch, planning the evening ahead, relieved that he wouldn't have to go home. He hadn't trodden this path for years, and with a sudden rush of pleasure, he realised that he was enjoying it.

Paul Winter was contemplating the prospects for the pub quiz when Morry Templeman phoned. The quiz took place on the second Monday of every month and August was especially good because so many of the better teams would be away on holiday. For Joan, in particular, the pub quiz had become the mainstay of her social diary.

The phone was in the hall.

'Paul? You got a pen there?'

Winter recognised Morry's thin wheeze at once. He reached for a Biro and closed the lounge door with his foot.

'Go,' he said.

Templeman gave him an address and a phone number in Port Solent. It was nearly dark outside, terrible weather for August, and Winter had to turn on the table lamp to read it all back.

'So who's that, then?' Winter was still peering at the address.

'Juanita. Her second name's Perez. And listen, Paul.'

'What?'

'It didn't come from me.'

By the time Faraday got to North End, Sandra

Maloney was preparing supper. Faraday offered to come back later but she said she wouldn't hear of it.

'I'm sure it won't take long.' She slipped the lettuce back into the fridge. 'Is there any news?'

Faraday was watching Emma laying three places at the table at the far end of the kitchen-diner. The girl darted to and fro with a deftness of movement that J-J had never quite managed to master, even now.

'I'm afraid not,' Faraday said at last. 'Are you sure you wouldn't prefer to do this later?'

Sandra shook her head and led the way through to the living room. Faraday shut the door behind them. The framed photo was still on the piano, the face beneath the enormous rucksack as stony-eyed and long-suffering as ever.

'About this new relationship of yours . . .' Faraday began.

'I beg your pardon?'

Faraday caught the chill in her voice. There was surprise there, certainly, but defiance as well. What had Sandra Maloney's private life got to do with the likes of Faraday?

Faraday settled himself in the high-backed armchair by the window. He wanted to know about Sandra's plans to move to Canada.

'I don't have any.'

'That's not the way I heard it.' He glanced round the big sitting room with its shadowed alcoves and brimming bookcases. 'Is this place on the market by any chance?'

'No.'

'You're not planning to sell up?'

'No.'

'Your partner, Patrick, is he—?'

'Friend, not partner.'

'Really?'

Faraday let the question settle between them. Two

decades inside J-J's head had given him a very special appreciation of body language. In situations like these, he always looked for the tell-tale signs of anxiety: tiny facial movements, especially around the mouth; a reluctance to risk full eye contact; trouble keeping the hands still. Clues like these often flagged the path to a successful result but so far, to his surprise, Sandra Maloney had evidenced nothing more revealing than anger.

She was perched on the edge of the Victorian chaise longue, her hands clasped together, her lips pursed. At length, she broke the silence.

'For the record, Mr Faraday, Patrick and I are extremely good friends. I don't know where you got hold of all this nonsense about me moving to Canada. If he hadn't disappeared, I'd put money on the fact that you've been talking to Stewart. That's the kind of thing he'd believe.'

'You're saying it's not true?'

'Yes, and it never has been true, either. Stewart's paranoic. He jumps to conclusions all the time.'

'But your friend *is* Canadian?'

'Yes.'

'And you're telling me he doesn't want to go back to Vancouver?'

Mention of Vancouver brought colour to Sandra's face.

'He does. That's true. He doesn't much like it here. And sometimes I don't blame him.'

'But you don't want to go with him?'

'What I want doesn't matter. I can't and that's that.'

'Why not?'

'Because of Em, of course. She loves her home. She's settled at school. All her friends are here. And then there's her dad. That's the irony, Mr Faraday, that's what poor, dear, deluded Stewart never quite understands. His best guarantee as far as Em is concerned is the girl herself. Do I *look* the kind of mother that would just pack her up and haul her away?'

'But otherwise you'd have done it?' Faraday said. 'Is that fair?'

'Done what?'

'Gone to Canada. With Patrick.'

Faraday's gaze strayed to the picture on the piano. Sandra was watching him carefully.

'I might,' she conceded.

'And he knows that? Patrick?'

'We've talked about it.'

'And he wants you to go?'

'Yes, he does. But men are like that, aren't they? Want, want, want. Need, need, need. Not a thought for anyone else, let alone Em.'

Faraday nodded, and produced a battered notebook. The interview was back where he wanted it. Sandra Maloney, for all her protestations, was the meat in the sandwich – not simply between two men, but between two men and her daughter. He hadn't been wrong after all.

'Do you happen to know where Patrick was on Friday afternoon?'

Sandra stared at him.

'For God's sake—' she began.

'It's a serious question, Mrs Maloney. You'd be well advised to answer it.'

There was a long silence while Sandra studied her hands. Faraday could sense her hauling the rope of days back through her memory. At last, she looked up. The defiance was back in her eyes again.

'He was here,' she said. 'With me.'

'Anyone else?'

'No. We were alone.'

'So there's no one else to . . . ah . . . corroborate that fact?'

Faraday's pen hovered over the notebook. In the

depths of the house, he could hear a clock chiming. Finally Sandra shook her head.

'Nobody,' she said.

'And you were both here all afternoon?'

'Yes, we had a bit of lunch. Patrick had brought a rather good bottle of wine.'

'And afterwards?'

'You really want to know?'

'Yes, please.'

'We went to bed. It's holiday time. The weather was miserable. Em was out for the afternoon. Oh, for God's sake, why do I have to justify myself? What are you after, Mr Faraday? The details?'

'He never left the house, then?'

'Not that I noticed.'

'You're absolutely certain about that?'

'Yes.'

'And has he ever been to your ex-husband's flat?'

'Never. In fact I don't think they've even met.'

'Never?'

There was another long silence. Then came the sound of a key in a door and Sandra was on her feet in an instant, a suddenly vivid smile on her face.

'Ask him yourself,' she said. 'He's just come in.'

Before Faraday could get to his feet, she was out of the room. Faraday heard the low murmur of voices in the hall, then the man on the footpath was standing in the open doorway. He was an inch or two over six feet. His scarlet anorak was dripping from the rain and what was left of his hair was plastered over his scalp. He ignored Faraday's outstretched hand.

'Can I help you?'

Faraday was still cursing himself for not being quicker into the hall. Five seconds was time enough to establish an alibi, especially if you were guilty.

McIlvenny was still waiting for an answer. Faraday explained briefly about Maloney, and about Emma's visit to the police station. He was here to help her find her father.

'Would you have any objection if I asked you for your fingerprints?' Faraday inquired.

McIlvenny stared at him for a long moment.

'For what purpose?' he said at last.

'Elimination.'

'Elimination from what?'

'I'm afraid I can't tell you at this point in time. If I could, it might be easier for all of us.' He paused. 'I understand you're thinking of going back to Canada.'

McIlvenny glanced at Sandra and then nodded. Trying to teach anything in this country had become a joke, especially in schools as appalling as Portsmouth's, and the higher you got in the pecking order, the more you realised that the problems were probably insoluble.

Faraday recognised the veiled threat.

'Where do you teach?'

McIlvenny named one of the big comprehensives. Then, for the first time, he permitted himself the ghost of a smile.

'At the moment I'm acting headmaster,' he said bleakly, 'until they find some other poor sap.'

Before he left them to their supper, Faraday took Sandra aside and told her that he'd appreciate a word with her daughter.

'Now?'

'Yes, please.'

Sandra looked him in the eye, wanting to say no, wanting him to leave, then shrugged, too weary to argue. Emma was upstairs in her bedroom. Faraday could ask her whatever he liked, as long as Sandra was there.

'No problem, Mrs Maloney.'

Sandra led the way upstairs. Emma was sitting on

her bed, watching television with the sound down. Faraday wondered whether she'd been at the top of the stairs, trying to eavesdrop.

Sandra explained about Faraday being a policeman.

'Detective, Emma,' Faraday murmured. 'Sounds more glamorous.'

The girl looked up at him. She was still a child, half frightened, half fascinated. Faraday reversed a chair and sat down, his chin on his folded arms.

'Just the one little question, Emma. Your dad's flat, those pictures on his wall in the front room. You know the ones I'm talking about?'

Emma nodded. The faint, whispery voice went with the freckles and the brace on her front teeth.

'You mean the photos?'

'Yes. Just imagine you're standing there now, looking out towards the window. OK?' Emma glanced at her mother, wide-eyed at this new game, then nodded again. 'Good. Now look just a bit to your left. There's a picture at the end of the row of photos, a bit bigger than the rest. Got it?'

Emma frowned with concentration, then began to giggle. Faraday was smiling, too.

'Know the picture I mean?'

'Yes.'

'What's the picture of?'

There was a long silence. Emma was still giggling. Then Sandra broke in, her patience exhausted.

'Just tell him, Em. Tell him what it is.'

'It's a lady.'

'A photograph?' Faraday asked. 'Like the rest?'

'No, a picture, a painting, something someone's done.'

'And what's it like? What's the lady doing?'

'She's sitting on a sofa thing. More lying down, really.'

'Is that all? Is that why you were giggling?'

'No, it's just that . . .' Her eyes went to her mother again. 'The lady hasn't got anything on.'

'Nothing at all? You mean she's naked?'

'Yes.'

Faraday nodded, letting the silence stretch and stretch. He felt Sandra stiffening beside him. Just one more question, he thought. Then we're through.

'This lady, Emma' – he gestured up at Sandra – 'is she your mummy?'

The child looked briefly startled at the suggestion, then shook her head vigorously.

'Oh, no, she's different . . . all over.'

There was a long silence, then Sandra manoeuvred Faraday out on to the landing and closed the bedroom door behind her. McIlvenny was at the foot of the stairs, waiting for them both to come down.

'I hope you've got a good reason for all these questions,' Sandra said icily, 'because you're sure as hell going to need one.'

Eleven

Faraday found the envelope on his desk when he got back to the station. The night shift had just booked on and the traffic crews were milling around the coffee machine along the corridor. Inside the envelope was a bunch of photographs secured with an elastic band. The top one showed a group of men clambering aboard a yacht, and it took Faraday a second or two to realise that these were the shots from Maloney's roll of film.

Cathy was next door in the CID room, bent to the phone. She gestured for him to come over, covering the mouthpiece with her hand.

'Checking on Pete again,' she muttered.

Faraday squeezed her shoulder and returned to his office, settling down to sort through the photos. They all seemed to feature the same yacht. The weather looked pretty similar throughout, so Faraday assumed that they must have been snapped on the Tuesday or Wednesday of Cowes Week. The name of the yacht – *Marenka* – was black-lettered on the crew's scarlet sweatshirts and, judging by the expressions on these men's faces, the day's racing must have gone well.

Towards the bottom of the pile, Faraday came across a shot that somebody else must have taken. *Marenka* was back on the pontoon amongst all the other yachts and the crew were crowded together in the cockpit for a victory pose. There were six of them in all, a mix of ages, two of them young, four of them older. With the exception of the man in the very middle of the group, they were all punching the air, Maloney's fist raised highest of all.

Faraday lingered for a moment on the three-day growth of beard that was rapidly becoming familiar, then he returned to the man in the middle. He was heavily built. He had a big, meaty face, and the same red sweatshirt and matching shorts, but unlike everyone else his head was turned to the left, his gaze directed elsewhere. One arm was up, his middle finger raised in a derisive salute, and the expression on his face was close to a snarl.

Trying to imagine the wider picture, Faraday half closed his eyes. *Marenka* had obviously won but for this man, at least, victory hadn't been enough. He'd spotted the opposition. And he wasn't going to let the moment pass. Something the girl in the Fastnet office had said came back to Faraday. 'They don't come more competitive than *Marenka*,' she'd told him. And here was the proof.

Cathy appeared at the open door, zipping up her anorak. When Faraday raised an inquiring eyebrow, she shook her head.

'Nothing,' she said. 'No one's heard a peep since last night.'

'Maybe the radio's out.'

'That's what they said.'

Faraday nodded, trying to think of something else to say, some other crumb of comfort, but Cathy was gone already, the clack-clack of her footsteps fading away down the corridor.

Reaching for the phone directory, Faraday found the number for Aqua Cabs and then dialled it. When he finally got through to the shift manager he asked what kind of records they kept.

'What is this?'

'Missing-person inquiry.'

The woman grunted then explained that a tally of

all calls and fares were kept on hard disc for a week. Then wiped. Faraday inquired whether she'd got a pen handy. When she asked why, he gave her Maloney's name, the address on the seafront and last Friday's date.

'I'm looking for a pick-up around four in the afternoon,' he said, 'Give or take.'

He heard the snort of laughter at the other end, then she was back on the phone.

'We're turning over more than a thousand calls a day at the moment,' she said. 'I hope you're not in a hurry.'

Back home by ten, Faraday found a scribbled note from J-J explaining that he'd gone to stay with a friend for the night. A couple of panes of glass in the greenhouse had been smashed by flying debris during the day, but he'd done his best to block the holes with sheets of plywood. He'd signed the note with a big loopy 'J' and added a pair of seagull wings underneath, and the gesture brought a smile to Faraday's face. It was the first sign of affection from the boy since his return from France.

Minutes later, standing in the lounge listening to the storm blowing itself out, Faraday answered the phone. It was Cathy. She was laughing. She'd just had a call from the Search and Rescue people telling her that *Tootsie*'s crew had been picked up by helicopter and flown to hospital in Plymouth. Pete was suffering from exposure but otherwise appeared to be OK. First thing tomorrow, she wanted to drive down to collect him.

'No problem,' Faraday said at once. 'Do it.'

'There's something else, too.'

She told him about another message she'd taken earlier from the race office at Cowes. The crew of a yacht called *Marenka* had also been hauled out of the water, and the girl at the Cowes office thought Faraday might like to know.

'So what's with this *Marenka*?' Cathy inquired.

Faraday muttered something about the misper, Maloney.

'You're really still interested?'

'Very much so.'

'How come?'

Faraday began to explain about the evening's developments, then broke off. If any bunch of guys could offer an intimate view of Stewart Maloney, then it would surely be *Marenka*'s crew. You could see it in their faces in the photographs. These guys were tight with each other. They'd sailed together, won together, celebrated together, got drunk together. There'd be few secrets on a boat like that.

'When are you leaving?' Faraday asked.

'First light. Say five.'

'Pick me up, then. I'm coming too.'

'What about the office?'

Faraday was still thinking about Maloney's photographs.

'Office?' he said blankly.

Next morning, Cathy and Faraday drove down to the hospital in Plymouth. The sky had cleared after the passage of the storm, leaving a clean, rain-washed blue, dotted with cotton-wool clouds. There were trees blown down in Dorset, and structural damage to houses around Exeter. Derriford Hospital was on the northern fringes of Plymouth. Staff at the reception desk directed them to the third floor.

Faraday accompanied Cathy along the corridor from the lift. Pete Lamb occupied a bed in a ward at the end. A glass partition screened the ward and Cathy paused to rearrange the flowers she'd bought from the shop downstairs. Faraday had expressed surprise at

Pete's fondness for flowers but Cathy, grinning, had told him not to be so naive. The bunch of blue iris was really for her.

Faraday saw the woman first. She was sitting at Pete's bedside, stroking his hand. She was young, with a knot of blonde hair pinned up at the back. She was wearing jeans and a blue scoop-necked T-shirt and when she reached out to get something from the cabinet on the far side of the bed, Pete leaned forward, nuzzling her breasts. A moment later, he caught sight of his wife.

Cathy's face had frozen. She stared at Pete a moment longer through the glass then moved to go into the ward. Faraday restrained her. The more she struggled, the more tightly he gripped her arm.

'Don't,' he told her. 'Not here, anyway.'

'You're fucking joking.'

'I'm not.'

'He's my husband.'

'It doesn't matter.'

'Doesn't *matter*?'

Cathy was staring at him. The sister behind the nursing station was getting to her feet. Faraday gestured for her to follow them both down the corridor. Back beside the lift, he asked where he could find the crew of a boat called *Marenka*.

The sister was still looking at Cathy.

'Are you OK, dear?'

Cathy couldn't take her eyes off the ward by the nursing station. Finally she tipped her head back and took a deep breath.

'No,' she said, 'but I will be.'

The survivors from *Marenka* occupied a ward on the floor below, and to Faraday's surprise there were just three of them. Faraday looked at Cathy, trying to judge how close she was to taking the lift back upstairs. She was very pale and the tension showed in the tightness of the skin around her lips.

'Come with me,' he said. 'We'll do this together.'

Faraday recognised the big, bulky figure in the corner bed at once. He'd been the one in the photo giving the finger to some rival or other. Now he was sitting up with a bowl of soup and the remains of a crusty roll. His jaw was swollen on one side and he had a livid bruise beneath his left eye. According to the chart hanging on the foot of the bed, his name was Charlie Oomes.

Derek Bissett, in the next bed, was a couple of years older, a smaller, slighter man. His eyes were closed, the blankets heaped up around him. Across the ward was the other survivor, Ian Hartson. He looked younger than the other two but Faraday was conscious at once of a wariness in his expression. Something about the eyes that followed them as they walked across the ward to talk to Charlie Oomes. Something this man was trying to forget.

No wonder.

Charlie Oomes turned out to be *Marenka*'s owner/ skipper, a gruff south Londoner with a florid complexion, huge, meaty hands and little time for small talk. Faraday and Cathy introduced themselves and then drew up seats beside his bed.

'What happened?'

Oomes studied them both for a moment with his tiny, bloodshot eyes and then told them the story of the yacht's final hours. How she'd pushed out into the Celtic Sea ahead of every other Class III boat. How she'd had to run before the storm on a tiny triangle of trisail, dragging a sea anchor to prevent a fatal broach. How he and Henry had taken turns at the tiller, half an hour on, half an hour off. And how a rogue wave had finally overwhelmed their tiny craft, roaring out of the darkness, pitch-poling *Marenka*, flooding the cabin, and finally breaking her up.

Oomes brushed crumbs from his borrowed pyjama top.

'Fucked,' he said, 'totally shafted. We didn't even have time to send a Mayday.'

'So how did they find you?'

'We had an EPIRB, an emergency radio beacon. We grabbed it off the back before we took to the life raft. Bastard thing didn't work at first. Derek had to fix it.'

He gestured at the inert figure huddled beneath the blankets and Faraday found himself nodding in sympathy. After a story like that he felt as if he'd been there.

'Who was Henry?'

'Our nav. Brilliant bloke. Total one-off.'

'And what happened to him?'

'Dead. Drowned.'

Henry Potterne, the navigator, had disappeared moments before the capsize. Sam, his nineteen-year old stepson, had stayed aboard to try and get a line around the sixth member of the crew, a university student, David Kellard. The last Charlie had heard from the life raft was a yell from young David as the storm swept them away. Turned out the lad had a terrible fear of drowning. Poor sod.

Faraday stole a glance at Cathy. She was miles away, staring blankly out towards the corridor. Another capsize, Faraday thought. Another little death.

'So what's with you lot? What are you after?' It was Oomes's turn to ask the questions.

Faraday explained about Stewart Maloney. He, too, had disappeared, though obviously not at sea. When did Oomes last see him?

Oomes frowned, picking at the last of the crumbs. Stu had broken his arm falling off that sodding bike of his. Felt like a year ago. Tuesday? Wednesday? Bastard must have been psychic, must have known the shit we'd be getting ourselves into.

'So where were you all on Friday?'

Oomes had started again on the soup, eyeing Faraday over the lip of the bowl.

'On the island. We rent a place at Cowes. Costs me a fortune.'

'And you were there all week?'

'Of course. That's what Cowes is about. We don't go there to tart about. We go there to race.'

'What about the rest of the year?'

'What about it?'

'Where do you keep the boat?'

'Port Solent.'

Faraday nodded, thinking at once about Nelly Tseng. Men like Charlie Oomes were exactly the kind of clients she wanted to attract. Probably a self-made businessman. Almost definitely wealthy.

'You've got a house there?'

'Bet your life. And a waterside mooring.'

Faraday made a note of the Port Solent address, then looked at Oomes again. Had Maloney turned up on the island after the injury? Had he come over to wish them good luck on Friday night or Saturday morning? Had he phoned or sent a card? Had Charlie or any of the rest of them had *any* contact with him?

Charlie shook his head. Maloney had been completely irresponsible, falling off the bike. Riding with a couple of pints inside him was asking for trouble when the man barely drank. He was bloody lucky it hadn't been more serious. Anyone with an ounce of common sense would have walked.

'Where was he going?'

'Back to the house, the place we'd rented.'

'How far was that?'

'About a mile. He was posing. He's always posing.

Leather strides and all that art-school garbage. Guy lives on another planet. Any woman with half a brain would walk away.'

Faraday glanced at Cathy. Her eyes were closed now. She looked exhausted.

'I'm not with you, Mr Oomes,' Faraday murmured. 'What are you telling me here?'

'Telling you?'

'About Maloney.'

'Stu?' He spooned up the last of the soup, wiped his mouth with the corner of the sheet, and shrugged.

'Nothing, really. We all have our little problems, don't we?'

In the end, Winter decided against phoning. The phone was too distant, too remote. It took nothing to mumble an excuse and just hang up. No, much better to pop along in person. That way, he'd get his foot in her door. Nice thought.

The address from Morry took him to the big horseshoe of apartments that looked west across the Port Solent yacht basin. A van from a glazing company was double-parked outside the main entrance and he stood waiting in the sunshine while a couple of workmen manoeuvred a big glass panel in through the door.

Flat fifty-seven had a security peep at eye level but Winter kept his head down when his second ring finally stirred a response.

'Who is it?' a woman's voice called.

'Management, love.'

'Your name, please.'

The voice sounded foreign, just the way it had been when she'd first phoned him.

'We're doing all the flats,' Winter called. 'Checking on damage from yesterday.'

Mention of the storm opened the door. Winter

found himself looking at a woman in her late twenties. She was wearing a red bikini and a pair of Kenzo shades. She had a deep tan, a wonderful body, and as far as Winter could judge, all her teeth seemed intact. Through an open door at the end of the tiny hall, Winter could see a sunbed on the balcony beyond the big lounge.

'Juanita?'

'*Sí.*'

'OK, are you?'

Without waiting for an answer, Winter stepped past her, walking through to the lounge. Looking round, he sensed at once that the place had been pre-furnished. The bamboo furniture and smoked-glass tables looked too new. Open any of the built-in cupboards, he thought, and you'd find yards of packing material and heavy-duty polythene.

'Been here long?'

The woman seemed nervous. She headed for the door across the room but Winter got there first. The last thing he needed was her making a phone call.

'*Policia*,' he said, showing her his ID card.

She studied it carefully, then nodded. She was clearly no stranger to subterfuge.

'OK, Mr Winter,' she said. 'You want coffee?'

Twelve

Faraday was in the middle of Dorset, driving back to Portsmouth, when Dawn Ellis finally raised him on his mobile.

'Couple of messages, sir,' she said crisply. 'One's from a Kate Symonds.'

The name snagged in Faraday's memory. Then he remembered the head-to-head with the journalist from *Coastlines*. Kate Symonds was the girl with lots of attitude who'd wound up Neville Bevan to such spectacular effect.

'She gave me a number.' Dawn was saying. 'She wants you to call.'

Faraday jotted the number down. The other message had come from Nelly Tseng at Port Solent. She'd been on three times this morning and the last of the calls had been fielded by the superintendent's office.

'What does she want?'

'You, sir. She's gone mental about the twocking last night.'

Twocking was CID shorthand for taking a car without the owner's consent. The Paulsgrove lads had obviously upped their game.

'How many vehicles?'

'Just the one, sir. But it was a Porsche Carrera – and they got involved in some kind of race afterwards. Rolled it on a bend at the top of the estate. The lads are OK but the car's a write-off.'

Faraday digested the news.

'And you say Bevan knows about all this?'

'Affirmative, sir. He wants to see you the minute

you get back. Just thought I'd pass the word.'

Dawn rang off and Faraday glanced across at Cathy. She was pale and tight-lipped at the wheel. So far she hadn't mentioned Pete and neither had Faraday but he sensed that now wasn't the time for a lengthy conversation. Better to stick to the business in hand.

Faraday pocketed his mobile.

'You think I'm barmy, don't you? Going to all this trouble about Maloney?'

Cathy glanced at the number he'd scribbled down. 'Yes,' she said, 'I do.'

On his return to Portsmouth, Faraday went straight to Bevan's office. Expecting a ruck over Nelly Tseng and the stolen Porsche, he found the superintendent brooding over a phone call from Patrick McIlvenny.

He explained that the two of them had shared a recent association under the auspices of an outfit called 'Common Purpose'. Like-minded high achievers met once a month to explore weighty civic issues, and over the course of a year he'd got to know the man. Bevan took a cautious view of friendships outside the job, but he clearly had a lot of respect for the acting head teacher.

Faraday was trying to work out where this conversation was going. Bevan at last got to the point.

'Patrick described events last night,' he said. 'He believes your behaviour amounts to harassment – and on the face of it, he just might be right.'

'What did he say?'

'He said that you gave his partner an extremely hard time about their relationship. He thought the word "intrusive" wouldn't have done the conversation justice.'

'I asked her some questions,' Faraday said woodenly. 'She had difficulty with some of the answers.'

'He disagrees. He says you upset her, disturbed the

child and virtually accused them of murder. All without a shred of supporting evidence. He said the inference you'd drawn from events was perfectly clear. You'd made up your mind that the ex-husband – Maloney? – had disappeared under suspicious circumstances and that they – he and his partner – were somehow implicated.'

'That's hardly murder.'

'In his eyes, I'm afraid it was. You took his fingerprints?'

'I asked whether he was prepared to be fingerprinted, yes.'

'For what reason?'

Faraday caught the menace in Bevan's voice. At first he'd thought that the superintendent was going through the motions, discharging a debt of friendship, but now he wasn't so sure.

'For the purposes of elimination,' he said evenly, 'and it doesn't stop there, either.'

'Meaning?'

'Meaning that we may have to search his house, and possibly hers too. If they choose not to co-operate, I may have to get a warrant sworn.'

'You've got the grounds?'

'Yes.'

'What are you after?'

'Correspondence, computer files, maybe even some forensic.'

'Relating to?'

'Some kind of struggle.'

'You're talking full forensic?'

'Perhaps.'

Faraday, with the greatest reluctance, found himself outlining the circumstances that had led him to McIlvenny. The sense of mutual awkwardness, embarrassment even, had gone. Faraday was beginning to get angry.

'He certainly has the motivation,' he concluded, 'and he may well have had the opportunity. Their alibi, such as it is, relies on each other.'

'You really think she's implicated too?'

'Very possibly.'

'After giving you the key to the flat? Dear God, Joe, what's this woman got? Some kind of death wish?'

'People do strange things.' Faraday shrugged. 'And murder isn't a rational act.'

Bevan stared into space for a moment or two. Faraday had always had the feeling that the superintendent had never quite come to terms with the darker side of human nature, which made him unusual for a policeman.

'I'm sorry he's a friend of yours,' Faraday murmured.

Bevan blinked.

'That's immaterial,' he said sharply.

'Is it, sir?'

'Yes. Listen, Joe. The last thing you need from me is a lecture about high-volume crime. You know the stats inside out. You know the battles we're fighting on the ground. Houses turned over. Cars nicked. All that grief. It might be boring, Joe, and it might be just a touch repetitious, but the fact is that these people pay our bloody wages. They have a voice. They use it. They matter. In the meantime, you're chasing shadows. He's probably shacked up with some other woman, this Maloney. It happens, Joe, in case you haven't noticed.'

Faraday ignored the sarcasm. High-volume crime was code for last night's events at Port Solent. He couldn't let that pass.

'I'm calling her this afternoon,' Faraday said. 'It's being dealt with.'

'Her?'

'Nelly Tseng. DC Ellis will be sorting it out.'

'She's done it already. Or put a phone call in, at any rate.'

'On whose instructions?'

'Mine, Joe,' Bevan said heavily, 'as if I didn't have enough to do.'

There was a long silence. This was rapidly turning into the kind of turf war that Faraday couldn't afford to lose. He was the DI. The DI managed the divisional CID. His call. Not bloody Bevan's.

He began to protest, but Bevan wasn't having it.

'There's a desk in the inspectors' office with your name on it,' he grunted, 'and by and large it's empty.'

'This morning it was empty.'

'Quite.'

'This morning was unusual.'

'It fucking well better be.'

Faraday returned his stare. He'd later spend hours trying to work out why this conversation had boiled over so quickly but just now they'd reached an impasse.

The real problem was simple. The real problem was that the DI's job had changed beyond recognition. High-volume crime wasn't sufficiently serious for him to get involved, not directly at any rate. Anything really tasty, anything at the other end of the scale, was declared a major inquiry and handed over to someone higher up the food chain, a detective chief inspector, or even a detective superintendent.

Either way, as Bevan was so forcefully pointing out, Faraday was trapped behind a desk, a prisoner of the ceaseless flow of paper that would otherwise choke the system. He'd joined the CID to clear up crime. He'd done well. He'd won promotion. And here he was, years later, pulling thirty-five grand a year and feeling like a well-paid clerk.

Bevan had relaxed a little.

'Maybe you should have taken the MIT board more

seriously,' he muttered, 'instead of pissing them about. A job's a job, Joe. All I'm asking is that you do it.'

To Winter's infinite disappointment, Juanita had disappeared to the bedroom to pull on a pair of jeans and a white sweatshirt before plugging in the percolator and making him a cup of coffee. One brew had led to the promise of a second and now – nearly an hour and a half later – the only memory of her near-naked body was the sight of her bare feet tucked beneath her. She'd used a vivid scarlet varnish on her toenails and the colour worked perfectly against the deep tan of her skin. Add the loop of thin gold chain around her right ankle, and Winter knew exactly why Marty Harrison had become so territorial.

They'd met on the quayside in Puerto Banus, where she'd been working for a yacht charter business. They'd spent time together and she'd introduced Marty to various friends, some of whom were English. A handful of the latter were expatriate criminals with excellent contacts in the drugs business, and for Marty Harrison Juanita had quickly become the perfect bridge between business and pleasure. She set up deals for him – tiny to begin with but rapidly getting bigger. She helped him find the waterside house that had long been his dream. And on the nights when he wasn't too pissed she was happy to share his bed.

Just now, she was on a kind of extended stay. Marty had leased the flat for her and bought a brand new Cherokee Jeep as a runaround. Last week, before he'd got himself shot, he'd even been talking about marriage. She nodded, flicking back the fringe of hair from her big brown eyes.

'Marriage,' she confirmed.

'Was he serious?'

'*Muy.*'

'Are you?'

'Maybe.'

Winter frowned.

'But he's an animal, isn't he? Marty?' He gestured at her, at her body, at those glorious feet. 'Why him when you could have the pick of the litter?'

She laughed. Perfect teeth.

'You're right,' she said. 'Animal is right.'

'You like all that?'

'I must do.'

Winter shook his head in mock-bewilderment. He was playing the naive old buffer who'd stumbled into a world he didn't understand. He'd no idea whether she believed him or not but it was certainly fun finding out.

'You said you got my name from a file.'

'That's right. It was an old file of Marty's. I found it in a drawer in the house down in Puerto Banus. He talked about you sometimes, too.'

'What did he say?'

'He said you could be bought.'

'How much?'

'Five thousand?' She shrugged. 'Ten?'

'Bollocks. That's way off. He always was a mean little toe-rag.'

She laughed again, throwing back her head, and Winter watched her as she hopped off the sofa and went to check on the coffee pot. At first he couldn't get over how up-front she was, how incredibly open about everything, but now he was close to accepting that this candour of hers was for real. That's the way things went, if you were foreign, and beautiful, and shameless, and had the misfortune to fall in with the likes of Marty Harrison.

'He's got a girlfriend, you know,' he called out to her, 'and a kid, too. You can read about it in the papers.'

'I know.' She was back with the coffee. 'I know about all that.'

'And?'

'It doesn't matter. I told you. If I wanted him all, I could have him like' – she snapped her fingers – 'that.'

'So what's the problem?'

She was pouring the coffee. Close to she smelled of sunshine and coconut oil.

'You think there's a problem?' she asked.

'There must be. You phoned me.'

She studied him for a long moment, then put the coffee pot carefully down on the low glass table and extended a hand.

'Come,' she said.

On the balcony, Winter followed her pointing finger. Beyond a forest of masts, executive houses lined the far side of the yacht basin.

'You see the one with the yellow curtains? The one with the sports car behind?'

'Yes.'

'That one.' She nodded. 'And he says you know this person.'

'What person?'

'The person he goes to see so much. The girl who screws for her living there. The *puta*. The whore.'

Winter stared at her, totally lost, then slowly the drift of this strange conversation became clearer. Marty Harrison had been visiting a call-girl. And his outraged mistress wanted to know why.

'You've got a name for me?'

'Of course.'

'What is it?'

She looked up at him, moist-eyed, and for the first time it occurred to Winter that she might be serious about Marty Harrison.

'She calls herself Vikki. Vikki Duvall. You know her?'

Winter fought the urge to give her a big hug. Results like this were sweetest when least expected.

'Her real name's Elaine Pope.' He smiled at her. 'How can I help?'

Faraday sent Cathy Lamb to sort out the totalled Porsche and spent the rest of the afternoon chasing the Aqua Cab lead. Cathy needed something to take her mind off her marriage and a face-to-face with Nelly Tseng would do exactly that.

By ten past four, Faraday had extracted the names of three drivers from Aqua, all of whom divvied up the shifts on car seventy-three. Car seventy-three had definitely been the cab that had responded to Maloney's call from the flat on Friday afternoon. On the phone, the first driver was guarded to the point of near silence. No, he hadn't been working on Friday afternoon. No, he hadn't a clue who might have been at the wheel. And yes, he'd be more than happy to bring this conversation to an end. Faraday's second call raised no response at all, not even an answerphone, and he was about to give up on the third, a mobile, when a voice finally came on the line. He sounded apologetic. He'd been asleep in bed. What time was it?

Minutes later, Faraday was on his way to Southsea. Barry Decker occupied a tiny basement flat in a sidestreet off Albert Road. He'd been on shift in car seventy-three all Friday, but he'd gone in for a silly tackle playing football at the weekend and had been laid up with a dodgy knee ever since.

Faraday roused him from his bed, put the kettle on, and then settled him on the sofa.

'Solent View Mansions,' he said. 'Flat seven.'

Decker was trying to raise a flame from his lighter. For the first time in his life, Faraday wished he smoked. Getting to his feet, Decker hobbled across to the kitchenette and lit the roll-up from the gas stove. A lungful of smoke, and his memory finally cleared.

'Bloke in a leather jacket,' he said, 'pissed off as fuck. Steaming, in fact.'

'How did you know?'

'You can tell. I talk to them all. I don't make a great thing about it. If they don't want to chat, that's cool. But this guy did. And he wasn't happy.'

'Any idea why not?'

'No. We talked about sailing mainly. He'd done his arm in and he was going to miss out on the Fastnet. But he wasn't really concentrating on what he was saying. He was miles away most of the time. Totally wound up.'

'Where did you take him?'

'Port Solent. You want to know where exactly?' He frowned and shook his head. 'I could take you there but no way have I got the address.'

Faraday drove Decker to Port Solent. The most expensive houses lay to the north of the yacht basin, a minute's drive from the entry roundabout. At the end of a cul-de-sac, Faraday found himself looking at a spacious executive house with an adjoining double garage.

He glanced over at Decker.

'Here?'

'Yep, and the boat was right behind the house, tied up like. You could see the mast.'

'Boat?'

'The boat he'd been crewing on. The boat that was doing the Fastnet. He told me the name but it's gone.'

'*Marenka*?'

'Dunno. Could have been.'

'Wait here.'

Faraday got out of the car. A narrow walk-through led him down beside the garage. Beyond it lay an empty wooden pontoon which served as a private mooring. Faraday peered up at the house, looking for signs of life, but no one answered when he knocked on the big patio door. He turned and looked out at the view. Beyond the forest of masts, he could see the row of tinted office windows above the Mexican restaurant where the marina's management were headquartered. Nelly Tseng, he thought, and her everlengthening list of trashed motors.

Back beside his car, Faraday at last checked in his notebook, flicking through the scribbled entries he'd made earlier in the hospital ward in Plymouth. Charlie Oomes, *Marenka*'s owner/skipper, had a house here. Seven, Muscovy Drive.

Faraday looked up. The big brass seven beside the hardwood door broadened the smile on his face. So what was the boat doing back in Port Solent on Friday? When, according to Oomes, they'd never left Cowes?

He bent to the open car window. Decker appeared to be asleep, so he reached in and gave him a shake.

'Name of the road?' he queried.

Decker opened one eye.

'Muscovy Drive,' he confirmed, 'and I gave the geezer a card in case he wanted a ride back later.'

Back at the police station, early evening, Faraday found Cathy Lamb sitting alone at a table in the social club. Within seconds, it was obvious that she was drunk. As best she could, she told him the bad news about Nelly Tseng – that she was about to lodge a formal complaint with the Chief Constable – and then insisted on buying him a double Scotch to celebrate.

'Leave it to the Chief,' she kept saying. 'His problem, not ours.'

Faraday explained the latest developments in the Maloney case. He needed to be sure that his memory of the conversation with Oomes at the hospital was correct.

'He definitely said the boat never left Cowes last week. Isn't that right?'

Cathy was staring into the middle distance, her eyes glassy.

'She's a probationer,' she said at last. 'From Fareham nick.'

Faraday remembered the girl at Pete Lamb's bedside. A probationer was a recent recruit to the force.

'You're pissed love,' he said. 'I'm asking you about Charlie Oomes.'

Cathy did her best to concentrate.

'He said they were in Cowes all week. Yeah.' She nodded. 'That's definitely what he said.'

Faraday watched her take another long swallow from her glass.

'Get a grip, Cathy,' he said softly. 'This is important.'

'Got a grip, sir.'

'I'm serious.'

'Surprise me.' She peered at him and then nodded. 'He definitely said they never left Cowes.'

'Then he was lying.'

'Or the taxi bloke got it wrong.'

'Sure, but he seemed pretty certain. And anyway, we can check when we do the house-to-house.'

'Oh yeah, when?' Cathy frowned. 'Are we talking major inquiry here? Incident room? The whole caboodle? Only if we're not, you just might get shitty about the overtime. Like last week. And the week before. Or had you—'

She broke off, staring across the room at a woman who'd just come in. She was small and pretty. She was wearing a thin blue cotton zip-up jacket over a white blouse, and when she turned her head, scanning the bar, Faraday recognised the face at Pete Lamb's bedside.

Finally, she made her way towards the table. Faraday's arm went out, steadying Cathy as she tried to get up. The girl was right beside them now, and looking up, Faraday could see how nervous she was.

'Can I have a private word?'

Faraday rose at once to leave them, but Cathy beat him to it. Lungeing across the table, she caught the lapels of the jacket in both hands then pulled the girl's face hard towards her own forehead. Faraday caught the briefest scent of perfume before the girl twisted her body, sparing her face, catching the force of the head-butt on her shoulder. Glasses crashed to the floor with the table. The bar went quiet, then erupted with roars of applause. By now, the young probationer was wriggling free from Cathy's crushing bear hug and running for the door. She was faster than Cathy, and probably a good deal fitter, but Cathy had been saving herself for this one moment for the best part of a day and no way was she going to let her rival go.

The double doors at the end of the bar crashed open. Faraday, in hot pursuit now, heard the clatter of footsteps on the concrete stairs beyond. The social club was on the fourth floor. Obscenities echoed around the stairwell as the women spiralled downwards. Cathy was back in her native Paulsgrove, all self-control gone.

'Fucking slag,' she was screaming, 'fucking whore.'

The route to the street took them out through the car park. At last, on the apron of tarmac at the front of the police station, Cathy finally caught up, trapping the younger woman against the brickwork.

'This is going to hurt,' she gasped, 'and afterwards you're never going to see my husband again.'

She went for the girl's face again, the heel of her hand this time, but the girl ducked and suddenly they were down on the tarmac, bodies intertwined, struggling for advantage, the classic playground brawl. Faces had appeared at windows immediately above them. Passers-by had paused to watch. A bus lingered at the stop across the road.

Faraday did his best to separate them and then stepped aside as a burly uniformed sergeant ran down from the front office. He stared at the two women, still flailing at each other, then glanced at Faraday for guidance.

'Cathy's not too well,' he said wearily. 'Leave it to me.'

He put the young probationer from Fareham in a taxi, and drove Cathy home. She was crying, humiliated and angry with herself, and when Faraday pulled up outside her house he could see in her face that it was the last place she wanted to be.

'Come back with me, Cath,' Faraday suggested. 'You can kip in the spare room.'

She looked at him a moment, grateful as well as surprised, then shook her head.

'You must think I'm a head-case,' she said.

Without waiting for an answer, she got out of the car and began to walk unsteadily towards the front door. When Faraday wound down the window and tried to call her back, she waved him away.

It was dusk by the time he got home. There were no lights on in the house and until he went upstairs he assumed that J-J was still out. Then, passing his son's bedroom, he saw the envelope pinned to the door. The envelope had his name on. Faraday ripped it open. The note was as brutal as it was brief. J-J had made a mistake coming home. He should have stayed in France, which was why he'd taken the afternoon ferry back to Caen. He'd be in touch soon. Love, J-J.

Love J-J?

Faraday read the note again, making sure he hadn't got it wrong. Angry now, he pushed the door open, finding the bed stripped to the mattress and both rucksacks gone. He stared at the discarded sheets, at the single sock the boy had never had time to pack, then his brain began to work again. Why this sudden decision? And where had J-J got the money from?

Another door gave on to the study they'd shared together. He stepped through it, standing in the gloom, staring up at the empty shelf. All nine volumes of *Birds of the Western Palearctic* were missing, doubtless flogged for a song to some second-hand shop. Just enough to pay for the ferry fare. Just enough to make good his escape.

Faraday gazed at the empty shelf a moment longer, then went downstairs again. He still had J-J's note. He read it one last time and then tore it into tiny pieces. If this was what the boy wanted, if this was the best he could do after all those years together, then so be it.

Thirteen

For once, Faraday ignored the overnight prisoner list. It was five past nine in the morning. Half a dozen officers, uniformed and CID, had gathered in the empty social club for the daily update, but Faraday wasn't interested in warehouse burglaries and a particularly violent affray outside a Southsea nightclub.

'Port Solent,' he said. 'Muscovy Drive.'

Cathy Lamb sat beside him, listening to his brief account of yesterday's developments in what Faraday now termed 'the Maloney inquiry'. A pair of sunglasses hid the worst of the swelling around her right eye, and the scratch marks down her cheek weren't as bad as she'd first feared. Even the smell of the social club – cigarettes and stale beer – made her want to gag.

'House to house,' Faraday ended. 'Any address with line of sight to number seven. That's front *and* back. We're interested in comings and goings on Friday afternoon, and we're especially interested in a yacht that was allegedly tied up round the back. OK?'

He was looking at Dawn Ellis. She and Cathy were to handle the house-to-house inquiries, while Paul Winter held the fort back in the CID room, getting to grips with the mountain of other crimes that were still awaiting attention.

Winter stirred. Ignoring Faraday, he looked across at Cathy Lamb.

'No disrespect, skip.' He touched his face. 'But wouldn't *you* be better off back here?'

Cathy shook her head and began to answer but Faraday stepped in.

'I want Cathy on the ground,' he told Winter. 'She's up to speed on the Maloney case and Dawn has a line to the management up there. It'll do them good to see us buckling down to a bit of serious coppering.'

Winter stared at him. He normally had no trouble hiding his real feelings, but this time something in Faraday's tone of voice had really got to him.

'Tell me,' he began. 'This Maloney business. Is it a private party, or can anyone come?'

Faraday ignored the gibe. He wanted Cathy and Dawn Ellis at Port Solent as soon as possible. The quicker they started knocking on doors, the quicker they might turn up something worthwhile. He gathered his papers and stuffed them back in his file, then looked at the watching faces.

'OK?' he said.

Winter cornered Cathy by the the staff notice board as she was on her way out of the building. Dawn Ellis was already warming up the unmarked Escort outside.

'Something I never mentioned back there,' he said. 'Your friend Vikki Duvall.'

'You mean Elaine?'

'Yeah. She's operating out of Port Solent now and she's not a million miles from Muscovy Drive. Look for a house with yellow curtains.'

'I thought she was still in London.'

Winter shook his head.

'She made a packet there but got sick of the Arabs. Port Solent's ideal. Good class of punter and nice place to live, too. She's driving a Megane convertible, by the way. You might look for that, too.'

Cathy filed the information away. Through the window she could see Dawn looking at her. She knew Winter too well not to ask the obvious question.

'Is this a freebie? Or are there strings attached?'

Winter looked briefly hurt, then shook his head.

'It's for you, skip.' He sighed. 'I'd have mentioned it earlier but the pillock never listens.'

Back in his office, Faraday lifted the phone and dialled the number of the local intelligence officer. The LIO manned a desk in the CID room. Faraday gave him three names to run through the Police National Computer: Charlie Oomes, Derek Bissett and Ian Hartson. He wanted details of any criminal records they might possess, plus any other information. Waiting for a response, he found himself looking at Bibi, Bevan's secretary. Kate Symonds, the journalist from *Coastlines*, was downstairs at the front desk demanding five minutes of his time.

'*Demanding*?'

'That's right.' Bibi rolled her eyes. 'And she seems to think you'll thank her for it.'

The LIO had finished accessing the national computer. His inquiries had drawn a blank on all three of the entries he'd typed in, but two of the names had triggered a personal memory.

'The man Bissett, sir,' he said. 'What kind of age is he?'

'Mid-forties, I'd say, but I'd be guessing.'

'Do you happen to know what he does for a living?'

'No, why?'

'We had a guy up at HQ at Kidlington. Same name. He bailed out early and joined a bloke called Charlie Oomes. Oomes ran an IT company. We bought a couple of systems from him.'

Faraday reached for a pad. The officer on the Intelligence Desk had come to Portsmouth North from the Thames Valley force.

'Tell me more about Bissett,' Faraday said. 'What did he do before he went?'

'He was an inspector, I think. Worked in one of the service departments.'

'Which one?'

'IT,' the LIO replied. 'Just a thought.'

Cathy Lamb had a minute or two alone in the car before she crossed the road to tackle Elaine Pope. Dawn Ellis was already busy in the next cul-de-sac, working slowly outwards, house by house from seven Muscovy Drive.

Swivelling the rear-view mirror, Cathy examined her face. She'd spent half the night boxing up Pete's possessions, surprised at how much they seemed to have accumulated over the years. She'd made a separate pile of his clothes, bundling them into black plastic dustbin liners, and before she'd driven to work she'd left them in the doorway of the Sue Ryder shop in Fareham High Street with a note telling them to help themselves. Later in the day, she intended to phone the Fareham nick and leave a message for Pete. Her ex-husband had always been keen on second-hand shops.

Ex-husband?

She gazed at herself in the mirror. It was easy to be strong in this kind of mood, easy to parcel up eleven years of marriage, give the house a good Hoovering and tell yourself that things could only get better, but she was too wise, and too level-headed, not to believe that the going was bound to get tough. There'd be times, lonely times, when she'd miss him. There'd be evenings when she'd want to sit him down, pour him a drink and generally make a fuss of him. That's what so much of their marriage had been about, snatched little moments in two busy lives when they could shut the door on the world and just be themselves. But those days, those moments had gone. They hadn't been enough for him and in consequence he'd looked elsewhere. As with so much in her life, it was simple logic. The marriage was over.

Strangely heartened, Cathy readjusted the mirror and got out of the car. Elaine's scarlet Megane was parked on the apron of hardstanding behind the house with the yellow curtains, just the way Winter had described. From the front of the property, as far as Cathy could judge, she'd have near-perfect line of sight to the waterside frontage of Charlie Oomes's place, less than a hundred metres away.

She crossed the road and followed the path to the front door. She'd known Elaine Pope since she was a kid. They'd lived within streets of each other in Paulsgrove, gone to the same scuzzy school, and in their separate ways they'd both battled out of the estate to make a better life for themselves. As far as Cathy had been concerned, that was definitely going to be the police force, but with Elaine Pope the options had been infinitely wider.

In an awkward, skinny kind of way she'd always had good looks, but the moment she hit adolescence it became obvious that she was going to be a stunner. Of five kids, she was the only one to have been fathered by the Swedish sailor with whom her mum had fallen in love. People on the estate had called him Blondie but he'd only stayed long enough to make Elaine's mum pregnant, and the day after she broke the news he'd disappeared back to sea. As far as Cathy knew, no one had seen him since, but the calling card he'd left behind – young Elaine – had inherited both his temper and his startling looks. Blonde, long-legged, and far too passionate for her own good, it was small wonder she'd earned enough to buy a pad like this.

When she answered the door, she was still wearing a dressing-gown. Cathy hadn't seen her for nearly three years, but London had done nothing to tarnish her looks. The same flawless complexion. The same perfect mouth. The same habit of theatrically widening those cornflower-blue eyes when she was taken by surprise.

'Cathy? Cathy Lamb?'

They talked in a big upstairs sitting room while Elaine rustled up toast and coffee. They both knew that there was business to be done but for the time being, like any women anywhere, they simply compared notes. Good times. Funny times. Bad times. A marriage as familiar as an old sweater, wrapped in a bin liner and left in a shop doorway that very morning.

'Shit.' Elaine shook her head. 'I'm really sorry.'

'Don't be. It was my own bloody fault. He must have been up to it for months, years probably. Fancy being that blind in my job.'

'Your face OK?'

'Fine. You should see hers.'

Elaine laughed her rich Pompey laugh. Three years in Holland Park hadn't quite eradicated her Paulsgrove accent and at moments like these it came muscling back.

'Men are lunatics.' She ground out her third cigarette. 'Fuck 'em all. What you doing?'

Cathy had gone to the window and seemed to be studying the view.

'There's a couple of questions I need to ask,' she said, 'about Friday afternoon.'

Faraday had left Kate Symonds waiting downstairs for more than half an hour while he talked to the Royal Ocean Racing Club people in London. As organisers of the Fastnet, they'd returned to their St James headquarters, and now they were sorting out documents for the official inquiry. Faraday wanted names and home addresses for Oomes, Bissett and Hartson, prior to arranging interviews, and when they faxed the information down he was surprised to find that it included next-of-kin. Charlie Oomes's main residence was on the Thames, west of Maidenhead.

The information filed away, he finally went downstairs to meet Kate Symonds at the front desk. When she insisted on somewhere private for them to talk, he swiped her into the station through the locked side door and took her up to the empty social club, settling her at a table by the window. She said no to his offer of coffee and told him at once why she'd come. In her view, Bevan had been offensive to the point of professional suicide during their last meeting. Answering the summons to return to the office was only one of the reasons she'd felt obliged to leave.

'Professional suicide? Bit strong, isn't it?'

'You were there, Mr Faraday. I'm not making this up. Describing someone you've nearly killed by mistake as scum isn't great PR.'

'Scum?' Faraday looked puzzled. 'I don't recall that.'

Symonds dug in her bag and passed over a long white envelope. Faraday could feel the shape of the audio cassette inside.

'That's a copy.' She smiled. 'I've still got the original.'

Faraday was thinking fast. An expression of outrage would be wasted on this woman. She was too ambitious, too driven to think of anything but her next precious headline. Whatever Faraday said would simply become part of the story.

'Are you taping this as well by any chance?' he inquired.

'No.' She pulled open her jacket. 'Search me if you want.'

'OK.' Faraday nodded towards the door. 'Then I suggest we widen the discussion. Mr Bevan's office is along the corridor there.'

'I'd prefer not.'

'Why? It's his call, not mine.'

Symonds leaned forward over the table. Faraday didn't move. In certain lights, he thought, she might almost be attractive.

'We're in a competitive business,' she said softly. 'It would be nice to steal the odd advantage.'

'Steal is a good word.'

'Just a phone call from time to time.' She ignored the sarcasm. 'And maybe the odd meeting.'

Faraday tried to hide his smile. The irony was too obvious.

'You're asking me to become a grass?'

'No, I'm asking you to compare notes.'

'That's what the briefing was supposed to be about.'

'Hardly, Inspector. I came in good faith. All I got was abuse.'

Faraday said nothing. Then he picked up the envelope again, weighing it in his hand. Bevan was in deep enough trouble with the media already. The after-shocks of the Harrison shooting were still rumbling on and quite soon he'd have to deal with the results of Pete Lamb's blood test. Add the possible consequences of last night's punch-up – two police-women brawling in public – and Kate Symonds might just be right. There comes a point in any man's career where the liabilities can tip the balance against him. Given Bevan's already volatile relationship with HQ, it might be wise to spare the world the contents of the audio tape.

Faraday got to his feet, pocketing the tape. Symonds reached for her bag.

'I'll be in touch,' Faraday grunted.

'Is that a yes?'

Faraday smiled for the first time, shepherding her towards the door, saying nothing.

*

Back in his office, minutes later, Faraday took a call from Cathy Lamb. She was still with Elaine but she'd hit a problem.

'What is it?'

'She won't talk without you being here.'

'Why not?'

'She wants some guarantees. From someone more senior than me.'

'Ah ...' Faraday nodded. 'Has she got much to say?'

'I think she may have, yes.'

'How come?'

'Charlie Oomes is one of her clients.'

Faraday drove to Port Solent. Cathy met him at the kerbside, and briefed him before leading the way back indoors. There were two potential hiccoughs. One was obvious. Elaine made a good living from her services and wasn't keen on interference from either the locals or the Inland Revenue. The other was more personal. Like a doctor or a lawyer, she had objections to discussing her clients, especially when it concerned a head-case like Oomes.

'Is that her description?'

'Yes. Apparently he pays good money but she says he can be difficult.'

'How come?'

'Strange tastes. She wouldn't go into it but I don't think four hundred pounds a pop buys him tea and sympathy.'

Cathy led the way indoors. Elaine was busy in the kitchen so Cathy took Faraday straight upstairs.

'By the way,' she said, 'Elaine's a good mate of Marty Harrison's, too. He's been using one of her brothers on various jobs. Dave Pope his name is. I think Marty keeps an eye on her just in case things ever get rough. That's the feeling I get.'

Faraday was looking round. The spotless lounge. The carefully lit marine watercolours on the pale grey walls. The rack of CDs beside the audio stack. This place could belong to any successful career woman, and in a sense it did, but not for a moment could he imagine the naked bulk of Charlie Oomes spread-eagled over the dainty Paisley-patterned sofa.

He walked across to the big picture window. The view across the marina pontoons was busy with yachts.

'That's Oomes's place, there.'

Cathy was beside him. He followed her pointing finger, recognising the back of the house. A pair of magpies were cavorting on the tiny square of turf. One for sorrow, Faraday thought. Two for joy.

'She had a perfect view,' Cathy was saying, 'and she definitely remembers the boat being there.'

'How come?'

'She was dreading Oomes being back and getting on his mobile. She knew he was away racing all week, but apparently he's the kind of guy who's always changing his mind. Some weeks he wants it all the time. Then she won't see him for a month. Sound familiar?'

Faraday glanced at her. With her sunglasses off, the damage to her face was worse than he'd thought. Maybe that was why these two women got on so well, comrades-in-arms on the same front line.

Elaine reappeared with a laden tray. Faraday couldn't mask his astonishment.

'They're chocolate biscuits,' Cathy pointed out gently, 'and I told her you like those.'

Elaine wanted a deal: a blind eye to her business dealings in return for whatever she could remember about Friday afternoon. On principle, Faraday hated this kind of bartering. To him it smacked of Paul Winter's style of detective work, creating a web of obligation and counter-obligation, but Maloney's disappearance was beginning to matter a great deal to him, and he sensed that the breakthrough would only come from a remorseless examination of events on Friday afternoon.

'OK,' he said in the end. 'Nothing to the management here and not a word to the Inland Revenue.'

'Can I have that in writing?'

'I'm afraid not.'

'So how do I know . . .?' Elaine looked to Cathy for help.

'You don't,' Cathy said quickly. 'You have to trust us.'

'*Trust* you? In my business that gets you screwed.'

There was a long silence. Faraday refused to go further. Finally she shrugged, then kicked off her slippers and sat on the sofa with her long golden legs tucked under her. The yacht, she said, had arrived around lunchtime. She'd known at once that it was *Marenka* because Charlie was subtle that way and had made a point of scrawling the name in huge white loopy script across the side. Marenka was his mum's name and he wanted the whole world to know how proud he was of her. White on red. You couldn't miss it.

Faraday helped himself to another chocolate biscuit. Marenka had been the next of kin on the fax from the RORC people in London. Only her surname was Dunlop, not Oomes.

'That's Charlie's real name, too.' Elaine was playing with the thin gold chain looped around her neck. 'His dad was some kind of gangster. Ronnie Dunlop?'

Faraday frowned. The name triggered a distant memory. Way back in the fifties, a Ronnie Dunlop had run with the Richardson gang, terrorising whole swathes of South London.

158

'Charlie hated him. That's why he got rid of Dunlop. He did it by deed poll. Oomes is his wife's name. He showed me pictures once. She's Dutch-Indonesian.'

'He's still married?'

'Far as I know. Though she never comes down here.'

Faraday at last produced the photos, spreading them on the low glass table in front of the sofa. Elaine had been watching the yacht on and off all afternoon, just in case Charlie was aboard.

'Did you spot any of these guys?'

Elaine studied the photos one by one. Finally, a scarlet nail descended on Maloney.

'He was the one who came later. He went on board the yacht. He was wearing a leather jacket and there was something wrong with his arm.'

'Had you seen him before?'

'No.'

'Not in Charlie's house?'

'I've never been in Charlie's house. Charlie doesn't mix business with pleasure.'

She returned to the photos. There were two other faces she recognised. One of them was Ian Hartson. The other was an older man, standing beside Charlie in the well of the cockpit. Faraday studied him closely, hearing Mrs Beedon's querulous tones. Tall man. Gaunt-looking face. And, yes, a red anorak.

'What was he wearing when you saw him on Friday?'

'That same top. The red thing.'

'You're sure about that?'

'Yes, he had it on when he brought the yacht in.'

'Did he stay here all afternoon?'

'I dunno.' She frowned. 'No, I don't think he did. I saw him come back from somewhere. That would have been later. Don't ask me when.'

Faraday was eyeing the remaining biscuit. According to Mrs Beedon, the stranger in the red anorak had left Maloney's flat just after half past three.

'Was he carrying anything when he came back?'

'Who?'

'This guy here.'

Elaine stared at the photo.

'Yeah.' She nodded slowly. 'He had something wrapped up in paper. Under his arm, like.'

'Big? Small?'

'Big enough.' She shaped an oblong in the air.

Faraday gazed at her for a moment, then asked for a refill from the cafetière. Eleven years on the CID had taught him never to jump to conclusions but sometimes, just sometimes, it was hard not to.

He knew that the stranger in the red anorak had come calling on Maloney. He knew that there'd been some kind of row. He knew that minutes later this same man had left carrying something under his arm. He knew that Maloney had pursued him back to Charlie Oomes's place here in Port Solent. And now, thanks to a nervous call-girl dreading a summons on her mobile, he also knew where the two men's paths had finally crossed.

He picked up the photo again.

'Maloney, this one, definitely went aboard?'

'Definitely.'

'And this other guy was already there?'

'Yes, I think so.'

'Did you see Maloney again?'

'No.'

'And when did the boat leave?'

'Around half five. *Home and Away* had just finished.'

Faraday exchanged glances with Cathy. This wasn't conclusive, far from it. Maloney could easily have slipped away but that would probably have meant another taxi, and with Barry Decker's card in his pocket, the chances were that he'd have called Aqua.

Faraday made the call on his mobile from the kitchen. The despatcher he'd talked to earlier was back on shift. He asked her whether she'd have time later to check for any other calls on Friday from a Mr Maloney, but she said there was no point.

'I looked already,' she said, 'and there weren't.'

Fourteen

For once, it was Faraday's turn to ask for a meeting with Bevan. When he got to the superintendent's office, his door was already open. Bevan turned from his computer screen and waved the detective into a chair. After their recent run-in, Faraday sensed at once that his uniformed boss was in the mood for building bridges.

'Beaten up any teachers lately?' Bevan grunted.

Faraday told him what had happened at Port Solent. After tracing Maloney to Charlie Oomes's house, and getting a positive ID on the stranger in the red anorak, he saw no reason to pursue the McIlvenny line of inquiry any further.

'How strong is the ID?'

'Strong enough.'

Faraday explained about Elaine Pope and her business links with Charlie Oomes.

'You don't think she's trying to put one over on him?'

'I doubt it. Henry Potterne is the one she ID'd.'

'Yeah, but even so, boyo. A tart in the witness box? Think it through.'

Bevan's views on call-girls were well known, a throw-back – Faraday assumed – to his chapel upbringing in the Welsh valleys. Given a choice, he'd run them all out of town.

Along the corridor, someone was ranting about the latest headquarters edict on overtime.

'You haven't found a body yet,' Bevan pointed out.

'No, sir.'

'So there could still be a million reasons for the guy going missing.'

'Absolutely.'

'What are we looking at then, resources-wise? Some forensic and a couple of extra hands?'

'Yes, sir. Plus a dive in the marina at the front of Oomes's property.'

'Dive? What are we looking for?'

'A weapon.'

'You really think this man's dead?'

'Yes, sir.' Faraday looked him in the eye. 'I do.'

'Some jump, isn't it?'

Faraday didn't answer. When Bevan inquired how everything else was going, he told him about Kate Symonds, the journalist from the freesheet. Mention of the audio cassette made Bevan wince.

'I knew she was trouble,' he muttered, gazing at the envelope Faraday had produced.

'You're right, sir. She's threatening to publish the transcript.'

Faraday outlined her terms for silence. Bevan shook his head at once.

'No can do,' he said. 'No way.'

He sighed, then got to his feet and went to the window.

'This Maloney business,' he said at last, 'what kind of time frame are we talking about?'

Faraday hesitated, knowing that this was the key question. No way would Bevan strip his division of CID cover for any length of time. If the inquiry were to go on and on, he might as well hand it over to a Major Inquiry Team now. And if that happened, Faraday would be back behind his desk in the inspectors' office, fenced in by street assaults, burglaries and serial shoplifters.

'A week should do it,' Faraday said lightly. 'Give me seven working days.'

Bevan, deep in thought, offered a slow nod. The other player in this game was Arnie Pollock. He was in charge of the divisional CID assets and the decision to call in a Major Inquiry Team would be his. Bevan didn't much like Pollock, but the two men had a grudging respect for each other and in view of the lack of hard evidence Bevan thought that Pollock might settle for staying with a low-profile, paper-based operation.

He looked up at Faraday.

'Leave it to me to talk to Arnie, then?'

'Glad to, sir.'

'Good.' His hand strayed to the envelope containing the audio cassette. 'And thanks for this, Joe.'

That afternoon, following a lengthy phone conversation with Pollock, Bevan strengthened Faraday's investigative hand by allowing him to poach two extra bodies to the Maloney inquiry. One, Duncan Pryde, was a young constable awaiting a posting after a successful CID board, while the other – Alan Moffatt – had just completed a lengthy stint on the force surveillance unit. Pryde and Moffatt would help out until Rick McGivern and Bev Yates returned from leave. With the addition of Cathy Lamb and Dawn Ellis, Faraday now had four detectives at his disposal.

In the CID room, at Faraday's insistence, Cathy Lamb created a nerve centre for the inquiry by pushing a couple of desks together and lining up the in-trays side by side. Each in-tray was labelled for a different form – Person Descriptive Forms, Message Forms, Action Forms – and the sight of this hastily improvised incident room brought a shake of the head from Paul Winter. Back in the office after hours of fruitless work trying to pin down a couple of guys working a roofing scam, he made no secret of his belief that Faraday had finally gone off his head. Decanting water from the chiller in the corner, he raised his plastic cup in a mock toast.

'This used to be a CID room once,' he told Dawn Ellis. 'Now it's fucking Toytown.'

Faraday wasn't around to hear the comment, and in any case he didn't care. The green light from Bevan had given him a focus, an incentive that he hadn't had for years. Seven working days to sort out the truth about Stewart Maloney. A week and a bit to become a detective again.

That evening, he and Cathy Lamb drove to Chiswick to interview Ian Hartson. Of *Marenka*'s three survivors, Faraday judged Hartson to be the most vulnerable. If there were to be a way into the mystery of Maloney's disappearance, then Hartson might supply it.

Hartson lived alone in a spacious first-floor flat in a quiet street off the Chiswick High Road. Faraday had already spoken to him on the phone and he'd had no objection to meeting them that evening. On the doorstep, inviting them in, he was taller and more imposing than Faraday had somehow expected from the figure he'd seen in the hospital bed in Plymouth. He wore jeans and an old cricket sweater and he walked with a slight stoop.

Upstairs, he offered them coffee and fig biscuits, only too happy to satisfy Faraday's curiosity about his connection with Charlie Oomes. As a television director, he explained that he'd contributed to a series of lavishly funded drama-documentaries exploring the London underworld of the 1950s. His film had traced the rise and fall of Ronnie Dunlop, Charlie Oomes's father. Hartson's treatment pulled few punches, portraying the gangster as a wife-beater and a psychopath, and Charlie Oomes had loved it.

Several weeks later, Oomes arranged a meeting with

the young film-maker. He wanted someone to work up an idea of his about the 1939 Fastnet Race. Charlie, fascinated by the challenges of ocean racing, had read a number of books about the race and was convinced that it would make a brilliant feature film.

Now, Hartson gestured at a pile of transcript lying on a low table beneath the window.

'Charlie was right,' he said. 'The race was a trailer for the war to come. The Germans entered a couple of boats, and the thing became a three-cornered battle between the Luftwaffe yacht, an American boat and the Brits. Our yacht was called *Bloodhound*. It was a lovely idea and Charlie wanted it developed to first script stage. No way was I going to say no.'

'Did he pay you?'

'Of course. There's a market rate for jobs like this and he paid on the nail. That bought me enough time for the research and a first draft. I started writing just after Christmas.'

He sank back into the chair. His Cowes Week tan was beginning to fade and his eyes kept straying towards the window, as if he yearned to be away from these questions.

'So what were you doing on the yacht last week?'

'That was Charlie's idea. He thought I needed to be hands-on, to do the race for myself. I started crewing back in June, just to get the hang of it.'

'So you knew Maloney then?'

'Yes.'

Faraday wanted to know more. Maloney had a reputation for chasing women. Was that something Hartson might be able to shed any light on?

Hartson looked pensive. He had a soft voice, with just a hint of a northern accent. His long body was folded into the armchair, and with his contemplative good looks and his mop of prematurely greying hair, he had exactly the kind of vulnerability that many women might find irresistible.

'Stu's just a regular guy', he said. 'He's divorced. He lives alone. Whatever he does is up to him.'

'You're telling me he does chase women?'

'I'm saying he's pretty normal. I'm sure he has his share of girlfriends.'

'Anyone in particular?'

'No.' He fingered the hem of his pullover. 'Not that he's ever said.'

'You never talked about it?'

'I can't remember. No, I don't think we did.'

'And when you were with him during Cowes Week, anything unusual then?'

'Not at all. In fact that first race on the Tuesday he had a stormer. He always took the foredeck. If you get it wrong up front, it can be a nightmare. Stu very rarely got it wrong. That was why Charlie was so pissed off when he blew it on the bike.'

Maloney's place on the crew had been taken by a nineteen-year-old called Sam O'Connor.

'Sam was Henry's stepson,' Hartson murmured. 'And he was pretty good, too.'

He explained that Henry Potterne had been the navigator on *Marenka*. Faraday remembered Charlie Oomes talking about him in Plymouth. He'd been swept to his death moments before the yacht capsized. Now, Faraday slipped the best of Maloney's photographs out of his jacket pocket and handed it across to Hartson.

'So which one was Henry?'

The sight of *Marenka*'s crew seemed to disturb Hartson. He studied it for a long time. Then the tip of his finger settled on the tall, gaunt-looking figure standing beside Charlie Oomes.

'That's him,' he said. 'We'd just won the Wednesday

race round the cans. Henry's doing, really. He called it perfectly.'

Faraday retrieved the photo.

'Did he always wear that red top?'

'When it was cold, or wet, yes.'

Faraday passed the photo across to Cathy, permitting himself the briefest smile. They had a name now, as well as a face. Henry Potterne.

'Was he a good navigator?'

'He was brilliant. That's Charlie's talent, really. He only goes for the best people and Henry was the best. Round the cans he was pretty outstanding, like I just said, but on a race like the Fastnet, the nav really earns his keep. The decisions he makes early on can win you the race within the first twenty-four hours. That's how good Henry was.'

'You knew him well?'

'Pretty well, yes. He was really helpful on the research for the film project. In fact I used to go and stay at his place sometimes, just so I could get a decent run at the thing. Charlie used to think he was a genius and in some respects I think he was right.'

'You sound like you miss him.'

'You're right.' Hartson studied his hands a moment. 'I do.'

The phrase had a dying fall, deliberate in its pathos, and Faraday began to wonder whether Hartson was always like this, investing memories with a wistfulness that was close to regret. Maybe it went with the territory, he thought. Maybe this was the way that film-making got to you.

Hartson was still talking about Charlie's star navigator. Henry Potterne had been in his early fifties. He'd learned his navigation in the Navy but for the last couple of years he'd been running a small art gallery in Southsea, specialising in marine pictures. In Hartson's experience he had an unusual combination of talents. On the one hand – afloat – he could be almost intimidating, sorting out problems with a hard, practical intelligence, whilst on dry land, away from the racing, it would be difficult to meet a more sensitive guy.

'Too sensitive, really.'

'How do you mean?'

'I don't know. Sometimes I just had the feeling that life was getting the better of him.'

'How?'

'I'm not sure. He had expectations, like we all do. Maybe some things hadn't worked out.'

'Like what?'

Hartson shook his head, not willing to go any further. Faraday shot a glance at Cathy, and raised an eyebrow.

'Was he married?' she asked.

'Yes. In fact it was his second marriage. First time I gather it was pretty much a disaster. She left him.'

'And now?'

'He married again. Her name's Ruth. They run the gallery together.'

'You know Ruth?'

'Of course. I used to stay with them in Southsea.'

'Did Henry have any kind of problem there?'

'How do you mean?'

'Was he a jealous man? And if he was, did he have cause to be?'

Hartson was studying his hands again.

'Henry was pathologically jealous,' he said at last. 'He'd been let down once and he was terrified it would happen again. But no, I don't think there was anyone else.'

'These were fears of his own making?'

'Yes, I think they were.'

There was a long silence. It was getting dark now but Hartson made no attempt to switch on the lights.

Faraday stirred in his chair.

'How did he get on with Maloney?'

'OK. They weren't bosom pals, but they were OK.'

'No antagonism there? No jealousy?'

'No.' Hartson shook his head. 'Not that I ever heard.'

'Does Maloney know Ruth at all?'

'I think they've met a couple of times, just socially. Charlie used to throw crew parties sometimes, and wives and girlfriends would turn up. But beyond that?' – Hartson shrugged – 'I don't think so.'

'Where does Ruth live?'

'Southsea. I just told you.'

'Like Maloney, then.'

'Yes.'

For the first time, Hartson looked Faraday in the eye, refusing to qualify the answer. After a while, Faraday nodded and made a laborious note in his pocketbook. Then he glanced up again.

'Charlie Oomes told us that the boat never left Cowes before the Fastnet,' he said lightly. 'Is that true?'

Now Hartson couldn't take his eyes off Faraday's open pocketbook.

'He told you that?'

'Yes, he did. He said you were over in Cowes the whole week. So let me put it to you again. Is it true?'

Hartson didn't lift his head.

'Why do you ask?' he said at last.

'Because it's material to our inquiries. Just give me a yes or no, Mr Hartson. Did the boat stay in Cowes, like Charlie said?'

'No,' he shook his head. 'It didn't.'

'So what happened?'

'We had to take her back to Portsmouth.'

'We?'

'Myself and Henry. There was a problem with our

life raft. We could have bought another one in Cowes but Charlie had a spare in his garage and saw no point in wasting money. He's got a place in Port Solent. We went over on the Friday.'

'So how long were you there?'

'Most of the afternoon.'

'And did either of you leave Port Solent?'

'I'm not with you.'

'To go into Portsmouth, say?'

Hartson tipped his head back and frowned. The frown, to Faraday, looked fake.

'Well?' It was Cathy this time.

'Yes. The answer's yes. Henry took a cab into town.'

'Why?'

'I don't know.'

Cathy glanced at Faraday.

'He didn't tell you?' Faraday didn't hide his disbelief. 'You were friends? You'd come over together? He suddenly takes a cab into town? And he doesn't tell you why?'

'It's the truth. I didn't ask and he didn't say. What's so sinister about that?'

'How long was he away for?'

'I can't remember. About an hour, I think.'

'Did he come back with anything?'

Hartson looked at the ceiling. Then his hand came out and switched on a small chair-side light, turning his head at once to shield his eyes.

'He came back with some kind of picture,' he said.

'Of what?'

'I don't know. It was wrapped up in newspaper.'

'You never saw it?'

'No.'

'You never asked about it?'

'No. I was busy. The new life raft had to be lashed down. There was a problem with the gennie halyard.

We were due back for supper. I had food to sort out, spare batteries, all kinds of stuff.'

'So what happened to this picture?' Faraday wouldn't let go.

'I don't know.'

'You don't *know*? You're squashed together on this tiny boat and you don't know?'

'It came back with us to Cowes. After that—' He shrugged. 'I never saw it again.'

'Did anyone else come along? Before you left for Cowes?'

'I don't understand you.'

'After Henry returned, were there any other visitors?'

'Yes.' Hartson nodded. 'Stu Maloney turned up. He knew we'd come over and he'd dropped by to wish us luck. It was a nice thought.'

'Did he seem angry at all? Maloney?'

'No. Disappointed, obviously, and pissed off about the arm, but not angry.'

'And what happened then?'

'He went.'

'Just like that?'

'No, we had a drink together.'

'What kind of drink?'

'I think it was malt whisky. Henry drank a lot of malt, Glenfiddich mostly.'

Faraday bent to his pocketbook again while Hartson waited for the next question. He had his hands linked around his knees now, his long body rocking slowly back and forth in the chair.

Faraday sucked the end of his Biro for a moment or two.

'So let me get this clear,' he said softly. 'You and Henry bring the boat over on Friday afternoon. Henry disappears for an hour. Maloney turns up out of the blue, just by chance, and – hey presto – you happen to be there. You all have a drink. Maloney pushes off. And then you and Henry go back to Cowes. Have I got that right?'

'I don't know about out of the blue. Maybe Henry phoned him or something.'

'On whose phone?'

'Henry's I suppose.'

'He had a mobile?'

'Yes.'

'So there'd be a record of the call?'

'I expect so. Yes, of course there would.'

Faraday gazed at him, openly sceptical. Then he went at Hartson's story again, different angles this time, different approaches, testing it this way and that, exposing little inconsistencies, pushing and pushing until Hartson finally dropped his head again and signalled no more.

'Listen,' he said in a low voice, 'I've told you everything I know. We took the boat over. Henry went off and came back again. Stu had a drink with us. And then he left and we took the boat back to Cowes.'

'Do you happen to know *where* Maloney went?'

'No.'

'He didn't say?'

'No.'

'Did he take a taxi? Did he walk?'

'I've no idea.'

'So he just went? Just like that? Just wandered off?'

'That's right.'

Faraday nodded, saying nothing. Cathy stirred in the shadows beyond the pool of light.

'You're sure there wasn't any kind of incident? Fight? Him and Henry?'

'No, definitely not. Why would they want to fight?'

He looked up at Faraday, almost pleading for an answer, for an end to this ordeal, and Faraday gazed back at him, nodding slowly, the friendly GP, ever patient.

'I haven't a clue,' he murmured at last. 'I was rather hoping you might be able to tell me.'

'He's lying.' Faraday stifled a yawn.

'You think so?'

'Definitely. And pretty soon he'll tell us why.'

They were still parked outside the house. Hartson had checked the street twice, a tall, stooped figure up at the window. The second time he'd appeared, Cathy had given him a little wave. An hour would be long enough to spook him. Then they'd go in again.

But it didn't work that way. The second encounter took less than half an hour. Hartson was a different man, taciturn, monosyllabic, giving nothing away. When Cathy asked him about the Friday afternoon, he simply referred her to his previous answers. When she asked him what he'd got to lose by going through it all again, he just shook his head, studied his hands and made pointed remarks about how late it was getting.

Driving south, towards the glow of Guildford, it was Faraday who finally broke the silence.

'He made a call,' he said thoughtfully, 'and I bet it was to Charlie Oomes.'

Fifteen

Faraday drove to Port Solent early next morning to supervise the naval dive team tasked to search the floor of the yacht basin around Charlie Oomes's waterside property. The lack of tide and current simplified the preparations and Faraday and the dive team leader agreed a throw radius from the yacht pontoon before the two divers submerged to begin a fingertip search. With visibility poor, the dive leader warned Faraday to expect a long wait.

Cathy arrived shortly before eleven. Two and a half hours had so far produced a single plimsoll. Cathy, who knew about plimsolls, judged it to be a Dunlop Green Flash, size eight or nine. It must have been submerged some time because the canvas was green with algae and the stitching was beginning to rot.

'Might as well put it back.' She smothered a yawn. 'I can't see this going to forensic.'

Faraday was watching the twin lines of bubbles in the murky brown water, expelled air from the divers working the basin floor. Despite the dive leader's warning, they were already some distance out from the pontoon. Any further, and Faraday would have difficulty tying recovered objects to Oomes's yacht.

He turned towards the back of the house. Two early-morning calls to Oomes's home address in Berkshire had so far failed to raise the man but Faraday would keep trying. A full forensic search, if it came to that, would be a declaration of war. Far better to go for a preliminary trawl, looking for signs of some kind of struggle, and to do it with Oomes's prior permission. In the meantime, a uniformed PC stationed outside would keep intruders at bay.

Faraday felt a tug on the sleeve of his jacket. It was Cathy. He followed her pointing finger, shielding his eyes against the glare of the sun.

'Over there in the upstairs window,' she said. 'It's Elaine. She's been watching us all morning.'

Cathy was right. Faraday recognised the scarlet bathrobe and the long blonde hair. He raised a hand and waved a greeting, but Elaine Pope turned away.

Faraday was driving back into the city when he took the call from Sandra Maloney. She wanted to know what was going on. She and Patrick had been steeling themselves for another visit. Nothing, thank God, had happened. In the absence of yet more harassment, might she assume that Faraday had lost interest?

Faraday accelerated into the outside lane. Off to the right, hundreds of seagulls were wheeling and diving over the municipal dump. From this distance, they looked like clouds of white paper.

'Yes and no,' he said.

'Meaning?'

'I don't think either of you were involved.'

'How comforting. And how nice of you to keep us informed.' She paused. 'Have you, by any chance, found the time to talk to anyone at the university?'

'Not yet, Mrs Maloney.'

'Then I suggest you do. We had a conversation last night. Her name's Jan Tilley and she is Stewart's departmental head.'

There was a long silence. Faraday inquired about Emma. How was she bearing up?

'Not well, Inspector. But then that's hardly a surprise, is it?'

*

Paul Winter had never had much time for hypermarkets. Under suffrance, at the weekends, he would occasionally volunteer to keep Joan company on a trip to the local Asda but he loathed the feel of the place – the lighting, the endless shelves, the slow, trancelike procession from aisle to aisle – and the bigger the store, the more irritated he became.

Tesco, on a huge site next to Port Solent, was the biggest of the local hypermarkets and he'd done his best to sell Juanita an alternative rendezvous, but on the phone she'd been adamant. If he wanted to meet her that morning, then it had to be Tesco. She was a busy woman. She was due at the hospital at noon but there was *muchas obras* to get done first. If he was lucky, she might even allow him to push her trolley.

To Winter's alarm, she meant it. He found her sorting briskly through one of the chill cabinets. Her handshake numbed his fingers.

'You don't mind?' She nodded at the trolley.

Winter looked down at the packets of langoustine and frozen squid. When Marty Harrison finally emerged from hospital, he was in for a treat. Winter began to push the trolley as Juanita zigzagged down the aisle. She did everything, he was beginning to realise, with an intense sense of purpose. Don't be fooled by the skin-tight white cut-offs and the curling smile. Here, very definitely, was a woman who knew her own mind.

Twenty minutes later, at Winter's insistence, they paused at the in-store coffee shop. Winter bought cappuccino and Danish for them both, hurrying back to the table in case she hit the aisles again, but he needn't have worried. Despite the 'No Smoking' notices everywhere, she'd already lit a cigarette, and now she was sitting cross-legged in her chair, ticking items on her shopping list.

Winter settled at the table, content to wait. He'd

been in touch with Harry Wayte, DI on the Drugs Squad, telling him he'd snared a Grade A informant. He hadn't mentioned Juanita's name, nor the fact that she was Marty Harrison's mistress, but he could tell from the quickening in Harry's voice that he was more than interested. Red Rum, despite all the Drugs Squad spin, had so far been a disaster. They had five of Harrison's colleagues banged up in the remand wing at Winchester nick but, if he was to be honest, the evidence against them was pretty thin. What Harry needed, very badly, was a headline or two. Something to justify all the money he'd spent. Something to redress the balance after the fuck-up at Harrison's place. Something to keep the suits off his back.

Winter lifted the cup to his mouth and sucked the froth from the top of the cappuccino.

'You wanted me to find out about Elaine,' he said, 'and Marty.'

'*Sí.*' Juanita moistened a finger and reached across, wiping the froth from the tip of Winter's nose. 'You've talked to her?'

'Yeah.'

'And?'

Winter hesitated. He'd rehearsed this conversation a number of times in his mind. Her English wasn't perfect, which meant there was more room for ambiguity than usual, but he still had to get the phrase exactly right because one day she would doubtless confront Marty with the evidence and Marty – being Marty – would want to know where it came from.

'It's difficult,' he began, 'but I think you could say that he's looking after her.'

'*Looking after her?*'

Winter nodded. It was like feeding pennies into one of those old pinball machines. The lights came on at once.

'That's why he's there so much.'

'You mean . . .?' Juanita bridged the gap between them with a plaintive gesture of her hand.

Winter nodded again, wondering whether it was too early to offer condolences. The essence of every sting was patience.

'He's known her a while,' he said. 'In fact they go way back. School, even. Same estate. Same friends.'

'Same bed. I can see it. I can see it from my place. You think that's some kind of joke? You think he does it deliberately? So close? So close I can almost *see* them? Behind those curtains?'

The thought of Marty looking after Elaine Pope brought a deep flush to Juanita's olive face and, watching her, Winter could imagine why Harrison had become so smitten. She'd be this way in bed, impulsive, uncontrollable, all over you the moment you stepped out of your kaks.

'You did ask,' he said carefully, 'and I'm sorry to be the messenger.'

'*Qué?*'

'The messenger. The bringer of bad news. Anything I can do—' It was his turn to gesture at the space between them, then he got to his feet. She stared up at him, in anger as well as disbelief.

'You're going? You're leaving me? You tell me news like that and then you go?'

The question, as ever, was direct, an unmistakable challenge, and for the first time it began to occur to Winter that he might be looking at the freebie of his dreams. Open house. Any time.

He looked down at her and smiled. On these occasions, the biggest mistake was to be too eager. If this incredible woman meant what he thought she meant, then only time would put her to the test.

'Must run,' he said. 'You've got my number. Give

me a ring and we could have a proper chat. Some-where' – he nodded at the mid-morning queue forming at the counter – 'a bit more intimate.'

From his desk back at the station, Faraday phoned the name Sandra Maloney had given him. Jan Tilley indeed worked at the university and it was plain at once that she was expecting Faraday's call. This morning she had just half an hour to spare, then she was off to London for the rest of the week. If they were to meet, then it had to be now.

Putting the phone down, Faraday went next door to the CID room, wondering whether Cathy was avail-able to do the interview. More and more, he felt a pressing need to talk to Charlie Oomes, but so far he hadn't even got through to him on the phone.

The CID room was empty. On the point of leaving, Faraday noticed a fax from the Force Intelligence Unit at Winchester, stamped with yesterday's date and wrongly filed in one of the in-trays. All requests for call print-outs on domestic phones went through the FIU, and this one listed calls over the last month from the phone in Stewart Maloney's flat. Faraday scanned it quickly, then glanced at his watch. Jan Tilley's train left at twelve-seventeen. If he was to catch her before she left, he'd have to run.

Jan Tilley was a thin-faced woman in a smart linen jacket with black-painted nails and a dry, slightly nervous cough. She occupied a small, cluttered first-floor office in the university's Department of Art, Design and Media and she numbered Stewart Malo-ney amongst her many administrative headaches.

'Sandra's not dealing with this at all well,' she said. 'I think it might pay you to treat her a little more gently.'

Faraday acknowledged the slap on the wrist with a

weary nod. A plea in mitigation would have been worse than useless. After half an hour on the phone to Sandra Maloney, this woman had obviously made up her mind about the CID.

'I understand you might be able to shed some light,' he said.

'Possibly. Possibly not. Let me explain.'

She began to slide the rubber band off a roll of sketches on her desk, then had second thoughts. With Stewart's work, she said, there'd never been a problem. He was a gifted teacher and brought out the best in many of his students. They liked his attitude, what she called his 'cultural take', and when they told her that he actually *cared* about them – about their problems and their difficulties and the challenges they were going to have to face in the world outside – she believed them.

She broke off, puzzled by Faraday's slow smile.

'You sound almost as defensive as me,' he said. 'What's the catch here?'

'Catch?'

'You're telling me he's a great teacher. You're telling me that he's conscientious, that he gets results, that he cares. So where does he go wrong?'

'I'm not sure I—' She looked warily towards the door. 'maybe he cares too much.'

'About?'

'One or two of the students.'

'Female?'

'Yes. I'm thinking of one in particular.'

'You're telling me he's been having some kind of affair?'

'Yes.'

'Is that a problem?'

'It can be, yes. He isn't married, of course. But some of these girls aren't as mature, as grown-up, as they look. And Stewart, bless him, is a great believer in looks.'

The girl's name she wouldn't reveal, but the affair had gone on for months and when Maloney began to hint that they might live together after her graduation, she'd believed him. Which made the inevitable parting – she called it the *dénouement* – all the more painful.

'What happened?'

'Stewart fell in love with someone else.'

'Another student?'

'No, not at all. A mature woman, this time. Someone his own age for a change.'

'She works here?'

'No, not really. He employs her occasionally as a model in his life-drawing classes. And it's apparently no secret that his interest goes way beyond . . . ah . . . figurework.'

At last the elastic band came off the roll. Maloney's student girlfriend had been especially gifted at life drawing. Her depictions of the human body had evidently been outstanding, a celebration of proportion and line. By the time it was her turn to sketch Maloney's model-friend, she'd become all too aware of the rumours.

Faraday nodded at the roll of sketches.

'Are they hers?'

'No, that's what made it all the harder. These are drawings of the same woman, but by other hands. Here. You ought to look.'

She cleared a space on the desk and flattened the roll. Faraday got up and found himself looking at a woman in the prime of her life. She was lying on a button-backed chaise longue. She had beautifully shaped legs and full breasts, and the way her hands lay interlinked over the roundness of her belly suggested a woman completely at ease with her own nakedness. It was a body that beckoned motherhood, eerily familiar, and as Faraday leafed through the rest of the drawings it became harder and harder not to think of Janna, his own wife. Some of the figurework was uncertain but the more gifted students had caught the expression on this woman's face and it spoke, at once, of vitality and a deep, deep sense of inner calm.

Here was someone who would rarely be bored with her own company. Here was a woman who well understood the effect she had on others and seemed prepared to face the consequences. No wonder Stewart Maloney had succumbed.

Faraday at last looked up. Jan Tilley was staring out of the window.

'So what happened to the girlfriend?'

'Hers was the best drawing.'

'And?'

'Maloney kept it.' She turned back into the room and took an envelope from a drawer in the desk. 'You might want to know who this woman is. I talked to the pay-roll people this morning.'

Faraday opened the envelope. Folded inside was a white sheet of paper with a single name. He stared at it. Ruth Potterne.

Cathy had returned to the station by the time Faraday got back. He produced the day-old fax from the Force Intelligence Unit. The CID office was empty.

'This was in the Actions tray,' he said briskly, 'and it would be nice to know why.'

Exhaustion had left its mark on Cathy's battered face. She nodded at the row of wire baskets straddling the two desks. Faraday was right. Paper was beginning to spill everywhere.

'Some people might say this is lunacy,' she said. 'And pretty soon I might be one of them.'

'You haven't answered my question.'

'I have. But you never listen.' She glared at him for a

moment, then nodded at one of the phones. 'Charlie Oomes has been on. Apparently you left a message on his answerphone.'

'Several.'

'Fine.' Cathy's gaze returned to the fax. 'I think he's wondering what all the fuss is about.'

Fifteen minutes later, Faraday was still sitting at his desk in the inspectors' office, gazing at the FIU printout of the numbers on Maloney's home phone. The recurrent number was so obvious that the processing clerk hadn't even bothered to highlight it. A local number: 842871.

Between Thursday and Friday afternoon, Maloney had rung it no less than nine times. None of the conversations had been long, but that didn't matter. If you were looking for patterns, for evidence of an affair, then here it was. Black and white. A line of digits: 842871.

So far, still haunted by Jan Tilley's roll of sketches, Faraday hadn't bothered to lift the phone. It would be her number, Ruth Potterne's number, it had to be. Maloney was in love with her, head-over-heels, ninecalls-a-day in love with her. They might have met at one of Charlie Oomes's parties. Or in a bar. Or in the street. Or any bloody place. They'd have shared a coffee, or a beer, and talked all that arty talk, and at some point thereafter – hours later, days later, maybe even weeks later – this relationship of theirs, this meeting of minds, would have tiptoed off to bed. Maybe her place. More likely his.

Faraday made a mental note, visualising the tousled sheets in Maloney's cluttered little bedroom. There'd be forensic there. Fingerprints. Curls of her hair. Her DNA on his toothbrush. He shook his head, trying to rid himself of the image of her body stretched out on Maloney's bed, the body on the chaise longue.

Faraday's hand finally found the phone. 842871. The phone rang and rang until a recorded message cut in. It was a man's voice, cultured, warm, almost amused. 'You have reached the home of Henry and Ruth Potterne,' it said. 'Please leave your name and number and one of us will call you back.'

Faraday let the print-out blur in front of his eyes. The voice of another dead man, he thought, slowly replacing the receiver.

Sixteen

Marmion Road, in the heart of Southsea, was busy at lunchtime. Faraday sat in his car, parked on a double yellow line, watching the shoppers swirl past. With their bulging Waitrose bags, and their fixed expressions, most of them seemed as walled-in and preoccupied as he was.

Across the road was the Henry Potterne Gallery. One of the two front windows was dominated by a handsome oil painting on a wooden easel. The canvas depicted an episode from the Battle of the Nile, catching the moment when Nelson's sweating gunners had found the French powder magazines. The treatment was a little operatic for his tastes – violent yellows and livid reds – but he knew exactly what the artist had been getting at. Put two combustible substances together, and the consequences could be incalculable.

Faraday got out of the car and crossed the road. Inside the gallery, it felt suddenly cooler. Dozens of marine prints hung on the calico-clad walls while at the back of the display space, softly lit, were a couple of decent watercolours together with a line of beautifully framed black and white photographs. Something about the composition and choice of subjects drew Faraday towards them. Photo after photo featured small, natural objects rendered in fine-grain detail, and a moment's study was enough to confirm Faraday's initial suspicion. This was the eye that had framed the shots on Stewart Maloney's wall.

A middle-aged woman appeared through a side

door. She looked nothing like the model on the chaise longue. When Faraday inquired about the gallery's owner, she confirmed that he was missing at sea.

'What about his wife?' Faraday said. 'Where might I find her?'

'She's still in Plymouth. She's been down there since Monday night, waiting for news. To be honest, it's looking pretty hopeless. I think she'd be better off back here now.'

'Do you have a number?' Faraday slipped out his ID.

She peered at the face in the tiny photograph then reached for a pen and a scrap of paper.

'I should know it by heart by now,' she said. 'It's a little B and B down near the Hoe. We talk at least twice a day.'

'And she's still there?'

'She was this morning.'

Faraday folded the number into his pocket, his eyes returning to the line of photographs. When he asked who'd taken the shots, the woman smiled.

'Ruthie,' she said. 'Terribly talented, don't you think?'

Winter was in a second-hand shop off Fratton Road, trying to nail down a couple of nicked stereos, when his mobile began to ring. The lad who appeared to run the shop was having difficulty explaining a shedful of bikes round the back, and was grateful for the interruption.

'Yes?' Winter barked.

Juanita was back at her flat in Port Solent. She'd unloaded her shopping and now she was lying on her bed, exhausted.

'Not surprised. That lot. Need a massage?'

'Yes, please.'

Winter laughed, sharing the joke, and it was several

seconds before he realised that she really meant it. Maybe this was the way things happened in Spain. Maybe this was why women like this were so bloody *sure* of themselves.

'Now?' He frowned, checking his watch. 'This minute?'

'If you want.'

'I want.' Winter nodded vigorously. 'But not now. No way, José. How about later?'

'Later I go to the hospital.'

'You're sure about that?'

'Yes. I'm there all afternoon. Now would be good. Now, before I see him.'

Winter scowled. He'd never underestimated his attraction to women, and he had dozens of conquests to prove it, but this was almost too good to be true. Part of him argued for caution, for a couple of deep breaths and a query or two about what she really wanted, but then the image of that golden body swam towards him and he found himself doing a rapid mental calculation, trying to work out how long it would take to get some sense out of the boy, take a statement, drive to Port Solent and still leave himself enough time to make it worthwhile.

'No can do,' he said regretfully, '*Comprende?*'

There was a long silence. When the youth made a move towards the shed door, Winter edged sideways, blocking the exit with his body. Finally Juanita came back on the phone. She named a pub in the country, out near Wickham.

'Half eight,' Winter confirmed. 'Drinks on me.'

Charlie Oomes lived in a sprawling Tudor-style country house west of Maidenhead, with lawns that ran down to the Thames. Savagely barbered poplars lined the gravel drive that swept up to the front door, and there was plenty of room beside a sleek red Mercedes for Faraday's Mondeo.

Inside, the house felt cold and over-furnished, and it was obvious at once that the place had become a monument to Charlie's business and sporting triumphs. Waiting in the lounge for Oomes to appear, Faraday and Cathy sat side by side on one of the huge sofas, eyeing the silver-framed photos propped on every available surface. Charlie at Ascot. Charlie at some industry function, receiving a customer service award. Charlie on a marina pontoon, hosing champagne in every direction. Charlie kissing Liz Hurley in a showbiz receiving line. Charlie getting ever richer.

Eventually, Oomes himself appeared, relaxed and expansive in slacks and a check shirt. The swelling around his jaw had gone down and the bruise beneath his left eye had virtually disappeared. He apologised for keeping them waiting. He'd been upstairs on the phone arguing the toss over some figures. The problem with bloody accountants was they never left you alone. He beamed at them both with his big, meaty smile and called for a tray of tea. It was several minutes before Faraday realised that the small, ghost-like, Asian-looking woman who'd let them in was in fact Oomes's wife.

Charlie made himself comfortable on the other sofa, warming to his theme. His company, Oomes International, was currently moving into CCTV and, although closed-circuit television was a natural fit with his other IT interests, there was never any satisfying the bean-counters. Many of his clients were in the public sector – local councils, National Health trusts, even the police – and the accounting standards were arse-tight. Take your eye off the ball for a single second, and these bastards would turn you upside down and shake the loose change out of your pockets. The public sector boys always wanted something for nothing. And playing that game was the shortest bloody cut to bankruptcy.

Mention of the police prompted a question from Faraday. Was it true that he'd stolen Derek Bissett from the arms of the Thames Valley force?

'Stolen's a bit strong.' Oomes grinned. 'He jumped at it.'

'Jumped at what?'

'The deal I offered him. He and I had done business together. In my line you get to sort out the tossers from the rest. Derek was never a tosser.'

'You sold him IT stuff when he was with Thames Valley?'

'Yeah, small systems at first, with maintenance contracts, then much bigger stuff. I forget which department but it was worth a bit.'

'And he's stayed with you ever since?'

'Yeah. In fact he's the guy who'll be heading the CCTV operation. I'm creating a subsidiary company, just for him. Derek thinks it's Christmas.'

'Is this recent, then?'

'I made him the offer yesterday. He'll be signing the draft contract tomorrow morning.'

Faraday reached for his tea. If you wanted to shackle someone properly, to bind them to you body and soul, you could do worse than hand them a company of their own. A deal like that could set Bissett up for life.

Cathy was sympathising about the missing members of Charlie's crew. Was there any possibility they might still be found?

Charlie looked abruptly grave and shook his head.

'I'm on to the Search and Rescue blokes every day. They've already scaled the search down. Tomorrow, they're jacking it in completely.'

'Must be hard for you.'

'Yeah.' Charlie nodded. 'It is.'

'What about a funeral?'

'Pointless, love. We haven't got any bodies.' He sniffed. 'There's talk of some kind of memorial service but I've been thinking of doing something private, as well. Don't know what, yet, but something tasteful, you know.' He frowned, then wiped his nose on the back of his hand. 'Maybe some kind of trust fund, I dunno. Money's not a problem but two of the guys were only kids. How can you compensate for that?'

Faraday was trying to decipher the lettering on a big silver cup, prominently displayed on the sideboard.

'Tell me about last Friday,' he said idly. 'That afternoon before the race. Where was the boat?'

'Henry took it over to Pompey. With Ian.'

'You told me it never left the island.'

'Did I?'

'Yes. I asked you in hospital in Plymouth and you said you'd all stayed in Cowes.'

'Then I was wrong. I was in a bit of a state. Sorry.' He helped himself to more tea, adding three spoonfuls of sugar. 'Actually me and Derek were buzzing around all day Friday, getting stuff organised for the off. Food and what have you. There was a problem with the life raft. They cost a fortune and I'd got a spare in the garage in Port Solent. Made sense for Henry to swap them over.'

Faraday nodded. He was writing notes now. It was important to keep Oomes on the record.

'Do you happen to know whether they met Maloney over at Port Solent?'

'Yeah, they did. Henry mentioned it. Stu dropped in to say goodbye. Why do you ask?'

'Because he's gone missing. Did Henry happen to say where he went afterwards? After Port Solent?'

'No.' He was looking Faraday in the eye. 'He didn't.'

'Did that strike you as odd?'

'Not at all. Bloke led a crazy life.'

'Led?'

'Leads.' Oomes hesitated for a second, then leaned forward, his elbows on his knees, and looked Faraday in the eye. 'What you have to understand here is that this guy's into serious fantasy. Five minutes with Stu and he'll be giving you a list of women he's shagging but it gets to be a joke in the end. He's piss and wind. He invents most of it.'

Faraday glanced at Cathy, then mentioned Ruth, Henry's widow. Did Maloney fancy her?

'Daft about her, stupid about her. I keep telling you, the bloke's a wet dream.'

'Do you think it's reciprocated?'

'Ruth? I haven't a clue. Listen, I provide the boat, I pay for everything, I give the guys a good time, and in return I expect to win. Mostly, they don't let me down. At Cowes we were creaming the opposition all week. A result in the Fastnet and we'd have cleaned up. Just like last year. No crew's ever done that before. That makes me very proud of them. The last thing I do is poke around in their private lives.'

'Maloney let you down,' Faraday pointed out.

'Stu let himself down. Next time he'll go a bit slower on that fucking bike.'

'You think he's still alive?'

'Of course he is. The only bit of Stu that's dead is his brain and he's been that way for years. He's gone off for a while. He's fallen in love again. He'll be back. Bet your life on it.'

Faraday bent to the notepad for a moment or two.

'What about Henry Potterne?' he said at last. 'Did he ever let you down?'

'No, never. Henry had his own problems. Fucking brilliant nav., though. The best. Just drank too much for his own good.'

'Oh?'

'Yeah, but you know something? That guy could drink a bottle of Scotch and still lay a decent course. Amazing.'

'Would you say he was an alcoholic?'

'Definitely.'

'A drunk?'

'No way. He could handle it. You think I'd put my boat, my crew, in the hands of a drunk? No kidding, other skippers were queuing up for Henry. He could have had the pick of the fleet. But he chose to stay with us. That's how tight we were.'

Faraday nodded, then asked about the two lads, David Kellard – the university student – and Sam, Henry's stepson. Charlie leaned forward again, warming to his theme, and for the first time Faraday realised that the man was a chancer, forever pushing the odds, forever in your face, making his case, telling you how good he was. Prudence would counsel him to say very little. But Charlie was a stranger to prudence.

'They hated each other. *Big* problem.'

'Who did?'

'Henry and Sam. In his own way, Sam was as good in a boat as Henry. But hands-on, unschooled, instinctive, you know what I mean? Sam was Ruth's boy, been afloat since he was a nipper, born to it.' Charlie was beaming now. 'Sam hated Henry, resented him like fuck. Often happens like that, doesn't it?'

Faraday inquired about David Kellard, his Biro racing across his notebook. According to Charlie, he'd been a nice lad, and straight as a die. His father was an old mate of Henry's. Lived down in the West Country somewhere. He'd been doing oceanography at Southampton University and was off to Africa for a year to sort out the fuzzies with some bunch of do-gooders before getting himself a job in the oil biz. Charlie just loved the combination. Rich by forty *and* guaranteed a place in heaven. Fucking wonderful.

Charlie barked with laughter and called for more tea. While his wife disappeared into the kitchen with the tray, Faraday quizzed him about the storm, and about the exact sequence of events that had led to the boat breaking up. Charlie nodded, drawing a deep breath, then talked him through it, describing the hours in the cockpit, the turns at the tiller, the towering seas, and finally the growing conviction that they were stuffed.

'Did you ever think of turning back?'

'Of course we fucking did.'

'So why didn't you?'

'First off, we're in a race. You want to hang in there. You think the wind'll ease. You think any fucking thing just as long as you keep going. Second' – he frowned – 'we were out beyond the Scillys, thirty miles give or take according to Henry. In a sea like that the last thing you want anywhere near you is land, especially somewhere as evil as the Scillys or Cornwall. We wouldn't have had a prayer.' Oomes broke off, studying his enormous hands, then he looked up again. 'Have you ever been in a sea like that? Bloody great waves coming at you from every direction? Rollers bigger than blocks of flats?'

Faraday was watching him closely.

'So who went over first?'

'Henry. On top of everything else, we had a problem with the rudder blade.'

'Was he roped on?'

'Obviously not.'

'Who was the closest?'

'Sam.'

'And?'

'Didn't lift a finger – but then he couldn't. One second Henry was there, the next he wasn't. And it was dark, remember. Pitch fucking black. Imagine being in the ring with a dozen Mike Tysons and then the lights go out. That's the way it was when we lost Henry.'

'And the two lads?'

'That was soon after. We'd gone arse over tit, pitchpoled. The cabin was full of water and we were broadside on. We were cream-crackered, whichever way you cut it. End game. *Sayonara*.'

'You'd got into the life raft?'

'Derek cut it free. Me and Ian piled in. Fuck knows how but we did. We had a rope to the yacht but in that sea you hadn't got a prayer. Someone must have let go.'

'Like who?'

Charlie stared at Faraday for a moment.

'That's a fucking stupid question, if you don't mind me saying so. We're in this storm. We've had the shit knocked out of us most of the night. We're knackered, we're cold, and we're frightened like you wouldn't believe because we think we're going to die. The fucking boat turns upside down and suddenly we *know* we're going to die. Somehow we get out of it. Somehow we're sitting in this life raft. And you ask who let go? Are you serious?'

This outburst prompted a long silence. Then Faraday leant back in the sofa and capped his pen. Charlie was helping himself to yet more tea.

'We need to take a look round your house,' Faraday said, 'down in Port Solent.'

Charlie finished with the sugar, stirred his tea, then dug in his pocket for a pair of keys.

'Be my guest,' he grunted, tossing them across.

It was still a beautiful evening by the time Winter pulled into the car park at the Forester's Arms. He reached back for the tan leather bomber jacket, then had second thoughts and decided to stay in shirt-sleeves. He could see Juanita's all-black V-reg Chero-kee Jeep up by the side entrance to the pub. She must be in there already, waiting for him.

He combed what remained of his hair in the mirror, then set off across the car park, grinning to himself. He still hadn't a clue what this women really wanted but it was going to be fun finding out.

On the point of going into the pub, he heard his name called from the shadowed garden round the front. Juanita was sitting alone at a table beneath a cherry tree.

The white Prada T-shirt was cut low around her neck and when she leaned forward across the table, reaching up to kiss him, it was obvious that she wasn't wearing a bra.

'Hmm . . .' she said.

Winter gestured at her empty glass.

'What is it?'

'Orange juice.'

Winter returned with the orange juice and a pint of Stella for himself. He'd asked the barman to put a double shot of vodka in with the orange but she didn't seem to taste it. Instead, she came at once to the point.

'I told him,' she said, 'I told him that I knew. And you know what? He just laughed. *Laughed*.'

She was talking about Marty Harrison. She'd spent most of the afternoon at the hospital with him, and the fact that he was back in a state to do anything even half-sensible wasn't altogether good news.

'How is he?' Winter asked.

'OK.' She shrugged. 'He takes a little food. He drinks a little tea. And every day he gets a little more better. He's a strong man. *Fuerte*.'

Winter looked down as she bunched her fist, remembering the message picked out across Harrison's knuckles. Noel Blake had taken no prisoners. And neither did Marty Harrison.

'He didn't deny it? About Elaine?'

'He laughed. I told you. He laughed so much it hurt him. How could I marry a man like that? How could I marry a man who laughs in my face about the whore he screws?'

She reached for her glass and sank half the vodka and orange juice at a single swallow. Moments later her eyes were shiny and moist.

'Nice,' she said.

They stayed in the garden, under the cherry tree, while the light drained from the sky. Juanita had a couple more vodka and oranges while Winter nursed himself along on refills of Stella. Her plan was to return to Puerto Banus just as soon as she decently could. She'd had enough of the English, with their crudeness and their aggression, and she'd certainly had enough of Marty Harrison. She'd been crazy, *loco*, to have believed anything he'd said in the first place. All he'd ever wanted was to screw her. All the plans to cut her in on the business, all the talk of partnership, had been lies. He'd never had the slightest intention of treating her like a real partner. Not in business, and certainly not in bed.

'How do you know?'

'I see him. I watch him. The house with the yellow curtains. I told you.'

'I meant the business.'

'The business? It's the same. He screws me there, too.'

'How?'

'By spreading himself everywhere. By going in with other guys. By selling more and more drugs.'

'Different drugs?'

'Sure. Cocaine, sure. Now heroin, too. All the time

he does it. That's why you'll never catch him. He's too clever for you, and maybe for me, too.'

Winter nodded. In these situations it was always cool to pretend more knowledge than you actually had. Marty Harrison was obviously making moves to stitch up the narcotics supply city-wide and the news that he was moving into heroin would cause a sensation with Harry Wayte's boys. But then Marty Harrison was that kind of guy, a born player who'd happily expand his cocaine and dope empire to include nests of skag-heads and little twists of brown powder.

Winter leaned forward. Names would be good.

'We're talking Portsmouth, here?'

'Of course.'

Winter waited. Would three double vodkas have been sufficient for Juanita to put her head in the lion's mouth? Was she angry enough to grass up her sometime lover? To blow the whistle on Harrison's fast-expanding empire? To light a rocket under Winter's career?

She beckoned him closer, naming three major players on the Portsmouth drug scene, plus someone else he'd never heard of. The names slipped effortlessly into that bottom drawer in Winter's mental filing cabinet, the one that no amount of Stella could ever touch. These were the men Harrison had gone in with. This was the secret he thought he'd kept to himself.

Winter watched as she leaned back, swaying slightly, delighted with herself. She'd done it. She was back in charge of her own life. And now she wanted to celebrate.

'You're serious?' Winter raised an eyebrow and reached for his glass.

'*Sí.*' Juanita had produced a set of car keys. 'You drive.'

Winter drove away from the pub, trying to remember the grid of local roads that led to the forest. He'd been here before, never with someone so obviously up for it, and never with someone so beautiful, but he knew there were woodland car parks where it was possible to disappear for a discreet half hour or so. It was dark by now, the roads virtually empty, just a single pair of headlights way back in the distance. Juanita had her tongue in his ear and her hand down his trousers. Revenge, Winter had decided. This woman wants revenge. And why not?

'Quick,' she kept whispering, 'quick.'

Eventually, he remembered a particular bend in the road. A minute or so later, he pulled into a clearing edged with tree trunks. With the engine off, he could hear the wind in the branches overhead.

Juanita had already clambered into the back, flattening the rear seats. When he joined her, she was naked. He caught a flash of white teeth in the darkness. She had a grin like a kid.

'You tell *me* something,' she said suddenly. 'How come you all knew where he lived that morning you shot him?'

'Who?'

'Marty.'

Winter frowned. In the cramped darkness, he was having trouble getting his shoes off.

'Everyone knew,' he said.

'But he was in his girlfriend's house, not his house. So who knew that?'

'Fuck knows, does it matter?'

At last, the knot in his laces shook free. He kicked the shoe off and tore at his trousers, then lay back on the mattress, gasping. Then came the taunt of her fingernails dancing up the insides of his bare thighs.

'Was it the boy at the police station?' she said.

'Why?'

'I want to send him a present, that's all. You think he'd like this? You think this would be a nice present?'

She was in Winter's lap now, her fingers teasing him. He squeezed his eyes shut, determined not to come.

'He'd love it,' he said. 'If he'd got any sense, he'd fucking love it.'

Abruptly, she reached up, unbuttoning the top of his shirt. Then she settled herself on his face, supporting herself on her arms. Looking up, Winter could see her breasts swinging gently back and forth as she ground herself into his mouth. He began to lap at her, faster and faster, not quite understanding how deftly she'd managed to reverse the roles. Seconds later, with a deep groan, she collapsed full length on his half-naked body.

There was an interior light switch on the roof above the passenger seat. She reached up for it.

'I have something special,' she said. 'Something you'll like.'

The light was on for no more than a second. She was holding an aerosol can of some kind and her other hand had found its way to Winter's crotch. She began to stroke him and her face came very close in the darkness.

'You know what's in this can?'

Winter shook his head. He thought he was going to burst.

'Tell me.'

'Spearmint cream. My second favourite taste.'

'Second favourite?'

'Sí.'

Winter heard the hiss of the aerosol in the darkness and a sudden chill in his lap. When he looked down, he could see nothing but white foam. Juanita was using the aerosol again, this time to cover her breasts. Her fingers uncovered her nipples and as the head-lights swung into the car park, she offered one to Winter.

'What the fuck's that?'

Winter was up on one elbow, peering out through the window. He could see the low outline of a car behind the headlights. The headlights were pointed directly at the Jeep, as steady as a gun.

'Shit.'

He reached for his trousers. He was four pints down. He was covered in spearmint foam. And he had an erection that made getting out of the car geometrically implausible.

None the less, it had to be done. He'd been in these situations before. The last thing you did was wait for the inevitable. He'd never in his life done that. Not once.

Zipping up his trousers, he found the rear door handle and got out of the Jeep on the blind side. The car was maybe ten metres away. He could hear the engine and it began to dawn on him that this wasn't, after all, a spoil-sport patrol car. They'd have been out by now, with their torches and their notebooks, and the minute they sussed he was CID they'd piss themselves laughing. No, this was a private job. And infinitely more menacing.

Cautiously, Winter circled round the edge of the clearing, hugging the treeline. The car was a big Volvo and as he approached the driver's door he could see a face behind the wheel. It was a face he recognised and he paused in the darkness, staring at it. Slowly, the driver raised a single middle finger and shook his head. Then the back tyres spun, showering Winter with loose gravel, and the Volvo accelerated hard towards the blackness of the country road. Seconds later, it had gone.

Winter made his way back to the Jeep. Juanita was still crouched on the mattress, dribbles of spearmint foam dripping onto her bare knees. She looked badly frightened.

'Who was it?' she whispered.

'Dave Pope. Elaine's brother.' He was trying to catch his breath. 'Works for Marty, doesn't he?'

She closed her eyes a second, then reached for her T-shirt.

'I want to go home,' she said.

Seventeen

For the first time that Cathy Lamb could remember, Faraday skipped morning prayers entirely, abandoning the usual nine a.m. meet in the empty social club for an earlier and more intimate conference in the CID room. She'd been in for nearly half an hour when he arrived, nursing a cup of black coffee as she re-read the letter from Pete for the umpteenth time. It wasn't contrite, or even apologetic, but she recognised the voice behind it from the old days. He'd made a mess of things. He was camping at his mum's in Gosport. If she ever fancied a drink, he had plenty of time on his hands.

Faraday had a list. He plugged in the electric kettle, readied a tea bag in an empty cup, and produced an envelope from the pocket of his jacket. As far as Faraday was concerned, Cathy knew that lists spelled trouble. The DI normally carried everything in his head.

'Maloney,' he said briskly. 'We need to talk to the Queen's Harbour master and anyone else who might have been on the water that Friday afternoon. Skippers on the Fast Cat. Guys on the blue boats. Fishermen. Anyone. I want to know exactly what was happening on the harbour between four o'clock and seven. Same for the coastguards, and guys out on the Solent. Ferry skippers. Big boats in and out of Southampton. Even the Navy. But push the times on a bit, add an hour at least. We're interested in Spithead to Cowes. The boat would have been back in Cowes by dark. Check out the exact time it got back. Find out which marina they were using, and which berth. That should give you the names of his neighbours – other skippers and crews. We need phone numbers and we need to talk to them. Anything odd they might have seen around *Marenka*, anything—' he frowned, glancing up – 'unusual.'

'Like what?'

Cathy was making a list of her own, a series of increasingly savage squiggles.

'Like lots of cleaning aboard, like sackloads of stuff coming off. That boat was a scene of crime. They had plenty to clear up.'

Faraday ploughed on. He was interested in the two lads on the boat, the ones who had been lost at sea. They might have noticed tensions amongst the crew – especially between Maloney and the navigator, Henry Potterne – and they might have buddied up with other crews. Find these guys. Talk to them. Nail down the gossip.

Faraday paused, struck by another idea.

'The boy David Kellard,' he said. 'His parents live in the West Country somewhere. Talk to them, too.'

'Why?'

'He might have made a pre-race phone call. Said goodbye. Shared the odd thought. It's a long shot, but give it a go.'

Cathy had nearly run out of paper.

'And just where do you suggest I start with all this?' she said finally.

Faraday was pouring hot water on to his tea bag.

'Get bodies working the phones, the new lads, Moffatt and Pryde. There's no one left in Cowes, the boats have all gone, but the marina people are still there and they must have kept records. The boy Kellard should be simple. The race organisers will have his details. I've got their number.'

Faraday stirred yesterday's milk into his tea and made for the door. Cathy watched him, bemused.

'I'm still not with you,' she said. 'What are we saying here? Where's Maloney in all this?'

Faraday glanced back at her. He was trying to nudge the door open with his foot.

'I think he was killed on the yacht at Port Solent,' he said. 'And I think they dumped him on the way back to Cowes.'

Bevan listened, plainly unimpressed.

'It's bollocks,' he said bluntly when Faraday had finished. 'The busiest stretch of water in the country? At the busiest time of year? All those ferries? Container boats? Warships? Trawlers? Yachties? You're telling me they'd dump a body when the whole bloody world's watching? It's half-baked, Joe. If I saw this in a movie, I'd want my money back.'

Faraday didn't shift an inch. He'd been in this situation a couple of times before in his life, not as a DI, not as top dog, but as a lowly DC working under a boss with – as he'd thought – more imagination than sense. On both occasions he and his mates had privately scorned theories that stretched the known facts to breaking point – and twice they'd been proved wrong.

Like the time when a psychopath with a passion for necrophilia had killed his girlfriend and then spent half the night screwing her dead corpse. The only evidence was an empty box of Kodacolour Gold at the scene of the crime but the DI had thought the crime through and was convinced that this was the kind of lunatic who'd take pictures of himself in action. Everyone thought the DI was crazier than the killer, but when they finally arrested the guy in a run-down North London bedsit, his camera was on the dressing table and the undeveloped pictures were still inside it. Just one of those shots was enough to put him away. Case closed.

Now, Faraday heard himself paraphrasing that same DI.

'Chuck out what's absolutely impossible,' he told Bevan, 'and in the mess that's left behind you'll somewhere find the truth.'

Bevan wasn't having it. His division was hurting badly from lack of CID cover and a couple of overnight burglaries hadn't helped.

'Chuck out what's absolutely impossible,' he snorted, 'and you're left with fuck-all.'

'You said seven working days, sir,' Faraday reminded him.

Bevan was staring out of the window.

'Did I?' he murmured.

Paul Winter found Harry Wayte in his office at Havant police station. Between calls on break-ins at three Cosham off-licences, he just had time to drive up there for a meet.

Harry had once been in the Navy and he still had the beard to prove it. Unkinder souls thought he'd kept it to hide the wreckage of his complexion and that, as Harry was the first to admit, wasn't too far from the truth. An appetite for good Scotch had veined a face already cratered with teenage acne, and under certain circumstances a first meeting with Harry Wayte could be a scary experience.

Paul Winter had known him for years. When Harry was still a lowly DC, they used to drink together – on and off duty – and Winter had a fund of stories about Harry that could, he'd assure young CID aides, guarantee the guy early retirement. So far, Winter hadn't managed to convert any of this leverage into a posting on Harry's Drugs Squad, but he was a born optimist and rarely gave up without a fight.

'They're kosher, these names,' he assured Harry. 'You're going to love 'em.'

'Where did they come from?'

'Can't say.'

'That's what you told me yesterday.'

'Just goes to show, then. Always trust a man who's consistent.'

Harry, as always, was a far from easy sell. He moved in a world where truth was a currency, traded for favours, distorted for gain, abandoned when plain fiction seemed more plausible. Dealing with junkies, and the suppliers who kept them in their cage, you got to disbelieve absolutely everything, even the evidence of your own eyes. See a man with one head, he probably had two.

'Harrison's on the mend,' Harry said dryly. 'We can't even shoot straight these days.'

'So I hear.'

'And the guy who did it was pissed. You hear that, too?'

'Yeah.'

'The blood tests are back and the suits are kakking themselves. Lots of shit.' He grinned. '*Big* fan.'

He sat back behind his desk, covering a typed field report with a copy of *Modeller Weekly*. Wayte built the most exquisite replica warships, authentic to the last detail, and sailed them on a local lake.

'Harrison's moved into smack,' Winter said lightly. 'You hear about that?'

Harry looked at him for a moment. His eyes were the lightest blue, diluted by Scotch and overtime. Underestimating that watery gaze had put a lot of guys behind bars.

'Harrison *wants* to move into smack,' he said. 'You've got to get the timing right in this game.'

'Wrong, Harry.' Winter at last produced his list of names. 'He's made his move. I don't know whether it's partnership or takeover, but these are the guys he's running with.'

'Says who?'

'Says my little friend.'

Winter studied his fingernails while Harry looked through the list. Juanita hadn't wanted to know about sex after the car park but he'd absolutely no doubt that she'd be there for him again. Tonight, as it happened, he was free. They might sink a bottle of wine or two before they went back to her flat. Or he knew a couple of places where even Dave Pope wouldn't find them.

Finally, Harry looked up.

'When did you get this?'

'Yesterday.'

'Where from?'

Winter grinned at him over the desk, refusing to answer.

'I'd knock on their door if I were you.' He nodded at the list of names. 'Quite early in the morning.'

Faraday picked up one of the life drawings from Jan Tilley's office, then drove to Marmion Road. The gallery was empty once again, and while he waited for someone to appear he began to browse amongst the pictures on the wall.

Towards the back of the gallery, amongst the stirring oils of J-class yachts and pre-war ocean liners, Faraday found a watercolour of the entrance to Portsmouth Harbour. It was painted from the Gosport perspective and showed a skiff outward bound for the Isle of Wight. There were elements in the picture that reminded him of the little pen-and-ink study he'd found in Maloney's bedroom, and he was still studying it when he heard a movement immediately behind him.

'It's a Clarkson Stanfield, 1829. But only a print, I'm afraid.'

He turned round to find himself face to face with the woman in the life class. She was smaller than he'd expected. She was wearing a long cotton dress loosely gathered at the waist and there were silver bangles on her wrist that looked faintly Indian. She had a twist of scarlet ribbon in her hair and enormous hoopy earrings. Her face was tipped up towards him, shadowed by the spotlights, and her smile revealed a line of perfect teeth. For someone so new to widowhood, she looked remarkably self-controlled.

'Ruth Potterne?'

She nodded. She was looking at the roll of drawing paper in his hand.

'Something we might be interested in?'

'I'm not sure.' He produced his ID. 'Could you spare me a couple of minutes?'

They talked in a back office, amongst a clutter of invoices, bank statements, glue, masking tape and rolls of corrugated cardboard. When Faraday offered his sympathies over the loss of her husband, she acknowledged it with another smile, ghostlier this time, and then hurried the conversation on. She wanted to know why he was here. She needed to know how she could help him.

Faraday explained about Maloney. A week ago, he'd disappeared. There was evidence that he'd met her husband, that there'd been some kind of row. Would that have surprised her?

'Yes, to be frank. Henry wasn't one for rows, in fact he hated them.' She frowned. 'Who told you all this?'

Faraday described his visit to Maloney's flat, and the woman who lived across the hall. Ruth looked even more perplexed.

'But what was Henry doing there? They weren't pals

or anything. In fact socially, they were miles apart. Always had been.'

Faraday caught the inflection in her voice. Did that mean they didn't get on?

'Not at all. They got on perfectly well. On a boat like that, you have to. All I'm saying is that he and Henry were just' – she shrugged – 'different. I wasn't even aware that Henry knew where Stewart lived.'

Stewart.

Faraday had been watching her hands. She had beautiful hands, small, expressive, bare except for a single ring in silver filigree on the thumb of her left hand. He could visualise that hand cupping Maloney's face. He could see it, minutes later, outstretched on the pillow, palm up, the fingers flexing.

The door opened behind him.

'Would you care for some tea, Mr Faraday?'

It was the other woman, the woman he'd met yesterday when he'd first come in. Faraday said yes to camomile. She disappeared again.

Ruth was still talking about her husband. To be blunt, she had absolutely no idea why he should have gone calling on Stewart Maloney. Neither did she know why he'd have taken a taxi to Port Solent. There was an edge of impatience in her voice now. She was a busy woman. She was under all kinds of pressure. Just where was this little chat of theirs leading?

'Might there have been any other kind of' – Faraday paused, trying to find the right word – 'antagonism between Maloney and your husband?'

'On what grounds?'

'I don't know. I was hoping you might be able to help.'

'Then I'm afraid the answer's no. I'm sorry but that's the way it was. They knew each other. They got on OK. And that was that.'

'No jealousy at all?'

'On whose part? Henry's? Stewart's?'

Faraday smiled. It was a good question. In their separate ways, both men would have had grounds for jealousy. Henry slept with this woman. Maloney made love to her. Or at least wanted to.

'I'm talking about your husband, Mrs Potterne,' Faraday said softly, 'and I'm simply asking whether or not he was the jealous type.'

Her guard lowered an inch or two. Faraday could see it in her eyes. She was genuinely curious.

'You're right,' she said at last. 'He was very jealous.'

'And did he drink a lot?'

'Yes, as a matter of fact he did. But then he'd always drunk. That's what ex-service people do. It's in the blood. It comes with the job description. Everyone does it.'

'Did it ever get out of hand?'

'A bit, yes, sometimes.'

'Why?'

This time the question was a direct challenge, and she knew it.

'Because—' She frowned. 'Because I suppose he couldn't always cope.'

'With what?'

'Everything.' She gestured around with one hand. 'This, the business. My son. Me.'

'What about you?'

'Nothing really. He was jealous, that's all.'

'Should he have been?'

'No, but there were times . . . I don't know . . . some men get funny and Henry was one of them. They don't need reasons. It's just the way they are. They get an idea in their heads and that's that. There's nothing you can say. They've just made up their minds.'

'About what?'

'About anything. Another man looks at you and instantly that becomes an affair. Or it would from

211

Henry's point of view. He was very possessive. He was always jumping to conclusions, always thinking the worst. And that can be difficult to live with, believe me.'

'But you loved him?'

'Absolutely.'

'And he had no reason to think that—' Faraday hesitated again. 'He might be sharing you with someone else?'

'God, no.'

Faraday unrolled the student's drawing. Ruth stared at it.

'Where did you get that?'

'The university.'

'It's me.'

'I know. Why did you do it?'

'For money,' she said hotly. 'Eight pounds an hour if you're interested. Have you ever tried to live off the takings from an art gallery like this? No wonder he drank.'

'Who asked you to pose?'

'Stewart Maloney.'

'Why?'

'I don't know . . . because . . . ask him.'

'Are you friends?'

'I know him, yes.'

'But are you . . .?'

'Friends like real friends? No, Mr Faraday, we're not.'

'He's got your photos on his wall. Shots of the city.'

'I'm flattered.'

'You're telling me you didn't know?'

'I knew he'd bought some. But I haven't a clue what he's done with them.'

'You've never been inside his flat?'

'God no, I'd never get out in one piece.'

'He phones you.'

'All the time.'

'Why?'

'Because ... Christ, why don't you ask him? Why me? Why do I have to spell it out?'

'Because he's disappeared. As I think I explained earlier.'

'Oh ... and you're assuming—'

'I'm not assuming anything. Actually, that's not true. What I'm assuming is that he had a thing about you. And that you knew it.'

'That's true.'

'You're saying he's been pestering you?'

'Yes.'

'Harassing you? Stalking you?'

'No, that's not his style. He's completely up front. It's not creepy at all. He just comes out with it.'

'With what?'

'I'd rather not say ... if you don't mind.'

'I do mind. Tell me.'

'OK.' She shrugged. 'He wants to have an affair. He'd like us to get it on.'

'And you've been posing for him? Knowing that?'

'I pose for the students.'

'Knowing the way he feels about you?'

'What he wants to do with me, yes. I'm not sure feelings come into it.'

'But is that wise?'

'Probably not.'

'Or even kind?'

'*Kind*?' She laughed. 'Maybe that's why I do it.'

'To taunt him?'

'Something like that.'

Faraday studied her for a long time. Not far away, he could hear the clink of china.

'And what about your husband, Henry? What did he think?'

'About Stewart?'

'Yes.'

'He thought what you're thinking. And he was as wrong as you are.'

'Meaning we have no grounds?'

'Meaning there's no way in the world I'll ever go with Stewart. None. Not ever. Not for money. Not for love. Not for the thrill of it. Not for anything. He knows that, by the way. Because I keep telling him.'

'Then you might be off the hook.'

'Why?'

'Because I think he's probably dead.'

Eighteen

Back at the station, Faraday compared notes with Cathy. She'd got the team working on the morning's actions and already Dawn Ellis had come back with a report on a conversation with David Kellard's parents. They lived in Exeter, but they'd come to Cowes on the Friday night to take their son out to supper on the eve of the race. They said that he'd been cheerful as ever and eager to get started. His special buddy aboard *Marenka* had been young Sam. He'd only known the boy a couple of days but already they'd persuaded the skipper to let them watch-keep together.

Faraday asked about Charlie Oomes. Had she checked with him exactly where the boat had been berthed, over in Cowes?

Cathy shook her head. She'd phoned Oomes's office but he'd been busy in a meeting. When she'd asked to talk to Derek Bissett, he was away on business and not back in the office until Monday.

'Where on business?'

'Germany.'

'How convenient. And Hartson? You manage to get hold of him at all?'

'No answer. I've rung three times so far and left messages.'

'OK.' Faraday nodded. 'Try Oomes again. We'll need another interview and before that see if you can lay hands on a plan of the boat. Get hold of the makers or something. We'll also need a warrant for Hartson's flat. We'll go up this afternoon. Can you talk to the magistrates?'

Bevan's secretary, Bibi, was standing at the door. The boss wanted five minutes. Now. Faraday followed her to the superintendent's office. The sight of Arnie Pollock sitting at the little conference table brought him to a halt in the open door. What was his CID boss doing here?

'Join us.'

Faraday sat down, exchanging nods with Pollock. Bevan stayed on his feet.

'That bloody woman's been on again,' he grunted.

'Which one?'

'Both, as it happens. Nelly Tseng is still threatening to write to headquarters, but that's not the real problem. It's the fact that she's been talking to our journalist friend. Kate Thingy. She phoned this morning.'

'And?'

'She says she's publishing regardless. I take that as a warning.'

'Publishing what?'

'She wouldn't say, not exactly. Except that it's about Port Solent and that it includes the dive search.'

'*Dive search*?' Faraday couldn't believe his ears. 'Who told her about that?'

'I did.'

Bevan at least had the grace to look shamefaced. He'd phoned her after listening to her audio tape and briefed her about the search for Stewart Maloney. At the time, it had seemed innocuous, a prime example of the lengths the police would go to when it came to missing persons. Treated the right way, it might even impress the likes of Nelly Tseng.

Faraday blinked, trying to get this thing straight in his head.

'So you gave her chapter and verse on Maloney? To keep her quiet?'

'I told her as much as she needed to know. She was

even talking about getting hold of a photo of Maloney. Under the circumstances, I imagined that might be helpful.'

'Did she ask for quotes from us? CID quotes?'

'Yes.'

'So who supplied those?'

'I did.' It was Pollock this time. 'Neville briefed me and I gave her a ring.'

'What did you say?' Faraday was staring at him. 'Sir?'

'I simply pointed out that Maloney was as entitled to his share of police time as anyone else. The man has gone missing. That, to us, may have serious consequences.' He studied his carefully buffed fingernails for a second or two, then looked up again. 'Unfortunately, this woman appears to be a loose cannon. We have absolutely no idea what she's going to write.'

'Does that matter?'

'Yes, I'm afraid it does.'

'Why?' Faraday was still thinking about Maloney. 'As far as the public's concerned, it's just like any other inquiry. We put divers down. We follow up various other leads. That's what they expect, isn't it?'

Pollock permitted himself a tiny frown. When events turned against him, he had a habit of steepling his hands together and resting his head on the tips of his fingers. Right now, he might have been at prayer.

'It's not the public we should be concerned about,' he said softly. 'It's HQ. There are sensitivities about media coverage. I don't want to go into it but we should be aware that they like to play it by the book.'

'Play what by the book?'

'Major inquiries. Like this one should be.'

Bevan nodded heavily and Faraday at last sensed where the conversation was going. Both men had a sudden interest in declaring Maloney the subject of a major inquiry, under the command of at least a detective chief inspector. That way, Bevan got his CID coverage back up to strength while Pollock would – in simple terms – cover his arse.

'You told me this morning you thought there was no case.' Faraday was looking at Bevan. 'So how come we're suddenly talking major inquiry?'

Bevan didn't even try to defend himself. Instead, he gestured towards the telephone and shrugged.

'She might change the equation completely,' he said. 'We just don't know.'

There was a long silence. Faraday looked first at Bevan and then at Pollock. Both remained totally expressionless.

'So how long have I got?' Faraday said at last.

'We understand she's publishing on Monday.' Bevan glanced at his watch. 'Give or take, I make that forty-eight hours.'

By the time Paul Winter found a moment to phone Juanita, it was early afternoon. He wanted to talk about uncompleted business. And he wanted to talk about Dave Pope. How come he'd tailed them to the car park? How come he'd just happened to be around?

At last she answered the phone.

'Me,' he said briefly, 'Paul.'

He settled behind the wheel of his car, letting the traffic sluice past. Just picturing this woman on the other end of the line was enough to give him the hots.

'You there, love?'

He could hear nothing. He held the mobile away from his ear, shook it, then tried again. Still nothing. Finally, he hit the redial button and waited for her to answer. When her voice came on, she didn't even give him a chance to start the conversation.

'You give me big trouble,' she said. 'Big, big trouble.'

The mobile went dead again, and Winter stared at it

for a full thirty seconds, his big face beaded with sweat.

Armed with a magistrate's warrant, Faraday and Cathy Lamb searched Ian Hartson's Chiswick apartment. The state of the place reminded Faraday of his first glimpse of Maloney's seafront apartment: a life abruptly interrupted. Amongst the litter of clothes, books, notes and newspaper cuttings about the Fastnet disaster, Faraday turned up a sheaf of bank statements. These revealed substantial transfers into Hartson's account. Faraday asked Cathy to take the details and commission further inquiries from the bank through the Force Intelligence Unit at Winchester. He wanted a source for the transfers, plus details of movements within the account over the last couple of days.

'If you push them, they'll turn it round in hours,' Faraday told her. 'Give them a ring.'

While Cathy talked to the FIU, Faraday dialled 1471 on Hartson's phone. His most recent call had come from a nearby travel agency. When Faraday phoned back, they confirmed an inquiry on behalf of Ian Hartson and despatch of ferry details for the crossing from Portsmouth to Bilbao.

Cathy had finished on her mobile. Force Intelligence were contacting NatWest with Hartson's details and expected a result before close of play.

Faraday nodded.

'Haven't come across his passport, have you?'

Cathy shook her head. Faraday had fired up Hartson's computer and she stood behind him, studying the files on the hard disc. He opened one marked 'Cape Clear' and found himself looking at the first draft for the feature film treatment commissioned by Charlie Oomes. He scrolled through the pages of dialogue, eavesdropping on the race that had caught

Hartson's imagination, and then stopped at a map showing the tracks of the lead yachts. There was an awful lot of ocean between Cowes and the Fastnet Rock.

Faraday stepped back from the screen, deep in thought. For the last twenty-four hours, he'd been trying to put himself in Henry Potterne's shoes. Say he'd killed Maloney at Port Solent. And say he'd sailed with the body aboard. Would it really have been that simple to slip it overboard on the passage back to Cowes? Or was Bevan right when he'd dismissed the possibility? Whatever the answer, a body on the boat at Cowes would have been even harder to dispose of. Hundreds of surrounding yachts. Partygoers by the thousands. And then, at dawn, serious last-minute preparations for the race itself.

Cathy was over by the window, thumbing through a pile of sailing magazines.

'Did you manage to lay hands on a plan of the yacht?' he asked her.

'*Marenka*?' Cathy nodded. 'It's in the car.'

'Good.'

Faraday returned to the PC. Within seconds, the printer had given him a copy of the map from 'Cape Clear'.

Cathy was watching him, puzzled.

'What's that for?'

'Reference.' He glanced at his watch. 'Let's hope Oomes is still at work.'

The headquarters of Oomes International were on a trading estate beside the M4 at Brentford. A high wire fence surrounded a car park, and a couple of spartan-looking warehouses bristled with closed-circuit television cameras.

At first, the receptionist dismissed the possibility of an interview. Without an appointment, no one got in to see Mr Oomes. Only when Faraday produced his ID did she consent to pick up the phone.

Charlie Oomes's office occupied a whole corner of the administrative block. The Venetian blinds were down against the hot slant of the late afternoon sunshine, and Charlie was at his desk, brooding over a spreadsheet on the computer screen. Back in the real world of profit and loss, he appeared to have dismissed the events of last week.

Faraday settled into a chair at the nearby conference table. He wanted an exact chronology of the race. He wanted to know everything that had happened from Friday night through to the moment when the yacht had gone down.

The back of Charlie's neck began to redden. He gestured impatiently at the grid of figures on the screen.

'Ever tried running a fucking business, by any chance? Ever tried keeping track of it all? Takes a bit of time. Time I don't have just now.'

'We could do this at my place or yours, Mr Oomes. Mine is in Portsmouth.'

Oomes spun round. For a split second, Faraday scented the possibility of physical violence. Then Oomes calmed down, tossing his pencil on to the desk.

'Class-wise we were odds-on to win,' he said. 'You wanna start there?'

Faraday declined the invitation. Painstakingly, he began to jigsaw the chronology of the Fastnet together. On Friday night, according to Ian Hartson, he and Henry had returned to Cowes in *Marenka*. True or false?

'True, obviously.'

'Where was she tied up?'

'The Yacht Haven marina.'

'What happened then?'

'They both came up to the Royal Corinthian. Me and Derek were already there. We all had supper.'

'How was Henry?'

'OK, perfectly normal.'

'Was he drunk?'

'No way. I've told you. Henry drank. He didn't get drunk, he drank. There's a difference.'

'Was he distressed at all? Upset?'

'No.'

'Was he ... did he look ... damaged at all? Bruised? Any signs that he might have been in some kind of fight?'

'No.'

Oomes was hunched at his desk now, his head tucked into his shoulders, the classic boxer's stance. He was playing it tight, giving nothing away. When Faraday asked which table they'd occupied, and exactly what time they'd eaten, he shrugged. It was mid-evening. It could have been any fucking table. He couldn't remember.

'Really?'

'Yeah, really. And you know why? Because since then we've all been to hell and back. I can't remember where the table was and I can't remember the name of the waiter's mother-in-law. Oh, and by the way, I just lost three good friends at sea. Does that sound reasonable to you?'

'But you had a booking?'

'I expect so. Henry handled all that. He was a member. Phone them. Ask them.'

'Was it busy that night?'

'It's always busy.'

'So other people would have seen you?'

'Of course. If they'd got nothing better to look at.'

Faraday watched Cathy scribbling notes. He'd make sure she had someone over in Cowes first thing tomorrow, testing every link in Oomes's story.

'So where were the two lads that night? Sam and David?'

'Dunno. Out, somewhere.'

'When did you next see them?'

'Saturday morning. Half past nine. We all met for breakfast.'

'At the house?'

'Of course. I gave them a pep talk. Not that they ever fucking listened.'

'So they wouldn't have been on the boat since . . . ?' Faraday frowned, waiting for an answer.

'Thursday. That was our last race round the cans. And we call it a yacht, by the way, just for the record.' Oomes nodded at Cathy's notepad. He was still combative, still angry, but he was stepping carefully now, doing his best to keep Faraday at arm's length.

Faraday wanted to know exactly where *Marenka* had been berthed in the Yacht Haven marina on Friday night.

'Why?'

'We may decide to send divers down.'

'Why would you want to do that?'

Faraday ignored the question. Were the berths numbered? Did you have to book ahead? There must have been a record, surely, of where the boat had been moored?

'We tied up alongside another yacht,' Oomes said. 'I think she was one of the Aussies.'

'Did you go out again that night?'

'No way. Another couple of guys made fast to us. We were tucked up for the night.'

'Have you got names for these boats?'

'No. And it's a big marina. You're talking maybe a hundred yachts. Every night you've got a different neighbour. God knows who it was on Friday.'

'We'll check, then.'

'Good fucking luck.'

Oomes had picked up the pencil again. When Faraday asked about the race itself, and the choice of course that first night, he began to tap it on his desk.

'You had a choice,' he said slowly. 'You either followed the herd and rock-hopped down the coast, or you put a good deep tack way down into mid-Channel. The coast can be tricky. There are loads of tidal gates. Miss one of them and you're going backwards. It's all down to the weather in the end, the weather and the wind.'

'So what did you do?'

Faraday produced the map he'd taken from Hartson's printer and now he spread it on the table. Oomes glanced at it without comment.

'We went south,' he said. 'Looking for the wind.'

'And the rest of them?'

'They mainly stayed inshore.'

'Why?'

'Because that was their punt. The Fastnet's a gamble. Saturday the wind was shit. It was coming at us from the south-west but there wasn't much to it. It could have done any fucking thing. The guys who stayed inshore were looking for a freebie on the tide. Like I say, we went south.'

'Who's idea was that?'

'Henry's. He'd been dialling up the weather people all afternoon. There's an outfit in Florida gives you read-outs from weather buoys and whatnot right down the Channel. That's all Henry needed. Give him the raw data and he could find wind in a vacuum flask. Guy was a genius.'

Faraday paused, struck by this piece of hi-tech wizardry.

'What do you mean, dialling?'

'Henry had a laptop and a mobile. That close to land, you can access the Internet through a modem. It's chicken-shit. Any kid could do it. Couple of seconds for the connection, and Henry could give you the weather anywhere in the world.'

'Henry used the laptop a lot?'

'All the time. Plus he had a couple of PCs, one for home, one for the business. I used to give him a deal on the hardware and bundled all the software he could handle. He loved it, loved it. Bloke was a natural around computers. Some of the nav programmes he actually offered to improve.'

Faraday nodded.

'So Saturday night, at Henry's suggestion, you went south . . .'

'Yeah, and you know something? He was right. Midnight Saturday the wind backed southerly, just the way he'd said it would. Little anticyclone, slipping eastwards, way out in the Channel. It was so small every other fucker missed it. The inshore boys were gutted. We'd stuffed them.'

'You were out there on your own?'

'Absolutely.'

'No other boats around?'

'Obviously not, that was the whole point.'

Faraday was staring at the map, trying to imagine the fleet thinning as they pushed west. Most of the boats had stayed inshore, tacking against the wind from headland to headland. *Marenka*, on the other hand, was way out in the Channel, cloaked by darkness.

From his briefcase, Faraday fetched out the plan of a Sigma 33 that Cathy had acquired from a local chandlery. He laid the plan beside the map, taking his time.

'You had a watch system?' he asked at last.

'Everyone has a watch system. Four hours on, four hours off.'

'The two lads, Sam and David, were they on the same watch?'

225

'May have been.'

'David's father says they were.'

'Is that right?'

'Yes. When they were off-watch, they'd get their heads down, wouldn't they?'

'If they were lucky, yeah.'

'Go to sleep even, down below.'

'Might do.'

'Where, down below?'

'In the main cabin. It's pretty much of a slum but that's where you kip.'

Faraday reached for the plan. Thick in the waist, *Marenka* tapered gracefully towards the bow. Forward of the tiny loo, beyond a bulkhead, lay the forecabin. Faraday's finger hovered over the bow.

'There's a hatch above the forecabin, isn't there?'

'Yeah. It's small, though.'

'But big enough for a sail bag?'

'Sure.'

'So if you wanted to get something out of the forecabin without using the main cabin . . . you could do it, couldn't you?'

Faraday waited for an answer. Oomes was staring at him.

'Like what?' he said.

Faraday ignored the question. He was still studying the plan of the Sigma when Oomes leaned forward, stabbing a thick forefinger at the very middle of the boat.

'Listen,' he said, 'this is a fucking garden shed you're talking about. Five paces end to end down below. It's tiny. I've measured it. This forecabin you're on about isn't at the end of some fucking corridor. It's just the other side of the bog. And the bog is smaller than a wardrobe. We're talking intimate here. You wanna keep something nice and private, forget it.'

'Why would you want to do that?'

'I wouldn't. Because I couldn't. And that's the whole point. OK?'

Faraday abandoned the boat plan and returned to the map.

'I need to know exactly where you went down.'

'I can't tell you.'

'You can't?'

'No way. We were south of Land's End around midnight, then we headed north-west. The weather was shit already. The wind backed to the south-east and we were flying. By one in the morning it was off the clock. I tell you, we were down to a storm jib and thinking of binning that. Huge fucking seas. Stuff coming at us from everywhere. Then the wind stops. Then it starts again. Bang on the nose, right out of the north-west. We didn't know where we fucking were. It was all we could do to keep the boat in one piece.'

'Yacht,' Cathy said quietly.

'Yacht, then.' Oomes hadn't taken his eyes off Faraday. 'They clocked those winds at force eleven. Force *eleven*. That's one down from a hurricane. It was unbelievable. You ask me where we came to grief I have to tell you I haven't a clue. The guys who picked us up will have a position but that was hours later.'

Faraday permitted himself a tiny frown. From Land's End to the Fastnet Rock was nearly a hundred and eighty miles.

'So she could be anywhere . . . ?' he said.

'*Marenka*?' For the first time, Oomes smiled. 'I'm afraid so, my friend.'

There was a long silence. Then Oomes glanced pointedly at his watch and got to his feet. He had an important client to meet in less than an hour's time. If he didn't get his figures together, the guy would have flown halfway across the world for nothing. Faraday nodded, then rolled the yacht plan inside the map and secured them both with an elastic band.

Beside the door was a photo of Charlie Oomes and Derek Bissett at some function or other. They were sitting at a table, sharing a bottle of champagne, their glasses raised to the camera.

Faraday paused, then glanced round. Oomes was sitting at his desk, his back turned, staring at the computer screen. Faraday mentioned the rumour he'd heard about Bissett when he was still with the Thames Valley force. Charlie had offered him bungs to put police contracts his way. Not just bungs but the guarantee of a job once Bissett's days in uniform were over. Did Charlie have a view on that?

Oomes didn't move. Faraday stood patiently by the door, awaiting a reaction. Finally, Oomes's left hand steadied on the computer keyboard. He didn't bother to turn round.

'Can you prove any of that drivel?' he said.

'Not yet.'

'Then don't waste my fucking time.'

They were nearly back on the M25 before Cathy began to voice her reservations. She'd listened to Faraday over the last couple of days. She'd listened to him building theory on theory, pushing his assumptions just as far as they would go. Some of the links he'd made were blind guesswork. Others were really shrewd. But was he really suggesting that Charlie Oomes and the rest of his crew had somehow volunteered themselves as accessories to murder?

Faraday nodded.

'Yes,' he said.

'But Bissett's a copper.'

'Was. Until Oomes bought him.'

'And Hartson?'

'Oomes has probably bought him, too. Have the FIU come back yet?'

'No.' Cathy stared out at the flaring sunset. 'So what was in it for Oomes?'

'Winning. He wanted to win. That's all that mattered. That's all that's ever mattered. Without a navigator, he'd have been stuffed. He's practically admitted it himself.' He paused to pass a convoy of Eddie Stobart trucks. 'And what's the risk? He dumps the guy at sea on night one. According to Kellard's parents, the two kids have buddied up. They're off watch. They're probably asleep. They don't even know there's a body aboard. The boat's way out in the Channel. There's no one else around. Looks foolproof to me.'

'You're serious? He sets sail with a corpse? You really think he'd take a gamble like that?'

'I know he would. He's been gambling all his life. That's what the firm's about. He's a guy who loves cheating the odds. Show him a challenge and he can't resist it. He'll square every circle. Just as long as he wins.' He glanced across at her. 'You don't see it, do you?'

Nineteen

Back in Portsmouth, Cathy found the details of the FIU inquiry waiting on her computer. The bulk of the major transfers into Ian Hartson's bank account had come from Charlie Oomes. The most recent, a sum of fifteen thousand pounds, had been deposited only yesterday when Hartson had also withdrawn eight thousand in cash from his local Chiswick branch. Cathy pointed out the time at which the counter transaction had been logged. Twelve forty-six. They'd missed him by barely an hour.

'Where do you think he went?'

Faraday was asking himself the same question. From memory, the Bilbao ferry sailed on Tuesdays and Saturdays. Tomorrow was Saturday, and he'd certainly get someone down to the ferryport to watch embarking passengers, but it seemed unlikely that Hartson would sail from here. With eight thousand pounds in your pocket there were a million ways of getting to Spain. Why risk Portsmouth?

Next door, in his own office, was a note for Faraday from Jerry Proctor, the SOCO. A preliminary trawl through Charlie Oomes's Port Solent house had produced nothing of any interest – certainly no signs of a struggle. He was quite prepared to give the premises a thorough turning-over but there were cost implications and he would need an overtime code before proceeding. Faraday thought about it for a moment or two and then scribbled a note in reply. He hadn't got the code Proctor needed and in any case he sensed that Neville Bevan had been right all along.

Anyone prepared to surrender their house keys had little to fear from the forensic boys.

Faraday looked up to find Cathy at the door. She was about to go home but he called her back.

'We need to check out the radio traffic,' he said. 'Messages from Oomes's boat during the race. I don't know how it works but you need to cover all the bases. VHF. Mobiles. Whatever. Then I need a look round a Sigma 33.' He smiled. 'I was wondering whether you could organise that, too?'

'Like how?'

'Like talking to Pete. He's bound to know someone.'

Cathy stared at him for a long moment, then rummaged in her bag for an address book. Taking the pen from his hand, she checked for a number and scribbled it on a pad by Faraday's elbow.

'What's that?' he said blankly.

'That's Pete's mum. I gather he's in most nights. Do you mind phoning yourself?'

Winter knew the geography of Port Solent by heart. From the terrace of a pub called the Mermaid, you could look across the water into the middle of the horseshoe formed by the apartment block. The balconies were all on the inside of the horseshoe and Juanita's place was up on the fifth floor.

The Friday night crowd were already three deep at the bar and after elbowing his way to a pint of Kronenburg, Winter settled himself on the terrace, abandoning his copy of the *News* for an occasional check on Juanita's flat. He had an intense respect for big Dave Pope. If anything, Elaine's brother was even more volatile, even more dangerous, than Marty. Quite why last night's events in the car park hadn't gone further was still beyond him.

It took another pint and a half before Winter had his answer. First on to the balcony was Juanita.

Tonight she was wearing a flame-coloured halter and she spent several minutes studying the view before glancing up at the darkening sky and disappearing inside. Fifteen minutes later, Winter was engrossed in a preview of Pompey's prospects for the coming season when his mobile began to chirp.

He answered it at once, still deep in the paper.

'I don't know why you read that crap,' said a voice.

Quicker than he should have done, Winter looked up at the apartment block. Dave Pope was standing on Juanita's balcony, one hand raised in a derisive wave.

At home by mid-evening, Faraday found a typed A4 envelope with a London postmark amongst his mail. Ripping it open, he emptied the contents on to the kitchen table. With the big colour photograph was a letter of congratulations. Mr J. Faraday had won second prize in a competition organised by a leading wildlife magazine. Enclosed was a cheque for three hundred pounds.

Faraday picked up the photograph. It showed a gannet that J-J had snapped on one of their birding expeditions to North Yorkshire. They'd joined a party of birders on a boat trip out of Bridlington. They'd spent most of the day at sea and towards the end of the afternoon they'd found themselves amongst a group of diving gannets in pursuit of a shoal of fish. It was only J-J's second outing with the 300mm lens that Faraday had bought him for Christmas, but as the birds began to feed he'd got lucky with the focus, catching a plunging gannet a split second before it hit the water.

Faraday looked at the photograph now, as amazed as ever at its power and impact. The gannet's long wings arrowed back from its body. Its neck was outstretched, its eyes were open, and J-J had captured perfectly the soft blush of apricot on its head. The wave at the foot of the frame was thrusting upwards, laced with spume, and half-closing his eyes Faraday was afloat again, gazing out as bird after bird plunged down, pocking the grey sea with little explosions of white. Janna would have been proud of a shot like this, and prouder still of the cheque. Three hundred pounds could have got J-J safely to France. Three hundred pounds would have kept *The Birds of the Western Palearctic* intact.

Faraday put the photograph and the cheque to one side, and sank into a chair. Making any kind of peace with J-J's absence was less than easy. Most of the time he was able to take Cathy's advice and push the boy to the very back of his mind. Other times he was just angry – angry with his son and angry with himself. But tonight, remembering the gannets, it was altogether more simple. He missed J-J. He missed his company, and his laughter, and his flailing arms. Without him, the house felt suddenly chill and empty, a tomb-like reminder that he was well and truly on his own.

Outside, it had begun to rain. On Friday nights, the traffic was streaming into the city but Faraday drove in a trance, oblivious to the blur of headlights around him. Ruth Potterne lived in Southsea. He had the address. He even knew the road, one of those sinuous tree-lined Thomas Owen streets that were the city's sole concession to gentility and good taste. When he found the house, a light in a first-floor window offered a glimpse of bookshelves and a corner of plaster coving picked out in buttermilk and soft reds. Janna's colours he thought, getting slowly out of the car.

Ruth Potterne answered his second knock. Barefoot, she was wearing a pair of jeans and a baggy old sweatshirt with 'Navy Gun Crew' across the front. She had a glass of wine in her hand.

It took her several seconds to recognise him. The rain had flattened his hair against his skull and drips from the lime tree were patterning his shirt. He began to apologise for calling so late, surprised at how tongue-tied he'd suddenly become, but when she stepped aside and invited him in, he felt unaccountably glad. The house smelled of joss sticks. The colours of the oriental rugs, and wall hangings, spoke yet again of a world he hadn't seen for twenty years. Janna's taste. Janna's daring. Janna's home.

Faraday heard himself talking about Stewart Maloney. Inquiries had reached the point where he had to be sure about events in his private life.

'Sure how, exactly?'

'Sure that you two weren't' – Faraday risked a smile – 'together.'

'You don't believe me?'

'It's not a question of belief, Mrs Potterne. It's a question of evidence.'

Something in that sentence made her flinch. Faraday could see it in her eyes. Was it the mention of belief? Was it the need for evidence?

'Call me Ruth.' She returned his smile. 'Would you like a glass of wine?'

Upstairs, in the living room, he accepted a glass of Chilean red. Her photos were everywhere, hung in random patterns against the deep, plum-coloured wallpaper. The contrast with the bleak white spaces of Maloney's seafront apartment couldn't have been more obvious.

'So how do you propose to acquire this evidence?'

Faraday blinked at the question. He hadn't thought this conversation through. For once in his life, he was completely lost.

'We'll need some DNA . . .' he began.

'Some what?'

'DNA. A mouthswab will do. Or hair, if it's easier.'

'But I thought Stewart had disappeared?'

'He has. It's your DNA we're talking about.'

Faraday tried to pull himself together, explaining how he'd look for a match on items from Maloney's flat. Something like a pillowcase from his bed. It was nothing more than a formality, a closing-down of a certain line of inquiry.

Ruth had settled into a chair beside the open fireplace.

'You want to do it now? Here?'

'We can do it whenever it's convenient. The kit's back at the station. I'll arrange for a policewoman to give you a ring.'

'Should I have a lawyer with me?'

'If you want to, of course you can. It's your choice.'

'Fine.'

'You don't mind?'

'Not at all. Why on earth should I?'

Faraday tried to think of an answer but couldn't. Ruth took a sip of her wine, then put it carefully to one side.

'So why are you really here?' she asked him.

Startled, he returned her gaze for a moment or two and then told her that he didn't know. It was a moment of absolute candour, and he felt all the more foolish because he couldn't account for the fact that he'd said it, for the fact that he'd even knocked on the door. Was it something to do with J-J? With memories of Janna? With working eighteen-hour days to no great effect? It was true. It was shameful. He just didn't know.

'My son left home a couple of days ago ...' he began.

She nodded and gestured for him to carry on, and moments later he found himself telling her about J-J, about his new French girlfriend, and about the boy's absolute conviction that his future lay with a virtual stranger in a foreign land. She was clever, this woman Valerie, much cleverer than J-J. She'd twist him this way and that, use him, take advantage of his innocence.

'I know she will,' Faraday said. 'I've met her. I've seen them together.' Ruth looked at him for a long moment, then shook her head.

'You're talking about loss, not innocence.'

'You're right.'

'Your loss.'

'Right again.'

'And it hurts. Of course it hurts. I lost my own son five days ago. It hurts a great deal.'

Faraday closed his eyes. He'd met this woman only yesterday. He'd met her in the gallery. He'd sympathised about the loss of her husband. Yet he hadn't said a word about her son. Sam had drowned at sea. And clever old Faraday had said bugger all.

'So what does that make me?' he said aloud. 'Apart from stupid?'

Ruth waved his apology away.

'It doesn't matter. There's nothing you can say anyway. Here' – she passed him the bottle – 'help yourself.'

Faraday hesitated for only a second. He liked the smell of this place, its warmth, the feeling that someone else in the world might understand him. He wasn't here to cross-question her, to push his working day still deeper into the evening, but as the wine slipped down he realised that it was happening anyway. He wanted to find out about Ruth Potterne. He wanted to know about her marriage, and her efforts to broker a peace between her son and her new husband. He wanted to understand where she'd come from and what it was that had first attracted her to Henry Potterne. Not because he was a detective, hunting for bits of the jigsaw, but because he felt old, and abandoned, and suddenly needful. Friendship would be good. He'd settle for that.

She was talking about the summer she'd first met Henry. She'd been living on a semi-derelict houseboat on the Isle of Wight with her ten-year-old son, trying to make a living for herself as a photographer. She did portrait work for friends, and friends of friends, and she even stooped to doing the odd wedding, but her real love was for art photography and to make a success of that she had to find an outlet.

'Henry had a gallery in Southsea,' she said, 'a tiny place in the back streets, totally chaotic. I'd heard of it from a painter friend so I just took an armful of stuff over.'

She'd been thirty-three years old. She remembered the date because it happened to be her birthday. She'd let the fact slip and Henry had taken her to lunch in a pub in Old Portsmouth. He'd liked her work a great deal. The word he'd used was 'compelling'.

'He was right.'

Faraday was looking at one of the shots on the wall. Unusually for Ruth, it was in colour. A low sun spilled shadows across an eternity of gleaming sand. In the far distance, a tiny row of beach huts.

Ruth laughed.

'That was Bembridge Harbour, just down from the houseboat. Imagine waking up to that every morning. It was a photographer's dream.'

'You've got more?'

'Hundreds. You'll regret this.'

She left the room and returned with a big fabric-bound album. Faraday began to leaf through them, pausing from time to time to study a particular shot. The younger Ruth had a thing about skies and the reflection of light in water. Time after time, Faraday found himself looking at a dizzying tumble of cloud, often framed by mud flats or sand, occasionally anchored by a thin strip of horizon. The album spoke of sunshine and space. Not one photograph contained a human being.

'Where's Sam, then?'

'He got snapped. Snaps are different.'

'And the houseboat?'

'Coming right up.'

She disappeared again. The next album was even thicker: page after page of tiny details from the houseboat, carefully lit and photographed through a variety of lenses. The pattern from the corner of a lace curtain, with a smudge of sand dune in the background. The eye of Sam's pet goldfish, later lost in a muddle over a change of water. The tip of an icicle, coldly blue against the rough nap of a hanging towel. Once again, there were no concessions to the obvious, no shots that might show the whole of the boat, that might help the casual observer get a fix on where this woman had once parked her life.

Was it deliberate, this lack of clues? Or had Ruth been deliberately reluctant to reveal anything as ordinary as an address?

The questions made her smile. She took the album and turned to a page near the back. It was an exterior shot this time, a close-up of the boat's name, either the bow or the stern, the grain of the wood clearly visible beneath the layers of carefully applied paint, but once again Faraday was denied the whole picture.

'*Kahurangi*?' he queried.

'It's a Maori word. It means something you really treasure. Sam was born in New Zealand. We didn't leave until he was nearly eight. He loved it there.'

She explained that his father had been a charter skipper, delivering yachts all over the world. He and Ruth had met in Australia and moved to New Zealand when she found out that she was pregnant.

'You divorced?'

'We never married. We just ran out of steam. He

238

came back here and took a job in Cowes and in the end we followed.'

'Why?'

'Because Sam missed him so much. It wasn't fair to stay out there. Here was much better from his point of view.'

Sam had seen lots of his father, staying over in Cowes with him and his new partner. That was where he'd learned to handle a dinghy. By the time he went to secondary school, he was regularly winning cups at local regattas.

The memories made her eyes swim and she looked down for a moment, embarrassed. They were on the second bottle of wine by now and Faraday's awkwardness had gone. This time he made a much better job of saying he was sorry. Losing a twenty-two-year-old to a French social worker was bad enough. Having your only son die was unimaginable.

'Where's Chris now?'

'In the Caribbean somewhere. He took a chartering job. I've been trying to get hold of him about Sam.'

Abruptly, she left the room again. He heard her blowing her nose, then came a series of kitchen noises. She was putting the kettle on. They'd have coffee. And then he would have to go.

He reached for the first album again. A section near the back was reserved for wildlife shots. Leafing through, he was trying to imagine her ten years younger when his eye fell on a bird. It filled the frame. It was on a pebbly beach at half-tide or less. There were growths of seaweed on the rocks and the mud flats behind still glistened in the low sun. The bird was a dark, mottled colour, perfectly camouflaged against predators, and Ruth had caught it exactly at the moment its head had turned. Most bird photographers judged the eye to be the test of a good shot. The eye was all-important. The eye was what you went for when you hunted for focus and resolution. Yet here was Ruth, breaking every rule, and coming up with a photograph that – to Faraday – exactly captured the essence of the bird. The sturdy little body bent forward, the tail tilted in the air, and a blur where the head should be. Like J-J, she should have put it in for a competition. And like J-J, she would doubtless have won a prize.

A movement at the door broke his concentration. Ruth was holding a tray and doing her best to peer over his shoulder.

'It's a turnstone,' Faraday said. 'I wake up to these little fellas every morning of my life.'

It was true. They lived on the mud flats below his bedroom window, dislodging stone after stone in the hunt for the food beneath. Watching them through his binoculars never failed to cheer him up. Their dedication. Their persistence. The joy he sensed in their brief moments of stillness after a particularly juicy beakful of lugworm. For his fortieth birthday, J-J had drawn him a turnstone and hand-coloured it in nuptial plumage before mounting it in a handsome frame. Four years later, it still occupied pride of place in Faraday's study.

He told her about it now, J-J's picture, and she knelt on the carpet before the hearth, easing down the plunger on the cafetière. Sam had been keen on them too. That first summer, in the evenings, he'd squelch across the mud flats, waving his arms, trying to catch them. He never did, of course, but he'd come back filthy, mud everywhere, trying to copy their call. She could see him now, back on the houseboat, sitting in the big wash tub, making his turnstone noise. It was loud and rattly. Trik-tuk-tuk-tuk, it went. Trik-tuk-tuk-tuk.

She poured the coffee, then turned her head away again, angry that she couldn't hide her grief.

'I've got turnstones,' Faraday murmured. 'You must come over to the house some time.'

Twenty

A call from Dawn Ellis awoke Faraday shortly after seven in the morning. He'd taken to sleeping with the mobile under his pillow and he rolled over with it clamped to his ear, trying to check the time. Saturday mornings used to be sacrosanct. Once.

'We had a serious wounding last night. I thought you ought to know.'

Faraday felt a deep chill, a coldness that reached way down inside. For some reason he wanted to defer the name. The name would be the worst news. He knew it would.

'Where did it happen?'

'Paulsgrove. You know that little cut off Alloway Avenue? Up near the shops?'

Faraday knew it only too well. Anson Avenue was only two streets away. He lay back against the pillows, listening to Dawn detailing the injuries. Knees pulped by a heavy concrete block. Lacerations around the head and shoulders. Ambush injuries. Pay-back injuries.

'Scott Spellar,' Faraday muttered. 'Has to be.'

Two of the four beds in the ward were empty. Scott Spellar lay in the corner, the bedclothes tented over his shattered legs. His face was bruised and swollen. He didn't seem to recognise Faraday at all.

Faraday drew up a chair and sat down. The boy's eyes had closed already, a gesture of infinite weariness, and Faraday looked at him for a long moment. The ward sister had shown him the X-rays from last night. In eighteen years, she'd never seen worse.

As gently as he could, Faraday tried to coax from the boy an account of what had happened. At first he refused to talk, even to acknowledge Faraday's presence. Then, half sentence by half sentence, a sequence of events began to emerge. He'd been drinking with some mates in a local pub. They'd played pool, had a laugh or two. Afterwards, he'd got a burger from a van. He'd been eating the burger, en route home, when the guys jumped him. There were three of them at least, maybe more. He could smell the drink on them. They'd dragged him into an alley and wrestled him to the ground. One of them had stood on his feet and another had sat on his head while the third guy did the business. He didn't think it had taken very long but he couldn't be sure. When he came round, it was raining.

He stared up at Faraday.

'What's up with my legs?' he said. 'No one'll tell me.'

Faraday, lying, said he didn't know. Care at the hospital was great. He'd be up and about in no time.

Scott's eyes were closed again. He didn't believe him and he didn't care. When Faraday asked for names, he shook his head. When he asked whether he knew them, he shook his head again. The denials meant he'd had enough.

Faraday bent towards him. Motive could wait. He wanted to find out first about Winter.

'Who?' The boy could barely muster the breath to answer but the shape of his lips told Faraday everything he wanted to know.

'Winter,' Faraday repeated, 'Paul Winter. The CID bloke who talked to you down at the Bridewell. After your dad died.'

Slowly, it dawned on Scott that Winter was the detective who'd made him trade details of Marty

Harrison's drugs operation in return for his own freedom.

'Fat bastard,' he mouthed.

'You remember him?'

Scott nodded. Then his tongue came out, moistening his lips. His teeth were a mess, three of them broken, a couple missing altogether. Faraday reached for the beaker with the plastic straw on the bedside cabinet but Scott shook his head.

Faraday glanced round for a moment. The ward sister was watching him from the nursing station. She tapped her watch and splayed both hands. Ten minutes. No more.

'Did you agree to work for Winter?'

'No way.'

'Did he approach you again? After the Bridewell?'

'Yeah.'

The boy's face twisted in pain for a second or two. Then he shifted his body weight beneath the sheets.

'I wanted my money off him. We had coffee. He said for me to talk to Marty, get in touch with him, like.'

'And did you?'

'Joking. I didn't want no more Marty.'

'But he still tried to persuade you? Winter?'

'Yeah. And I played along, like.'

'Why was that?'

'He still owed me.'

'He was paying you?'

Scott took a deep breath and gritted his teeth. Then the spasm passed.

'Yeah, but it was my money all along.' He stared up at the ceiling. 'Know what I mean?'

Faraday bent towards him, trying to follow the logic.

'You're telling me Winter was paying you with your own money? The money from your bedroom? And you're saying he still owes you?'

Scott nodded, his battered face grey with pain.

'Two hundred quid,' he muttered.

Paul Winter was sorting out an overnight break-in at a video store when Faraday caught up with him. Fratton Road was thick with Saturday shoppers and Winter was less than thrilled at surrendering part of his weekend to tossers who thought that nine boxes of worn-out videos were worth nicking. Faraday led the way to his car.

'Get in,' he said.

Winter was still musing about establishing patterns. These guys were into bulk theft, chiefly teenage horror. Did that make them middle-aged retards or adolescents off the Buckland estate or what? Faraday ignored the sarcasm. Winter had been winding him up for too long.

'Tell me about Scott Spellar.'

Winter was eyeing a fat blonde on the pavement with two kids and a doll in a triple buggy.

'Gone to ground,' he said. 'Haven't heard a peep.'

'Wrong. He's in the QA, as of last night, and he won't be playing football for a while.'

'Oh?'

'So who put him there? Any ideas?'

Winter shrugged. The blonde had crossed the road. When she turned to grin at him she gave him a little wave. It was the wave that did it for Faraday.

'I asked you a question. It would be nice, just for once, to get an answer.'

'I haven't got one. Because I don't know.'

'You're lying.'

'I beg your pardon?'

The question hung between them while Faraday wound the window down. Winter's aftershave was overpowering.

'You seized the eight hundred quid from his bedroom,' Faraday went on, 'and the boy says you kept two hundred back.'

'He's right.'

'So why didn't you give him the lot? Like I asked?'

'Because he's a scrote. And scrotes need incentives.'

'Incentives to do what?'

'Grass.'

'So you *did* try and turn him?'

'Of course I did. That's my job. You know this city. Without informants, we'd be fucked. Unless you think there's a better way.'

Faraday looked across at him. Winter was still staring out at the swirl of shoppers on the pavement. He seemed a million miles away.

'We took the two hundred quid back up to Anson Avenue,' he said at last. 'Dawn came with me.'

'Was Scott there?'

'No. Some twat mate of his.'

'And you were two-handed?'

'Yeah, me and Dawn.' Winter smiled. 'You wanted the money witnessed, boss. I was just following orders.'

Faraday tipped his head back and closed his eyes.

'So where's the money now? The two hundred he never got?'

'It's back in the crime property store. Check, if you want.'

There was a long silence while Faraday fought to contain his temper. Winter, as ever, had covered his arse. The best Faraday could do now was take the money to the hospital himself. That way, at the very least, he'd make sure the boy got it. Two hundred pounds might make a big difference if you were in a wheelchair for six months.

Winter was staring out through the windscreen. The smile had gone.

'Paulsgrove's no mystery,' he said softly. 'They sort things out themselves up there. The kid got a smacking. That's the end of it.'

'But from whom? Who did it?'

Winter shot him a look that was close to pity.

'Do you want a list? We pulled young Scottie at the weekend, right? We banged him up in the Bridewell and half of Paulsgrove were banged up with him. That's what happens on a Saturday night. That's where they all end up. They're not stupid, these people. They knew we were talking to him. They knew he ran all kinds of shit for Harrison and half of them had him well sussed already. They knew we had him by the balls. They knew he could have gone down for murder. So instead, he chose to grass up Harrison. There's a price for touting round his way. And he's just paid it.'

'As simple as that?'

'As simple as that. The moment he started telling us about his little trips to London, he was stuffed.' He nodded at Faraday. 'We both put him in that hospital, boss, you as well as me.'

Against her better judgement, Cathy Lamb phoned Pete at his mother's house. It was nearly eleven o'clock. He'd just got up.

Recognising her voice, he began a conversation but she cut him short.

'Has my boss been on to you? Joe?'

'No.'

'He wants to pick your brains about the Fastnet. He's got some weird idea about carting a body along and he needs someone to tell him he's talking crap. He seems to think you're some kind of expert.'

'Thanks.'

'I meant the Fastnet.'

'Really?'

Despite herself, Cathy laughed. She'd had a couple of conversations with Pete's mum about her new lodger and she couldn't believe he'd suddenly learned to do the washing-up. Not only that, but he'd volunteered for the shopping as well.

Pete was asking about Faraday. What, exactly, did he want?

'An hour of your time and a look round a Sigma. Can you handle that?'

'No problem.'

'You want me to give you his mobile number?'

'No thanks. I'd prefer to do it through you.' He paused. 'If that's OK.'

Cathy eased her chair back from her desk and stretched her legs. Her plans for a long walk on Hayling Beach were rapidly receding.

'I don't know,' she said. 'I think that counts as overtime.'

Minutes later, Faraday appeared in the CID room. When Dawn Ellis inquired about Scott Spellar he simply shook his head and changed the subject. He wanted to know about developments over in Cowes. What had the marina people come up with?

Dawn reached for her notes. According to the management's records, *Marenka* had berthed on the outer pontoon late on Friday, tying up alongside one of the Aussie boats. A trawl through the paperwork had unearthed the crew's details and Alan Moffatt had come away with a handful of phone numbers, most of them in Sydney. The bulk of the Australians had flown home by now.

'And?' Faraday was impatient.

'We've phoned them all, got hold of maybe half of them. Nobody remembers anything.'

'*Nothing*?'

'Lots about the storm. Nothing about *Marenka*.'

'Nothing about the crew? Henry Potterne? Hartson? Nothing odd they were up to?'

'Nothing.'

'What about the Royal Corinthian? Dinner that night?'

'Oomes had booked four covers for half eight. The waiter remembered two of them starting before the others arrived.'

'What time did they get there?'

'Soon after nine. The kitchen was still open. Just.'

'Did anyone get a good look at the two who were late? Potterne especially?'

'The waiter did, and I got hold of the people on the next table. The tables are quite close together. You can hear what's going on if you've nothing better to do.'

'What did they say?'

'The guy I talked to remembered Potterne and Hartson arriving. He thought Potterne might have had a drink or two but he wasn't outrageous or anything. In fact he was anything but.'

'What does that mean?'

'He scarcely said a word. According to this bloke.'

'Any marks on him? Bruising?'

'Not that he remembered.'

'Did he drink anything else?'

'Plenty. I saw the bill. They had four bottles of wine between them. Plus lots of Scotch afterwards.'

'Doubles?'

'Yes, and trebles.'

Faraday wandered across to the window and stared down at the car park. As hard evidence this was worthless, but the pictures it conjured in his mind were all too vivid. If Potterne had really killed Maloney, and if Maloney's body was still on that boat, then you'd very definitely be in need of a drink or two. Potterne, according to Charlie Oomes, had played the elder statesman aboard *Marenka*. He was the one with the ocean-going experience. It was his judgement they'd rely on in the Fastnet. The race was due to start in less than twenty-four hours. Yet here he was, quiet as a mouse, with absolutely nothing to say. How come he was so preoccupied? What kind of problem had he just given himself and the crew?

Faraday turned away from the window. Dawn Ellis was back on the phone, talking to the coastal radio station at Falmouth, trying to nail down radio traffic from *Marenka*. Cathy had abandoned her phone for the kettle.

'Pete's happy to have a meet about the race,' she said. 'But I don't suppose he'd want to do it here.'

Pete Lamb turned up at Faraday's house at lunchtime. He was nearly an hour and a half late, blaming the delay on his sports car. The temperature gauge was off the clock. He'd had a poke around under the bonnet and eventually found a leaking head gasket so in the end he'd had to abandon the bugger in Gosport and come over by ferry and cab.

Faraday accepted the apology with a grunt. Pete's hands were spotless – not a trace of oil – but just now, a sloppy alibi for being late was the least of his problems. The results of the blood test were back from the lab, and according to Jerry Proctor he'd be lucky to escape with the sack. If the Police Complaints Authority had appointed an investigating officer who knew his business, Pete Lamb could be down for attempted murder.

Under these circumstances, Lamb seemed remarkably cheerful. Cathy had hinted at the onset of depression but Faraday had rarely seen him so buoyant. He was more than happy to help Faraday out. He'd brought a chart. Clear some space on the table and they could get going at once.

The chart showed the English Channel from Selsey

Bill to way out beyond the Scilly Isles. A series of pencilled zigzags led from Cowes to the Needles passage at the western tip of the Isle of Wight. From there, the zigzags broadened, following the shape of the coast as far as the toe of Cornwall. Off Land's End, the line angled north-west, coming to an abrupt end at a pencilled cross roughly a third of the way towards the Irish Sea. Faraday stared at the cross, fascinated.

'What happened there?'

'We capsized. Twice.'

'And?'

'Abandoned ship. After the second time.'

Faraday peered harder at the chart. There was a line of tiny numbers where *Tootsie*'s crew had taken to the life raft.

'Our position,' Pete explained. 'This isn't the original chart, of course. I've transferred all the details from memory.'

'But the position's right?'

'It's spot on.' Pete offered him a rueful smile. 'That was the GPS read-out the second time we went over. It's like winning the Lottery. You never forget the numbers.'

GPS was a hand-held electronic marvel carried nowadays by most yachts. Fed by data from satellites, it could fix your position anywhere in the world, accurate to a hundred metres.

'You had time to make a distress call?'

'Too right. In weather like that, you have someone sitting on the VHF. Beyond a certain sea state, it feels odds-on that you'll go over. The last thing you need is to be floating around in the middle of nowhere with the world looking the other way.'

Faraday told him about Charlie Oomes. For *Marenka*, the end had come so quickly that no one had managed to get a message out on the yacht's VHF.

'They got the life raft away?'

'Three of them did.'

'And they had the EPIRB with them? And a grab bag with a mobe?'

'The EPIRB definitely. I'm not sure about the grab bag.'

The EPIRB was a hand-portable radio beacon, lashed to the pushpit on the stern. Stowed elsewhere would be a grab bag stuffed with survival essentials, including a mobile phone. If you still had a brain, they were the last things you snatched before you jumped for the life raft.

'The EPIRB sends a position?'

'Yes. It's linked to a GPS and keeps transmitting the latest fix. It's good kit.'

Faraday produced a series of numbers Dawn Ellis had passed on from the Rescue Co-ordination Centre. They'd logged the position of every rescue and this one had featured Charlie Oomes.

Pete was studying the co-ordinates.

'When were they picked up?'

'14.16 on the Monday.'

Pete was using a ruler to calculate the exact position of the rescue. Finally, he pencilled a tiny cross due west of the Isles of Scilly and then stepped back from the chart, a frown on his face.

'That's well south of the track,' he said. 'What was he doing down there?'

'The yacht went over in darkness, just before dawn. I gather they had some problem with the beacon. Otherwise they'd have triggered it at once.'

'What was the matter with it?'

'Dunno. Apparently one of the guys fixed it. He's an electronics buff.'

'Fixed the EPIRB?' Pete glanced at Faraday. 'It's a sealed unit. You can't get at it.'

Faraday studied him a moment, and then went back

to the chart, trying to estimate the distance between the track to the Fastnet Rock and the point where the rescue helicopter had plucked Oomes and the others from their life raft. According to the scale, it was nearly thirty miles.

'You're telling me that's a long way to drift?'

'A helluva way. But then' – he shrugged – 'you're talking exceptional weather.'

'Force eleven winds? Out of the north-west?'

'After the eye had moved through?' He nodded. 'Yes.'

'And that would be enough to account for the drift? If they were in the raft for ten hours?'

'Yeah ... maybe ... what sort of state were they in?'

Faraday thought about the hospital ward in Plymouth. Nearly a day later, Oomes had been sitting up in bed with soup and a crusty roll but his face had been a mess and the other two were still suffering.

'Not good,' he said. 'Would that make sense?'

'Definitely. We were in the raft for less than an hour and I wouldn't want to go through that again.'

Faraday took him back to the start of the race. It was Saturday afternoon, just after lunch, and for the rest of the afternoon, the smaller yachts were tacking down the Solent towards the Needles.

'We cleared Hurst Castle around late afternoon,' Pete said. 'The wind was eight knots or so, maybe less. We wouldn't have been through the Needles Channel until six or maybe seven.'

Tootsie had been a twenty-nine-foot Sadler, broadly comparable to *Marenka*. Faraday's pencil had come to a halt at the very tip of the Isle of Wight. Ahead lay the passage across Poole Bay to St Alban's Head and the distant swell of the Purbeck Hills.

'Still lots of boats?' Faraday was looking at Pete.

'Everywhere. The maxis and the multi-hulls had

buggered off by then but you couldn't move for us weekenders.'

Faraday nodded. Returning to the chart, he wanted to know about the decision awaiting skippers beyond the Needles. According to Charlie Oomes, this was the moment when the race could be won or lost. You either stayed inshore with the lemmings, or drove south in search of glory.

'That's true. But it was a brave man who went for the starboard tack.'

His finger slipped down into mid-Channel. By abandoning the coast, he said, you were taking a huge gamble. The weather had been dominated by an anticyclone over northern France. Hence the light south-westerly winds. There was no evidence that this area of high pressure was about to move so the long tack south would serve no purpose at all. Later in the race, a deepening low-pressure system over the eastern Atlantic would come into play, changing the weather completely, but on the Saturday night, the smart money was on the inshore route. That, at least, had been the consensus aboard *Tootsie*.

'And were you right?' Faraday asked carefully.

'Yes. Unless you know different.'

'Oomes says there was a wind shift in mid-Channel. He says Potterne was right. He says it backed.'

'That's news to me.' Pete was staring at the chart again. 'Off-hand, I can't think of anyone else who went south. Who's this Potterne?'

'The navigator. One of the guys who died.'

'And he really found wind down there?'

'So his skipper says.'

'Then he must have been psychic. Maybe it was some local effect. A fluke breeze. It can happen.'

'Can we check? Are there records?'

'Sure. Talk to the Met Office. Or one of the private outfits. They pick up data from the weather-buoys.

Someone'll know. Someone always does. I'll make some inquiries, if you like.'

'*You* will?'

'Why not? It's not time I'm short of.'

Faraday studied him for a moment, puzzled by his tone of voice. It wasn't self-pitying, or even wistful, but totally matter-of-fact. There was a job to be done here. And Pete was glad to lend a hand.

He drew Faraday back to the chart.

'So your guys are down to the south here somewhere?' He drew an imaginary line into mid-Channel. 'Then what?'

Faraday shrugged. West of Pete's finger he could see nothing but white space, dotted with tiny figures.

'What are these?'

'Depth readings.'

'This one?'

'That's sixty-nine metres. Over two hundred feet.'

Faraday sat back, feeling suddenly pleased with himself. His theory, after all, had been right. They'd shipped Maloney's body out of Port Solent aboard *Marenka*. They'd wrapped him up and hidden him aboard, and at some point the following night, with the race under way, they'd slipped him quietly overboard. Weights would have taken him to the bottom. The bottom was hundreds of feet beyond the reach of a mere detective. Game, set and match to Henry Potterne. A genius indeed.

Faraday strolled to the tall glass doors and slid one back. He kept a bagful of stale crumbs for exactly moments like this one, and he took a handful now, tossing them on to the lawn. A couple of starlings appeared from nowhere, pecking savagely at the bread while Faraday shared his conclusions with Pete Lamb.

'You're telling me they *all* knew?'

'Not necessarily.'

'How come?'

Faraday explained about the watch-keeping system. If it was the middle of the night and both the young lads had their heads down, the others could have bundled Maloney overboard.

Pete glanced at the map again, unconvinced.

'I don't know the crew,' he said, 'and I don't know the personalities involved. But from where I sit—'

Faraday butted in.

'Oomes is a monster,' he said. 'He dominated them all.'

'Sure, but even so it's a hell of a gamble. OK, you can maybe hide the body but it's bloody uncomfortable down below and there's no guarantee the kids will get to sleep. For a start, there's all kinds of crap lying around and most of it's soaking wet. You've got spare sails, and boxes of food, and all sorts. Plus you're out in the ocean. The sea will be running from the west and on a beat like that the boat is taking it on the bow, thump-thump-thump, hour after hour. I don't know about a Sigma, but trying to kip on *Tootsie* was a nightmare. The mastfoot for one thing. It's rotating all the time, right above your head. Squeak-squeak-squeak. One of our guys even tried squirting washing-up liquid under it. Drives you insane in the end.'

'But you have to sleep sometime,' Faraday pointed out.

'Sure.'

'So maybe they did.'

'Yeah,' Pete said, 'and maybe they didn't.'

They were both still gazing at the chart when there was a knock at the front door. When Faraday opened it, he found himself looking at Cathy.

'Is Pete here?' she said. 'Only I've just had his mum on.'

Faraday stood aside, inviting her in. Pete was still in

the living room. The sound of Cathy's voice had brought a smile to his face.

'Hi,' he said, nodding at her.

She might have been a stranger. She was polite, but distant. Quickly, she told him about the call that his mum had taken. His divisional commander wanted him to ring urgently. Something about the inquiry into the Harrison shooting. Faraday nodded towards the phone, drawing Cathy into the kitchen. When he suggested coffee, she shook her head.

'I've talked to the race people again,' she said. 'They say they had no contact at all with Oomes during the race.'

'And the radio stations?'

'Dawn and one of the lads are still working on it. The favourite seems to be Pendennis. Channel sixty-two. When they get a moment, they'll check their records. Every boat has a call sign, by the way. *Marenka*'s was Bustler.'

'Nice.'

Faraday smiled. Next door, he could sense the conversation coming to an end. Seconds later, Pete was with them in the kitchen.

'My super,' he explained to Cathy, 'suggesting I get myself a good lawyer.'

'Why's that?'

'Positive on the blood tests.' His eyes found Faraday's. 'Fucked up big-time, didn't I?'

Twenty-One

Faraday was back in his office, waiting for a return call from Pendennis Radio when his mobile began to trill. It was Ruth Potterne. She got to the point at once. She'd been catching up on her paperwork and she'd found an e-mail that Faraday might like to take a look at.

'What does it say?'

'It's odd. It seems to be about a Wyllie.'

'A what?'

'He's a marine artist. Did lots of stuff round here. He's becoming hugely collectable.'

Faraday was trying to visualise Maloney's cramped little bedroom. The framed print beside his PC.

'Pen-and-ink stuff? Skiffs in the harbour entrance?'

'That's him.' She hesitated a moment. 'This e-mail came last Friday. I've only just seen it.'

'Is it signed?'

'Yes.'

'So who sent it?'

'Stewart Maloney.'

The PC was in a big first-floor study at the back of the house. It was obvious at once that the room had been chiefly used by Henry. There were dried flowers in extravagant vases, shelves of books on various naval campaigns and a couple of exquisite watercolours he'd obviously kept back from public sale. Watching Ruth at the keyboard, Faraday was reminded of a blind person in a strange room, every next step fraught with danger.

'I hate these things,' she admitted. 'Henry was the whizz with all this stuff.'

'He had a laptop as well?'

'Yes, he'd just bought himself a new one. He took it to sea with him. He'd send me messages sometimes, but I always forgot to check for them. We've got a perfectly good phone. Why didn't he use that?'

At last she managed to find the e-mail. 'Picked you up a Wyllie,' the message went. 'Guess who's home this afternoon? Love, Stu. P.S. Wipe this soonest!'

Love Stu?

Faraday stared at the screen. If he needed proof that she really had been involved with Maloney, that they knew their way around each other's lives, that they swapped fond messages and spent time together, then here it was, white script on a blue background, dancing in front of his eyes.

She held her hands wide, a gesture of helplessness.

'The man lived in his head. I'd no more go and see his bloody Wyllie than fly to the moon. And he knew that.'

Faraday waved a hand at the screen.

'Love, Stu?'

'Fantasy.'

'You never saw him? Never met at all?'

'Never. He used to phone me when he knew Henry was away. I think I told you. Listen to those calls, and you'd think we'd been lovers for years.'

'How did he know Henry was away?'

'Because he was with him. They were out sailing together. He'd sneak off before they left the marina. Or phone as soon as they got back. On Sunday mornings. It became a kind of joke. I could set my watch by it.'

'What did he say?'

'Pretty much anything. How good he'd be for me.

How natural we'd be together. How he just wanted the one chance. Lucky old me, eh?'

Faraday fought the temptation to believe her. Was it really credible that she'd fended him off all this time? That curiosity or boredom hadn't got the better of her? She was studying his reflection in the window. She could be almost psychic sometimes.

'I needn't have shown you this,' she pointed out. 'I needn't have phoned.'

It was true. Faraday indicated the P.S. on the screen.

'Do you know how to wipe an e-mail? Get rid of it?'

'No. But I could have found out. If it was that important.'

'Sure.' Faraday nodded. 'Maybe he wanted to tell you how to do it, talk you through it.'

'Here, do you mean?' Ruth looked startled.

'Why not? It gets him past the door.'

Faraday peered at the message again. It had been logged in at ten forty-six on Friday morning, the sixth of August. By the time Henry Potterne was bringing *Marenka* across, Maloney's billet doux would have been sitting in his wife's e-mail box for several hours.

'Did Henry ever access your mail with his laptop?'

'I've no idea. Could he have done?'

'Unless you protected it, yes.' Faraday paused. '*Did* you protect it?'

That same gesture again, utter helplessness.

'I wouldn't know how to,' she said, 'so the answer's no.'

Faraday glanced at his watch. The guy in charge down at Pendennis Radio was going off shift in less than an hour. Maloney's apartment was barely five minutes away.

'This Wyllie . . .'

'Yes?'

'Maybe you ought to take a look at it.'

*

He drove to the seafront, fighting the temptation to look at her. Had she been this way before? Had she walked or driven this tight little grid of streets? Would her eyes, or that tiny hint of amusement that sometimes curled her lips, give her away? She sat beside him, totally impassive, explaining about a monument she wanted to build for Sam, her dead son, on one of the lonelier reaches of Bembridge Harbour.

'Something simple,' she murmured. 'Maybe just a cairn of stones or something.'

Faraday parked on the seafront opposite Maloney's block of flats. He still had Emma's key, and standing on the pavement, looking up at the window of Maloney's flat, he knew that this was the moment of decision. As soon as he unlocked the big communal street door, as soon as he invited Ruth inside, the building would bear traces of her presence. Contaminated like this, the evidence that she might have been here with Maloney would be useless. Any half-decent defence lawyer would tear the prosecution case to pieces. Of course Mrs Potterne had paid a visit. She'd come with DI Faraday.

Ruth glanced up at him.

'Where now?' she inquired.

Maloney's flat smelled even worse than before. Ruth stood in the front room, her eyes drawn at once to the sunshine outside the window. The contrast to Faraday's last glimpse of the view couldn't have been more vivid. A car ferry was churning past one of the old mud-pie sea forts. Weekend yachtsmen stitched back and forth, white sails against a deep blue sea, while immediately below the window couples were sprawled semi-naked on the vast expanse of the common, the grass a rich emerald-green after all the rain.

Faraday touched Ruth lightly on the arm.

'Yours,' he said, indicating the row of photos on the wall.

It was a statement, not a question, and Ruth nodded, giving each one a moment or two's attention, a gesture – Faraday thought – of disassociation. By coming here, by being on these walls, these pictures had betrayed her.

'Strange,' she said.

She was looking at the debris on the table, at once fascinated and repelled. A tableau frozen in time. A still frame from the movie of someone else's life.

At length, she wrinkled her nose and pulled a face.

'The milk's gone off.'

Faraday was watching her carefully.

'It's in the fridge,' he said.

She glanced back towards the door.

'Where's the kitchen?'

'You really don't know?'

'No.'

The kitchen was jigsawed into a narrow galley beside the bathroom. Faraday led the way then stood aside. The fridge was opposite the sink beside the window. Ruth stepped towards it, then paused.

'Is it OK to touch things?' she queried.

'Technically, no.'

'So what shall I do?'

Faraday looked at her for a moment, then grinned. For the first time in days he felt he was making progress.

'Open it,' he said. 'It's a bloody awful smell.'

The picture was still in the bedroom. Ruth held it up to the light, her mouth curling in amusement.

'It's lovely,' she said, 'but it isn't Wyllie. The artist's name is Rowland Langmaid. Typical really. Stewart couldn't even get that right.'

'You got off lightly,' Faraday said dryly. 'You think it's a coincidence he kept it here?'

He waved a hand. A week later, the litter of clothes around the unmade bed looked even more tawdry.

Ruth was shaking her head.

'You really think I'd come to a place like this?' she said.

Faraday shrugged. He realised he felt wonderful.

'People don't let decor put them off,' he said. 'Not when they're in love.'

She eyed him for a moment, amused.

'Is that the detective speaking?'

'No.' Faraday shook his head. 'It bloody isn't.'

On the way out of the flat, Faraday's mobile began to ring. He stepped out into the hall and pulled the door shut behind him. It was the shift leader from the radio station in Pendennis. He'd at last had a chance to go through the log and he'd come across a note of a contact on the Sunday night.

'The yacht *Marenka*?'

'That's right.'

'She came through at twenty twenty-one. Channel sixteen. It was a bit of a mystery, actually.'

'Why?'

'We thought it was a Mayday at first. The person went through all the right procedures. Then it was cancelled.'

'Same voice?'

'No, definitely not. There's a note on the log here. It says "Skipper apologised". It seems there'd been some mistake.'

'*Skipper*?'

'That's what it says.'

Marty Harrison had been out of intensive care for a couple of days by the time his lawyer, Morry Templeman, paid a visit. The single-bedded private room was tucked away at the end of a corridor on the third floor. An extravagant display of flowers brightened the bedside cabinet and the nursing staff had run out of space for the dozens of cards that had arrived since the shooting. One of them, featuring a black-and-white scene from *Reservoir Dogs*, had come from the Unofficial Pompey Supporters Club. 'Back in the Pink with Mr Blue', went the message inside.

Templeman pulled up a chair and made himself comfortable. The afternoon was beginning to cool at last but even the walk from the lift had left him gasping.

Harrison eyed him from the pillow.

'You wanna be careful, Morry,' he said. 'They might never let you out.'

'You think that's funny?'

'Yeah.' Harrison nodded. 'I do.'

He wanted to laugh at the old man but laughter still hurt. His fingers crabbed down the front of his pyjama top.

'Here,' he said. 'I know why you've come.'

Templeman peered at the big square of gauze bandage taped to Harrison's chest. The bullet had passed beneath his heart, shattering a couple of ribs. The entry wound was neat enough but the serpent tattoo that coiled down his back would never look the same again.

Templeman reached out for the bandage. He wanted to touch it.

'They change it every other day,' Harrison told him. 'Stings like a bastard.'

A trolley clattered by outside, the orderly pausing to have a word or two with Dave Pope. Pope turned up at the hospital for a couple of hours most days, standing guard in case one of Harrison's many rivals decided to simplify the local pecking order. It was highly unlikely to happen, but Marty's entourage knew it was good for the boss's ego and that alone was enough to justify the pantomime. Harrison was watching Dave Pope now. His enormous bulk cast a long shadow through the slatted Venetian blinds on the door.

'We should have asked the police for protection,' Templeman said. 'It's the least they owe us.'

'The Filth? You're joking. Given half a chance, they'd finish the job.'

It was Templeman's turn to smile. He'd come armed with half a bottle of whisky and a couple of good books, but the best present for his client was the news he passed on now.

Harrison couldn't believe it.

'Pissed? You're winding me up.'

'It's true, my friend.'

'The guy that shot me?'

'Indeed.'

Harrison took a moment or two to absorb the news then, with a patience that surprised his lawyer, began to button up his pyjama jacket.

'We'll have them,' he said thoughtfully. 'Bastards.'

Mid-evening, Faraday abandoned the office and drove down to Old Portsmouth. All afternoon, he'd been trying to think through the sequence of events that might have led to the cancelled Mayday from *Marenka*. A mistake was out of the question. On a boat that professional, with veterans like Henry Potterne aboard, you simply didn't fool around with something as serious as a distress call. No, it had to be something else, some sudden drama that had driven one or other of the crew to dial channel sixteen and call for help. After thirty hours banged up on a thirty-three-foot yacht, someone's nerve had broken. But whose? And why?

Faraday parked his car and wandered down

through the maze of cobbled streets towards the water. This was the corner of the island where the city had begun, an arm of shingle that curled in from the harbour mouth, enclosing a tiny pocket of sheltered water that had become the Camber Dock.

For eight hundred years, merchants had traded from here, and the scents and sounds of the tiny harbour-side settlement lived on in the street signs and the names of the pubs. Spice Island. Oyster Street. The Still and West. The naval dockyard had expanded to the north, hundreds of acres of dry docks, mast lofts, victualling stores and all the other facilities that had made this battered city indispensable in time of war, but Faraday's favourite haunt was still Old Portsmouth with its chaotic mix of ancient fortifications, cobbled streets and gimcrack post-war infilling. Until very recently, no one had very much bothered about Old Portsmouth, which was altogether in keeping with the neglect that had settled on the rest of the city.

Faraday bought himself a beer and settled on one of the new stone plinths on Point, the tip of the tiny promontory of Spice Island. From here, the view of the harbour was uninterrupted. He loved this place, not simply the waterfront but the city itself. He loved its busyness and its blunt, unvarnished ways. He loved the rough pulse of life that pumped through the pubs and endless terraced streets. Portsmouth wasn't a city you'd choose for sparkling dinner parties or dainty conversation, and for those two blessings Faraday was eternally grateful. In a country which had largely sold its soul, it remained uncursed by money.

Faraday thought about Charlie Oomes. If Portsmouth sometimes felt like a state of mind – stoic, gruff, implacably stubborn – then Oomes would understand that because Oomes came from a very similar culture. Life in South London must have been Pompey without the seaside, but Oomes had turned his back on all that and Faraday despised him for it. He'd seen what success had brought the man, how success had fenced him in, and what angered Faraday more than anything else was the assumption that money, his money, could buy anything. It wasn't just jealousy that had killed Stewart Maloney. It was the arrogance that came with Oomes's assumption that you could simply cover it up. Money had delivered Ian Hartson. Money had handcuffed Derek Bissett. But money, in the end, couldn't buy the perfect murder. Not if Faraday's job meant anything at all.

At the end of his second pint, he wandered back from Point, pausing at the foot of the Round Tower on the harbour entrance. In the gathering darkness, the last of the day-sailors were ghosting in on the tide, their sails white against the bulk of the submarine base on the other side of the harbour mouth, while closer still a fishing boat puttered past, outward bound for the scallop beds off Selsey Bill. Listen hard, and he could hear the swish and suck of water in its wake.

Faraday watched the lights of the fishing boat disappear, thinking about Charlie Oomes again. The investigation had become a chess game, one on one. So far Oomes had played a blinder, his pieces still intact, but the first tiny cracks were beginning to appear in his defence and the aborted Mayday was an opening Faraday couldn't afford to ignore. Like all good chess players, he should come at Oomes obliquely, from the direction he least expected.

He took out his mobile and dialled a number he'd written on the palm of his hand. When a woman's voice answered, he turned from the view, sheltering the conversation from the sudden rumble of a passing ferry.

'Mrs Bissett? My name's Frank Terry. I'm an old colleague of Derek's from his Thames Valley days. I'm just wondering whether he's there?'

He listened while she explained that he was away on business in Hamburg. He was due back tomorrow. Might Mr Terry be able to return his call?

Faraday did his best to sound disappointed. He was on holiday in the area with his wife and kids and he was rather looking forward to a lunchtime pint or two with Derek and a chat about the old days. What time was he due back?

'Late, I'm afraid. The flight gets in to Heathrow about four. That's cutting it a bit fine for lunch, isn't it?' She paused. 'What was your name again? I'll make sure I mention it to him.'

'Just tell him Frank.' Faraday turned to watch the ferry. 'I expect I'll catch up with him in the end.'

Twenty-Two

The Hamburg flight was ten minutes early arriving at Heathrow the following afternoon. Faraday barely had time to find a spot by the exit gate before the first passengers came hurrying out. Bissett was amongst them, carrying a holdall and a briefcase. He was smaller and slighter than Faraday remembered from the hospital, and he looked exhausted.

Faraday stopped him on the concourse. Bissett recognised him at once.

'What are you doing here?'

'I've come to meet you.'

'Why?'

Faraday took his holdall in one hand and an elbow in the other. At the foot of the escalator, Bissett tried to shake him off.

'You want me to call the police?' he said.

Faraday laughed.

'I am the police.'

Upstairs, on the main concourse, Faraday steered him towards the bigger of the two snack areas. There was a table vacant beside one of the big picture windows.

'Tea or coffee?'

Faraday was still holding his bag. Bissett shrugged, resigned now, and elected for tea. Back at the table, balancing a tray of tea and doughnuts, Faraday sat down. He wanted to talk through one or two things about the Fastnet Race. And it might just be in Bissett's interests to listen.

By the time he'd finished, the tea had gone cold. He

sat back, awaiting a reaction. As an ex-policeman, Bissett – above all – would understand the implications.

Bissett at last picked up his doughnut. He had a sallow, slightly oriental face, and affected a thick Burt Reynolds moustache. His eyes were a deep, deep brown, settling on Faraday for a second or two and then slipping away.

He finished his mouthful and carefully brushed the sugar from his fingertips.

'You should know why we all got into this,' he began. 'It might help to understand.'

Faraday listened to Bissett describe his early sailing days. He'd bought a second-hand Laser and learned to race it on the Welsh Harp reservoir, just off the North Circular Road. In a way, he'd been responsible for Charlie's conversion to the sport because the two men were friends by then and Charlie used to wander down on Sundays and cheer him on.

'Charlie used to sail dinghies?'

'No. He was only ever interested in the big stuff. He got into that through Henry. But it was me who planted the seed.'

Bissett was still in the Thames Valley force at this stage in his career, but the department he headed was doing a lot of business with Oomes International and it was easy for Faraday to imagine the policeman sucked into Charlie's boiling wake. Bissett had a natural flair for IT, and Charlie liked that. He also had an eye for a deal, and Charlie liked that even more.

'Thin ice?'

'Not at all. I drove a hard bargain.'

'In whose favour?'

'Ours. Thames Valley's. Take a look at the accounts. I squeezed him for more product and tighter service agreements than we'd ever achieved before. Charlie thought I was crucifying him.'

'Sure.' Faraday nodded. 'And he couldn't wait to buy you out.'

'He made me an offer. I'd got twenty-five years in. Charlie knew that.' Twenty-five years' service gave any policeman what the personnel people called 'career flexibility'. Bissett could go at any time of his choosing and still keep his pension. 'It was a brilliant move,' he said. 'Even my DCI admitted it.' Bissett toyed with the remains of his doughnut. If anything, he looked smug. 'I've been with the man for nearly three years now and I haven't regretted it once. The guy's a genius. That's why we win.'

Genius. Charlie had used the word, too, this time about Henry Potterne. Was that a judgement that Bissett shared?

'You wouldn't want for a better nav.,' he said. 'And that certainly takes something pretty special. But Henry was unstable and we all knew it.' He paused for a moment and stared out of the window as a big jet rolled slowly past. 'He also saved my life, so maybe you're talking to the wrong guy here.'

With some reluctance, he described *Marenka*'s final hours. In the bedlam of the storm, Bissett had damaged his safety harness beyond repair. Without the ability to clip himself on to something solid, he was as good as dead.

'So what happened?'

'Henry offered me his. Insisted, actually.'

'Why?'

'I don't know. I've thought about it a great deal and I don't know. But it doesn't alter the facts. I owe him my life.'

'He gave you his safety harness?'

'Yes.'

'So he wasn't secured at all?'

'No.'

Faraday remembered Charlie Oomes telling him

that Henry had been unclipped when he tried to sort out the rudder, but he'd never realised that Henry had discarded his harness altogether. This was a new development and Faraday took a couple of moments to let it sink in.

Why on earth would a man like Henry Potterne, with all his years at sea, take a decision that verged on the suicidal? Was he wrestling with the consequences of what he'd done to Maloney? Was death by drowning a better option than a life sentence at the hands of a judge and a jury?

Faraday stared out across the concourse.

'You used the word unstable,' he said at last. 'Do you mean during the race?'

'No. In general.'

'How, exactly? In his behaviour? In his judgements?'

'Neither. Maybe unhappy is better. Henry was a disappointed man. If you spent time with him you got to recognise it. There were things he wanted that he couldn't have.'

'Like his wife?'

Bissett's eyes settled on a passing stewardess and a smile briefly warmed his face. Faraday wanted to go into detail about Friday, about the likelihood of Henry reading Maloney's e-mail to his wife, about the revenge he'd taken on an assumed rival, about Henry's state of mind when he returned from Port Solent, about the watch-keeping arrangements that first night at sea, but the harder he pushed Bissett, the less the man said. He was a copper. He'd spent years in the CID. He knew the ways to cosy up to a man, to trick him into tiny lapses of concentration, to sweet talk him into lowering his guard, and then to pick over his story again and again until the first inconsistencies began to appear, hair-like cracks that a good interviewer could lever wide open in seconds.

Bissett knew all of that and he made it plain that Faraday had a choice. If he wanted to do this thing properly, then it had to be formal. If he was down for an interview, then he needed advance warning, and a tape recorder running, and his solicitor present.

'Why?'

'Because you have no case. You know that and I know that. Maloney has disappeared. That's all you know for sure. The rest is conjecture. To make anything stick you need evidence. Forensic's hopeless. There isn't any. If you're suggesting a scene of crime then I suppose you might be talking about the yacht, but there's no point doing that because the yacht's gone—'

'OK.' Faraday leaned forward, interrupting him. 'Let's talk about that, then. The yacht went down. Pretty unusual, wouldn't you say?'

Bissett conceded the point with a nod. Over a twenty-four-hour period, more than two dozen crews had been rescued but only one yacht – *Marenka* – had completely disappeared. The rest, in various stages of disrepair, had remained afloat, awaiting salvage.

'We took a couple of huge seas,' he said. 'It's like being under shell fire. The cabin was completely stove in.'

'I thought Sigmas had a reputation for build quality?'

'They do. Just goes to show what we had to survive.' He revolved the plastic stirrer between his fingers. 'You have another theory?'

'Yes. I think you might have sunk it on purpose.'

'Scuppered the yacht? In conditions like that? We were pretty desperate, you're right, but we weren't suicidal.' He began to laugh. 'This is crap,' he said. 'You're talking crap.'

Faraday ignored him. Given that *Marenka* foundered, he wanted to know exactly where.

The laughter died. Bissett tipped his head back, staring up at the roof.

'North-west of the Scillies,' he said at last. 'We were heading three three five.'

'How far north-west?'

'Thirty, forty miles? I wasn't counting.'

'So when did you go down?'

'Just before dawn. Four? Four-thirty?' He shrugged. 'The eye of the storm had just passed through. The seas were chaotic. We were all over the place then the wind came back – bam! – stronger than ever.'

'OK, let's say four-thirty.' Faraday was visualising the chart of Pete Lamb's. 'Ten hours later you were winched out of the raft way down to the south.'

'That's right.'

'So how come the time gap?'

'That's what we wondered.'

'Have you asked them since?'

'Yes.'

'And what did they say?'

'They said they didn't pick up our EPIRB until just before noon.'

Faraday leaned back in his chair, nodding. The EPIRB was the emergency radio beacon Oomes had snatched from the cockpit seconds before he jumped for the life raft. Faraday had checked a number of models that very morning in a boat chandlery in Old Portsmouth. Pete Lamb had been right. They were all sealed units.

'So how come the EPIRB wasn't working properly?' he said.

Bissett was watching him carefully now, trying to anticipate the next question the way a helmsman might study a following sea. One mistake, one over-correction on the tiller, and he might lose it completely.

'I've no idea,' he said. 'Nothing electronic is ever perfect.'

'Did you try and mend it?'

'Of course I didn't.'

'Oomes says you did.'

'Then he's wrong. It's impossible. You'd need a test bench and specialist kit even to get inside it. I expect you know that by now, don't you?'

Faraday permitted himself the beginnings of a smile. *Touché*, he thought.

'So how come it just started working?'

'I've no idea,' he repeated. 'It might have been a loose connection, saltwater damage, some problem at the other end. God knows. As far as we were aware, the thing was OK. The mystery was that nothing happened. No choppers. No lifeboats. Nothing. You start taking it personally after a while, believe me.'

'What about the mobile?'

'What mobile?'

'You have a grab bag, don't you? For emergencies like this?'

'That's right.'

'And it included a mobile?' He was gazing at Bissett. 'Didn't it?'

Bissett shook his head, emphatic now.

'On this occasion, it didn't,' he said. 'Don't ask me why, but it didn't. If we'd have had a mobile, we'd have used it. Wouldn't you? Under those circumstances?'

'Of course.' Faraday beckoned him closer again, trying to bridge the gap between them. 'But look at it another way. The yacht's gone down. You don't know the depth of water. You don't know how easy it might be to salvage. So the sensible thing would be to put as much distance between you and it before anyone came to the rescue. Then no one can even find it, let alone salvage it. Doesn't that make sense?'

'Only if you've got something to hide.'

'And did you?'

'No.'

'Nothing? You had *nothing* to hide?'

Bissett shook his head, refusing to qualify the statement. There was nothing to talk about, nothing to discuss. *Marenka* had foundered in a force eleven storm. They'd taken to the life raft. They'd drifted south. They'd been picked up. End of story.

'Sunday night,' Faraday began, 'around twenty past eight.'

'What about it?'

'You were off Falmouth.'

'Yes.'

'And someone sent a Mayday. Or tried to.'

'Really?'

For a second, Faraday almost believed the surprise in his eyes.

'You didn't know?'

'Absolutely not. I was on the helm. What happens down below is a mystery. No one mentioned it afterwards.'

'Charlie Oomes says there are no secrets aboard a racing yacht. He told me himself.'

'Then he's wrong. If someone did send a Mayday, then I never heard about it.'

'It's on the log, black and white, Pendennis Radio Station.'

'Then why didn't they take action?'

'Because Charlie cancelled it.'

'Why would he have done that?'

'You tell me.'

'I can't. Because I never knew in the first place. Listen' – he bent forward on his chair, a man whose patience has suddenly been exhausted – 'I know where you're coming from and I know what you're after. Like I say, the forensic's nonexistent. Your only

276

realistic hope is some kind of witness statement and to get that you've got to assume guilt and then trip someone up.'

'Witness to what?'

For a second, Bissett looked almost sorry for Faraday. Then he glanced pointedly at his watch and bent down to retrieve his holdall.

'We sailed a good race,' he said quietly. 'We did as well as we could and we lost three guys in the process. If I were you, I'd leave it at that.'

Back home, mid-evening, Faraday took a call from Dawn Ellis. She sounded hesitant, almost nervous. She'd been making some inquiries on the Paulsgrove estate after the assault on Scott Spellar and now she wanted a private word.

'Scott phoned me a couple of times before he got done. He wanted to ask me about Paul Winter.'

'What did he say?'

'He was really worried about what Paul could do. Paul was talking about arrest on a Class A drugs charge.'

'Unless he turned informer?'

'Unless he got close to Harrison again.'

'Same thing.'

'I know. Apparently Paul said he could put him away for seven years. Scott wanted to know whether that was true or not.'

'And what did you tell him?'

'I said Paul was right. It wasn't a hundred per cent guaranteed but seven years wouldn't be far out.'

Faraday closed his eyes. Paul Winter had been close to the truth in the car. It might have been kinder to have put Scott Spellar away at the start instead of playing Harry Wayte's game. At least his legs would have stayed intact.

'Letting him run was a terrible idea,' he muttered. 'We're all so sure that money will sort it.'

'Whose money?'

'Ours. As well as Harrison's.'

'Well, he didn't take either. Not after we arrested him that night.'

'I know. He told me that in hospital.' He paused. 'So who set him up for the beating?'

There was a long silence. Informing was strictly for the scrotes. Detectives were better than that. Unless the circumstances were truly exceptional.

'I think we did,' Dawn said at last, 'the day Paul and I called round to give him back his two hundred pounds. There was a guy there. He sussed us. He knew what we were about. I know he did.'

'Friend of Scottie's?'

'I doubt it.' She paused. 'Paul was that keen to get the money witnessed. He told me you were insisting. Is that true, sir?'

Faraday was watching the shadows lengthen as dusk stole over the harbour. At length, he sighed.

'Sort of,' he said.

Twenty-Three

The meet, this time, was at Harry Wayte's insistence. His summons caught Paul Winter at home.

'It's my day off,' Winter said. 'I'm down to cut the bloody grass again. You want me to come to your office?'

'No. You're still living in that poxy bungalow in Drayton?'

'Yeah.'

'You know the car park by Farlington Marshes? Meet me there in half an hour.'

Winter was at the car park with time to spare. It was a cloudy day, almost completely windless, and he gazed out at the big grey expanse of Langstone Harbour, wondering what had prompted Harry Wayte to leave the office. He'd been rather hoping for news of a series of dawn raids, mounted on the assurance of the names Winter had passed on. That, and a quiet invitation to apply for one of two vacancies on the Drugs Squad which Winter happened to know were imminent. A couple of years working under Harry Wayte would see him nicely into retirement. The thought of saying goodbye to Faraday's strange interpretation of detective work brought a smile to his face.

Wayte was driving one of the Escorts the Drugs Squad had recently acquired for long-term surveillance work. It had once been a patrol car and although the support mechanics had stripped off the decals and red and yellow stripes, it was still possible to read the word 'Police' against the white paintwork. When Winter pointed this out, Harry Wayte just laughed.

'It's double-bluff,' he said. 'So fucking obvious everyone assumes it can't be true.'

They were sitting in Winter's Honda Prelude. He'd played the Chris de Burgh cassette so much lately, it was starting to wear out. Harry reached for the controls and turned it off. Winter had rarely seen him so businesslike.

'Listen. Those names and addresses you gave me.'

'Yeah?'

'One of them was a no-show, but we busted the other two this morning and you were right. They were both doing smack.'

Winter nodded. On these occasions it paid to show no emotion, simply a lift of the eyebrow and the kind of quiet professional curiosity that would give Harry a chance to show off.

'How much smack?'

'Couple of dozen bags at one address, all sealed up and ready to go, and . . . you ready for this?'

'Yeah.'

'Nearly a kilo at the other.'

This time Winter permitted himself a low whistle. The sums were awesome. Nearly a kilo, scaled into tiny bags for sale at ten pounds on the street, would be worth in excess of quarter of a million. Harry Wayte, at the very least, owed him a drink.

'A pleasure,' Harry grunted, 'but just tell me one thing.'

'What's that?'

'Where did you get the names?'

Winter eased the window open. It was low tide and the car was suddenly flooded with the tang of drying seaweed. Harry waited for a second or two, then saved Winter the bother of answering.

'It was that Spanish tart, wasn't it? That Juanita.'

Winter looked at him for a long moment.

'How come?' he said at last.

'Because all the stuff about Harrison going into partnership is bollocks. The guy's flat on his back in hospital. He's kakking himself that these guys are going to muscle in and he's gone in for a spot of early revenge. Us taking them out suits him nicely. Just a shame we didn't shoot them.'

Winter was thinking fast. The implications of what Harry was saying were obvious. Juanita had set him up.

'She thinks Harrison's shagging Elaine Pope,' he began.

Harry shook his head, emphatic.

'That's bollocks, too. She's big mates with Elaine, and Dave as well. In fact it was her idea to get Marty a private room at the hospital and put Dave Pope outside. She's genuinely terrified someone's going to knock Marty off, and after this morning I don't blame her.'

'But she hates Marty. She thinks he's an animal. She's had enough of him.'

'Wrong, mate. She'd do anything for him. Short of getting screwed herself.'

Winter dismissed the thought. He'd been there. He'd had her.

'Not the way I hear it, you didn't.'

'What do you mean?'

Harry shook his head and reached for the door handle. Then, halfway out of the car, he paused.

'That motor of hers you were in. Didn't happen to turn the light on, did she? Just when you thought it was your turn?'

Winter stared at him. The light was a signal. Dave Pope's cue. Harry Wayte was laughing now, his big face scarlet.

'You should send her a bill,' he said. 'Services rendered.'

Pete Lamb was waiting for Faraday at the end of one of the wooden pontoons in the Hornet Marina, a five-minute walk from the Gosport end of the harbour ferry. Tomorrow, Faraday knew that Pete would be tucked up with his solicitor, waiting to be formally arrested by the investigating officer sent down by the Police Complaints Authority. The charge, almost certainly, would be attempted murder – and if a court found him guilty, Pete would be facing a long spell behind bars. Under the circumstances, Faraday could only marvel at the way Pete seemed to have taken this possibility in his stride. Shaking Faraday's hand, he even managed a grin.

The cabin of the Sigma 33 lay open for Faraday's inspection. He climbed over the low rails, steadying himself on one of the backstays. According to Pete, the yacht was identical to *Marenka*, same rig, same layout down below. Faraday glanced around the cockpit, marvelling at how small it was. Six grown men would fill this space. Easily.

Pete explained that very rarely would the whole crew be together in the cockpit. On a reach or a beat, every available spare body would be sitting out on the weather side, their legs tucked under the bottom wire, their arms folded over the upper rail. That way, their weight would help nudge the yacht back towards the vertical. The better the balance the better the performance, and on a race like the Fastnet, with its long beats to windward, a quarter of a knot could mean a six-mile lead after the first twenty-four hours.

Faraday went through it in his head, trying to match the theory against the real world of offshore racing. The learning curves might be steep but already he could sense the way a crew might divide and then subdivide: a couple in the cockpit, a couple sitting out, a couple down below. Apartness could make for friction. Especially when there might be a corpse aboard.

'No,' Pete said. 'Often four are sitting out.'

'So when do they sleep?'

'On the wire. I've done it thousands of times. You just nod off.'

'All night?'

'Occasionally. Take a look below. It's a black hole. Some guys prefer to stay up top.'

Faraday clambered down the steps and into the main cabin. Pete was right. It was tiny: a bench seat to port with a table; a couple of bunks, one on top of the other, to starboard. Aft of the bunks was a cramped little galley with a stove mounted on gimbals. Every available space was filled with cupboards and other storage.

'And this?'

Faraday gestured at a table and chair tucked into the space behind the steps on the port side.

'That's where the nav. lives.' Pete indicated the electronic log, sonar read-out and VHF radio consoles on the shelf beside the table. 'And this is the closest you get to privacy.'

Faraday was looking at the row of charts stacked vertically on the back of the table. Eastern Channel. Western Channel. Needles to Start Point. North Brittany Coast. Pulling open a drawer, he found himself looking at a collection of rulers, protractors, dividers, and a battered box of carefully sharpened pencils. This is where Henry would have sat. This is where the man would have powered up his laptop, studied the weather print-outs and spent long reaches of the night worrying himself stupid about his wife. Faraday picked up the dividers and tested the points against the tip of one finger. The irony was all too clear. As far as Ruth was concerned, Henry Potterne, the master navigator, had completely lost his bearings.

Faraday shivered. Even in port, at the height of the summer, it felt cold down here. So what must it have been like for Henry at sea? Tormented by thoughts of his wife's betrayal? And by the rough justice he'd meted out to Stewart Maloney?

Pete was standing behind him. He gazed around at the tiny cabin, everything tidied away, everything shipshape.

'This is as good as it ever gets,' he said. 'Imagine six blokes with all their gear. Then sails dumped in the middle here. And food. And wet towels. And everything else. Believe me, the place becomes a slum in minutes.'

Faraday wasn't listening. Forward of the main cabin lay a hand-pumped toilet and a saucepan-sized basin. For a big man, it would be difficult to even turn round in the space available. Beyond that was another door. Faraday opened it. The yacht narrowed in front of his eyes. This was the forecabin. At knee level, filling the triangular space towards the bow, were two bunks.

'What happens here?'

Faraday was on his hands and knees, peering at the cluttered space beneath the bunks.

'Storage. Spare anchor chain. Plastic buckets. Sails. Whatever.'

'And during a race?'

'You keep everything as central as possible. Lug it into the main cabin.'

'So it's empty?'

'More or less, yes.'

Faraday took a closer look. It was difficult to estimate measurements but if there was room for a man on the bunk above, then surely there'd be space for Maloney underneath.

'Would anyone sleep in here during the race?'

'No.'

'Why not?'

'It's weight again. We keep the bow riding as high as possible.'

'So this would be empty?'

'Yes.'

'No reason for anyone to come in here?'

'Probably not.'

Faraday was peering up at the hatch. Releasing the clamps, he pushed hard. The perspex hatch swung up, nearly to the vertical, and the damp, claustrophobic little cabin smelled suddenly of fresh air.

'What happens up there?'

'That's the foredeck.'

'Could you get a rope down here? To haul something out?'

'Of course.'

'Excellent.' Faraday glanced triumphantly over his shoulder, then gestured up at the open hatch. 'See? It's plenty big enough.'

Pete Lamb was crouched awkwardly in the tiny doorway. He'd lost the plot completely.

'Plenty big enough for what?'

'Maloney, of course.' Faraday grinned at him, a moment of the purest pleasure, then reached up to pull the hatch shut.

A copy of *Coastlines* was lying on Faraday's desk when he returned to the office. The entire front page, cleared of advertising, was devoted to Kate Symonds's Port Solent story. The story was headlined 'So Where Were The Police?' and featured a grid of photos, including a number of vandalised cars and – much more importantly – a photograph of Elaine Pope snapped on a long lens through a window of her waterside house. Elaine was revealed to be four-hundred-pound-an-hour call-girl Vikki Duvall, and the thrust of the story implied that her continued presence in Port Solent was somehow tied to her cooperation in an on-going CID inquiry. Of the Maloney inquiry there was absolutely no mention.

The front page had Nelly Tseng's fingerprints all over it. In a series of blistering quotes, she detailed instance after instance when calls to her local police station had produced nothing more than assurances that matters were being dealt with. Port Solent, she pointed out, was attracting more and more money into the city. As a leisure opportunity it had been a brilliant success. Its marina facilities were second to none. Buyers were queuing for the coveted waterfront homes. Yet foreign investors might well pull out unless something was done to stamp out the current plague of trouble-makers. 'The development that put a smile on the city's face is now under threat,' thundered the accompanying editorial. 'Is it beyond our policemen to deal with the vandals and the high-class tarts?'

The call to Bevan's office came minutes later. Detective Superintendent Arnie Pollock sat beside him at the eight-seat conference table and it was obvious at once that the meeting would be under his control. He'd just come off the phone from HQ. He'd been talking to the Assistant Chief Constable (Operations) and Pollock's face was the colour of putty. Headquarters wanted a full report on the division's current CID workload by close of play and it was his job to make sure they got it. Issue number one was Faraday's bloody misper. He wanted a detailed account of progress to date and he wanted some solid thoughts about developments to come. His tone of voice left no room for ambiguity. The future of the Maloney inquiry was on the line.

Faraday ignored the threat. He'd brought his copy of *Coastlines* with him and he was looking at Bevan.

'Who gave them Elaine's name?'

'I did. I think I told you.'

'And you gave Symonds the OK to use it?'

'That's irrelevant. She uses what she wants to use. What you or I might say wouldn't make the slightest difference. The bloody woman's out of control.'

'And you *still* gave her Elaine's name?'

'I had to. It was—' He frowned. 'Germane.'

'Germane, bollocks. Germane to us, maybe. Germane to Nelly Tseng, very definitely. I gave Elaine certain assurances. She hasn't got a prayer now. Thanks to this.' He tapped the paper and turned away in disgust.

Bruised himself, Bevan dismissed Faraday's outburst with a shrug. Elaine Pope was trash. Tarts deserved what they got. There was a long silence, then Pollock cleared his throat. His distaste for scenes like this was legendary. There wasn't a problem in the world that couldn't be solved by the careful application of cold logic.

'Tell me about Maloney,' he said again.

Faraday was still fighting to control himself.

'It's difficult . . .' he began.

'Everything's difficult, Joe. Just give me the facts.'

Faraday started to review the way the inquiry had gathered pace. Going after McIlvenny had been a mistake. He admitted that. But the circumstantial evidence was strong and he'd have been foolish to ignore it.

'Facts, Joe.'

'I'm giving you facts.'

'No, you're not. You're giving me waffle. Fact number one. How can we be sure that Maloney's come to any harm?' Faraday blinked.

'We can't,' he admitted, 'but it's a reasonable supposition.'

'Think court, Joe. Would a defence brief agree with you? Would a jury?'

'These are early days. Once I've put bodies in the dock, they'll go down. I guarantee it.'

'What bodies?'

'Oomes and Bissett. And Hartson, too.'

'On what charge?'

'Conspiracy to murder. Aiding an offender. They all knew about Maloney. They knew the background, and once Hartson had told them what happened, they knew the guy was dead. The problem they had was disposal. Getting rid of the evidence.'

Faraday bent across the table, describing his morning's visit to the Sigma across the harbour. He'd gauged the available space beneath the bunks in the forward cabin. He'd peered up through the open hatch. He'd tested his theory every which way he could and he'd found nothing to rule it out. It wouldn't have been easy, but with a helping or two of darkness, and exhaustion, and maybe a bit of luck, it might have been possible.

'So how do you prove that?'

Pollock was getting impatient. Faraday might have been a difficult child, refusing to put his toys away.

'We keep plugging on,' he said, 'just like we always do.'

'And you really think you'll get a result?'

'Yes.'

'How can you be sure?'

'Because I know that Maloney came to grief. He got himself into a fight over another guy's wife and the other guy killed him. That's murder. It says so in the book.'

'Wrong. It's supposition. Just like your McIlvenny was supposition. We could argue this all afternoon but facts are facts, Joe. And what we know so far, know beyond reasonable doubt, is fuck all.'

The phrase hung like a death knell over the conversation. Faraday, all too clearly, saw the inquiry slipping away. He'd anticipated this moment, and with great reluctance he played his last card.

'Why not hand it on to a Major Inquiry Team?' he suggested. 'Throw some decent resources at it?'

Pollock and Bevan exchanged glances. They'd obviously been this route as well.

'Out of the question,' Pollock said bluntly. 'We've got one team up at Petersfield on the stabbing. The Aldershot stranger rapes are going into their third week. And the DNA job in Woolston has turned into a nightmare. We haven't got the bodies, Joe. And neither have you.'

'So we pack it in? Is that what you're saying?'

'No, I'm not saying that at all. I'm just asking you to justify it, to give me one shred of evidence that there might, at the end, be some kind of result. So far, we've done the decent thing. Thanks to you, we've had a real go at it. But we haven't even got a body. The guy could be anywhere. He could be in Rio, Timbuktu, North End, anywhere. This isn't a murder inquiry. It's an obsession. And obsessions don't come cheap.'

'So it's money, is it?'

'Of course it's money. Everything's money. Don't play the innocent, Joe. You know that. The guy's disappeared. We've looked for him. We can't find him. Inquiry binned. OK?'

Bevan was gazing up at the ceiling.

'Arnie's right, Joe,' he said at length. 'Resource-wise, we're cleaned out. The bloke's an adult, for God's sake. He should have known better.'

'Better than what?'

'Better than to have disappeared.'

'And caused us all this trouble?'

'Yes. If you want it from the shoulder, then yes.'

Faraday had a sudden image of Emma, Maloney's daughter. She was up in her bedroom, that first and only time he'd talked to her. She'd been nervous, of course, and a bit uncertain, but there was something else in her eyes and he'd never doubted for a moment what it was. She loved her dad a lot. And she wanted him back.

'Maloney was murdered,' Faraday said softly. 'Dress it up whichever way you like, but that's what happened. I know it and I think you do too.'

Pollock steepled his fingers, his face half hidden behind his hands. The conversation with HQ must have been even more brutal than Faraday had thought. At length, his eyes appeared over his fingertips.

'Let me get this straight, Joe. Let's say I agree with you. Let's say Maloney *was* murdered. You think the guy Potterne did it?'

'Yes.'

'And he drowned at sea?'

'Yes.'

'So what's the problem?'

Faraday stared at him for a long moment. He wanted to ask a thousand questions. He wanted to ask about the others, the accessories to murder, Charlie Oomes, Derek Bissett, Ian Hartson. He wanted to tell them about the holes in their story, about the aborted Mayday call, about the EPIRB that suddenly mended itself. He wanted to suggest the importance of a link between crime and punishment, between involvement in murder and the inside of a prison cell. And he wanted, above all, to ask whether there was any longer any point in trying to do his job. Maybe Paul Winter was right. Maybe they should restrict themselves to the budgets and the paperwork and let the bad guys sort each other out.

Pollock got to his feet. The meeting was obviously over.

'You should be thinking of a holiday, Joe.' He offered Faraday a thin smile. 'Especially this time of year.'

Twenty-Four

Faraday slept late next day. He got up at twenty past nine, determined to build a dam between himself and the events of the last ten days. Maybe Pollock was right. Maybe obsession had begun to warp his better judgement. Jesus, even Neville Bevan's patience was running out.

He made himself sandwiches and a flask of tea. Before he'd left the office last night, Bevan had secured from him a promise to take the day off as a down-payment on a proper holiday. Pollock would try and sort out some cover from one of the other Eastern Division DIs. There was no suggestion that he'd failed, or that he'd in any way wasted resources, but there were some inquiries that would never work out and Maloney, alas, was one of them.

In his heart, Faraday knew that they were wrong but he knew as well that there was no longer any point in arguing. Every life had a price – measured in man hours, and overtime, and backfill – and Maloney had simply run out of budget. Leaving the house, Faraday glimpsed a flash of green from the grass beside the harbourside path. Woodpecker, he thought. Good sign.

Titchfield Haven nature reserve flanked the estuary of the River Meon, half an hour's drive from Portsmouth. A three-pound ticket bought Faraday a day of solitude in any of the purpose-built hides that looked out on to the ponds and tall stands of reeds. Seated on the wooden bench, his elbows propped on the shelf beneath the viewing slot, he watched cormorants, moorhens and a family of grebes shepherding their young. Black-tailed godwits poked about in the shallows. Flocks of dunlin pecked at the mud. A lone grey heron stood sentry over a trickle of sluggish water. Everything in place, he thought. Everything tied together by the simple imperatives of hunger and procreation.

This ever-changing tableau never ceased to work its magic on Faraday. Occasionally, fellow birders slipped into and out of the hide. Conversation, if it happened at all, was limited to a whispered exchange of information. Sightings of a spotted crake in a nearby reedbed. Talk of the dazzling little egrets over at Thorney and Farlington. The atmosphere was reverent, almost churchlike.

In the heat of the afternoon, the rough-cut wood began to sweat beads of resin and Faraday basked in the warmth, savouring the sharp, tangy smells. Happiness was yet another page of his notebook, filling up with jotted observations. A water rail, half hidden by the rushes. Above it, a bearded reedling, swaying in the breeze from the sea. Soon, in September, the Arctic skuas would be passing through, dramatic shadows in the morning mists, while later still – back home – he'd be waking up to the first flocks of Brent geese, grunting at each other across the eel-grass after their long flight from the Siberian tundra.

On the way home, peaceful at last, he phoned Ruth Potterne from the car. He'd got some seafood in the freezer and a bottle or two of decent Chablis. Why didn't she come over for the evening? Make it by seven, and he'd walk her up the harbourside path, show his separate kingdoms: the grasses and scrubland fringing the harbour itself, busy with stonechats and dunnock; the freshwater ponds, home for moorhen and coot; and – of course – the mud flats and shingle beach beneath his very own windows. Paradise for a wader-nut like himself.

To his intense delight, she said yes at once. The day had been awful, far too much time spent thinking about Sam, and getting out would be a godsend.

'You know how to get to my place?'

'No problem.'

'Scallops OK? And salad and French bread?'

'Lovely.'

'And turnstones?'

'Yes, please.'

Ruth arrived on her bicycle. Faraday gave her the tour, as promised, and afterwards she settled in the kitchen while he busied around the stove. Conversation, to Faraday's surprise, was effortless, not the question and answer of their previous encounters but something infinitely less forbidding. She wanted to know all about him. She wanted to know about Janna, and J-J, and the reasons he'd abandoned their gypsy life for a career as a policeman. She wanted to know about this house of his, and his passion for birds, and just where he'd learned how to master *Coquilles St Jacques*. Each fresh inquiry unlocked another door in Faraday's past and he pushed through them one by one, glad of the opportunity to show her around, flattered by the depth of her interest.

While he washed lettuce and chopped tomatoes for a salad, Ruth drifted next door again, taking another look at Janna's photographs. When she returned, her glass was nearly empty.

'How long were you together?'

'Fourteen months and three days.'

'And was she always that good a photographer?'

'Yes. If anything, I was a distraction.'

'But a welcome distraction.'

'Yep, I guess.'

293

This sudden gust of America made him smile. Ruth, simply by asking the right questions, had brought it all back. The first weeks in Seattle. The wild afternoons in a borrowed dinghy in Puget Sound. The evening she hid his precious tickets for Pink Floyd and took him to bed.

'I like her.' Ruth was laughing now. 'I like her a lot. No bullshit about prior arrangements. Just do it.'

'Yeah. And we did.'

'Better than Crazy Diamond?'

'We never made it to the concert so I never got the chance to judge.'

'Serves you right. She obviously spoiled you.'

Faraday nodded.

'Spoiled is good.' He poked a scallop. 'Spoiled is right.'

'Spoiled how?'

'Spoiled afterwards. Nothing could be that good again. Ever.' He glanced up at her, an eyebrow raised, wanting confirmation, but she shook her head.

'Not from where I sit,' she said simply.

She'd met Sam's father on a blind date. She'd been doing a lot of dope and it had taken her for ever to get organised enough to realise that she fancied him.

'His name was Chris. He was blond and kind of craggy – incredibly good-looking. He had women queuing round the block and that really put me off because he'd stopped trying. Underneath, though, he was really quiet, really thoughtful. Guys like that shouldn't have good looks. It makes them lazy.'

She laughed to herself, and reached for the bottle. Chris had earned a living delivering yachts to far-flung locations. They'd gone halfway round the world before they'd slept together.

'That was good, though. Because by then it mattered.'

'You think we rushed it, me and Janna?'

'I'm sure you did. And I'm sure it was brilliant. Just look at you. It *was* brilliant.'

Faraday caught sight of himself in the kitchen mirror. Ruth was right. He was grinning fit to bust.

'Here,' he said, reaching for the plates. 'Soul food.'

They ate at the kitchen table. At Faraday's prompting, she told him about New Zealand and the place she and Chris had rented in Doubtless Bay. Sam had been born there and for several years she'd been so happy she'd simply vanished.

'I was part of the landscape. I was a rock or a ponga fern or something and the strange thing was that I never gave it any thought. I'd become Polynesian. The place we had was miles from anywhere and we'd hang out half naked in the summer, just the two of us, Sam and me. I had a little veggie plot round the back of the house. We'd spend the mornings there, digging and weeding and planting, and in a way it got to be a bit like school. I taught him everything. I taught him the names of the plants, and the dishes you could make with them, and the bits you could eat and the bits you couldn't, and then in the afternoon we'd go out on the beach and I'd teach him about the shells and the driftwood and what it took to splash around in the shallows and dream you were a dolphin. Most of his toys were driftwood and he really treasured them. He'd give them names and then we'd make up stories about them. Sounds loopy now, but at the time it was amazing.'

She garnished the story with that same quiet laugh and looking at her, Faraday saw the woman on the chaise longue, heavy-breasted, slender-legged, her hands cupping her belly. Tonight she was wearing jeans again, with an Indian cotton shirt in deep olive greens and swirly blues. The shirt was opaque to the light but he could imagine the contours of her body beneath the thin cotton.

'And Chris?' he murmured.

'He'd gone back to sea. In fact he was at sea most of the time.'

'Did you miss him?'

'No, not really.'

'Did Sam?'

'Yes, especially when he got older. That's why we came back. I think I told you.'

She pursued the last of the scallops with her fingers, then licked the sauce from each individual fingertip. She had a sense of inner calm that Faraday found almost mesmeric. He'd never met anyone so obviously at peace.

'Tell me about Henry,' he said.

'Henry?'

For a tiny moment she looked guarded. Then she shrugged and helped herself to another hunk of bread. After she'd shown Henry some of her portfolio, he'd begun to invite her across to Southsea regularly. She had practically no money so he'd send a twenty-pound note in an envelope. At first she'd taken Sam across, too, but then she found it worked better *à deux*. Henry wasn't good with kids. Especially Sam.

'Why not?'

'Because he was jealous.'

'Of Sam?'

'Of me. Of his time with me. It wasn't a love affair or anything but we were good together. He was a great storyteller. He could make me laugh. He had money, too, and he began to sell a lot of my work. I liked him. He made me feel I was worth something. Not as a person. I'm OK with that. But as an artist. Believe me, that's a very sexy word if you say it properly.'

A couple of months later, Henry had proposed marriage. They weren't even sleeping together but for Ruth that hadn't been a problem. By now, she liked

Henry a good deal. And more than that, she felt sorry for him.

'Why?'

'He'd had a rough time. He'd married his first wife in America. He was in the Navy and they met at some embassy cocktail party or other. She was Hispanic – Consuela – and really beautiful. See photos of her and you'd understand.'

'What happened?'

'He brought her back here and it all went wrong. She wouldn't make friends. She couldn't settle down. And like an idiot he got himself way into debt trying to keep her happy. I can see him doing it now. If she wanted a country cottage, he'd go off and buy her one. In fact that's exactly what happened. Henry was a bit of a high-flyer and took a couple of risks he shouldn't have done on the money side. The cottage turned out to be a wreck and he needed even more to sort it out. He never told me the details but he got himself chucked out of the Navy in the process.'

'What about Consuela?'

'She went off with the builder. It broke his heart.'

Faraday nodded. Over the last few days, Henry Potterne had become an almost physical presence. He could visualise the tall stooped figure in Maloney's photograph and every word of Ruth's story rang true. Life had put those lines on his face, and life had doubtless driven him to the bottle.

'So you married him? Out of sympathy?'

'No, of course not. Partly, maybe, but other things too. We were good together. I was flat broke and it was a bit of security for Sam. Then there was the gallery, and everything he was doing for my career. It all seemed to add up. None of those are desperately important on their own, but put them all together and you end up with a marriage.'

While Faraday opened another bottle of wine, she

told him the rest of the story. How the gallery had prospered. How they'd found larger premises. And how Charlie Oomes had walked into their lives.

'He came in one day to buy a picture. It was a hideous thing, a huge oil painting. It was a present for his mother. She was in a nursing home on the Isle of Wight and he was always popping over. In fact that's why he got the house at Port Solent.'

'And her name was really Marenka?'

'Yes. According to Henry, she was a Polish Jewess with an amazing past. Charlie was devoted to her. He'd hated his father but his mum could do no wrong.'

'Is she still alive?'

'As far as I know, yes.'

Charlie had named his yacht after his mother, and he'd enlisted Henry's help to teach him how to sail. When it came to money, Charlie was always more than generous and the stake he'd taken in the gallery had enabled them to buy the old Victorian house where she now lived. For a couple of years even Sam had been happy, but then she'd slowly come to realise that there were demons inside Henry that would never go away.

'Demons?'

'Ghosts. I don't think he ever got over Consuela.'

'Or you?'

'I was first reserve.'

'That I doubt.'

'It's true. He tolerated me. I pleased him in various ways. It's not such a hard thing to do.'

'Have you ever thought you were more to him than that?'

'No.' She held out her glass. 'I thought so once, but no. He had an idea about me, like most men, but it happened not to fit.'

'How come?'

'He wanted all of me. He wanted sole possession.'

'Isn't that reasonable? If he was your husband?'

'Of course it was, but we're not talking fidelity here. It wasn't a question of other men. Or even of Sam. What Henry wanted just wasn't possible. He wanted all of me and then something else as well. It obviously mattered a great deal but I was never quite sure what it was.' She paused, sipping at the wine, then she looked up again, an expression of absolute candour on her face. 'He used to say I was beyond reach. Does that make sense to you?'

After supper, Ruth and Faraday lay together on the sofa, listening to old records that Faraday hadn't played for years. More relaxed than he could remember, he mused about his fortnight's leave. He fancied somewhere abroad, hunting for bearded vultures on the Spanish side of the Pyrenees above Benasque. Or maybe a week in Gibraltar watching the autumn passage of raptors, heading south to winter in Africa. Thousands of white storks. Hundreds of black kites. Dozens of honey buzzards. Maybe even the odd Bonelli's eagle. The thought made him sigh with pleasure and Ruth nestled closer to him, listening to the music. After a while, he drifted off to sleep.

Past midnight, Ruth kissed him softly on the lips, slipped her sandals on and tiptoed out of the house. By the time Faraday woke up, she'd gone.

Next morning, returning briefly to work, Faraday discovered that Cathy had put the remains of the Maloney inquiry to bed. The in-trays were back in the stationery store. The paperwork had been cross-indexed and tucked away in a master file tagged 'No Further Action'. All that remained of Maloney himself was a single comment in red Pentel on the bulletin board: 'Serial shagger,' it read. 'Gone to heaven with a smile on his face.' The handwriting was Paul Winter's.

Faraday finally found Cathy by the photocopier. He wanted a word or two with Winter about young Scottie, but she hadn't a clue when he'd next be in. His wife had reported him sick this very morning and she didn't think he'd be back on his feet for at least a couple of days.

'Anything serious?'

'I don't think so.'

'Shame.'

Cathy was running off a dozen dupes of Kate Symonds's front-page splash for *Coastlines*. Faraday picked one up, still hot from the machine.

'Who are these for?'

'Us. We all have to read it. Bevan's instructions. He thinks we need motivation.'

Faraday wondered whether she was joking. She wasn't.

'You're supposed to be on leave,' she said pointedly, 'or hadn't you heard the rumour?'

'I'm off tomorrow.'

'Anywhere nice?'

'No idea. I think I'll just follow my nose.'

'Nothing changes, then, eh?'

She gave him a smile and when he asked what else there was to do on the Maloney inquiry she told him it was all done. Then she changed her mind.

'You might pop up to see Elaine,' she said, 'if you were really brave.'

Elaine Pope opened the door to Faraday's knock. It was obvious at once that she'd been beaten up. Her face was swollen and purple, and there were more bruises on her arms. She tried to shut the door on Faraday but he wouldn't let her. He wanted to know what had happened.

She wouldn't tell him. They stood in the hall, shouting at each other. She said she'd been crazy ever to have talked to him in the first place, crazier still to have believed his promises of immunity. She'd had the management round twice now. The place was rented. They were threatening to terminate the lease, to run her out of town, to send her back over the tracks to fucking Paulsgrove. And if that wasn't bad enough, she'd now got this to put up with.

She looked at herself in the hall mirror, too angry to cry. Faraday tried again but she shook her head and told him to fuck off.

'You want me dead or something? Isn't this good enough?'

Faraday didn't answer. On the table was a copy of *Coastlines*. Faraday picked it up.

'Where did you get this from?' he asked her.

Elaine stared at him, then shook her head in disbelief.

'Everybody gets one,' she said. 'Hadn't you even worked that out?'

Charlie Oomes was out in the sunshine barely a hundred metres away, sprawled in a deckchair in front of his waterside house, his face shadowed by a baseball cap. He had a mobile phone in one hand and a tall glass of something pink in the other. There were documents piled on the briefcase beside the chair, and every now and then he'd clamp the glass between his knees while he referred to a figure or a line of text.

Faraday watched him for a minute or two. He'd walked down the path beside the house, alerted by the sight of Oomes's Mercedes parked outside. Oomes had done the damage to Elaine Pope, he knew he had. He'd picked up his copy of *Coastlines*, read the front page and drawn the obvious conclusion. Elaine had told Faraday about Henry coming to the boat. And now she'd paid the price.

Oomes ended his conversation and began to dial another number. Faraday, approaching from behind, lifted the phone from his hand.

'Moved offices?'

Charlie heaved himself out of the deckchair and snatched the phone back. For a big man he could move surprisingly quickly.

'They ever tell you about private property?' he said hotly. 'Or is it another fucking search?'

Faraday ignored the question. He was looking at the yacht moored beside Oomes's private pontoon. It looked bigger than *Marenka* and it looked new.

Oomes was back in control of himself.

'Hundred and seventy grand,' he said, 'in case you were wondering.'

Faraday was still studying the yacht. A burgee sporting the logo of Oomes International fluttered from one of the mainstays.

'Any thoughts about a crew?' he said. 'Anyone daft enough to risk it?'

'What's that supposed to mean?'

'Work it out.'

He turned to face Oomes for the first time. The scratches down his left cheek looked barely hours old. No wonder he was wearing a baseball cap.

'At least she fought back,' he said. 'Must be a change, not getting everything your own way.'

Oomes didn't flinch. He took a tiny step forward, his nose inches from Faraday's face.

'You've got fucking nowhere,' he said softly, 'and you know something else? You never will.'

Faraday held his gaze for a long moment. He could smell the bacon on Oomes's breath.

'I just called to share the good news,' he said at last.

'And what's that?'

'They've doubled my resources,' he said. 'We'll be in your face for a while yet.'

It wasn't true, of course, and Faraday knew that it was a measure of his failure that he should be driven to a lie as infantile as this. Back at the station he made a final check with Cathy, asking her to call on Elaine again. She seemed determined to keep her mouth shut, but at the very least they should get photographs of her injuries in case she changed her mind.

Faraday looked round. Bev Yates and Rick McGivern were back from leave. CID was nearly up to strength again. Cathy caught his eye, and nodded towards the corridor. She wanted a private word.

'I wouldn't do a Maloney again,' she said. 'Not if I were you.'

'Meaning?'

'Meaning the management's mega-pissed off. And one or two others, as well.' She indicated the newly tidied office. 'Were you thinking of taking a lot of leave?'

'Not really. Couple of weeks at the most.'

'That's probably wise.' She touched him lightly on the shoulder. 'Have a great time.'

Back home, Faraday found a parcel waiting for him beside the front door. It felt like a picture. He settled in the warm sunshine, easing back the Sellotape, and found himself looking at the photograph of the turnstone he'd admired at Ruth's place. She'd mounted it in a wooden frame and added a note. 'One turned stone deserves another,' she'd written. 'Thanks for a brilliant evening.'

Twenty-Five

It was a while since Paul Winter had tried his luck with some serious surveillance and the whole day watching Juanita reminded him how tedious it could be. Whether parked outside her Port Solent apartment block, or tracking her Jeep on her occasional excursions, he'd stuck rigorously to the rules – forever hanging back in traffic, forever masking his interest behind a newspaper or a feigned conversation on his mobile – and the sum total from all those hours of rigorous sentry work had been the dawning conviction that she'd become a very hard lady to intercept.

In her flat, she appeared always to have company. In public, she walked or rode with another heavy – occasionally Dave Pope, more often other members of Marty Harrison's entourage. Either way, after the conversation with Harry Wayte, Winter had no appetite for being humiliated yet again.

She'd suckered him twice. She'd fed him all kinds of crap about Marty screwing around with Elaine Pope, and when he'd been daft enough to believe her she'd dug stuff out of him about Scott Spellar that had very nearly amounted to a death sentence. Winter had rarely paid much attention to his conscience but this little episode left him little choice. All he wanted was thirty seconds of her time. Alone.

Now, mid-morning, she was off to see Marty again. Three cars back in heavy traffic, Winter watched as Dave Pope indicated left, pulling the gleaming Jeep into the street that led uphill to the hospital. If they repeated yesterday's routine, Winter might just lever himself into her busy, busy day without the risk of a confrontation.

Parking at the hospital was a nightmare. Outside the main entrance, Dave Pope slowed and then stopped completely. Juanita got out, shut the door and turned for the big double doors. This morning she was wearing brown leather hot pants and a spray-on vest, and watching her cross the pavement Winter realised why Marty had been so keen on a private room. This woman would be far more therapeutic than any antibiotic.

Winter waited for the Jeep to depart in search of a parking place, then slipped his Prelude on to an oblong of yellow hatching marked 'Ambulances Only'. Hurrying into the hospital, he spotted her across the concourse, buying a huge bunch of flowers from the League of Friends' shop. With the flowers wrapped, she picked up copies of the *Sun* and the *Daily Sport*, and then made her way towards the lift. Winter followed, praying that the lift would give them the privacy he needed.

It didn't. The moment the steel doors opened, a couple of porters pushing beds stepped in, then a fat woman of uncertain age and a slim, harassed-looking man who appeared to be a priest. The last two passengers for the ride to the third floor were Juanita and Winter.

The lift was moving before she realised who had squashed against her. Winter had been hoping for thirty seconds. With luck, he might get half that.

The lift juddered to a halt. Second floor. Winter stepped aside to let the priest out. With more room inside the lift, Juanita made no attempt to make space between them. She loved to taunt him, even now, and bodily contact was infinitely better than anything she could say.

The lift was on the move again. Winter reached inside his jacket. She didn't flinch.

'You owe me one,' he said. 'Here. Give it to Marty.'

He produced a folded copy of *Coastlines*. Her hand brushed his, hesitating a moment longer than was necessary. Winter gazed down at her. All he could smell, all he could think about, was big puffballs of spearmint foam.

The lift came to a halt again. Her hand gave his a little squeeze.

'One what?' she asked.

In the end, Faraday chose the Isle of Wight for what Bevan, in an unguarded moment on the phone, had called his 'convalescence', and the moment he tucked himself into cover on the edges of Newtown Creek, he knew that it had been the right decision. No problems getting up at some ungodly hour for an early flight. No hassles with holiday crowds at the airport. No aisle seat beside the talkative granny or the squalling kids. Just the solitude of the salt marsh and the sweet knowledge that the next seven days were his for the keeping.

The morning passed in a satisfactory muddle of waders. There were greenshanks, the purest elegance, chest deep in water; and black-tailed godwits striding around the glistening mud flats; and away in the distance, a pair of ruffs, wandering aimlessly between the tidal pools. Each bird had its own special place in this tableau – no duplication, no wasted effort – and as the hours slipped by Faraday felt himself at one with a pageant that made a great deal more sense than the world he'd left behind. Passage on the car ferry across the Solent had dug a moat between himself and the past couple of weeks, and he wasted not a single second on regret or frustration. He'd done his best, he'd failed, and that was that. Some you won, some you lost. Maloney, in all probability, was lost for ever.

At lunchtime, when the sky to the west began to darken with the threat of rain, Faraday made his way back to a pub in Shalfleet. He treated himself to a crab salad and a pint of Goddard's Fuggle-dee-Dum and then drove south, to Freshwater Bay. From here, a footpath climbed the long green humpback of Tennyson Down, and he put on his anorak against the thin drizzle, striding across the springy turf, his body bent forward as the climb began to steepen.

He'd once lived here with Janna, those first months when they'd returned from North America, renting a half-derelict bungalow in Freshwater Bay. The kitchen offered glimpses of the sea between neighbouring properties. There'd been no hot water, barely any furniture, and they'd conducted a permanent war against a family of mice which nested in the attic. Even on windy nights you could hear them scurrying back and forth.

The memories brought him to a halt. Away to the left, a black-headed gull was riding the updraught from the cliff face. Ahead lay the tall, sturdy monument to the dead poet, and beyond that the bared chalk teeth of the Needles. Faraday hadn't walked this path since Janna died, a deliberate parcelling-up of sights and smells and sounds too painful to contemplate, but he remembered her now, on this very stretch of downland, taunting him with verse after verse from *In Memoriam*.

They'd first met in a bookshop in Seattle, and wherever they lived had always been littered with paperbacks. She'd read anything. Anything from trash recipes to Peruvian poetry to hard-bitten American crime thrillers. Her books were piled high by the bed and she'd reach down sometimes, those freezing winter mornings in the bungalow when they never got up, choosing a volume by touch. He could hear her voice now, feel the warmth of her breath on his ear. She read verse like she tackled everything else, with a gay ironic lilt, committing long passages to memory. Janna was the woman who'd touched him like no other. Janna was the woman who could read him Tennyson in the dark.

Hours later, the rain heavier, Faraday picked his way through the quiet village streets, hauling himself back along the rope of years. The bungalow had occupied a corner plot. More than two decades later, it was virtually unrecognisable. The roof had been reslated and at the rear of the property, where the penetrating damp had blistered the wallpaper in the tiny living roof, there was a brand new conservatory in gleaming PVC. The garden was beautifully tended, brimming with flowers, and there was even a decent car in the drive, with two little baby seats strapped side by side in the back.

Faraday stood in the rain for minutes on end, staring over the dripping hedge. On the left was the bedroom where he'd nursed her through those final hours. The oncologist had done his best to insist that she should die in hospital, with every last ounce of hi-tech support, but neither Faraday nor Janna would hear of it. Here was where they'd belonged. Here was where she'd given birth to J-J, where they'd sunk their roots. She'd died on a Sunday morning, early, with the sunshine on her face.

> Let Love clasp Grief lest both be drown'd
> Let darkness keep her raven gloss
> Ah, sweeter to be drunk with loss,
> To dance with death, to beat the ground.

That night, Faraday booked into the Farringford Hotel, a mile away up a lane overhung with elms. The house had once been Tennyson's family home and the hotelier had preserved a little of the comfortable Gothic gloom of the period. Faraday sat in the library with a drink, staring out through the mullioned windows, transfixed by the memories. There was a different view of the Down from here. On the far side of the hotel grounds was a wooden door inset into a brick wall. Beyond the door, he could see where the path tracked away between fields, hedged on both sides, then zigzagged up the swell of grassy chalk to the bare ridge that ran west towards the Needles. Just occasionally, he thought, you can take the past by surprise and even – if you're very lucky – survive it.

He ate alone, avoiding conversation, thinking of Ruth. She was part of this, part of the gamble he'd taken by coming here. Meeting her, talking to her, being with her, had handed him the key to the gate at the foot of the garden. She'd reminded him of what was possible, and what was good, and the overwhelming temptation was to phone her, and invite her over, and see where the relationship might lead. Twice, during the meal, he nearly did just that. Twice, he pushed his plate away and checked to see whether the phone in the hall outside was free. But both times another instinct stayed his hand. He didn't need her. He didn't need anyone. Not yet.

Early next morning, he awoke to bright splashes of sunshine on the duvet. By ten o'clock he was back on the road again, driving east along the coast towards the distant prow of St Catherine's. Past Ventnor, he picked up signs for Shanklin and Sandown. He had no plans, no fixed itinerary, and was more than happy to ride along in little knots of holiday traffic, letting the day sort itself out. Maybe he'd do a little more birding. Maybe, for once, he wouldn't.

On the main road out of Sandown, he spotted a

signpost for Bembridge Harbour. Traffic had slowed to a crawl and he could see the turn-off fifty metres ahead. He began to indicate right, changed his mind, then changed his mind again. Seconds later, he'd left the traffic behind, settling behind the wheel for the long descent towards the sea.

He hadn't been to Bembridge for many years, but very little had changed. The road still wound down the hill to a causeway on the landward side of the harbour, and there was still a collection of scruffy houseboats drawn up on the foreshore. One of them, he knew, was Ruth's. *Kalaringi*? *Kaluwhundi*? He couldn't remember.

Faraday parked the car outside a café at the foot of the hill and slipped the binoculars into his pocket. Way out in the harbour he'd spotted a raft of duck. Were they eider? Even through the glasses, he couldn't tell. He abandoned the ducks and began to walk along the causeway, passing the houseboats one by one, eyeing their names, trying to imagine what this place must have been like in the depths of winter. Towards the end there was a boxy little houseboat with curtained windows and an old bicycle padlocked to a stanchion on the foredeck. The colour – a deep, deep blue – struck a sudden chord. Close enough to read the name, he stopped. *Kahurangi*. Ruth's place.

Had she sold it? Did it still belong to her? He didn't know. A sudden squawking attracted his attention and he lifted his binoculars to find half a dozen seagulls locked in a dogfight over a beakful of food. It looked like a sliver of mussel. The bird in possession twisted in the air and then dropped it. A couple of other gulls dived in pursuit but quickly lost interest.

Faraday crossed the road, putting the traffic between himself and the blue houseboat, then studied each of the windows through his binoculars. Behind the biggest, he sensed movement. The curtains blurred the detail, but the longer he looked, the more convinced he became that there was someone aboard. Ruth?

The café where he'd left the car sold sandwiches. Faraday bought two, eating one and tearing up a triangle of bread from the other. Passing *Kahurangi*, he tossed the bread on to the afterdeck. Within seconds, a cloud of seagulls descended, wheeling and shrieking as they fought for the bread. By now, Faraday was back across the road, half concealed behind a car, his binoculars trained on the door at the back of the cabin. Moments later, it opened and a face appeared. Faraday tweaked the focus. It was a man's face, a face he'd last seen in an upstairs flat in a suburb of west London. The mop of grey-streaked curls. The suggestion of wistfulness around the eyes. The slight stoop as he stepped carefully on to the afterdeck. What was Ian Hartson doing on a houseboat in Bembridge Harbour?

The door was wide open now as he shooed the gulls away, and through the binoculars Faraday was able to glimpse the interior of the saloon. It looked cosy enough and even from this distance he could recognise Ruth's handiwork. The rich terracotta finish on the wood panelling. The handpainted scrollwork around the full-length mirror. On the table was an open laptop, the screen glowing blue amongst the shadows.

The gulls gone, Hartson kicked the remains of the bread on to the foreshore and retreated back inside, leaving Faraday with an ever lengthening list of questions. How long had he been here? Had Henry once given him a key? Had Ruth? Faraday shook his head, knowing only that he faced the simplest of decisions. Either he arrested him now, at once, or he called for help. Help would be wise. There might be others aboard. Another pair of eyes and ears might be useful, too. Corroborated testimony always survived better in court.

Keeping the houseboat in sight, Faraday walked back to his car and called Cathy on his mobile. She was on the point of leaving for an early lunch. Things were quiet for once and she'd arranged to meet a friend. Faraday explained what had happened and asked her to come over. Quickest would be the hovercraft from Southsea and a taxi to Bembridge. She was to look for his Mondeo outside a café at the bottom of the hill.

'But why are we doing this?' Cathy couldn't keep the impatience out of her voice. 'Inquiries have been suspended. You're supposed to be on bloody holiday.'

'It doesn't matter. It's important. Just do it.'

'I'm scheduled to see Bevan this afternoon. Annual assessment.'

'Then tell him you can't make it.'

'You're serious?'

'Of course I am.'

'And you want me to tell him why?'

'Absolutely.'

Even on leave, he was still a DI, still her boss. Get down to the hovercraft. Bring some handcuffs. He'd expect her within a couple of hours.

Reparking the car to give himself a better line of sight, Faraday settled down to wait, wondering what Hartson might be writing on his laptop. Was he still in touch with Charlie Oomes? Was it another draft of the feature film he'd researched? Or was there something buried amongst the debris of the past couple of weeks that Faraday had somehow missed? The longer he thought about it, the more convinced he became that summoning Cathy had been the right decision. One way or another, the next couple of hours would draw a line under the Maloney inquiry. If he'd got it wrong, if Hartson and the rest of them were indeed in the dark about their missing crew mate, then Faraday would have dug an even deeper hole for himself. If, on the other hand, this was the breakthrough he'd been praying for, then there might yet be some prospect of nailing Charlie Oomes.

To Faraday's astonishment, Oomes himself appeared within the hour. Faraday caught sight of the Mercedes in his rear-view mirror as it coasted down the hill behind him and he recognised the bulky silhouette behind the wheel. Oomes drove past without giving the Mondeo a second glance. He swung the Mercedes on to the grass verge beside the houseboat and clumped aboard. He pushed the cabin door open without bothering to knock and then slammed it shut behind him. Minutes later, he was out again, carrying the laptop. He put the laptop in the boot of the Mercedes, locked it, then returned to the houseboat.

Faraday glanced at his watch. It was early afternoon and Cathy was due any time. He waited and waited, lifting the binoculars to try and tease some clues from behind those net curtains, but the sun was reflecting off the glass now and the explosion of white light through the lens gave him nothing more than a headache.

At last the taxi arrived. Cathy had obviously dressed for an important lunch date. She rarely wore a skirt.

'This had better be important,' she warned.

'Says who?'

'Says Bevan.'

Faraday gestured towards the line of houseboats and the red Mercedes parked at the far end.

'Guess who,' he said.

He started the Mondeo and drove slowly past the houseboats. Beyond the Mercedes, he turned the car in a cul-de-sac and then parked on the grass verge. With the engine off, Faraday could hear gulls again.

'You're serious about arresting these guys?'

'Yep.'

'On what grounds?'

'Conspiracy to murder. The least I want out of it is the laptop – and the chance to search the houseboat.'

'Do we have a warrant, by any chance?'

'Of course not.'

Cathy gave him a last, despairing look and then got out. There was no plan beyond gaining access to the boat. She'd follow Faraday just the way she'd always followed him, and when things became a little clearer she'd enjoy a word or two of explanation. Bevan's parting advice had been to take a precautionary can of CS with her. From the expression on his face, she half suspected that his target might have been Faraday.

Access to the houseboat took them over a couple of builder's planks, laid side by side. The afterdeck was still littered with crumbs. Faraday hesitated for a moment at the door, then knocked twice and stepped inside. Cathy was right behind him.

Charlie Oomes was sitting behind the table, nursing a tumbler of Scotch. Recognising Faraday, he made no move to get up. Faraday began the formal caution. When he'd finished, Oomes lifted his glass in a toast.

'You're like one of my mum's old records when the needle gets stuck,' he said. 'If you weren't so pathetic, I'd think this was a joke.'

Cathy pushed past him, looking for Hartson. She disappeared through a door at the other end of the tiny saloon. Faraday heard voices. Then she was back again.

'Come here, sir,' she said urgently.

Faraday followed her into a tiny bedroom occupied almost entirely by a double mattress on the floor. Hartson was slumped against the pillows with his head in his heads. When he looked up, the lower half of his face was a mask of blood.

He showed no signs of recognising Faraday, but nodded just the same.

'Hi,' he said thickly.

Faraday bent to help him to his feet. Cathy had found a cubbyhole with a sink beyond the bedroom and returned with a wet flannel. As she reached to mop Hartson's face, Faraday heard the stamp of heavy footsteps from the saloon, then the slam of the door as Oomes left.

'Shit.' He looked at Cathy. 'Stay here. Clean him up. I'll be back.'

Faraday was out of the bedroom in seconds. By the time he was up on the afterdeck, Charlie Oomes was back behind the wheel of the Mercedes, pulling it into a tight U-turn. As he accelerated past the houseboat, he turned to look at Faraday. His big, jowly face was twisted in a snarl of triumph and he had one hand raised, the middle finger erect. It was exactly the pose he'd struck on the photo Maloney had taken in the cockpit of *Marenka*. It meant more than the scent of victory. It meant that he'd won.

The Mondeo started first time. By now, Oomes was at the foot of the hill, stalled by a long queue of holiday traffic. Catching him up, Faraday reached down for his mobile. The sensible thing would be to phone for assistance. He needed a road block, extra hands, local knowledge. Instead, he dialled Oomes's mobile.

'Who is it?'

'Faraday. You're under arrest.'

Faraday watched as Oomes adjusted his rear-view mirror. He began to pull out to overtake the traffic queue, but an oncoming bus made him change his mind. Instead, he settled back behind the wheel. Faraday could suddenly hear music in the background.

'Arrest, bollocks,' Oomes said. 'What is it with you,

Faraday? Why don't you just let it go? Like any other fucker would?'

Faraday didn't give him the satisfaction of an answer. He could hear the anger in Oomes's voice but there was something else there as well, something close to weariness. Faraday seemed to genuinely puzzle him.

'I've just cautioned you,' Faraday said. 'Pull over.'

'No.'

'It's finished. Just do it.'

'Fuck off. I'm going to see my old mum. You gotta problem with that?'

At the top of the hill, Oomes hauled the Mercedes on to the main road south, using his lights and horn to try and shift the endless convoys of family cars en route to the beaches, but few would budge. Holiday traffic clogged the roads at every bend and Faraday simply rode in Oomes's wake, matching him move for move. Every time Oomes checked in his mirror, Faraday was there, three car-lengths back, happy to take the risks he took, happy to wait for the next development. It was a tactic calculated to test Oomes to the limit, and at Sandown his patience finally snapped.

Without warning, he plunged right, crossing the oncoming stream of traffic, and disappeared up a narrow lane. As soon as he could, Faraday followed. The road wound uphill, and he could see the scarlet Mercedes maybe half a mile ahead. At the top of the hill, set back from the road, was a white-painted mansion that Faraday first mistook for a hotel. Only when he turned in at the drive did he realise that Oomes had meant it about visiting his mother. 'Vectis Nursing Home', read the gold-lettered board beside the big brick pillars.

Oomes was already standing beside the Mercedes when Faraday pulled to a halt on the circle of gravel in front of the house. In an upstairs window, an elderly figure in a yellow dressing gown was peering down at them both. Her face behind the glass was a mask of rouge.

'My mum,' Oomes grunted. 'Good for eighty-nine, eh?'

Faraday was looking at the Mercedes. The keys were still in the ignition.

'Open the boot,' he said.

Oomes shook his head.

'No.'

'Then I will.'

Faraday stepped towards the car but Oomes blocked his path, pale with anger.

'You,' he said, 'are a fucking lunatic.'

A thick finger stabbed Faraday in the chest, then Oomes was on top of him, pushing him backwards, big powerful shoves. He felt the Mondeo's bumper against the back of his calves. One more poke from Oomes and he'd be lying on the bonnet, totally helpless. When Oomes came forward again, he side-stepped to the left, catching the bigger man off-balance. Seconds later, Faraday had the Mercedes keys out of the ignition and was circling round the car on the blind side. Oomes met him by the boot.

'Give me those keys.'

'You're under arrest.'

'I said give me those fucking keys.'

There were more faces at the windows now. Dimly, Faraday heard the front door open. Then came the patter of footsteps and a sudden silence.

'Mr Oomes? Is everything all right?'

Oomes didn't answer. His eyes never left Faraday's face and Faraday knew that violence, serious violence, was now inevitable. Charlie Oomes had reverted to type. Goaded beyond endurance, he'd become Ronnie Dunlop.

The first swing was wild and high. Faraday ducked

it with ease, stepping in close, driving hard for the big man's throat. Oomes twisted sideways, absorbing the force of the blow on his shoulder. At the same time, he locked his arm around Faraday's neck, using his weight to force him to his knees.

'I'm going to fucking kill you,' he hissed. 'You're gonna regret you ever started any of this crap.'

Faraday was choking. Dimly, he could see the rear bumper of the Mercedes coming towards his face. Any moment now, Oomes was going to batter him to death on the back of his car. So much for heroic exits.

Inching his mouth open he forced his head down and then bit hard when he sensed flesh. Oomes bellowed with pain as Faraday felt the blood trickling into his mouth and he bit again, harder this time, until the pressure on his neck suddenly slackened. Wiping his mouth, he struggled to his feet and turned in time to parry a lunge from Oomes and then a wild kick that caught him high on his left thigh.

Oomes was breathing hard now, his face scarlet with anger, and he hurled himself forward, all restraint, all calculation, gone. Faraday waited until the bulk of the man was only inches away before trying to side-step him again but Oomes's sheer bulk forced him to the ground.

For what seemed an eternity, they rolled around on the gravel, first Oomes on top, then Faraday. Twice Faraday thought he'd pinned him in an armlock but both times Oomes broke free. He was breathing harder and harder, his face scarlet, his hands desperate to choke the life out of his tormentor, but by the time Faraday heard the wail of the sirens, his strength was beginning to flag.

Moments later, he found himself looking up at a young uniformed policeman. Behind him, a circle of watching faces shuffled warily closer.

'CID,' he explained wearily, fumbling for his ID.

'And in case you're wondering, I've just arrested this guy.'

'What for, sir?' The policeman was examining the ID.

'Conspiracy to murder.'

The nearest cloakroom was a couple of steps inside the front door. Faraday soaped his face and then gargled with cold water, ridding his mouth of the coppery taste of Oomes's blood. Oomes himself had been bundled into the back of the patrol car and driven to Shanklin police station. Later Faraday would be pressing personal charges of assault, but first he wanted a look at Hartson's laptop.

Opening the boot of the Mercedes, he lifted it out. With his back to the sunshine, he steadied it on the bonnet of his car and powered it up. The last file Hartson had used was tagged '*Fastnet*', and the first page was dominated by a title in heavy italic script. '*Marenka*', it read. '*The Truth*'. Faraday smiled, resisting the temptation to scroll any further. The file extended to thirty-eight pages. Hartson must have been working on it for days.

Faraday closed down the programme and slipped the laptop into his car. Closing the passenger door, he glanced up. The elderly woman in the yellow dressing gown was back at the window, gazing down at him. The moment their eyes met, she shook her head and turned away.

Before he checked in at Shanklin police station, Faraday drove back to Bembridge. Unless Hartson admitted that the laptop was his, its value as evidence would be zero. Whatever it contained.

When he got to the causeway, he parked in the Mercedes' wheelruts and eased himself out of the car. Already his neck was stiffening, and Oomes must have kicked him harder than he remembered because his hip was beginning to throb. Stepping aboard the houseboat, he paused by the cabin door, wondering whether Cathy had found time for a thorough search.

The saloon, to his surprise, was empty. The tumbler still stood beside the bottle of Scotch but there was no sign of either Cathy or Hartson. Faraday reached for his mobile, meaning to ring her, when a woman's voice came from the bedroom next door. It was a voice he knew. She was calling for Ian.

Faraday rubbed his neck, wondering whether the damage had been worse than he'd thought. He'd never believed in ghosts. Until now.

'Ian?' The voice came again. 'Is that you?'

Very slowly, Faraday limped forward through the saloon. The door opened with a small sigh when he pushed it with his foot. For a moment he just stood there, rooted, then he stepped forward again. Ruth Potterne was lying full length on the mattress. Naked against the whiteness of the sheets, she might have been brought here from the empty space on Maloney's wall. Exactly the same pose. Exactly the same message.

She stared at Faraday, then brought her knees towards her chin. It was a reflex movement, instinctive, defensive, fending him off.

'Why you?' she queried softly.

Twenty-Six

By seven in the evening, back in Portsmouth, Faraday had read Hartson's file twice. His account of the events surrounding the loss of *Marenka* covered everything from his first meeting with Charlie Oomes to the afternoon nearly a week ago when he'd fled from his Chiswick flat. In terms of evidence – names, dates, even motivation – Faraday had rarely been so spoiled. But one question still haunted him.

'Why her?'

The tiny interview room felt even more oppressive than usual. Faraday sat on one side of the table, Ian Hartson on the other. Hartson had waived his right to a defending solicitor.

'Because she is who she is,' he said simply. 'Meet a woman like that and she changes your life.'

'How?'

'I don't know. It's impossible to say. Her face? Her eyes? Her conversation? Her body? The fact that you get it on? The fact that you can't stop? The fact that you go to bed with a certain expectation, and then you find yourself blown away by what actually happens? I don't know. You tell me.'

The invitation was rhetorical, Faraday knew it was, but the implications made him look away. Time and again Hartson had led the interview back to Ruth, to the strange spell she'd woven, not in a bid to shift the blame, but in an almost detached fascination with the chain of events that had led him from a London media career to a holding cell in a provincial police station.

He'd fallen in love with the woman. They'd had an affair. And months and months later, it had led to this.

'Who made the first move?'

'It doesn't matter. I did, by accepting Henry's invitation to stay. She did, by being there. Stuff happens. It's pointless trying to analyse it.'

'But that's what we're doing, isn't it? That's what you said you wanted?'

'That's true.' He nodded.

'So answer my question. Who made the first move?'

Hartson sighed. His face had ballooned round the jawline where Oomes had beaten him up, but so far he'd had four paracetamol and the pain didn't seem to worry him. Far more important was Ruth.

'I did,' he said at last. 'It was around Christmas time, maybe just after. Henry had some kind of sale at the gallery and he wasn't around a lot. He'd been kind enough to lend me his study at home. That's where the reference was. He had Fastnet stuff coming out of his ears.'

'And Ruth was there?'

'Most of the time, yes. She'd bring me coffee, rustle up a spot of lunch. We found we liked the same food, the same books. We talked at first. That's all. Just chatted. It was easy. And we laughed a lot, too.'

Faraday found himself nodding in agreement. He'd been there. Only a couple of days ago, in his own kitchen, he'd been there. Laughter was where it began. Laughter was the real aphrodisiac.

'And then?'

'Hard to say. It just grew. A kind of closeness. I can't describe it. I felt I'd known her for years. I even used to talk to Henry about it. It was that innocent.'

That innocent.

Was this what Faraday had stumbled on? The guilt-free murder? The slaying so hedged around with wonderful moments that it ceased to have anything to do with crime and punishment?

'You cheated,' Faraday pointed out. 'She cheated on her marriage and you cheated on your friend.'

'I know. That's what was so unbelievable, so hard to grasp. It was never in the game plan, never what we intended. What we had was simple. It felt good. It felt whole. The last thing we wanted to do was hurt anyone.'

'Maloney died.'

'I know. I was there.'

'He died because you lied.'

'By omission, yes.'

'Because you let Henry believe that Ruth was screwing Maloney.'

'Yes.'

'And you never told him otherwise.'

'That's true.'

Faraday leaned back, letting the implications sink in. It was no longer a question of formal admission. Already, earlier on the tape, Hartson had described in great detail exactly what had happened on the Friday afternoon before the race. How Henry had accessed the e-mail message on the passage over from Cowes. How he'd gone looking for Maloney and returned with a picture of his wife posing naked on a chaise longue. How Maloney had pursued him back to Port Solent, outraged in his innocence. And how Henry, maddened by drink and jealousy, had smashed an empty bottle of Glenfiddich over his head and sliced his face to ribbons with the jagged remains. Maloney had done his best to defend himself but a broken arm hadn't helped. After the fight, there'd been blood and tissue everywhere. Even making a film about Ron Dunlop had never prepared Hartson for this.

Now, he was still tussling with the implications of

323

what he'd done. Faraday shook his head, putting the record straight, his finger in Hartson's face.

'What you'd both done,' he said.

'Of course.'

'Does Ruth know about Maloney? What actually happened?'

'Christ, no.' He seemed startled. 'Absolutely not.'

'You're sure about that?'

'Yes. As far as she's concerned, he's done a bunk. He was that kind of guy. Forever dreaming of the next affair.'

'And she'd never ... ?' He left the question unfinished.

'No, God no. Not Maloney. If you knew Ruth at all, at *all*, you'd know there'd be absolutely no way.'

Faraday gazed at him. He was right. She'd never cheapen herself with the likes of Maloney. The silence stretched and stretched.

'So what does that tell you about Henry?' he said finally. 'He seemed pretty convinced about Maloney.'

'He was.'

'And you didn't bother to put him right?'

'Not at all. Maloney was a smoke-screen, a cover for us. Henry was jealous anyway. He was just made that way. He didn't really know Ruth, not the way I knew her. He couldn't get close to her – and that simply made him more manic. The slightest symptom, he'd think the worst.'

'You *were* the worst.'

'No. That's just it. That's the paradox. We were the *best*. How come all this' – he gestured at the tape machine, at the log, at the bars on the single window – 'comes out of all that?'

At the custody sergeant's insistence, they broke for forty minutes to let Hartson have something to eat. Faraday was under instructions to keep Pollock and

Bevan informed of progress, but instead he stepped out of the police station and walked to Old Portsmouth. He wanted to be by himself. He wanted to know exactly what had happened to Maloney's body.

'We put him in a sail bag,' Hartson said. 'Big black thing. Have you ever tried doing something like that? It takes for ever.'

They were back in the interview room. Hartson's swollen chin was smudged with ketchup.

'The cabin would have been a mess,' Faraday prompted.

'It was. We did our best to clean it up on the way over to Cowes but you're right. It was. I'd no idea. Absolutely none.'

'No idea of what?'

'No idea how much blood there is inside a human body. Henry must have hit an artery. The stuff was everywhere—' He broke off, studying his hands. 'You know something? I can't look at kitchen roll any more. I can't bear the sight of it. At home I had to throw them out. Ruthie had some on the houseboat.' He shuddered at the memory.

Faraday pretended to make a note on the log. Ruthie, he thought. This man's property. The little gem he'd spotted in his travels. The magical village way up in the mountains, hidden from view, undiscovered by the world. He'd moved in and made her his own. His, and his alone.

'You got back to Cowes,' Faraday said. 'What did you tell Oomes?'

'We cooked up a story about a tart, a young kid, a junkie down from Liverpool. Henry had screwed her for twenty quid. She'd tried to nick his credit cards. He'd had too much to drink—'

'And *killed* her?'

'That's right. It happens. Believe me.'

Hartson sat back at the table, nodding. This is the way it would have been, Faraday thought. The older man, driven half insane by his own demons, and the cool young writer, cooking up an alibi to hide his own guilt. Hartson worked in the invention business. He invented people. He invented plots. Deep in his head, he may even have invented his precious Ruthie, with consequences he can never, for a second, have imagined. At some point along the way, Ian Hartson had confused real life with his own elaborate fantasies and this was the result.

'What did Charlie Oomes say?'

'He bought it. He wanted to do the race. That was what mattered. The last thing he cared about was some young skag-head who no one had ever heard of.'

'And Bissett?'

'He thought it was crazy.'

'And criminal?'

'Sure. But he went along with it in the end because Charlie made the decisions. On that boat, you either did what he said or you waved goodbye. Bissett couldn't afford to wave goodbye. Not with the business and everything. Not with the opportunities Charlie had put his way. He was mortgaged to the hilt. He *liked* working for Charlie. And he liked the money, too.'

Bissett had been arrested at his home in Beaconsfield. Like Charlie Oomes, he'd be available for interview later in the evening.

Faraday pushed the story forward.

'Did the other two know? Sam? David Kellard?'

'No. We'd stuffed the sail bag away in the forward cabin. There was no need to go in there, so there was no need for them to know. We were going to dump it at sea, just as soon as we could, the further out the better. There was anchor chain in the bag to help it sink, and a couple of old car batteries.'

'Heavy, then?'

'Sure. But Henry came up with a lift using a spar and the gennie halyard. We could have got it out through the forward hatch. No problem.'

'So what happened?'

'Sam and Dave never went to sleep. Not that first night. And Charlie wasn't prepared to involve them. The second day we were on a long beat down to Land's End and it all got a bit edgy. Sam and Henry were always having a go at each other. Sam was Ruthie's boy. He resented Henry, always had done, and Henry knew it. They'd pick a fight over anything. What course to sail. How many tea bags in the pot. Anything. Being around them both was like the holiday from hell. You just wanted to hide.'

'But on a boat like that?'

'You can't. There's nowhere to go. You're forever on top of each other. Plus you've got a body stashed away. Nightmare.' He shook his head. 'Total nightmare.'

A patrol car whined past on the dual carriageway outside, its two-tones slowly receding into silence.

At length, Hartson looked up. The light was fading now and Faraday was reminded of the evening he and Cathy had first interviewed him at his Chiswick flat. His voice was lower, his tone less certain, and Faraday wondered whether the consequences of what he'd done, of what he was saying, were beginning to dawn on him.

'Maloney started to smell,' he said. 'Henry had locked the forward cabin but the smell must have got into the bilges. It was everywhere. You couldn't avoid it. The cabin smelled like a butcher's shop. Sam wanted to find out why.'

'So he looked?'

'Eventually. Charlie kept giving him jobs to do, silly jobs, stuff to keep him out of the cabin, but that only made it worse. Sam wasn't stupid. He knew something was up and he wanted to know what it was.'

By now, they were closing the Lizard. According to the weather reports there was a storm on the way.

'Sam and Dave were talking about putting in to Falmouth. I think they'd both had enough but Charlie wouldn't hear of it. He said we were going on. We'd come to sail round the bloody Fastnet Rock, and that was that.'

'What did you think?'

'Me? I thought it was surreal. It was like being in some film, some movie. I couldn't believe what was going on. In a way it was all logical. I knew the background. I knew exactly why everything had happened. Yet to end up on this tiny yacht, with a body up one end and a bunch of guys who were driving each other barmy at the other, was beyond belief. On top of that, there was this storm coming. I'm no sailor but you could almost feel it. There was something about the sea, the wind. It was like an animal, stirring . . .'

He fell silent again, contemplating that awful evening. Sam had gone to the heads and then broken into the forward cabin and discovered the sail bag under one of the bunks. He'd dragged it single-handed into the main saloon and unzipped it.

'We were all down there except Derek Bissett. He was on the helm. Maloney's face had gone black. I've never seen anything like it. Charlie went potty, absolutely potty.'

'Why?'

'Because Henry had lied to him. That was even more surreal. Charlie hadn't seen anything wrong in getting rid of some girl Henry had shagged, some junkie, and I'm not even sure he'd have objected to dumping Stu. It was the fact that Henry had lied. He just kept yelling at him. Betrayal. That was the word he used. Henry had betrayed him. He completely lost it. He was completely off his head.'

'How did Henry react?'

'Henry had been out of it most of the day. It was my job to get rid of the bottles.'

Marenka ploughed on. The wind backed to the south-east and the yacht began to ship the biggest waves over the port quarter.

'That's when Sam tried to send a Mayday. He thought Charlie was busy in the forward cabin. We'd chucked Stu overboard by now and Charlie was making Henry clear up the mess. While he and Henry were up forrard, Sam tried to get the call out. Charlie caught him and cancelled it. Then he put a rigging spanner through the VHF and dumped the flares overboard. That did it for Sam. He turned on all the gas jets on the stove and tried to set fire to Henry's charts. Charlie doused them with a towel but it was chaos. They were just swinging at each other. Mad. Completely mad.'

Faraday remembered the state of Oomes's face the morning after he'd been rescued. The damage had come from Sam, not the storm.

'And this message he tried to get out? You've got a time?'

'I'm not sure. It was coming on dark.'

'No other boats around?'

'Nothing close.'

Faraday grunted in agreement. According to the Pendennis Radio, the beginnings of the call had been received at 20:21. Within the hour, the wind had been blowing at gale force.

'That's right,' Hartson said. 'I think we all knew we were in the shit. Then we lost Henry.'

'How?'

'He was hanging over the stern, trying to sort out a problem with the rudder blade. He wasn't wearing a safety harness and he wasn't roped on. One minute he was there, the next he'd gone. Thinking about it now, I wonder whether he'd just had enough.'

'You think he went over on purpose?'

'I think he may have done. Like I said, he'd been drinking all day. I don't think he could cope any more.'

'Could you see him in the water?'

'No chance. We were surfing by then, the wind behind us, huge waves.'

'What did Charlie say?'

'Nothing at first.'

'Then what?'

'He went crazy again. Not just that, he—' He broke off, studying his hands.

'He what?'

'Nothing, really.'

'Tell me. Tell me what he did.'

There was a long silence.

'Will Ruth get to know about all this?'

'No,' Faraday lied, 'she won't.'

'OK.' Hartson didn't look up. 'Charlie threw Sam off the boat.'

'*What*?'

'He just did it. I was there in the cockpit, as close to him as I am to you.'

'He did it deliberately?'

'Yes.'

Faraday leaned forward.

'You're sure about that?'

'Positive. Charlie had simply had enough. The body and everything. The fact that it was Maloney. The fact that Henry had lied. The fact that Sam had tried to set us on fire. He was through with it. He just picked him up and chucked him over. I couldn't believe it.'

'Did anyone try and help? Did you turn the boat round?'

'It was blowing a gale. It was as much as we could do to keep the thing in one piece.'

'Who was on the tiller?'

'Derek, still. He was keeping out of it as much as possible. I don't think he said a single word that night.'

'And David Kellard?'

'In shock. He was mates with Sam. He couldn't believe it either.'

The weather had gone from bad to worse. In those conditions, said Hartson, you think of nothing but the next wave. It was obvious by now that they ought to have put in to Falmouth or Penzance but they were out beyond the Scillys and there was no chance of turning round. The wind was still blasting out of the south-east. Beam-on to those seas, and you were in serious danger of capsizing.

'So you had no choice?'

'None. We just had to run before the storm. You get to the stage where you've got past being frightened. You're just cold and numb and hanging on for dear life. You know you're going to die. It's inevitable. It's just a question of when.'

Around half past three in the morning, the eye of the storm had passed directly over the yacht. Briefly, the wind had dropped. Then it picked up again, more violent than ever, blasting out of the north-west. For a while, they'd run south-east. Then Charlie had decided to scuttle the yacht.

'You mean sink it? Deliberately?'

Hartson nodded.

'He was quite calm about it. There wasn't any drama. He just went round each of us, telling us the way it would be. I remember him having to shout to make himself heard. First we'd get the life raft ready, and the EPIRB, and then he'd put an axe through the inside of the hull up towards the bow. There was no argument. We just did it.'

'And it worked?'

'Perfectly. The cabin began to fill with water. We chose our moment. And then stepped into the raft.'

'All of you?'

'No.'

'Where was Kellard?'

Another silence. Hartson's face was like a mask now, his eyes pouched in the swollen flesh.

'He got snagged in a rope,' he said softly.

'On the yacht?'

'Yes.'

'Anyone help him?'

'We couldn't.'

'Couldn't?'

'We were in the raft.'

'So what happened?'

'I don't know. We never saw him again.'

'You mean he drowned.'

'Yes.' He looked down at his hands. 'He must have done.'

The three of them – Charlie, Derek and Hartson – had spent the night bailing for their lives. Only by late morning would Charlie let Derek trigger the EPIRB. By then, they were miles from *Marenka*'s last sighting. Not that they had a clue exactly where they were when she went down.

Faraday stared at the ceiling. This was the way Hartson had described events on the laptop. The body had been disposed of. The yacht, the scene of crime, was somewhere at the bottom of the Irish Sea. One witness had gone down with *Marenka* while another had been lost in the wastes of the English Channel. The near-perfect murder.

Faraday reached for the light. The interview room was suddenly bathed in neon.

'Why the stuff on the laptop?'

'Because I needed an insurance policy. I was a

witness too, and I've seen what Charlie can do. I've made a film about his father, for God's sake. If push came to shove, if Charlie thought I was about to do something silly, then I'd be in deep shit. I was going to send one copy to him. The other would go to my solicitor. If anything happened to me, he had instructions to read it.'

Faraday was back in his car at Bembridge, watching Oomes park the Mercedes and storm on to the houseboat.

'And Charlie thought you *had* done something silly?'

'Yes. Apparently you had a map of mine, a chart of the Fastnet. You brought it along to his office. He thought I'd given it to you. He thought I'd been talking.'

Faraday remembered the second time that he and Cathy had interviewed Charlie Oomes. Hartson was right. Faraday had used the map from Hartson's film script to try and pin Charlie down.

'But I thought you'd gone abroad.'

'That was the plan. That's what we'd agreed. But then Charlie realised I hadn't got a passport. We carry them on every long race, just in case. They'd all gone down with the yacht.'

'So how did he know you were at Bembridge?'

'He'd put two and two together about me and Ruth. He'd been watching me over the last couple of months. He thought she was up to something and he knew it would never have been with Stu. Plus he also knew she had the houseboat because he'd been aboard a couple of times when she and Henry were staying there and he was visiting his mum at the nursing home. Charlie isn't stupid. When needs must, he knows where to look.'

Faraday made a final note, then got to his feet and stretched. His neck was hurting badly now and he wondered whether there were any more paracetamol in the custody sergeant's drawer. Hartson was slumped in the chair, gazing into nowhere.

There was a quiet whirr from the tape machine. Faraday reached down and turned it off.

'Tell me something,' he said softly. 'Who do you think killed Stewart Maloney?'

Hartson answered without hesitation.

'Henry Potterne,' he said.

'And who's equally guilty?'

'Me.' He closed his eyes and shook his head. 'I just want to know why.'

At Pollock's insistence, Winter and Dawn Ellis interviewed Charlie Oomes. The assault charge had given Faraday too personal a stake in confronting Oomes, and a warm note of appreciation from Harry Wayte had given Pollock every confidence in Winter's abilities.

Faraday was therefore back in the room next door, the interview relayed to him through speakers, and he knew at once that Oomes was never, for a second, going to admit anything.

'Hartson made it up,' he grunted. 'That's what the guy does for a living. He makes up all kinds of crap. Good money in it, too. I don't blame him.'

Faraday could visualise the scene: Winter and Ellis on one side of the table, Oomes and his brief on the other. At Oomes's insistence, they'd had to delay the interview until his solicitor got down from London. Eleven o'clock at night was late to be starting a conversation like this.

Winter was at his most persuasive, and listening to him Faraday realised that these two men came out of the same mould. They were used to taking the shortest cuts. They had absolutely no fear of turning the truth on its head and pretending that black was white.

'You're a winner, mate. Winning's what counts.'

'Too fucking right.'

'So the race mattered. Come what may.'

'Absolutely.'

'So when laughing boy turned up with a story about some tart he'd shafted, that Friday night, you weren't much bothered. Isn't that right?'

Next door, Faraday tried to people the silence that followed. How was Oomes reacting? Shock? Disbelief? Outright denial?

'I know where you're coming from, son,' Oomes said at length, 'and you're talking bollocks.'

'How did he put it? Was he pissed? Did he look guilty? Did he say sorry? Did *anyone* mention the police at all?'

'The who?' Oomes was winding him up now.

'The police. The Old Bill. Us.'

'Ah. You lot.'

Winter changed tack.

'Conspiracy to murder isn't a parking offence,' he began. 'You could make things a lot easier for yourself.'

'I could?'

'Too right. Your buddy, Bissett, he's ex-CID, isn't he?'

'Yeah.'

'Then he'd have known the form, what to avoid, how to get this thing done properly. He might have advised you. Talked about forensic. Talked about getting everything squared away. He might have pushed you into it. Say that's true. Say that's the way it really happened. That might put a different slant on your involvement. You wanted to do the race. You wanted to *win*, for fuck's sake. Winning's not a crime. The rest you might have left to him. His doing. His fault.'

Faraday bent towards the speakers, trying to inter-
pret what he was hearing. Finally he realised that
Charlie Oomes was laughing.

'You guys crack me up,' he said. 'You want to do
something about that dialogue of yours. You need a
good writer. Happens I know just the bloke.'

The interview went on, Winter taking the lead,
Dawn Ellis occasionally trying to appeal to Oomes's
better nature. It wasn't just Maloney they had to
account for. Aside from Henry, two other lives had
been lost, young lives, and Hartson's version was
absolutely clear. Not that Charlie Oomes saw it that
way.

'They copped it when the boat went over,' he said.
'Like we nearly did. It was a lottery. End of story.
That's the way it happens at sea. It's got fuck-all to do
with strength or stamina or any of that shit. It's where
you happen to be standing. And what you happen to
do next. Life's a game, love. The lads had a lousy
hand. A lousy hand means you end up dead.'

Dawn dismissed the speech with a snort of derision,
but when she started to press hard, and Winter came
in behind her, Oomes just yawned. He was tired. He'd
had a long day. A muttered conversation with his
solicitor, and the interview was at an end.

Pollock, alerted by the despair in Faraday's voice,
drove to the station. It was two in the morning. He
reviewed the tapes, and talked to both Winter and
Dawn Ellis. A separate interview team – Cathy Lamb
and Alan Moffatt – had confronted Derek Bissett with
Hartson's account, but the ex-CID man, ably repre-
sented, had declined to answer any questions at all.
Instead, he'd supplied a half-page statement that
couldn't have been clearer. They'd had a successful
Cowes Week. They'd competed in the Fastnet Race,
they'd been caught in the storm, they'd lost their

navigator over the stern and later the same night they'd also lost two crew mates in a catastrophic capsize. They owed a debt of gratitude to the rescue services and one day, God willing, they might venture afloat again. Until then, he'd be obliged for a little peace and a little quiet.

Faraday was still sitting in the empty interview room, staring at the tape cassettes. Pollock had just fetched another round of coffees from the machine up the corridor.

'I don't think they'll budge, Joe,' he said. 'And without corroboration, we've got nothing but Hartson's word.'

'He's telling the truth, sir.'

'I think he is. I think you're right. But we're talking lawyers here. Oomes can afford to buy the best. They'll crucify Hartson. They'll tear him to pieces. We've all seen it a million times. It's not about the truth, it's about money.'

Faraday picked up one of the audio cassettes, weighing it in his hand. In his heart, he knew Pollock was right. The CPS wouldn't even risk a trial unless he could come up with something else.

'He assaulted me,' he pointed out. 'And I've got witness statements to prove it.'

'Sure,' Pollock pushed one of the coffees towards Faraday in a gesture of sympathy. 'And talking to his lawyer, I get the feeling he'll be suing you for harassment.'

By the time Faraday left the station, the sky over Fratton was beginning to lighten. He'd been locked in conference with Winter and Dawn Ellis. Winter, for once, had been nothing but helpful. He wanted another crack at Oomes and maybe Bissett in the morning. He wanted to go over every last particle of Hartson's statement, in the search for some tiny

337

fragment of evidence that might nudge Oomes into making a mistake.

Faraday had helped him as best he could, setting out the chronology, detailing the inquiries that he and Cathy had been making, but the more he gritted his teeth and tried to step back from the case, the more he realised that Pollock and the rest of them probably had a point. Not one perfect murder, but two. Maybe even three, if you included David Kellard.

On the steps of the police station, Faraday produced his mobile. At Pollock's invitation he'd succumbed to three hefty Scotches, and the last thing he needed was a pull for driving under the influence.

'Cab, please—' he began.

He felt a hand on his arm. It was Winter. He nodded at the Honda in the car park.

'Give you a lift, boss?'

They drove in silence through the empty streets. Faraday had seldom felt so exhausted, so completely drained. Both physically and mentally, there was nothing left. In Milton, Winter inquired where to turn, and for the first time it occurred to Faraday that Winter didn't know where he lived.

'Next right,' he said, 'then down to the bottom. I've got lots more Scotch.'

Winter accompanied him into the house. He accepted a small Scotch and stood in the big living room, staring out as a steely grey light settled on the mud flats beyond the window. Faraday had collapsed on the sofa. After a while, Winter glanced down at him.

'We've got twenty-four hours from last night,' he said thoughtfully, 'plus another twelve if Bevan gives the say-so.'

Faraday nodded. They could hold all three men for a day and a half without having to go to a magistrate and face a legal argument.

'What's the point, though? Pollock's right. Oomes and Bissett won't crack.'

'They won't get bail, though. And that means Winchester nick.'

'So?'

'Marty Harrison's mates are in there. The ones the drugs squad busted the morning they shot the boss. They're banged up on the remand wing. One big happy family.'

Faraday was up on one elbow now. Winter was right. Charlie Oomes would spend at least a night on the remand wing at Winchester prison.

'So?' he said again.

Winter moved towards the window. He'd seen movement out on the harbour. He wanted to know what it was. Faraday peered over the back of the sofa.

'Cormorant,' he said briefly. 'Tell me about Winchester.'

Winter shrugged, then emptied his glass.

'I got word through to Marty about the state of Elaine Pope's face,' he said. 'And I don't think he was best pleased.'

Faraday studied him for a long moment, then smiled.

'Result,' he murmured.

For the next week or so, Faraday pulled together the file on Maloney. He'd thought about getting a statement himself from Ruth Potterne, but in the end he asked Cathy Lamb to do it. Ruth confirmed receipt of Maloney's e-mail, described Henry's state of mind as 'troubled', and admitted a relationship with Ian Hartson. Reading her statement, Faraday was uncomfortably aware of looking for clues about her current feelings. Was she still seeing Hartson? And if so, was it as all-consuming as it had been before?

With the file readied for despatch to the Crown Prosecution Service, Faraday resumed his vacation, buying himself a ferry ticket to France and running J-J to earth in a borrowed flat on a housing estate outside Caen. To his immense relief, the boy seemed genuinely happy and by the end of the evening he was beginning to suspect that he'd got Valerie wrong. She wasn't, after all, a threat to J-J. *Au contraire*, she seemed – in ways that Faraday didn't fully understand – to be in love with him.

Before he left Caen, Faraday invited them both to stay and bought a pair of open ferry tickets to seal the invitation. When J-J took him aside, wanting to know whether there were any strings attached, Faraday shook his head. J-J was twenty-two. For both of them, life had moved on. J-J looked delighted and then kissed him on both cheeks.

'Very Gallic,' Faraday signed in return, beaming.

In early September, a French fishing boat trawling for

hake thirty miles north of Roscoff recovered a body from the sea. The face and flesh were largely eaten away, but a British passport in one of the pockets of the weatherproof jacket yielded a name and next of kin. Sam O'Connor, Ruth Potterne's son.

The body was taken to Roscoff and stored overnight in a big freezer full of gutted fish. Inquiries were made next day by the local *Chef de Police* and a telex was despatched to the CID Superintendent at Portsmouth. That evening, Ruth Potterne answered a knock on her door. It was Faraday. He'd spent the best part of a month trying to work out what he'd say when this moment arrived, but the French police had spared him the trouble.

'I'm afraid I've got some bad news,' he began.

The following morning, he drove her to the airport at Southampton. A chartered Cessna flew them to Roscoff, where an unmarked police car was waiting on the tarmac. The body had been transferred to a mortuary in the city's hospital.

When the green-suited attendants slid the gurney out of the big fridge, Ruth needed only a second to confirm that the body was indeed her son. A sturdy silver chain still hung around what was left of his neck. He'd bought it in Brighton only weeks before his summons to replace Maloney on the Fastnet Race.

Outside the mortuary, Faraday conferred briefly with the pathologist who'd already examined Sam's remains. His English was far from perfect but he left Faraday in no doubt that the body held few clues to the circumstances that had led to the boy's death. He'd doubtless come to grief in some kind of accident. Water in his lungs indicated death by drowning. *Aucun mystère.*

Before they returned to the airport, Faraday took Ruth to a nearby hotel for a drink. They sat at the bar and he did his best to comfort her while choosing the best moment to ask about Ian Hartson. Hartson, like Bissett, was currently on bail, charged with conspiracy to murder. In the absence of further evidence, CPS lawyers were close to dropping the case.

'Have you seen him at all? Hartson?'

'Yes. We met in London last week.' She smiled. 'Why do you ask?'

'No reason really. I felt a bit of a fool, that's all.'

'Why?'

'For not asking the obvious question. Henry was right. You *were* having an affair. I made his mistake. I never looked further than Maloney.'

'Was that your fault?'

'Of course it was. I'm a detective. That's why they pay me.' For the first time that day, she laughed.

'Men are funny,' she said. 'They're always getting things in a muddle. Ian's the same. He's no more idea of who I am than Henry had. He's got an image in his head and he's too lazy or too insecure to get beyond that. Men should take a closer look sometimes, and maybe listen a bit harder.'

Faraday rocked back on his stool. The last thing he'd been expecting was a speech like this and it was hard not to take it personally. He reached for his glass, suddenly keen to change the subject.

'I'm sorry about Sam,' he said. 'Just when you might have been coming to terms with it.'

She shook her head very slowly, a gesture tinged with pity, then leaned forward on the stool and touched him lightly on the hand.

'Not at all,' she said. 'I wanted a body. I wanted a funeral. I wanted to say a proper goodbye. I think psychiatrists have a word for it ... closure?' She smiled at him. 'Isn't that what they call it?'

Faraday swallowed a mouthful of Kronenburg, saying nothing. He thought he'd got this woman out of his system. He thought the last couple of weeks would have been quite enough to have loosened the grip she'd taken on his life. He was wrong.

'What about Charlie,' she was saying, 'Charlie Oomes?'

There was a big gilt-framed mirror on the wall behind the bar. For a second or two, he studied their reflection. Should he tell her the truth about her son? That Oomes had thrown him overboard? That otherwise he might have survived?

Of course he shouldn't. He studied the remains of his lager. According to Winter, Oomes's blood had been all over the showers on the remand wing, and the latest reports from the hospital had confirmed the need for plastic surgery. A life sentence, after all.

Faraday raised the glass in a toast.

'Closure.' He smiled. 'I'll drink to that.'

If you have enjoyed
TURNSTONE
don't miss

THE TAKE

Graham Hurley's second novel
featuring DI Joe Faraday.

Price: £6.99
ISBN: 0 75284 807 0

One

Unable to sleep, Faraday was up by half-past five, nursing his second cup of tea. It had been light for over an hour, a pale grey wash spilling over the mud flats of Langstone Harbour. At half-tide, from the upstairs study, he could see turnstones strutting across the pebbled flats, pausing from time to time to poke around in the pools of standing water. Several of them seemed to follow the mooring lines that snaked out to dinghies and larger craft marooned by the sluicing tide, and he watched a group of three as they squabbled over a yellow smudge of mussel. Aggressive behaviour was rare among turnstones, but over the last few months he'd noticed a number of episodes like these. Must go with the territory, he thought. Inner-city turnstones. Bred to be stroppy.

He turned back from the view, eyeing the mountain of paperwork on his desk. All the years he'd been living with J-J, he'd made it a rule never to bring work home. That, of course, was impossible. It was a rare evening when the phone didn't ring at least a couple of times. But paper was different. That belonged in his other world, and with the challenge of bringing up a deaf child to meet, he'd made bloody sure it stayed there.

But Joe-Junior had been gone for the best part of a year now, a gangly, loose-limbed twenty-two-year-old who'd blissfully surrendered himself to a sharp-faced French social worker from Caen, and the months of living alone had nagged away at Faraday's resolve until it was rare not to return with his battered briefcase bulging with stuff he never seemed to have time to sort out at the office. Minutes of meetings he could barely remember. Agendas for meetings he'd do his best not to attend. Amendments to Force Standing Orders. Thick briefs on upcoming European legislation. Incomprehensible strategy papers from the Social Services policy group on child abuse and the At Risk register. Home Office updates on service performance indicators. Risk assessments on more or less everything. Hundreds of thousands of words that were somehow expected to make him a better detective.

Faraday emptied his mug and picked up the yellow pad he normally kept by the telephone. The duty DC had answered the call from the control room about last night's Donald Duck incident. By the time he'd got to the woman, she was up in Accident and Emergency at the Queen Alexandra hospital getting her injuries sorted out. She'd evidently gone straight home after the incident because she'd left her kids by themselves, and by the time a uniformed patrol had made it to her house, she'd changed into a dressing gown, dumping all her clothes in the washing machine. She'd felt dirty, she'd said. This pervert had touched her. Pawed her. Pressed himself up against her. All of which, in the DC's dry phrase, was a bit of shame. Because even with the washing machine's filter for examination, nothing makes forensic evidence more difficult to recover than a cupful of BioSurf and the hot-spin cycle.

At the hospital, X-rays had confirmed two broken fingers and a fractured wrist and the DC had piled insult on injury by arranging for a police surgeon to take scrapings from under her fingernails, plus a couple of hairs from her head, for later matching if they were lucky enough to pull in a worthwhile suspect. After discharge from the hospital, he'd driven the woman back to the ponds by the harbour where three uniforms were waiting to identify the scene of crime. The woman had done her best to try and work out exactly where she'd been jumped, but in the dark she'd got hopelessly confused and in the end they'd taped off the whole area, waiting for daylight before beginning a proper search.

This was the third time this year that someone in a Donald Duck mask had exposed himself to local women, but so far there'd never been any suggestion of rape. The DC, on the phone, was still unclear in his own mind whether the guy had simply been trying to defend himself from the flailing dog lead or had had something more substantial in mind, but either way, it didn't really matter. The woman's injuries turned a potential nuisance into grievous bodily harm. Crown Court, for sure.

Faraday made his way downstairs, musing on the irony of the case. The incident had taken place barely a hundred yards from his house, here beside Langstone Harbour. Had he been in on Sunday night, he'd probably have heard the woman yelling. A piece of luck like that could have saved him the chore of organising a proper inquiry, getting bodies out there, knocking on doors, asking questions, taking statements, raising actions, looking for leads. They'd have the bloke locked up by now, tidied away, not too much paperwork, minimal fuss. Luck like that might even have stirred a modest herogram from headquarters. Exemplary vigilance. In the best traditions of the force.

As it was, though, Faraday had driven out to the New Forest, beyond Southampton, and spent a couple of priceless hours wading through the still-wet heather, waiting for the first churring of a pair of breeding nightjars. He'd visited them last year and the year before. They arrived in May from Africa, shy, dun-coloured birds, almost impossible to spot in their daytime scrapes among the gorse. Only at night would they emerge, fleeting silhouettes against the last of the sunset as they hunted for insects and moths. They flew in spurts, twisting and gliding, the churring noise issuing from the syrinx in their throats. Stand absolutely still, as Faraday had done, and a couple of handclaps might bring on the birds in big swoopy circles, curious to check out this stranger in their midst. He'd played the game for the best part of an hour, the birds softening his rage about Vanessa, and with the light finally drained from the night sky, he'd driven back down the road to a favourite pub and offered a private toast to her memory with three pints of Romsey bitter. Allies like Vanessa were hard to find. Dead, he knew that the ongoing war would be that much more pitiless.

He put a couple of slices of bread under the grill and looked half-heartedly for bacon. The fridge, like so much else in the house, was beginning to fall apart. The place needed a thorough going-over. Sills and window frames on the weather side of the property were showing signs of rot and he'd known for months that it was time to get out the ladder and the sandpaper, but the one thing he was

9

never short of was excuses. Another ruck about overtime allocations. Another outbreak of vehicle thefts. Another crisis with a dodgy informer.

The thought of bacon finally abandoned, he buttered the toast, wandered through to the living room and stood in front of the big glass doors that opened on to the harbour, disappointed to find a thick grey ledge of cloud where the sun ought to be. The light was flat and lustreless. The water was the colour of lead. Even the oyster-catchers, normally so pert, seemed to have difficulty stirring themselves. Sometimes, just sometimes, Faraday felt his whole life could do with a stiff scrub-down and a coat or two of Weathershield. Something to keep the rain away, for Christ's sake. Something *bright* for a change.

Paul Winter, against his better judgement, finally agreed to accompany his wife to the hospital. It wasn't about taking the time off (though that was the excuse he'd offered her) and it wasn't that he didn't think she meant it when she woke him up early and asked him to be there. It was just this thing about the Queen Alexandra. He hated the big hospital on the hill. He hated the kind of people who went there: overweight, ugly, greyfaced. He hated the bossy, in-yer-face posters on the corridor walls: don't smoke, don't drink, don't shag. He hated the heads-down weariness you encountered in the lift. And he hated, most of all, the feeling of resignation, of *defeat*, that overwhelmed you the moment you stepped inside the place. Life was about seizing opportunities, about playing the game to maximum advantage, about staying ahead of the pack. Hospitals, especially big anonymous ones like the QA, were for the also-rans.

Joannie's appointment card directed them to the gastro-intestinal clinic. She'd been to the GP twice since Christmas, complaining of pains beneath her rib cage. The first time, she'd come away with tablets for dyspepsia. The tablets had made no difference at all, and the second time the GP had referred her to the QA for tests and a scan.

By now, she wasn't eating properly or sleeping well. Winter, cheerfully dispassionate, put it down to her ongoing failure to get on *Who Wants To Be a Millionaire?* As an ex-teacher, she was certain she could get at least as far as £64,000, a conviction which made Winter a willing accomplice when it came to making the calls to the contestants' line after the show. Sixty-four grand would make all the difference. Sixty-four grand might even put daylight between himself and the likes of Faraday.

The fact that he'd been paper-sifted out of contention for the DC vacancy on the Drugs Squad – the fact that he hadn't even made it to the fucking interview board – still rankled, and the knowledge that it was Faraday who had shafted him made the insult even worse. 'Fails occasionally to see the big picture', Faraday had written, a form of management-speak that suggested Winter was a law unto himself. This was a judgement Winter himself wouldn't necessarily dispute, but that wasn't the point. The point was that Winter had got Faraday a result on the Oomes case, and Faraday *still* didn't understand that one good turn deserved another. '*Fails occasionally to see the big picture*'. A killer phrase like that, and Winter was lucky not to be back in uniform, posted to traffic cones and the challenge of the lost-property store.

Winter had read last January's copy of *OK!* twice before Joannie's name was called. She took his arm and followed the nurse into the office at the end. The consultant got up the moment they appeared at the door, extending a hand to Joannie, and as soon as Winter saw the expression on his face he knew something terrible had happened. Bad news was like a smell. There was no disguising it.

The consultant was tall, with a long, bony face and the hint of a northern accent. While Joannie made herself comfortable, he ducked his head to check a file.

'What is it?' Winter heard himself say. 'What's wrong?'

Despite everything, he hadn't once given the possibility of anything serious a moment's thought. Joannie was as strong as an ox. Twenty-four years of marriage – countless fallings-out, countless makings-up – told him that she was immortal. However badly he treated her, whatever he got up to, she'd been there for him. Her capacity for punishment, for forgiveness, was infinite. Now this.

The consultant took a tissue from a box on his desk and went through the motions of blowing his nose.

'Mrs Winter,' he began at last, 'you'll forgive me, but I'm afraid there's no point in beating around the bush. Conversations like this can be difficult. If you feel you need . . .' He left the sentence unfinished, nodding at the box of tissues.

Fucking Kleenex? Winter was on his feet now.

'Just tell us,' he said. 'What is it?'

For the first time, the consultant spared him a glance.

'Mr Winter?'

'That's right.'

'Please sit down. There's no reason to make this more—'

'I asked you a question.'

'And I'm about to answer it.' He turned his head. 'Mrs Winter, I'm afraid . . .'

Joannie reached up for her husband, tugging him back. With some reluctance, Winter sat down. The consultant's tone had changed. His eyes were on the file again and he sounded like he was reading a death sentence. Winter had heard judges more sympathetic than this.

'Pancreatic what?' he said.

'Carcinoma, Mr Winter.'

'What's that?'

'Cancer.'

'*Cancer?*' Winter stared at him, suddenly chilled. 'You're joking. Joannie? *Cancer?*'

There was a long silence. From the waiting room came the rattle of a tea trolley. Then Joannie's voice, smaller than Winter had ever heard it.

'You're sure?'

'Positive, Mrs Winter.'

'Can you' – she hesitated – 'do anything?'

'Alas, no. We can try and make life easier for you, maybe a small operation, just to tidy things up . . . but no, long-term, I'm afraid no. This is a particularly aggressive cancer. You have secondaries in the stomach and liver. There are drugs, of course. Palliative treatment. The hospice. But I wouldn't want to mislead you about the outcome.'

'So . . .?'

'About three months, Mrs Winter.' The consultant inched the box of Kleenex towards her. 'Though even in a case like this it's hard to be precise.'

*

Faraday had been at his desk at Southsea police station for several hours by the time Cathy Lamb arrived for their regular Monday conference. She'd driven down from Fratton nick where she had an office of her own. The old divisions of Portsmouth North and South were in the process of amalgamation into a single super-division, and in the consequent administrative uncertainties, Cathy had seized her chance. CID was short of Detective Inspectors to fight the rising tide of so-called volume crime, and with Faraday's support Cathy had made it to acting DI. Responsibility suited her. She'd been in the job a couple of months now, and she plainly loved it. A big woman, crop-haired with an open, outdoors face, her gaze was steadier than ever.

'How's your little treasure, then?' She nodded back towards the big open-plan CID office along the corridor where Vanessa's replacement was punishing the photocopier.

Faraday pulled a face.

'She's got some kind of agency for Beanie Babies,' he said. 'She brings the bloody things in every day, trying to flog them. Drives the blokes mad.'

'Why don't you tell her not to?'

'I did. She doesn't listen.'

Faraday got to his feet and shut the door. The new management assistant was called Joyce. She was an overweight American in her early forties, the kind of woman who from day one had presumed an intimacy which didn't exist. With Vanessa, Faraday had been only too happy to offload endless administrative baggage, includ-ing material which was extremely sensitive, freeing up precious time he could devote to something worthwhile. With this woman, that kind of trust was out of the question.

Cathy seemed amused.

'I hear her husband's in the job.'

'That's right. He's an Inspector at Southampton. As useless as she is.'

'Nice to keep it in the family, though.'

'Yeah, kind of two-for-one offer. Makes life twice as bloody difficult.'

'Is she here for ever?'

'No idea.' Faraday nodded at the file on Cathy's lap. 'What's the score, then? Anything interesting?'

Faraday's own CID boss was Willard, and the Detective Superintendent had made it clear that he expected Faraday to keep a watching brief over Cathy's stewardship of Portsmouth North. Acting DI at twenty-eight was going some. The girl would need supervision.

Cathy ran quickly through the usual tally of minor crimes: thefts from vehicles, vandalism, shoplifting, house burglary, warehouse break-ins, and, from the weekend, four serious assaults. In theory, she had six detectives and a couple of Sergeants to do the legwork, but as an ex-Sergeant herself she knew that the staffing figures were largely fiction. It was a rare week when at least a third of her guys weren't either abstracted for major inquiries elsewhere, sorting out the backlog of training courses they'd missed, or filling in for other divisions stripped even barer than hers.

'Then there's Winter,' she added. 'Called in sick this morning.'

'Nothing minor, I hope.'

'Actually, it's his wife. He had to take her to the hospital.'

'Winter? Looking after his missus? You're sure it was him?'

'Had to be. Said it might take all day.'

Faraday made a note on his jotter. It took real determination to resist change, but in his early forties Paul Winter was still an old-style DC, wholly unreconstructed, a man for whom the difference between criminality and innocence was never less than subjective. As such, he was the perfect specimen of the old Portsmouth Mafia, a brotherhood of like-minded detectives who'd thrived on alcohol, patronage and favouritism in more or less equal measure. Unlike his ex-colleagues, though, Winter had survived the CID culture changes of the eighties and some of the newer intake still viewed him with awe. Winter, they said, had a rare talent for getting inside the heads of the bad guys, for winning their trust and opening their mouths, for tying them into schemes so complex, so byzantine, they defied description. This interpretation of Winter's MO was both colourful and compelling, but to Faraday, the truth was altogether simpler. On a good day, just, Winter stayed legit. The rest of the time he was as bent as the low-life he gloried in putting away.

'Give him a call,' he said briskly. 'No hospital appointment lasts all day.'

A frown ghosted across Cathy's face. She was about to dig in, but Faraday didn't give her the chance.

'How's Pete?' he said. 'Climbing the walls yet?'

Pete Lamb was Cathy's estranged husband, a uniformed Sergeant from Fareham nick. As leader of one of the forces tactical firearms units, he'd been suspended pending the outcome of an internal inquiry after shooting a suspected drug dealer on an early-morning bust. That was bad enough, but what had turned poor threat perception into a potential jail sentence was the result of a subsequent blood test. Breaking every regulation in the book, Pete had been drinking. Thanks to some inspired work by Pete's lawyer, the inquiry would probably take a couple of years to resolve certain issues about the admissibility of evidence from voluntary blood tests, but in the meantime, still on full salary, he was forbidden to take other paid work.

'He's fine,' Cathy said.

'Not bored out of his skull?'

'Never. It's June. He's still got shares in the boat, and Cowes is coming up.'

'Is he still living with his mum? Over in Gosport?'

'Not any more. He's just got a flat in Southsea. Whitwell Road.'

'Nice?'

Cathy gave him a look, then softened it with a smile.

'Oldest trick in the book,' she murmured. 'How would I know?'

For the third time in as many weeks, Pete Lamb made his way through the second-hand book shop, pushed past the boxes of *Reader's Digest*s at the back, and clumped up the bare wooden stairs to the office on top. He'd known Malcolm Garrett from Mal's days as a DS at Fareham, and now that Mal had turned early retirement into a new career, Pete saw every reason to develop the relationship. A tatty room overlooking Southsea's Albert Road wasn't the greatest commercial address in the world, but, as Mal kept pointing out, this was just the start. After decades of neglect, the city was beginning to boom. And big money always brought with it the need for special kinds of investigative expertise.

'Bird called Liz Tooley.' Mal gestured towards the kettle on the shelf by the door. 'Water's still hot. Help yourself.'

Liz Tooley headed the residential sales operation at Gunwharf Quays, an enormous harbourside redevelopment scheme that was fast turning thirty-three acres of ex-Navy land into an aspirational lifestyle fantasy. Already it had sucked in a hundred million pounds' worth of investment. Retail names like Ted Baker, Tommy Hilfiger and Gap had finally secured a unique retail niche in the city, and plans for three hundred luxury harbourside apartments would no doubt do wonders for Portsmouth's social mix.

'They're flogging the penthouses for half a million quid,' Mal grunted. 'You put down a grand for starters, then ten per cent, then the balance on completion. They've got people queuing round the block. Half a million quid. For some poxy flat. Can you believe that?'

Pete could. Living in Gosport, on the other side of the harbour, he'd regularly been taking the ferry across, and the view on a sunny morning from the upper deck was more than enough to explain the rush to buy. Gunwharf Quays lay between the cobbled streets of Old Portsmouth, huddled around the harbourmouth, and the national treasure trove that was the Navy's Historic Dockyard. The site was still chaotic, a busy muddle of diggers and piling-crews beneath the soaring construction cranes, but even without a look at the glitzy brochures the potential was obvious. A couple of minutes' walk, and you'd be sitting on a train at the harbour station. Ninety minutes later, you'd be at Waterloo. For someone with a London job and a yearning for premium maritime views, Gunwharf Quays would be the dream address.

Pete was trying to get the lid off the Kenco jar.

'So what's the problem?'

'She's lost a buyer. Not lost him, exactly. It's more complex than that.'

The guy had taken an option on three flats, two of them penthouse apartments, all of them with waterside views. One had been for himself. Another for his mother. The third for a South African chum. Once the apartments were ready, the guy would be parting with nearly a million and a half pounds.

'That makes him worth finding,' Mal pointed out. 'Because his time is up.'

He'd signed and paid for the thousand-pound options on 23 May, making an appointment to hand over the ten per cent deposits two weeks later. The appointment had been for late afternoon on Tuesday, 6 June, and he'd made a little joke about D-Day, inviting the sales girl to mark the occasion by accepting his invitation for dinner. The sales girl had pleaded pressure of time so he'd settled for a meet on site instead.

'He didn't show?'

'No. And when they tried the numbers he left, they got nothing. His option expires tomorrow, but they're naturally bolloxed about pissing him off if there's some genuine reason he never made it on the sixth. So, sunshine, I just thought . . .'

Pete had abandoned the coffee jar for a packet of Jaffa cakes, fumbling in his leather jacket for a notepad.

'Name?'

'Pieter Hennessey. Spelled P–I–E–T—'

'He's South African too?'

'Yeah. I've got the numbers and stuff on a sheet from Liz. Guy's a surgeon of some kind. Been in the UK for years now. Here.'

Pete looked briefly at the sheet. With the phone numbers were three addresses, one in Beaconsfield, one in the New Forest and the third in Harley Street.

'Private practice?'

'So I gather. Apparently the guy earns a fortune, though at their prices he'd bloody have to.' He paused, impatient as ever. 'What d'you think, then?'

Pete glanced up, wiping a smear of chocolate from the corner of his mouth. Had they tried the other two buyers? His mother? His mate?

'Yeah. They've got phone and fax numbers in Cape Town but no reply so far. It could be they don't exist, of course. Hennessey says he's acting as proxy but there's no real proof.'

'So he could be buying these places as a spec?'

'He could be. They don't like that, but he could be.'

'OK.' Pete scribbled himself a note. 'How long have I got?'

'Couple of days.' Garrett relieved Pete of the Jaffa cakes. 'That's all the Gunwharf lot are prepared to pay.'

Paul Winter was contemplating yet another pot of tea when his mobile rang. It was Cathy Lamb at Fratton nick, wanting to know where he was.

'At the QA.' The lie was automatic. 'Why?'

'How's it going?'

'Crap, love. You know what these places are like. Wait, wait,

wait.' He paused. Next door, in the lounge, he could hear Joannie crying again – tiny, choking sobs. He closed his eyes and put the phone to his ear. 'They want us now, boss. Call you back?'

Without waiting for an answer, Winter ended the conversation.

Joannie was curled into her favourite recliner. Already, in less than an hour, she seemed to have physically diminished. She looked pale and thin and beaten. The spark had gone, the energy, the life. She was a stranger in their little bungalow, not Joannie at all.

'Love,' he began, 'it'll be—'

'Don't.'

'Don't what?'

'Don't say it. Don't say anything. It's just the shock. I'll get over it in a minute. Just give me a bit of time.'

She looked up at him, doing her best to summon a weak smile, then buried her face in her hands, her whole body rocking back and forth. Winter was on his knees beside her, carefully moving the empty cup to a safer place, feeling hopelessly inadequate. On the shelf above his head their single goldfish flapped slowly around the bowl. He put his arms round his wife and watched it for a moment or two, trying to work out what to say, realising that he didn't know. He thought he'd got the world sussed, and he'd been wrong. He thought life owed him no surprises, and here he suddenly was, completely helpless. Not an operation. Not a week or two in hospital. But a death sentence. Delivered, in Winter's view, without a shred of compassion.

'Wanker,' he said softly. 'Complete tosspot.'

'Who?'

'That bloke. Your specialist.'

Joannie, who'd rarely seen anything but the brighter side of life, shook her head. It wasn't the consultant's fault. He was only doing his job.

'His *job*? His job is to make you better. Not sit you down like that and tell you there's no point even bloody trying. What are these people *for*, for God's sake? We pay their wages. We build them all these bloody hospitals. There are drugs. Machines. All kinds of stuff. All he's got is a white flag. Fuck him. Just fuck him.'

He shut his eyes, close to tears himself. Rage and self-pity. Then he felt Joannie's hand on his, stroking and stroking.

'It'll be all right,' she was saying softly. 'I'm still here.'

A minute or two later, standing in the kitchen, Winter realised he'd just washed the same cup three times. Can't cope with this, he told himself. No bloody way.

Opening a drawer, he pulled out a drying-up cloth. Beautifully ironed, it smelled of fresh air. Shutting his eyes again, he visualised a line of washing in the garden, the way Joannie pegged the big stuff in the middle, the way she planted the pole so the sheets never snagged on the rose bushes. Twenty-four years she'd been doing that. Twenty-four years he'd taken it all for granted, every single time. And now she was next door. Dying.

He'd left the mobile on the side. Cathy was in her office.

'We're through at the hospital, boss.' He tried hard to sound normal. 'What have you got for me?'

Faraday was reading the front page of the *News* for the second time when the duty DS from Fratton phoned. Joyce, ever gleeful, had left the midday edition on his desk. DONALD DUCK RAPIST STRIKES AGAIN ran the headline. MOTHER FLEES IN TERROR.

'We've had a bloke at the front desk, sir,' the DS was saying. 'Not sure about the strength but we thought you might be interested.'

'What's it about?'

'His daughter. He thinks she's been molested.'

Faraday was leafing through the paper. A search of the area around the ponds was still going on, but the *News* editorial left it in no doubt that the city's women deserved a better deal from the police. Three incidents in a row. Three chances to nail the guy. And absolutely nothing to show for it. This was the kind of nonsense that sent the suits at headquarters racing to their PCs. Any minute now Joyce would be bending over his shoulder, reading the first of the e-mails.

'Molested by who?'

'Her lecturer.'

The DS named a college in the city. The girl was on some kind of media course. The lecturer taught drama and film studies. According to the father, she'd been pressured into sleeping with him. She was a good girl, weak-minded but a good girl. Bloke needed sorting out.

19

Faraday at last closed the paper. The college was up in the north of the city, part of Cathy Lamb's patch.

'So why me?' he enquired drily. 'Can't you lot cope?'

'It's not that, sir.'

'What is it, then?'

'His address, for a start, and hers. They both live down your way. She's in some kind of bedsit in Southsea. He's got a place in Milton.'

Faraday reached for a pen. The Donald Duck incidents had all occurred around the edges of Langstone Harbour. Milton was half a mile away.

'And?' he said.

The DS paused a moment, then laughed.

'This is the father talking,' he said, 'but apparently he's got a thing about dressing up.'